Sally Brampton was born in 1955 in Brunei and spent her childhood in the Middle East and Africa. She studied fashion at Central St Martin's College of Art and Design before joining *Vogue*. Four years later she went on to become the fashion editor of the *Observer* and in 1985 she launched British *Elle*, which she edited for four years. She is currently the editor of *Red*. She has written three previous novels, *Good Grief, Lovesick* and *Concerning Lily*. She lives with her husband and their daughter in London.

Also by Sally Brampton

Good Grief
Lovesick
Concerning Lily

SALLY BRAMPTON

Love, Always

ARROW

Published in the United Kingdom in 2000 by
Arrow Books

1 3 5 7 9 10 8 6 4 2

First published in the United Kingdom in 2000 by William Heinemann

Arrow Books
The Random House Group Limited
20 Vauxhall Bridge Road, London, SW1V 2SA

Random House Australia (Pty) Limited
20 Alfred Street, Milsons Point, Sydney, New South Wales 2061, Australia

Random House New Zealand Limited
18 Poland Road. Glenfield
Auckland 10, New Zealand

Random House (Pty) Limited
Endulini, 5a Jubilee Road, Parktown, 2193, South Africa

The Random House Group Limited Reg. No. 954009

www.randomhouse.co.uk

A CIP catalogue record for this book is available from the British Library

Papers used by Random House are natural, recyclable products made from wood grown
in sustainable forests. The manufacturing processes conform to the environmental regula-
tions of the country of origin

Printed and bound in Great Britain by
Bookmarque Ltd, Croydon, Surrey

ISBN 0 09 940628 4

For my parents
with love

One

It is past midnight. I am awake, worrying about death. Not my own, but Rebecca's.

There is a long dent on the other side of the bed. I stretch out my hand, curl my fingers into it. It is still faintly warm from Ben's body, although he has been gone for over an hour. I glance up at the clock. One hour and twelve minutes exactly. It feels longer. It feels as if I have known about Rebecca for ever.

When he tells me, we are lying flat on our backs on the bed, our heads turned towards each other. I can see from his face that he wants to make love but I won't. He's too distant tonight. He doesn't belong to me. I see a flicker of impatience, perhaps anger in his face.

'She's done it again.'

I rouse myself, consider the possibilities. 'Done what?' Sometimes I see us, not as lovers, but as parents saddled with a wayward child.

'She's tried to kill herself again.' His arms are stiff at his side, the fingers hard.

I imagine a hospital. White sheets. Bright lights. 'Where is she?'

'At home.'

I grow impatient. 'Yes, yes. I mean where is she now?'

'At home.'

'Be serious.'

His gaze flickers to me, slides across my face and away.

1

I see then that he is serious and let out a long, slow breath. 'You mean, she's dead?'

He turns his head, stares up at the ceiling. 'I don't know.'

I sit bolt upright. 'What do you mean, you don't know?'

He will not look at me. 'I panicked, got in the car. I didn't know where else to go. I thought you'd understand.'

'You must go back. We can't just leave her there.' He smiles briefly and I see, too late, that I have included myself in this decision. 'She may not be dead.'

'No,' he says after a while, 'she may not.'

Taking him by the shoulder, I shake him with fingers made hard with panic. 'You must go and see.'

Ben does not move. 'In a minute.'

'No. Now. You must go now.'

He turns his head, looks at me beseechingly. 'Please. Just one more minute, then I'll go.'

I stare down at him but he closes his eyes. For a split–second I imagine that he too is dead. 'Please,' I say. He is utterly still.

I lie down again, my limbs folded in on themselves, clamped fast to my body. For a moment I imagine that if I stay like that then the moment will pass, the knowledge will skitter over my body, fly out of the window, ricocheting down the street to lodge itself in somebody else's head. I shall be free of it. A memory floats into my mind, of when I was a child at school and forced to keep still for what seemed like hours on end. I learned then to empty my mind, to rid my body of its glorious, bursting energy. How wasteful it seems now, that binding of our youthful limbs. Now that I am older, it is easier to sit still and watch life pass by. Too easy. I think of Rebecca and the life flooding out of her, and make an awkward angry gesture with my hand.

2

'In a minute,' Ben says, aware of the sudden shift of movement although his eyes are still closed.

Should I call an ambulance? The police, perhaps? And if I do, what will I say? That her husband, who found her, is lying in my bed? I think of Rebecca's face, the pale, luminous quality of her skin and the eyes, which are neither blue nor grey but some colour in between, smudged with a dusty bloom of violet, that give her a faintly bruised look. A helpless, innocent look although there is nothing innocent about Rebecca. Nor helpless either. A vein, a faint tracery of blue, runs from the corner of her right eye, threading into the silvery blonde hair that grows at her temples. 'Fairy hair,' Beattie called it. Her little fingers itched to stroke it, to tangle themselves through the long silken skeins that ran from a widow's peak arching off the wide, pale forehead and swept down the length of her back.

Men dream of such hair, of such a face. So do small children. So do I. I dream of slapping that face. Even now.

The bed creaks under me. 'I'm going,' Ben says. His face looks bleary, as if some giant's finger had poked out from the clouds and smudged his features. It is the blurry caress of shock.

I get up to follow him to the door, but he motions me back with a sharp gesture of his arm. The door bangs and he is gone.

I go back to bed, lie down, calculate how long it will take him to get home to her. Thirty minutes, maybe twenty at this time of night. I think of Ben's long body, hunched over the steering wheel, his pale eyes fixed on the dark, empty streets.

Then I think of Rebecca lying in a bath, cloudy pink water lapping at white breasts, her face obscured by a faint, vaporous steam, silvery blonde hair darkening at the temples. Jagged cuts criss–cross her thin white wrists, the

3

edges of the torn skin curling back like sea anemones as blood coils into the water.

Is she dead? Nearly, perhaps.

My heart is beating too fast, sending the blood jerking through my body. I sit up, then lie down again, knowing there is nothing for me to do but wait. *Wait*. It's such a small, quiet word, the opposite of what I am feeling. Knowing I will not sleep, I pull on an old dressing-gown, walk quickly through the silent house. A door is open on the landing. The dim glow of a night–light creeps over my long, bony feet. I look down and see white toes flashing in the light. The glow is coming from Beattie's room. The compulsion to stop and stare is overwhelming, but I turn my head and keep walking. I have lost too many nights like that.

I count the stairs that lead to the ground floor; an awkward combination of three steps followed by five followed by two, twisting through the centre of the old house. The unwary are often wrong–footed in that house. The kettle is still warm. I made tea for Ben when he arrived. He must have been here for an hour before he told me about Rebecca. I look up at the clock in the kitchen, try to remember what time it was when we stood here, talking easily, mugs of hot tea in our hands. The hands say it is twenty minutes past twelve. Was it ten when he arrived, or a little earlier? I try to remember what it felt like not to know, but I can't. All I can think of are Ben's fingers reaching into the cooling water to find Rebecca's pulse.

I drop a camomile tea-bag into a mug, hunch over the kettle waiting for it to boil, waiting for the telephone to ring. Will he telephone, once he's found her? Perhaps not. There'll be an ambulance to summon, paramedics to deal with. And he'll have to accompany the body to the hospital, of course. Will it be a body that he is taking, or Rebecca herself? Frightening how quick death is to rob a person of their identity.

4

The kettle boils. I pour water over the tea bag. It rises to the surface like a balloon, then deflates, bubbles slowly fizzing out of its papery skin. The old wood floor is rough and cold. I wish I'd put my slippers on but I can't be bothered now to go and get them. I curl my feet against the cold, flexing my toes. They look yellow under the neon light. The second toe is much longer than the big one. A sign of madness, so they say. Or genius. Opinion is mixed on this point.

I think again of my slippers but it's cold upstairs and dark, except for Beattie's room where it's cosy. The curtains are drawn. I made them for her, out of blue glazed cotton printed with white clouds, carefully stitching in a heavy inner lining to keep out the light. She hated any light at night. The glow of the night-light is for me, not her. There's a sheepskin rug by the bed, ready to warm her toes in the morning, and the Noddy duvet is smoothed back ready. Her bears, the three favourites, are lying on the pillow, waiting.

Beattie was still with me when we first met Rebecca. We were in Margaret's garden. Well, it's our garden, really. We have more right to it than Margaret, who is a sitting tenant and occupies the flat downstairs. Not that we ever say so. Margaret is passionate about the garden and we are not. Perhaps it's fair, then, that passion should triumph.

Margaret is in her seventies but still sprightly. She's small, but appears tall because of her regal bearing and the size of her head, which is too large for her body and seems larger still, crowned as it is with an abundance of white hair, pulled back in a rough bun. She has an imperious face, a bold, hawked nose and piercing small blue eyes. Her skin is creased like a map that has been folded and refolded many times. She looks, I think, like the sort of woman on whom empires were founded.

Margaret was Beattie's best friend, or so Beattie liked to

claim, despite the enormous age difference, but such considerations never deterred Beattie. When we moved into this house, Beattie was only five, but the two of them made friends immediately, spent hours together huddled in secret conversation.

The afternoon that we met Rebecca was Beattie's first day at school. It was September, an unusually hot September, just as it had been an unusually hot summer. So hot that it seemed to us then that the long warm days would be with us for ever. They weren't, of course. The weather broke that day, just like everything else.

Beattie appeared, limping, at the school gates. Her knee was badly grazed, a stretchy pink plaster stuck haphazardly over the wound, but I could see scratches extending like the rays of a violent red sun. I kissed her and made some joke about wounded soldiers to hide my alarm as we walked slowly through the hot streets, her fingers threaded through mine, one leg dragging slightly. I wanted to pick her up, carry her poor wounded body, but she would not suffer the indignity. Not on her first day at school. When we got home, I cleaned the graze with a pad of cotton wool and warm water, then smeared antiseptic cream across it. My fingers worked gently to disguise my anger at the teacher who hadn't seen to it better.

'How did it happen?' I asked, peeling papery wings off a pink plaster and sticking it gently across the cut. I needed to use the largest plaster in the box. It was a surprisingly big graze, and quite deep.

Beattie patted the plaster proudly. 'Can I wear it tomorrow?'

'Yes, of course. Now, what happened?'

'Mary pushed me over. She says she doesn't like me.'

The breath caught in my throat. I imagined slapping Mary until she bled and turned away from Beattie, shaken by the violence of my thoughts. 'And do you like Mary?' I asked, trying to keep my voice even.

'No. She's ugly.'

'That's no reason not to like her.'

Beattie shrugged, distracted by a dead fly on the floor. Squatting down, she lifted it by a wing, laid it on my hand. It looked very black against the pink skin. I flinched involuntarily, wanting to throw it away.

'Can I keep it?'

Not being able to think of a good reason why she shouldn't, I went to a drawer and pulled out a box of matches, shaking the matches back into the drawer. Then I laid a piece of cotton wool in the empty matchbox and handed it to her silently.

'Thanks, Mum,' Beattie said, tenderly depositing the dead fly on the lint. I longed to cup my hands over her fragile skull, the soft pink tops of the ears peeking through the gold, curling hair. She was still young enough to have that rare, inhuman beauty that all small children possess. But I knew that Beattie would shrug away my touch. She was an independent child. I taught her that much. So I said instead, 'Will you tell me if Mary hurts you again?'

'She won't.'

'But you'll tell me if she does?'

'OK. Can I go and show Margaret my plaster?'

'Will you tell me about school first?'

'It was fine.'

'What's your teacher like?'

Beattie gazed at me patiently. She had eyes the colour of a summer's morning; a clear, untroubled blue. 'Fine.'

'All right. Go and see Margaret. But don't disturb her if she's busy.'

I went and sat at my desk, staring at the manuscript on which I had been working, but could not settle to it. I kept seeing the asphalt peppering Beattie's tender flesh. In the end, I wandered downstairs.

'Ah,' Margaret said, 'I wondered how long it would take you.' She was wearing a dashing blue silk turban and red baggy trousers. Beattie was sitting at the kitchen table, her head bent over a drawing. 'Hi, Mum,' she said, without looking up. 'I'm doing a picture of my school for Margaret. She's so old she can't remember what they look like.'

Margaret smiled.

'Margaret's seventy–eight,' Beattie went on, 'so she'll die first.' She looked on us with serene eyes. 'Then you'll die and then me.'

'Not for a long time, I hope,' I said.

Beattie shrugged and turned back to her drawing. 'Margaret's got a good ten years left in her.'

Margaret's mouth twitched. 'Or at least, she hopes she has.' She turned to me. 'Why don't you go and sit in the garden? I'll make us both a cup of tea.'

The tiny garden is paved, with narrow beds running around the walls. Clematis, jasmine and everlasting sweet-peas cover every inch of brick. There are containers, dozens of them, transformed from anything that Margaret can lay her hands on; old yoghurt pots, broken-handled buckets, a butler's sink, each densely planted with flowers. The scent is overwhelming.

I submitted to it, sprawled in a chair, my face tilted to the sun, still uneasy about Beattie's knee, the blood congealing like sticky jam.

A memory appeared, of being bullied at school. I must have been about Beattie's age, maybe a year older. It was my first visit to England. Home, my parents called it, their voices taking on a vague, unfocused yearning. I did not understand what they meant. Home to me was Arabia.

The thing I remembered most was the absence of light, the way it lent everything a depressed, leaden quality. I woke that first morning to a bright light shining in my eyes from a bare bulb poking out of a grimy nylon shade, pink and frilly as a petticoat. My mother was at the window, drawing back the thin curtain.

'Is something the matter?' I asked, scrambling to my knees to peer out at the pitch-black gardens.

My mother looked at me with surprise. 'No.'

'Is it morning, then?'

'In England it's always dark in the mornings at this time of year. Now hurry up and get dressed.'

A pile of clothes was arranged neatly on a chair at the end of the bed. She must have come in during the night and laid them out.

'Are we going somewhere?' I asked, but my mother had already gone. Her voice floated up the narrow stairs.

'School.'

I stared stupidly at the blank doorway. 'School? What school?'

No reply. There was nothing for it but to get dressed and go downstairs. 'What school?' I asked, pushing porridge around the bowl.

'Gypsy Road Primary. It's just down the road. And do eat that up, Janey, there's a good girl.'

'Are they expecting me?'

'Your father wrote, before we left.'

So this had been planned, then. 'I won't know anybody.'

My mother smiled vaguely. 'You'll be fine. You'll see.'

I am standing at the front of the class, the teacher's hand resting heavily on my shoulder. 'This is Jane Rose. She will be with us for the next few weeks.' There is a sour note of disapproval in her voice. My heart lurches despairingly. Mysteriously, I have already done something wrong.

The teacher, whose name is Mrs Malcolm, eyes the two empty desks in the class. 'Claire? Tommy?' she says, her voice false and bright.

Nobody stirs. Mrs Malcolm sighs. 'Very well, go and sit next to Claire,' she says, propelling me forward with a sharp push.

Claire is a square, dumpy girl with a prim mouth and

9

small, lashless eyes. She has a double desk, right at the front of the class. I sit down in the empty chair next to her and smile eagerly, holding out my hand in the way I have been taught to do. Claire's eyes flicker towards my outstretched hand, then she sets her face to the blackboard, her mouth pursed in a smug pink smile.

A few children snigger. Claire blushes proudly. I let my hand drop and hunch over my desk, picking at the splintered wood and trying to concentrate on what Mrs Malcolm is saying.

A bell sounds. I jump to my feet. Nobody else moves.

'Milk monitors,' Mrs Malcolm calls. Two children rush to the front of the class and begin hauling bottles out of a crate. Mrs Malcolm takes two and hands one to Claire and one to me.

I stare in astonishment at the small, squat bottle, the milk curdling yellow at the neck. 'What's this?'

Mrs Malcolm eyes me cautiously. Perhaps I seem as strange to her as I do to the children; skinny and brown, with an odd accent and an uncomfortably exotic past. 'Milk,' she says, attempting a pleasant smile, 'to make you big and strong.'

Back home, milk comes in cardboard boxes marked Long Life in huge green letters. It is disgusting, even in tea. The two milk monitors grin, nudging each other with sharp, six–year–old elbows. I bend my head and suck nervously on the waxy straw. English milk is disgusting too.

I follow the other children out to the playground, stand against a wall, the bottle growing warm in my hand. Occasionally, one of the children runs over and jabs me with a hard finger. Otherwise they leave me alone. The bell rings and we queue to go back inside. Claire comes up behind me and pushes hard. I skid down onto the scratchy asphalt. Miraculously, the bottle does not break. Still more miraculously, when I pick it up it is empty.

That evening, my mother dabs antiseptic on my wounded knees. Her hand is not quite steady. Nor is her voice. 'People are unkind about difference,' she says, easing asphalt out of the graze. The antiseptic hurts, but I am too distracted by her face to notice. My mother's soft pink mouth has tightened to a hard red line and her kind, short-sighted eyes are watery. Then, I thought that it was the smell of the disinfectant that affected them. But when I was grown, and had a child of my own I understood it had nothing to do with that at all.

'It's their loss,' my mother says, stoppering the small brown bottle firmly and giving me a kiss. 'You'll see.'

My mother haunts the school gates every lunch break. She tries to hide, does not know that I see her drooping anxiously against the wide, red-brick pillars or peering through the gates to see if I am playing with anyone.

I never am, but when I see my mother I skip into the nearest game and shout and laugh until I think my lungs will burst. The others see her too and let me play, obeying the curious code of honour that children observe to protect grown-ups from unpleasant truths.

It is only later that they beat me, in the passageway by the bike sheds where no adult ever goes. It is always Claire leading the pack, her small lashless eyes blinking with pleasure as she thrusts a fat fist into my stomach or tugs at my hair until my eyes water.

I never fight, just wait patiently for them to finish, so there is little pleasure in it for them. I know, from the lonely double desk, that nobody likes Claire but they follow like small animals, attracted by the scent of her excitement.

Claire enjoys herself, grunting with satisfaction at each blow. 'Aay-rab,' she chants, 'filthy dirty Aay-rab.'

I am found out in the end, of course, but by then it is nearly over.

11

My mother is brushing my hair. Most of it comes out in the brush. 'Oh,' she says, blinking sadly at the hairbrush.

The next morning my mother marches into the classroom, in the middle of Reading Time. Ignoring Mrs Malcolm's surprised face, she comes and stands in front of my desk, staring out at the children. There are two bright spots of colour in her cheeks and her beautiful hands tremble like leaves, but her voice is strong and clear. 'You are bullies,' she says, 'and cowards, and when you are grown I hope that you will remember this moment and be ashamed.'

She takes my hand and leads me from the classroom. I cast a last look over my shoulder and see on Claire's plump, smudgy face an expression of sad and infinite envy.

A shadow fell across my face, blocking out the sunlight. I opened my eyes to find Beattie standing over me, her face a dark shape against the bright light.

'Mummy!'

I struggled upright, hearing the thread of urgency in her voice.

She patted my hand distractedly, frowning in excitement. 'Mummy, there's a lady with fairy hair in the house.'

'What's fairy hair?' I asked, amused.

'You know, curly and long and –' her arms bunched out at her sides, as she struggled to convey the magic of this hair. ' – like candyfloss, but golden.'

I craned my head, intrigued by this description, but Beattie's hand tightened on mine. 'Shh,' she whispered urgently, 'she's coming.'

A woman stepped from the house. She scarcely made a sound. Her white dress billowed around her long, slender body but the first thing I noticed about her was the light that seemed to cloak her in a pale, luminous aura. It was only then that I noticed her beauty, which was excessive.

As she moved towards me, I saw that her face was as familiar to me as my own, although I knew only the newspaper version of it, a smudgy black-and-white print that I had brooded over for eight years. She held out a hand. It was cool to the touch. 'I'm Rebecca.'

A faint movement came from the french windows. I looked up to see a man, staring down at me with appalled fascination. I dropped the hand as the blood jerked in my veins. It was Ben.

He stepped into the garden followed by Margaret, carrying a tray piled with cups and saucers. I turned away from him to help her, depositing the heavy load on the table and carefully sorting out cups and saucers. None of them matched. My hands were shaking slightly, but on the whole I was pleased by my composure.

'Have you all introduced yourselves?' Margaret said. 'Jane and Beattie moved in upstairs a couple of months ago. I suppose you might say she is my landlady.' She smiled at me. The landlady line is a joke between us. 'Ben is my great-nephew.'

I looked at him. It seemed impossible, but there he was, his pale hair still flopping over his eyes, his face a little older. We did not smile. Nor did we say that we knew each other. Some things are better not told.

Beattie edged closer to Rebecca. 'Are you a fairy really?'

Everyone laughed except Rebecca, who reached out long, slender fingers and twined them around Beattie's small hand. 'Why, yes,' she said, 'and if you'd like it, I'll tell you the story of how I came to be one.'

Beattie's face dazzled with ecstasy. It was rare for her to be offered a story. Usually, she had to plead.

Rebecca tugged gently at Beattie's hand, leading her to the far end of the garden. 'Come and sit in the shade with me. I hate the sun.'

'Would you like tea?' Margaret called, but Rebecca shook her head. 'No thank you.' Her gaze flickered to Ben.

'A glass of water would be nice.' He smiled obediently and I watched him walk up the garden, wondering at her words, how careful the phrasing. It was only later that I learned that Rebecca never made demands. At least, not directly.

Ben returned with the glass of water, bending over her attentively while he fussed about, trying to find a flat piece of ground to put it on. My stomach cramped at the sight of his humility and I wondered what the price would be for clumsiness.

Rebecca's voice reached out, soft but insistent, 'Thank you, my darling,' then Ben was back with us, his gaze still lingering on the dappled shade where Rebecca sat, her white dress glowing slightly. At her wrists she had wound pale-blue satin ribbons. They rose and fell like silvery fish as she described to Beattie how it was she came to be a fairy princess.

Ben did not look at me.

Two

We were young when we first met, although we believed we were already old. Ben was twenty-five. I was twenty-three. We weren't together long, a matter of months. We parted badly. He says it was my fault, that had I never run from him all this would never have happened. By all this he means Rebecca. It is a fair summary. Rebecca is a force to be reckoned with. Or, perhaps, *was* a force. Is she dead yet?

It is past one o'clock now. I watch time swarm across the clock face, then glance at the window, as if I can see into the darkened garden below, can hear Rebecca's maddening, insistent voice. Ben still has not telephoned. I sip my cooling tea and think about death. Not Rebecca's. Not even my own. I think about the first death I ever saw.

I close my eyes and the smell is with me at once. It is the smell of home, the spicy, scented air of Arabia. How I love that smell, how I miss it even now. I have tried sometimes with cardamom pods and amber resin, with cumin and coriander, to recapture the sweet, brackish scents of my childhood. I think perhaps that the missing ingredients are urine and a certain thick, dusty quality to the air.

It is just after six in the morning, but the sun is already hot. It burns down on my neck as I scuff my school sandals through the sand, feeling it seep through the daisy punched in the leather toe of the shoe and trickle warmly between my toes.

There is a sharp screech of brakes, then nothing, only

silence: not a calm absence of noise but the silence of terror, like the bated nothingness before an explosion. I run out to the road, stumbling a little, hampered by the sand in my shoes. Little Johnny Johnson is lying half-way under an army lorry. He looks as if he is asleep, his mouth curved in a small, puzzled smile. The only mark on him is a wide black tyre track decorating the front of his white Aertex school shirt.

I hear the sound of running feet, soles slapping urgently on the stony ground. 'Get a blanket,' the headmaster, Mr Foster, says. He takes me by the shoulders, his face as bleached as Johnny's shirt. 'My wife will have one in the flat.'

I do not move, my attention is riveted by a man climbing slowly out of the lorry. He is crying, his face twisted in a strange, ugly pattern. The tyre is so big, it comes up to his shoulder. The air around him burns with the smell of scorched rubber, sharp and acrid. I have never seen a grown man cry before. Certainly not one in army uniform. He doesn't even try to hide his tears, lets them flow down his face, his big hands hanging by his khaki knees, red as hams. Noticing me, he raises his hands imploringly. 'Nothing I could do, ran out right in front of me, he did. Right in front.'

A small group gathers around, staring. A woman knocks me with her elbow as she pushes forward, trying to get a better look.

I run for the blanket. When I get back, the headmaster's wife at my heels, I see Johnny's mother coming up the road, her feet slipping and sliding in the loose sand. Her face has disappeared, swallowed up by the gaping hole of her mouth.

Mrs Foster sees her too. I feel the shock of it go through her, like a bolt of electricity. 'Go back to the classroom,' she says, taking me by the shoulders. I twist away from her towards the sound, a high, thin, screaming noise.

'Now,' Mrs Foster says, giving me a gentle shove.

It was years later that I came across Edvard Munch's painting, *The Scream*. I thought, why, it's Mrs Johnson.

The night that little Johnny Johnson dies I cry in my bed. At the same time that I am crying a part of me is thinking how it was that nobody ever mentioned Johnny Johnson's name without saying little Johnny Johnson. Why was that? Was it because everyone knew he would die young? And if so, how did they know? I am conscious, as I am crying, that I am not devoting myself fully to my task. It seems a bad thing to be doing, to be thinking of something else while your face is occupied with tears.

A shadowy shape appears in the doorway, my mother's scented darkness slips over me. 'What is it, darling? Is it little Johnny Johnson?'

I nod, although it is not Johnny Johnson I am thinking of but the world, which is no longer benign. I fumble for words but find none to explain.

The next morning I am up early, making coffee. I haven't slept. Nor, from the look of him, has Ben. His face is waxen. He comes and leans against me as if I am a lamppost. I shift slightly under the hot weight of him but he does not budge. I wonder, if I moved, whether he would topple like a felled tree.

'She's dead, then?' The words come out in a whisper.

Ben pushes me away and blunders across the room to slump heavily in the chair. He places his hands on the table carefully, as if they are something heavy and precious.

I wonder if he has heard, say again, 'Is she dead?'

'Yes.'

The word drops between us like a stone. I want to hear everything, every tiny detail. I need to hear them to make it real but Ben just goes on staring at his hands and I think that this is not the time. 'You didn't sleep,' I say, pouring strong coffee. The burned acrid smell of it swirls around us. 'Hot or cold milk?'

Ben does not look at me. 'I'd like to make love,' he says in a low voice. 'Now.'

I stand motionless by the cooker, a carton of cold milk in one hand, an empty saucepan in the other. 'Hot, then,' I say.

He looks up at me. 'Is that very wicked?'

My mouth quirks. 'Perhaps inappropriate.'

'How very prim you are sometimes.' He is staring at me, and I wonder what he feels for me, after all that has happened.

'Perhaps,' I say.

'I didn't mean that.' He looks away. 'What are we going to do?'

I put a cup of coffee in front of him. The surface is streaked with the white scum of heated milk. He stares into it, not moving. 'You don't need me,' he says.

I sigh. We have been through all this before. 'You don't need anyone.'

'Not now, Ben, please.'

'I love you.'

I know what he wants me to say, but I don't.

He waits, then gives up. 'Never mind. Think I'll go down and see Margaret.'

'Have you told her?'

'I rang her first thing this morning.'

'The whole story?'

'No. Not yet.'

After he has gone, I sit at the table thinking about Ben. He's right, of course. He always is about things like that. I don't need him, or not in the way he believes I should, clinging to him for dear life, for dear love. There was a time, just after Beattie left, when I felt like that, felt that the waters would close over my head without him. Ben thought I would be that way for ever.

He says I've changed since we first met. I say that I haven't, but there is an edge to my voice; a faint hum, like the high-pitched whine of a buzz saw. He hears it too. It sets his teeth on edge. 'It's Rebecca, isn't it?' His face is set, white with intensity.

I don't answer. Who was it who left, anyway? Who was it who married somebody else? Not me. I thought I would die of it when I heard. I didn't, of course. Ben's right. I never lose control. Not me. But then Beattie was born and I discovered passion of a different sort. Before she was born I would never have believed that another person's flesh could be so familiar, but when I was with her I could not tell where hers ended and mine began. Sometimes, when some dream or childish infection drove her to my bed, she would curl up beside me, her small, sturdy body stuck to mine like a limpet. We would sleep like that the long night through and, in the morning when I woke, I would wonder that I felt no consciousness of another person in the bed beside me. It was as if I had slept with my hand resting on my own leg or arm.

It was only after Beattie left that Ben and I came together again, as if she had made a space for him. As to whether I would *want* to live without him, well, that's a different question, but it is not one Ben asks. We see love differently. When Beattie left, I was destroyed. The me that exists now is a different person. Ben knows that – he was the one who put me back together and I'm grateful to him for that. But now he wants to be loved in the way that I loved my child, in that enveloping, physical, greedy way most people think of love.

I can't do it and it angers him to know that, hard as he tries not to let me see. It shows in the faint hardening of his jaw, in the static that sparkles sometimes in his eyes. It's always there, even during the weeks when I can't keep my hands off him. Ben says I ebb and flow like the tide, one moment I'm crashing up against him and the next I'm sucked away to some other place. He says the crashing times don't make up for the rest, the days when I separate myself from him, withdraw into a space all my own. He blames my childhood for my coldness, for my way of closing down when things get difficult, when I think I am going to have to give away too much. Perhaps he's right. I don't know. Who knows what makes us? All we know is what others tell us. We can't be witnesses to ourselves, we lack the clarity that distance brings.

He's right about one thing. It was a fragmented childhood. Shards of it are embedded in my soul like splinters. We lived on the hoof; house to house, school to school, country to country. We travelled light, as nomads must, discarding belongings, clothes, toys and people like sloughed-off skins. Ben says it was that early restlessness that gave me my fine talent for saying goodbye. And my disdain for sentiment in matters of the heart.

A door bangs violently. I move to the window, look out to see Ben hurrying up the steps that lead down to Margaret's flat. He takes them two at a time, his knees jerk up and down like pistons. I can tell, from the set of his head, that he is angry. Or perhaps upset. He has a right to be. His wife has just committed suicide. He is angry because he couldn't save her – and because he did not want to. He is angry because Rebecca needed him, angry because even need was not enough. He is angry because life is unfair. And death is unfairer still.

As he reaches his car, Ben stops and stares up at my window. I duck down, crouching below the wooden sill.

I am not sure why.

There is silence, then the cough of an engine turning over, firing into life. It fades quickly. I get shakily to my feet and go downstairs.

Margaret never locks her front door, which I tell her is foolish, but she says that although she is old and can do

20

nothing about that, she refuses to be old and frightened too.

It makes me nervous, thinking of her down there with nothing between her and violence. I suggest buying her a personal alarm, the sort you can get to terrify would-be rapists. Or not. A man whose reason is clouded with violence is hardly likely to be frightened by a shrill piece of plastic. Even so, it would make a noise. I would hear it.

'And how about a help button for when I break my hip?' Margaret says crisply. I sigh and leave it.

There is silence in the flat. I hurry down the corridor towards the kitchen, which is at the back of the flat, overlooking the garden. It is empty, but I am relieved to find the french windows locked. I wonder what it is that is making me so nervous. Then I remember. Rebecca is dead. Death makes everyone nervous.

The sitting-room is empty and the bathroom. Eventually I find Margaret in her bedroom, sitting on the edge of her bed with her hands folded squarely in her lap, her feet dangling over the edge. She looks small and very old.

I sit next to her. The bed heaves under me and I realise how little Margaret must weigh, scarcely anything at all.

'He told you, then,' I say, after a while.

She shakes her head. 'I never thought she'd do it. Or rather, I never thought she'd succeed.'

I say nothing.

'She was always so careful to be found. She must not have realised how strong those pills are.'

I have the picture of Rebecca all wrong, then. All night I imagined blood-clouded water lapping at white breasts.

'Pills? I thought she'd cut her wrists.'

'Oh, no. Ben said, quite distinctly, that she had taken sleeping pills.'

A pot of loose face powder is standing on Margaret's dressing-table. By its side is a pink swansdown puff. A scattering of powder blooms on the surface of the dark wood.

'And then, of course,' Margaret is saying, 'she would have timed everything for Ben's arrival. It's just bad luck he got caught up in a meeting.'

I keep my silence.

'Well,' Margaret says with a sigh, 'she wasn't to know.'

'No,' I say. 'She wasn't.'

I go upstairs, try and settle to my work, but my mind will not be still. All I can think of is death. It is Rebecca who is dead, but it is my mother I think of, can even now hear the clatter of her heels on a wooden veranda.

She always wore shoes a size too large.

The clattering gets louder, my mother's voice thin and high as if she is out of breath. Then she's upon me, tumbling through the door of the bedroom, scooping me up in her arms. 'Home!' she exclaims, in that same queer, breathless voice, 'we're going home!'

I wrestle myself away and look up to see the lines on my mother's usually careworn face smoothed away with excitement, her cheeks young and pink. Pleased to see her looking so well, I scoot back over and hug her. Even then, I always preferred to be the one doing the hugging. Mother pats my back absently. She has gone into one of her reveries, dreaming as she so often does through the days.

'When?' I say. 'When are we going home?'

For a moment she looks blank, then releases me with a startled cry, exclaiming that there is so much to be done. Hurrying over to the wardrobe, she throws it open. Her glance is despairing, every particle of her thin, pliant body seems to droop. My mother is beautiful, even when she droops. Especially when she droops. Everybody says so, unable to resist a furtive, bewildered swivel of the eyes as they seek us out, comparing our two faces.

Today she is wearing a fitted dress with a wide scooped

22

neck, neat cap sleeves and a tight skirt that slides over her hips. It is in a splashy rose-print cotton and she has matched the red of the roses to her lipstick, and to her sandals, which are made of fine leather straps and have low, pointy heels. She looks with despair at the boy's shorts and soft cotton shirts stacked in neat piles in my wardrobe. Heaving a sigh she says, 'We'll just have to send to England for some warm clothes and hope they arrive in time.'

Her beautiful hands delve into the back of the wardrobe, emerge clutching a cardigan. Beckoning me over, she holds it up against my skinny chest. I cast a last longing glance at the book I was reading, then go and stand obediently in front of her. The cardigan doesn't fit, of course. It was mine when I was three and now I am six, and tall for my age.

'It doesn't fit,' my mother says, wrinkling her nose.

I look up at her. 'Will I see snow?'

Mother looks doubtful. 'It will be spring, but I've known it to snow, even in April.' Her face clears, her gaze going out over my head to the flat, changeless landscape of cracked rock and brown thorny shrubs outside the window. 'That's the thing about the English weather,' she says, kissing me absently. 'You never know what it will bring.'

She leaves in a flurry of words, trailing shopping lists as she goes. 'Cardigans and woollen trousers. And shoes. Oh God, she must have shoes.'

I gaze disconsolately at a pile of shorts. No snow. What is the point of an England without snow? I long to see it, to see a landscape transformed into a glittering fairyland. It has been described to me often enough: white and very cold, with a crunch like sugar under your feet.

Every year, my mother sends home to England for an advent calendar that she hangs on the wall in my bedroom. It is always the same picture of a group of houses in a forest, their lighted windows twinkling cosily, their roofs iced with snow. I lie in bed, staring at the calendar, picture myself scooping snow off those low sloping roofs and eating it like ice-cream.

Cold is harder to imagine. We live on the Tropic of Cancer. 'The hottest place in the world,' my father says, tracing his finger across a page in the big, heavy world atlas, following the faint blue line that bisects Muscat, the nearest town. The heat outside is tremendous. We know never to go out in the mid-day sun, to brace ourselves as we step out of the door for the heat that scorches our throats and knocks the air from our lungs. My father says that in England it is the cold that rips at your throat and stings your eyes. In even colder countries the tears freeze on your eyelashes.

I huddle against the air-conditioner in my parents' bedroom, my face thrust into the blasts of icy air as I try to imagine how frozen tears would feel, chipping at my eyelashes.

'What are you doing, you little goose?' my father asks.

'Trying to imagine cold.'

He laughs merrily. 'Good God, this isn't cold. This is like an English summer.'

'Good God,' I say, through chattering teeth.

We live among Arabs, handsome men and women with flashing eyes, smooth brown skins and strong white teeth. We live among them but apart, creating our own little England where there is always the six o'clock BBC World Service news, gin and tonics on the veranda and boiled eggs and cocoa for the children at tea.

We are like concubines, protected from the life that chatters, noisy and colourful, outside the gates of the compound. There is a social club, cinema, swimming pool, tennis courts, beaches, a school and one shop – a low grey concrete bungalow, stacked with shelves of imported English food – which my mother visits weekly, bringing home packets of dusty tea, flour that we sieve for weevils, meat frozen hard as rocks and packets of sour, metallic Long Life milk that she dribbles sadly into the endless cups of tea that punctuate her day.

Two hundred families live inside the barbed-wire fence, most of them English, their fair skins protected by air-conditioners and long shady verandas. There are about two thousand outside, crammed into the dusty, crowded souk, living five to a room. The low, mud-walled houses are surprisingly cool inside and clean, the smooth sand floors patterned with the brush strokes of twig brooms. We visit them rarely, once a year, during the celebrations that mark the end of Ramadan.

'Best behaviour,' my father warns, ducking through a low door. 'We mustn't let Mohammed down.'

Mohammed is our houseboy. He leads us through the narrow jumbled streets of the souk, one bony wrist emerging stiffly from the sleeve of his white cotton robe as he beckons us on. Herding us into his house, he settles us on rugs, claps his hands imperiously. A cluster of women and children appear, carrying trays of food. They lay them at our feet, crowding around, hands hovering over heads and faces as if they would like to touch but don't quite dare. Mohammed gazes proudly, as if we are trophies he has brought home.

One old woman starts to shriek 'aye! aye! aye!' and is led away in disgrace. My family is all fair, with blond hair and blue eyes.

Mohammed says later that his grandmother thought we were ghosts, so devoid are we of colour. 'She knows nothing,' he says matter-of-factly. 'She never leaves the house.'

The parcel of warm clothes arrives.

'In the nick of time,' my mother exclaims, unpacking scratchy woollen trousers and cardigans with glass buttons shaped like flowers.

The next morning, just as the sun is turning the earth pink, we drive to the airport, bumping over gaping potholes where the tarmac has melted into the porous yellow sand. A faded signpost, on which somebody has painted the words International Airport, lurches drunkenly in the loose, shifting sand. We walk into a tin hut where we show our passports to uniformed officials who finger them with solemn curiosity.

As we clamber up the rusted iron steps into a looming Dakota ten-seater, my mother cast a triumphant look over her shoulder. 'Thank God,' she says, but she whispers it under her breath so that my father won't hear. She loves him and so she must love everything that he does.

The aeroplane heaves itself into the sky, its thin walls shuddering alarmingly. My mother, indifferent to our certain death, keeps mouthing something at me and pointing excitedly at the windows. I can't hear above the din of the propellers, so I press my face to the cold, sand-blasted windows and stare at the desert below. It flows beneath us like a sea, its surface swept by the wind into billowing ripples, stretching on and on to infinity.

Infinity, as it turns out, is not so far away. The oceanic expanse of the desert has an end after all, slipping into a straggling shore of mud-coloured houses and half-finished buildings, the steel rods of their innards poking out the eye of the sky. The aeroplane swoops down over a dusty patch of earth and lands with a tremendous bump.

'Are we there?' I say, looking out at the arid earth.

My mother laughs and hugs me. 'England is green.'

We get on another plane, then another. Each time they get bigger and bigger, and each time my mother covers me with another layer of clothes until the only bare skin I can see are my hands, yellow and dirty under the aeroplane's harsh lights. I wriggle uncomfortably in my cocoon of wool until an air hostess with hair like a helmet and eyelashes as black and stiff as spiders' legs takes pity on me and hands me a colouring book and a set of miniature coloured pencils. I struggle to fill in a few blocks but my arms, encased in unfamiliar layers of wool, itch too much from the effort. I lie back, closing my eyes while my mother chatters excitedly about cousins whom I have never met, and all the thrilling things we will see and do. 'Home,' she says, her voice filled with longing. 'Home.'

I am soothed by the sound of her voice but my feet, clamped in their cruel leather prisons, will not be still. As we hurtled through the darkening skies they wriggle constantly, longing for the abandoned pleasure of sand between the toes.

Home turns out to be a damp, grey place. England is not green at all but filled with the skeletons of trees brooding under a lead-white sky and narrow, undernourished streets clustered with thin, blank-eyed houses. There is no snow.

When at last the taxi pulls into a narrow grey street, we tumble out to burrow down in the dark, nocturnal afternoon in a strange, cold house filled with furniture that is not our own.

'Careful,' my mother says. 'We'll have to pay for it if anything gets broken. Careful!' she calls again as I scurry through the rooms exploring. For a long time afterwards I associate that word with England; England the careful, a country full of care.

'I suppose I should go and see about the beds,' my mother says. 'I expect they'll be damp.'

My father moves towards her, gently circles an arm around her head and bends it to lie in the crook of his neck. They sway against each other like pale statues in the dim afternoon light. 'I'll light a fire,' he says. 'That'll make us more cheerful.'

I look at his bright, false smile and feel puzzled. We are cheerful. We are home.

Three

The police have been informed.

Ben says they want to talk to me. He leans against the front door, passing the information on as casually as if it were a telephone message. He won't come in. There are things he needs to attend to.

I gaze at him in astonishment. 'But why do they want to talk to me?'

'I don't know. Something about the pills they found in Rebecca's handbag.'

'What pills?' I say, although there is no need to ask. I know the answer already.

His expression draws in, grows furtive. He will not look at me. Does he hold me responsible, because of the pills? But, no, it's something else. 'I told them I was with you that night.'

Now I understand. We are conspirators. I say slowly, 'You didn't tell them that you went home first?'

He shakes his head. 'No.'

So I am an accomplice, then. Or some such thing. Can you be an accessory to a suicide? I don't know. There's so much I don't know. 'You might have asked me first.'

'Yes, I'm sorry. Things happened so fast. I didn't know what else to say.'

There are questions I want to ask. How fast did things happen? What time did Rebecca die? I understand they can work it out to the minute these days. I think of something Margaret said. Has he lied to her too, as well as

29

to the police? 'Margaret thinks you were at a meeting. That's why you got home late.'

He looks bewildered. 'Does she? I think I just said I was late getting home. I don't recall telling her where I'd been.'

I say nothing. It is not my place to judge him. I, too, have my reasons for staying silent.

The policeman looks tired. Surprisingly so for such a young man. He leans forward, hands me a small brown bottle with a slightly faded label stuck on the front. I have to squint to read it. My name is on the label. 'Are these yours?' His tone is gentle, pleading almost. I can see he wants no trouble.

There is no need to examine the bottle. I know it contains sleeping pills. Or, at least, it used to. It is empty now.

A vision of Rebecca's face floats into my mind, her smooth brow puckered in a slight frown. 'Would you think it the most awful cheek if I asked you to let me have some sleeping pills?'

She is standing in my bedroom, plucking at the thin sleeves of her blouse with long, nervous fingers. 'It's just that I haven't slept in weeks and it's hell. If only I could get a few hours, I'd find everything much more manageable.'

I look up at the young, tired policeman. 'Yes, they're mine.'

The expression on his face is half regretful, as if he had hoped that there might be some mistake.

I show him the label. 'My name's on it.'

He takes the bottle with a sigh.

Down at the station, the Detective Inspector is less friendly. Not that he's unfriendly but he's distant, reserved.

He holds out the small brown bottle again. 'Did you give this bottle to Rebecca Robinson?'

'Yes.'

'Were you aware that she had a history of suicide attempts?'

I nod.

'But you still gave her sleeping pills?'

'She said she was desperate.'

The Detective Inspector lets out a short laugh, like a bark. 'All the more reason, I would imagine, not to let her have them.'

I can see what he is getting at. In the past twenty-four hours I have wondered myself what my motivation was. What was I thinking? Perhaps I did hope she would take them and die.

I try to recall that afternoon.

We were standing in the kitchen. Rebecca had come to visit Beattie. She had a passion for Beattie – her words, not mine. Rebecca always did overstate the case. She mentioned the sleeping pills, said, 'You don't mind?'

Her face was in profile. She raised a hand, tucked a gilded thread of stray hair behind her ear. The movement displaced a sleeve, long, with a trailing handkerchief point, of a style worn by Anne Boleyn. Rebecca affected them too, although poor Anne only wore them because they disguised an embryonic sixth finger, a boneless fleshy protuberance that jutted from her fifth finger. It was that harmless extra appendage that had her branded and beheaded as a witch. These days they remove them a few hours after birth, unless you happen to be Arab, in which case they are thought to be lucky. Rebecca had no extra fingers, although about the witchiness one could not be too sure. She wore the sleeves to hide the scars that gleamed pale on her thin wrists like the silvery trails left by slugs. She had attempted suicide twice before.

I thought of the scars and said, 'I'm not sure I have any sleeping pills –'

'Oh, but you do,' Rebecca exclaimed. 'I saw them in the bathroom cabinet earlier –' She trailed off, biting her lip like a small child caught out in some act of wrongdoing. 'I was looking for some soap.'

I knew there was a bar of soap lying on the cold enamel of the basin, so new that its make was still embossed on its smooth waxy surface.

'I really am desperate.'

I said reluctantly, 'Well, perhaps I could let you have a couple –'

But Rebecca's hand was already in the pocket of her dress. It emerged, clutching the brown bottle.

'I'll let you have them back, once this ghastly insomnia's gone.'

There were two things I could have done. I could have fought Rebecca for them or I could have told Ben. I did neither.

The Inspector's voice breaks in. 'So you admit that you supplied sleeping pills to Mrs Robinson, knowing that she had, on various occasions, attempted to take her own life.'

I nod.

The tape whirrs in the empty room. The Inspector leans back in his chair, threading his fingers together across his stomach. It is an inappropriate gesture for such a thin man. He grows impatient. He needs my voice, to feed life into the whirring tape. The fingers move to the table, begin to drum insistently. 'Miss Rose, did you or did you not supply Mrs Robinson with sleeping pills, knowing that she had twice made attempts on her life?'

'She took the pills from my bathroom cabinet.' My voice is loud, blanketing the drone of the tape.

'You did nothing to stop her?'

'No.'

The Inspector is silent for a moment, then he says, 'In his

statement Mr Robinson claims that he was with you that evening.'

I feel a slow creep of unease.

'Yes or no,' the Inspector says reprovingly, his eyes fixed on the tape.

'Yes.'

'And what time did he leave?'

'Just after eleven.'

'And when did he arrive?'

'Just before ten.'

'You are very precise about time.'

'I am very conscious of time.' I realise, as I say it, that this is true. Being late for anything makes me so excessively nervous that I keep a constant eye on the clock, albeit subconsciously. Perhaps it's because I live my professional life to deadlines.

He nods, satisfied. 'And may I ask what your relationship is with Mr Robinson?'

I gaze at him steadily. 'We are friends.'

Another impatient shift of his chair. 'Mrs Robinson seems to have thought it was more than that.'

'We have known each other for many years.'

'According to a letter written by Mrs Robinson, you were lovers and had been for some time.'

I imagine the letter, written in Rebecca's round, childish hand. A suicide note, I suppose. It doesn't surprise me. People rarely depart this life without wanting to leave their mark on it. Not, that is, unless they have touched the blankness of despair. 'No,' I say, 'it wasn't like that.'

Looking back on my young self, it is as if I was asleep until I was twenty when I was roused from my dreaming to see the world through wakeful eyes. I suppose it must happen to other people too, that sense of sudden wakening. Perhaps I simply came to it late.

It is absurd to say that one day my life began. My life

began when I was born and will go on until I die. Yet, one Thursday morning (I was born on a Thursday, so perhaps it does have some significance) something occurred that was to mark the beginning of the passage of my own life, as opposed to the passage of my life with my parents.

In those days I earned my living as a secretary, doing temporary work. Some jobs I stayed in for three weeks, some for three months. They were all the same to me.

It was early morning. I was standing at a bus-stop, on my way to work. The bus, as usual, was nowhere in sight. I waited, gazing unseeingly into the window of a shop nearby. Letters formed with sudden clarity. I read a small advertisement: 'Publisher needs help'. There was something endearing in the phrasing. Help seemed so much more persuasive than work. I looked up at the shop frontage and saw that I was standing in front of an employment agency; a small, shabby place that I must have passed a hundred times. As I stared in through the grimy window, a woman approached the door on the other side of the glass and twitched a sign to read 'Open'.

I pushed the door and walked in.

The woman looked up, irritable at the intrusion. She had blonde hair, the texture of dried grass, and lips painted a chalky pink. They gave her an odd appearance, as if she had been sucking on a pot of cream. 'Can I help you?' she said unwillingly. I heard the whine of a kettle coming to the boil. 'Won't be a sec,' she added and disappeared.

When eventually she emerged from behind a flowered curtain at the back of the shop, I explained about the card in the window.

'Oh, *that*,' she said, but her tone was less irritable. Tea has a calming effect on many people. She leaned forward confidingly. 'Between you and me, it all sounds most unsatisfactory. I've asked until I'm blue in the face but they still can't seem to say what this help is that they need.' She gave the word a sarcastic spin, her starched blue-and-white blouse rustling as if affronted by this display of amateurism. 'Is it a domestic? A bookkeeper? A clerk?'

Amused by her disapproval, I smiled. 'I'm interested anyway.'

She raised an affronted eyebrow. 'Well, it's up to you.' The chair swivelled as she turned away and picked up the telephone receiver, polished fingerails drumming on the wooden desk. After a while she leaned forward, spoke in hushed, confidential tones.

Putting the phone down, she swung back to face me. 'Nobody there yet.' Her expression indicated that she could have told me this without the bother of picking up the telephone.

I waited expectantly.

' . . . nobody in a position of any importance anyway.'

With a slight sigh she reached down behind the desk, snapped a small white card on the surface in front of her and wrote with brisk efficiency. 'I told whoever it was to note the appointment in George Curtis's diary. Whether they will or not is anybody's guess.' Her mouth, set in a pale, tight line, said that at least she had done *her* job.

She handed me the card. Allen Marshall Goodheart, it said, Publishers of Fine Books. I was expected at twelve noon the next day.

'Thank you.'

She shrugged. I could see that she had lost interest in me.

The next morning, at eleven fifty-five precisely, I presented myself at the offices of Allen Marshall Goodheart at number one Albion Mews. It was at the furthest end of a terrace of small white Georgian houses, approached down a cobbled street. A small brass plaque bearing the name was screwed into a red door, flanked on either side by tubs of roses. Two young women sat on a wooden bench, gossiping idly and flicking cigarette ash over the roses.

I looked towards them for help but they were engrossed with the night's conquests, so I pushed at the door tentatively and let myself in.

I found myself in a small hallway, painted white, with a scuffed grey carpet. In the middle of the room was a plain wood desk. On it sat a small telephone exchange and surrounding it a quantity of large cardboard boxes in various stages of packing, or unpacking. A young man was bent over a box, thin arms working furiously.

'Hello,' I said.

He grunted, furiously ramming books into the box. 'They won't fit.'

I walked towards him, stared down at the piles of books waiting to be packed. 'Perhaps there are too many of them.'

He stood up, pushing irritably at his hair, which immediately flopped back over his eyes, and aimed a kick at the box. He was tall and excessively thin, with a mouth that would make angels sing. 'Of course there are too many of them. There are always too many of them. You'd think they'd buy bigger boxes.'

'I have an appointment for a job.'

He looked at me properly for the first time. 'Are you help? They will be pleased.'

'I don't know.'

He shrugged, turned to glare at the box of books. 'Maybe you could help me.'

'I don't have a job yet,' I said patiently.

His eyes flicked over me appraisingly. 'You will.'

He was right. I did have a job. It was to start on Monday at nine thirty sharp. When I arrived, the same young man was standing in the hallway, gazing stonily at a pile of books. It must surely have been a different one but his stance was so much the same that I had a sudden dizzying sense of unreality. I tried to shake it off, stamping my shoes firmly on the worn grey carpet, but only succeeded in drawing attention to myself. The angelic mouth curved in a smile.

'I am to report to George Curtis. Could you tell me where I can find him?' Nervousness always makes me formal.

His eyes signalled some secret amusement as he pushed at the hair that flopped over his forehead. I wondered why he didn't get it cut if it bothered him so much. 'Up the stairs, second door on the left.'

I didn't know his name, nor he mine. This seemed awkward if we were to be working together. I held out my hand. 'I'm Jane Rose.'

He raised his in a casual salute. 'Ben.'

My hand filled the space between us, looking awkward and forgotten. I flipped it into a stiff salute. 'I'm new here.'

His amusement grew. 'Obviously,' he said, before turning back to the books.

I discovered the source of Ben's amusement when I mounted the stairs. George Curtis was not a man, but a woman. 'Are you help?' she asked, banging a pile of papers down on an already congested desk. I leaped forward, rescued a page of manuscript as it slid into certain oblivion. 'Thank God. Can you proof-read?'

I shook my head regretfully.

'Ah, well,' she said. 'Small mercies, then.'

Ben is waiting for me outside the police station. As I emerge and walk down the stone steps, I see that his face is crumpled.

When I reach him, his mouth buckles in misery. 'It's what she wanted,' he says. He puts his head down, swings it like a wounded bull. 'It's what she wanted.'

'Is it?' I say, reaching forward to hook his head so it lolls on my shoulder, hard and heavy. He opens his mouth, presses a hot tongue to my neck then cries with that deep belly noise that men like him make.

At first I cannot make out what he is saying, but then he pulls his head back and bellows at me: 'She never fucked me. She never fucking fucked me. Not in seven years. Not ever.'

I put my hand over his mouth, clamp it shut with hard fingers. 'Stop it,' I say. 'Stop it.'

His fingers slide between our bodies, worming under the scratchy wool of my jumper, past the elastic lace of my bra until my nipple is hot and sharp in his hand. I feel the pull of it in my stomach and glance around, aware that we are still standing outside the police station.

I pull my hand away, cradle him in my arms, rocking back and forth on the wet pavement, as car wheels hiss past. My legs are spattered with dirty water. 'Come on,' I say. 'We can't stay here.'

He groans and I slip from under him leaving him standing on the wet pavement, still swinging his head from side to side like a wounded animal. I take his chin in my hand, push it back. His eyes are bruised with exhaustion.

'We're going home,' I say more gently, slinging his arm over my shoulders and half carrying him towards the car.

We don't speak on the journey home. He is shaking violently but pulls himself together enough to climb the stairs to my bed and fall on it, breathing heavily. I pull off his shoes, lift a corner of the duvet and twist it over him, then go off in search of a blanket. There are none. I have lent them all to Margaret, who recently had friends to stay. I consider going downstairs to ask her for them, but decide against it. I am in no state to face Margaret now. Taking a deep breath, I walk into Beattie's room and snatch the Noddy duvet from the bed. Resisting the temptation to bury my head in it, I walk back to my bedroom and fling it on the bed.

Noddy's face leers up at me. I lie down, keeping my face turned to the ceiling although I want to gather the duvet in my arms, wrap my body around it. I have not washed it, or the cover, since Beattie went. I think of the way she used to sleep, tangled in the bedclothes, one arm flung protectively across her eyes. Or the way she used to hit me if I woke her, squealing in outrage as I tried to ease her limbs from their cotton embrace.

I hit out too, if people try to take me from my dreams.

I turn over, bury my head in Beattie's duvet and breathe in sharply. It smells slightly stale, the musty sourness of unwashed sheets. I open my eyes to see Big Ears beaming up at me. 'Fuck you,' I say and push my hand into his fat red face. Beattie has gone. There is nothing left of her. I rear up, weeping.

Ben lurches out of the bedclothes like a drowning man, pulls me down beside him. 'It's all right,' he says, stroking my hair. His hands are heavy, clumsy with exhaustion. 'It's all right.'

It is not all right, but we sleep.

Four

I wake early and lie watching the morning light expand into the room. Ben's arms are flung above his head, his breathing easy, his face smoothed to a boy's with sleep. I reach out a finger, trace the air above his mouth, careful not to wake him, then lie watching his sleeping face, remembering how I used to imagine mornings like these, the steady, consoling warmth of his body beside me.

I slide my feet out carefully, encounter something soft on the floor. Looking down, I see it is Beattie's duvet. It must have slipped off the bed as we slept. For a moment I feel a wash of tears and brace myself for the usual flood that follows. Nothing happens. I feel a surge of exhilaration. Maybe I'm getting better after all. Bundling the duvet under my arm, I resolve to wash it.

When I get downstairs, a pale-blue light is flooding into the kitchen. It is going to be a beautiful day. I rip the duvet from its cover, the Velcro makes a most satisfying noise, and push both pieces into the machine, loading in powder and fabric conditioner before I change my mind. The machine coughs into action. Noddy's face slowly disappears under a rising tide of soapy water.

Buoyed up by my mood, I go into the sitting-room and settle down at my desk to do some work. I am late with a manuscript, promised for Monday. It is Thursday already. I dash through it, enjoying the sensation of familiarity. The words rise and fall beneath my eyes, mistakes are gently ironed out by the smooth motion of my hands. Order is being restored.

A noise behind me alerts me to Ben who is in the kitchen making coffee. He appears in the doorway, tiptoes over, pantomiming silence, and drops a kiss on the top of my head.

I smile up at him. 'I thought I'd let you sleep late.'

He yawns, stretches hugely and for a moment it is as if we have always lived like this, Ben and me, me and Ben. I feel a sudden wash of tenderness and wonder if, after all, everything will be all right.

He peers down at the manuscript. 'What is it?'

'A concise history of underwear.' Costume is my speciality, mainly because it is no one else's.

'Brief,' Ben says, grinning. 'A brief history of under-wear.'

I smile back as it if were a new thought. 'Do I smell coffee?'

'There's some in the pot, but I must go. I'm late already. I'll leave you to it.'

His face is closed suddenly. I catch his hand, just as he turns away. He doesn't move, keeps his back to me as if he wants me to release it. I let go.

'The autopsy results are due this morning,' he says, rubbing his hand as though he had burned it.

'Will you be back?' I ask, but he doesn't answer. The air crowds in on us, dense and choking. Ben shoves his way through it, his shoulders held out like a man in a crowded department store.

I turn back to my work, but the words leap before my eyes, refusing to settle. I push the manuscript away, feeling as if I have been in some way let down and go to the kitchen to make tea, rifling through the cupboards in search of something sweet. My store cupboard is a disgrace. A half-used packet of spaghetti, a shelf's worth of spices, their lids capped by a crust of grey dust. I sweep them into the dustbin, load a cloth with gritty cream cleaner and rub at the sticky circles in a fury of distaste.

41

There was a time when the cupboards were full, when even a spare inch of wood made me uneasy. When I was a good cook, even a great one. There was a time, but it was long ago.

I remember Beattie, standing on a chair at the counter in the kitchen, pressing biscuit cutters into a circle of sweet shortbread dough; stars and hearts and Christmas trees. Her tongue edged out of her mouth, its pale-pink tip caught between her teeth as she grunted with concentration. It was the only way in which she resembled her father.

It was our first Christmas in the house. We were very happy. Margaret was to spend the day with us. Beattie was overjoyed. So, I think, was Margaret.

She telephoned as we were stuffing the turkey. Ben and Rebecca, who had planned to go to the Caribbean for Christmas, had cancelled their trip at the last minute. 'She really is being very insistent about me spending Christmas with them,' Margaret said.

'Oh,' I replied, wondering how I was going to tell Beattie who had been counting the days and was now busy on the hours.

An itch of irritation surfaced in Margaret's voice. 'I believe I told you that my niece – Ben's mother – lives abroad and Ben and his father are not close.' Dear Margaret, never one to overstate a case. Ben hates his father. She went on, 'As for Rebecca, her parents died some years ago. She says she feels the need of family around her at Christmas. Anyway, I'm the closest thing they've got.'

I thought how like Rebecca it was to mislay her own family and lay claim to somebody else's. 'Never mind,' I said, disappointment making my voice brisk. 'Another time, perhaps.'

Her voice tailed off mournfully. 'I'm so sorry to spoil all our arrangements.'

I put down the phone and walked into the kitchen where Beattie was manfully loading stuffing into the huge turkey. It was the smallest the butcher could offer us but it still looked enormous. I had considered buying a chicken instead but couldn't bring myself to make the substitute. As a child, my mother cooked turkey religiously each year, which we ate solemnly, and Christmas pudding too, even as the temperature outside reached a hundred and thirty degrees in the shade. Later, we would pile into my parents' bedroom, which had blessed air-conditioning, and lie on the bed recovering.

Beattie looked up, her small arm swallowed up in the bird's chest cavity. 'What's the matter? Your voice sounded funny.'

I said carefully, 'That was Margaret. Ben and Rebecca haven't gone away after all. Rebecca says she wants family around her so Margaret ought to be with them instead.'

Beattie's mouth curved into a circle of distress. 'Well, why can't they all come here?'

I thought of Ben at the table, a paper hat on his head, long legs dancing a jig, willing his body to follow and escape from us all. I remembered his eyes fixed on Rebecca, the loving absorption of his gaze and said, 'Oh, darling, they wouldn't want to do that.'

Beattie extracted her arm from the turkey's fleshy interior, then moved over to the sink and washed the stuffing from it. Frowning with concentration, she dried it carefully on a towel and walked out of the kitchen.

I finished stuffing the turkey, stitched down the flap of pink skin, securing it with a vicious double knot, then hurried along to Beattie's bedroom. It was empty. I went into my bedroom, the bathroom and the sitting-room, where the Christmas tree lights winked cheerily at me. Moving to the telephone, I dialled Margaret's number, heard her voice enunciating carefully; 'Double two one three double six four.' I could hear laughter in the background. 'Margaret,' I said, my voice coming in little bursts of fright, 'I'm so sorry to bother you but is Beattie with you by any chance? She was a bit upset earlier and she –'

'She came to invite us all to Christmas lunch,' Margaret said. She left a tactful silence. I knew then that she sensed the awkwardness between Ben and me, although neither of us had spoken of it. 'Ben's here. He's just telephoned Rebecca. We all think it's a good idea if you can bear it.'

I thought of Beattie's face and tears of shame pricked at my eyes. 'I can bear it.' My voice came out more harshly than I intended.

'Will you come down here for a drink?' Margaret said gently. 'We'd all like to see you.'

I went into the bathroom to wash my face and smooth on some lipstick. Changing out of my old jumper and jeans, I put on a pair of black trousers and a new jersey of fine crimson wool with a fleck of glitter running through it, which I had been saving for Christmas Day.

'Lovely,' said Beattie, who was very conscious of clothes. She was sitting on the floor, surrounded by Margaret's china animals from the mantelpiece. They were staked out in small groups around her legs. I recognised the arrangement. It was a farm. 'I had some champagne,' she announced proudly.

'A little white wine with a lot of lemonade,' Margaret said, handing me a glass of the real thing.

Ben looked at me warily. 'I'm sorry to crash in on your arrangements.'

'There's plenty of food.' I was aware of how stiff my voice sounded, starched and creaky as newly pressed linen. Beattie looked up at me uncertainly, Margaret's gaze swung back and forth between the two of us, beady with alarm. 'Anyway, I was dreading two weeks of cold turkey.'

Ben smiled faintly.

'Well, at least you can carve,' Beattie said to Ben, before going back to her farm. 'Mummy says it's the only thing that women can't do.'

On Christmas Day Rebecca flickered like a candle flame, flaring up in eddies of vivacity, then dying down until she was as pale and mute as a corpse. By the end of lunch her plate was piled with four cones of finely cut-up turkey and a radiating sun of minced-up roast potato. Only the Brussels sprouts had been eaten. Beattie's eyes grew round as saucers as she considered this breach of table manners but she said nothing, perhaps sensing that Rebecca was not like the rest of us.

Nobody wanted the Christmas pudding although I spooned brandy over it and lit it so the flames crackled and burned the holly and we all gasped dutifully.

After lunch Rebecca claimed the sofa for herself, spreading her golden head on a velvet cushion so the hair lay against it in gilded threads. She had taken off her shoes and her toes gleamed with silvery pink polish, as though they had been dipped in sugar. Ben sat next to her, idly stroking her bare feet while she stretched and arched beneath his hands and the rest of us looked away, pretending not to notice. It was only later that I understood that what I had taken for desire was revulsion. Rebecca hated to be touched.

'Why did you do it, then?' I asked Ben. We were lying on the same sofa, a few months later, my feet cradled in his lap. Rebecca was not yet dead. Our sin was still pure, uncomplicated by guilt. At least, it was uncomplicated by our guilt over her death. Guilt over adultery seems almost sweetly innocent now.

Ben sighed. 'They are beautiful. Rebecca has beautiful feet. It's hard not to touch them.'

I felt a worm of disgust wriggle in my belly and shifted position slightly. Noticing it, Ben twined his fingers through my toes, which hurt a bit. They are not used to such treatment. 'I don't want to but I have to,' he explained. 'It's like some awful compulsion.'

I understand. Beauty is an awful compulsion.

Even Beattie felt it that Christmas Day, and went and kneeled by Rebecca's head, taking the long strands of silvery hair between her fingers and stroking it gently while Rebecca lay like a cat in front of a fire, dozing luxuriantly. Her wrists were bound with blood-red satin ribbons. Back then I thought it was just an unusual fashion, did not know the ugly truth they hid. Rebecca never dressed like anyone else. Her clothes were mostly antique and very expensive, velvets and satins, and rare and wonderful embroideries stitched with gold and beads. She spent hours looking after her clothes, entrusted them only to specialists adept at cleaning the fragile fabrics, kept them swathed in boxes lined with tissue or hanging from padded satin hangers in her long cedar-wood wardrobe. Or so Ben said. I think they were her raiments, the garments she wore to be worshipped in. Rebecca loved to be worshipped. She could bear no less.

Oh, but Rebecca was clever. She was determined to win me. The ruder I was, the sweeter she became. She was the suitor and I the unresponsive lover.

The first time I knew that she was up to something Ben had called in unexpectedly at Margaret's, to find me in the garden, repotting plants. I remember the crumbling black compost between my fingers, the rows of fresh green shoots waiting to be knocked out of the old earth, bedded down snugly in the new. I don't know where Margaret was. Pottering about in the flat, perhaps. And where was

Beattie? I don't know, perhaps with Margaret. I feel now that I should have known where Beattie was every minute of the day. Then I would have had all those extra minutes to recall. But still they wouldn't be enough.

Never enough.

It was a Saturday in early March. Spring was coming. You could feel it in the air, see it in the fuzz of green inching along the branches of the trees, in the lovely wild purple of the crocuses, the clear blue of the scillas in Margaret's garden. Her little patch of heaven, as she calls this tiny green square of hers.

Ben knelt down beside me, dug his hands into the bucket of fresh compost. 'When are you going to stop ignoring me?' he said in a low voice.

I said nothing, just went on scraping away at the top of a crust of earth, squirrelling my fingers around the delicate new growth just breaking under the surface.

'Janey –'

It was what he always used to call me. Nobody else used the diminutive except my father.

'Where's Rebecca?' I asked, my cheeks flaming.

I suppose it was then that he knew.

'She's at home. She likes you, you know. She thinks you're magnificent.'

I considered the word, wondering what game this was of Rebecca's. 'Magnificent?' My voice sounded hollow.

A faint, mocking smile hovered on his face; the ghost of a smile from the Ben I used to know. We looked at each other, locking into each other's gaze, not glancing away as we usually did.

I was the first to break the silence, so complete it felt almost like a pact. 'I can't imagine why she should think that.'

But if I was the first to break the silence, Ben was the first to drop his gaze. 'She says it's because you're so self-contained, so independent.' I glanced at him sharply, to

47

see if he was mocking me, but he seemed embarrassed, humiliated even, and I wondered what demands Rebecca made on him.

I reached out to touch his hand. He jumped as if he had been burned. I jumped too, responding to his nervousness, to the heat of his skin.

He let out a shaky laugh. 'Sorry.'

I wanted to ask him if that's what he thought too, but it was Rebecca's question so I held it back. In any case, it felt too intimate and neither of us had a right to be like that. So I said instead, keeping my voice light, 'My fault. I took you by surprise.'

He looked up at me. 'Yes, you did.'

I did take him by surprise. He took me too, back then. Both of us astonished by that small collision of our souls. I knew if I put out my hand again the years would drop away and we'd be back where we started, and all the defences I'd built up against him would be worse than useless. So I turned my head away, pressed my fingers back into the damp earth.

He chose Rebecca. But Rebecca knew that, first, he chose me. That's why she would come after me, to try and win me like a trophy to lay before her husband, because she knew it would please him.

Sometimes I think that memory's a curse. It stops you greeting every new day like the first. So nothing's ever new, everything's plated over with a silvering from the past. But they say it's useful when you're old, when there's nothing much else to do except remember.

I feel old now, the way I keep looking back to the past. It's just that the future feels so unsteady.

I wonder what Ben's doing, if the autopsy is going well and laugh mirthlessly at the thought. Autopsies go neither well nor badly, they just go. I wonder where he is, what sort of room he is sitting in, whether his chair is wooden and hard or one of those sway-backed plastic-moulded things that stack so cleverly, so usefully, for institutions. Or do they give you a soft chair to sit in, to ease the pain? They're serving up his dead wife to him in neat morsels; how she died, what time she died, precise to the minute, the contents of her stomach, the contents of her lungs. The only thing they can't tell him is the one thing he wants to know: the contents of her mind. Or perhaps he did know, perhaps that's why he left her there, the pills fizzing through her blood, cancelling out the future. Well, her future, anyway. Ours is still intact, as intact as any future is.

Ben's changed these past few days. There's a sly look to him, a faintly furtive air. It's the pressure, Margaret says. You can't expect a man to stay the same, not after his wife's suicide, not with a police inquiry, an inquest and a funeral still to face. But it's more than that. I know it, just by the way he is with me, the way he stands a little sideways to me, the way he makes love, sliding into me, body clenched, eyes tight shut. There's something he's not telling me.

What?

Nobody really knew what Ben did at Allen Marshall Goodheart. He just did anything that came his way, running errands, collecting manuscripts, taking turns on the switchboard or packing up those eternal boxes of books. He took the job because he considered himself to be a writer. 'The only difference between them and me', he said, savagely stuffing more books into another box too small to take them, 'is that they are published and I am not.'

He kept at it because he believed success would rub off on him; maybe some of the magic too. 'There are thirty authors published in this building and, while their muses might not be with them at all times, you'd think a small host of them might be hovering over this building during some part of the day.'

We were sitting in the pub. It was our lunch break. I was on my way out for a sandwich when he said that he was going to the pub and, if I felt like it, I could go too. The careful way that he phrased it, as if to say it didn't much matter to him whether I went or not, told me how much he wanted me there. I went.

'But don't you need your own muse? Surely you can't go around borrowing other people's.'

'Perhaps. Then again, where best to find one than a place where they are known to congregate?'

His hair had just been cut, revealing an exquisitely tender line of new skin at the nape of his neck. It gave him a helpless quality. When he was younger there was something alarming about Ben. At least, it alarmed me. Something in the quality of his gaze – tender, but at the same time mocking – and the way he held his body, as if it was precious yet something to be treated with casual contempt. It's gone now, that easy confidence. I wonder if Rebecca is to blame for that.

'How's The Egg going?'

'It's going badly. Very badly indeed.'

'That's good. It's how it's supposed to go.' I knew this much about novels even after a few short weeks hunched over a temperamental photocopier. The Egg was Ben's work in progress, seen with him at all times, carried to and from work every day on the Tube, ('amazing how much you can get written on the Circle Line') and laboured over at any snatched moment he could find in the day. The title was a nickname dreamed up by George – a diminution from *oeuvre* to *oeuf* and so forth – and which had come to stick. Ben laughed about it but there was a faint air of tension to his laughter, as if he thought he should be taken more seriously than he was.

All the published authors who visited the offices

enquired regularly after The Egg; a kindness that ceased to amuse Ben. 'We'll see who's laughing when it tops their shoddy little efforts in the best-seller list.' The Egg had been in progress for almost two years.

He stretched, shaking his long body irritably. The gesture displaced the fabric of his shirt – an old dress-shirt, bereft of its hard collar, shirt studs and cuff-links. It flapped around his thin body like a night-dress. I could see the sparrow breadth of his collar bones through the opening of the shirt, where the studs should have kept it fastened. His skin was very white, with a slight bluish tinge to it.

He looked so gloomy that I said, 'I know it'll be good,' although I had not read one word of it.

'You know, do you?' The same tender, mocking gaze. Smiling at my blushes, he said, 'Shall we get some food?'

The menu was short. Three sorts of pies, all served with chips and baked beans. The woman serving dolloped extra chips and beans on Ben's plate and handed it to him with a wink. I blushed, remembering the blue-white skin under his shirt.

Ben ate with the concentrated fury of a starving man while I picked shreds of grey chicken and mushroom out of the middle of my pie, then amused myself by building the soggy pastry into walls, barricading the baked beans to form a small lake. There was a comfortable quality to his silence and the quick, swooping movement of his knife and fork. It was a long time since I had eaten with somebody. I don't remember eating with my father after my mother died. He was never hungry, or at least not during the day. In the morning I would sometimes find evidence: a piece of nibbled cheese abandoned on the counter in the kitchen, an empty packet of digestive biscuits thrust down the back of the sofa during his nocturnal ramblings around the house. I tried cooking nutritious stews and things with eggs, but I was rarely hungry either and after I had dumped the fifth casserole of meat in the dustbin, I abandoned the pretence of eating proper food and took to eating in fits and starts, like my father.

A sudden movement made me start and I looked up to see that Ben's plate was wiped clean. His eyes were fixed on the fortress I had built, was still building, out of the pie and beans.

Blushing slightly, I dropped the fork.

He picked up my full plate and put it in front of him. 'Do you mind?' he asked, almost as an afterthought.

I watched him eat my food, using the fork that had been in my mouth and felt, oh, I don't know, *happy*.

People ask me sometimes if I am affected by wanderlust but this, I think, is to misunderstand human nature entirely. Adventurers have homes to go to, if only of the heart. It is the dispossessed who cling to their small patch of earth. My wish is not to travel but to arrive.

Until that first visit to England, I had not been aware of the terrors that difference arouses. At home – or rather, in whichever country we lived, for they were all home to me – I was not different. We were all different there, all of us children. We were cemented by our difference. And later, when my father finally counted on two hands the number of countries I had lived in (five) and the number of schools I had been to (ten), he hurriedly arranged to send me off to an English boarding-school, where I was to remain for eight years.

We were different there too, shared a mutual language of BOAC Aunties and comforted each other over childish complaints and the questions left unanswered while our letters laboured through the long, tedious journeys home. In those days the long-distance telephone was a rarity, an event connected only with tragedy and celebration. For three months we had little or no contact with our parents.

We were like little adults: contained, independent, watchful. Then we climbed on a plane for the long haul home, where we became children again.

But that was later. During my first visit to England there was one duty to be borne. We were to call on one of my father's sisters. He had six, which amounted to an intolerable amount of visiting, most of which he did alone. All except his youngest sister, Sue, who announced that she couldn't live in peace if she didn't once clap eyes on me.

She exaggerated. No sooner had she clapped eyes on me than I was sent off into a dark corner with my cousin Janet while the grown-ups shrieked and laughed, and drank tea together. After a while they noticed our awkward, reproachful silence and Auntie Sue bustled over. 'Why don't you both write a nice little story?' she said, clattering pencils and scraps of torn paper onto the table in front of us.

Janet and I sucked thoughtfully on the pencils, bending our heads dutifully to the table. We scratched quietly at our work while the talk around us bubbled up with the shrieking whistle of Auntie Sue's laughter. Janet kept her hand cupped around her paper, her face bent so close to the page her nose was nearly touching it. Sighing, I went back to my story. It was about a pig with a vicious nature who is chopped up and made into sausages. I described in loving detail the knife slicing into the fat pink flesh and thought about Claire at my first English school while I was writing.

I looked up to see Auntie Sue's thin, frosted smile.

'Joined up writing! How very advanced Jane is.'

I glanced over at my cousin's scuffed paper, littered with clumsy, smudged capitals, folded my piece of paper into a small hard wad and stuffed it into my pocket.

'They push them quite hard,' my mother said apologetically. 'Terrified they'll turn into little savages, I expect.'

'No doubt,' Auntie Sue said, her voice cool. Perhaps she expected me to write in sand with a stick.

The rest of the scraps of paper and pencils were quickly cleared away and Janet was told to take me to her bedroom to play with her dolls.

The room was pink and white and very tidy. There were curtains sprawling with pink roses and a bed studded with pink nylon ruffles. The door closed on us. Janet kicked me hard. 'Show-off,' she said, her face ugly with spite. 'My mum says you think you're better than we are, with your servants and your name-dropping.' She adopted a high, singsong voice. 'When I was in Arabia ... When I go to AF-RI-CAAA.'

'Africa?'

'That's where your dad says you're going next, stupid.'

I had seen her leaning against his leg, her plump face screwed up in a smile as she squirmed against him. He patted her treacherously, gave her half a crown.

'He's mad, your dad, taking you and your mum to live in a dirty place like that.'

I turned away from her, reaching out a hand for a doll, but Janet snatched it away. 'Don't touch. My mum says there's no telling what germs you've got.'

I spent the rest of the afternoon sitting on the scratchy nylon ruffled bed, staring out at a chill grey afternoon while Janet played with her toys on the floor beside me.

During future visits home I became adept at lying. At each new school I learned to cover my English exercise book with smudgy capitals, until I got the measure of their ways. It was then, too, that I got into the habit of silence, one that I have never quite abandoned.

Five

Margaret is inquisitive. She knows there's more to Rebecca's death than is being said. 'But why the police, dear? Why must Ben go and see them again?'

Her tone is faintly querulous. I feel a sudden sense of shock. She sounds so old. I look at her closely now. She is hunched in an armchair, next to the fire, her fingers plucking aimlessly at the frayed edge of the loose cover. Everything in Margaret's flat is frayed and shabby. She is of the generation that believes a new set of loose covers will do for twenty years. As she is no longer convinced that she herself will do for another twenty years, she does nothing about replacing them.

'And this inquest business,' she says fretfully. 'Is it really necessary?'

I murmur something about the police having to investigate every death, but Margaret casts me a hooded, suspicious look. 'Why won't you tell me?'

'It's not for me to say.' I sound too prim. She gives me a look that recalls her long career as the headmistress of a girl's school. 'Because I don't know the whole story,' I say, imagining generations of young women wilting under that gaze.

'The part you know, then,' she demands imperiously.

Ben is her family. It's only fair that she should know. 'On the night Rebecca died he wasn't at a meeting. He was with me. That's why he was late getting home.'

She digests this slowly, absorbing the implications.

I do not say that Ben went home and found Rebecca

55

dying, then visited my bed. There's only so much truth a person can take. 'She took the whole bottle of pills. She would have died anyway, whether Ben was there or not,' I say, although I do not know if it is true. I say it partly to reassure myself.

Margaret fixes me with a measured stare. 'I have often suspected that you and Ben are lovers and have been for many years. Is that correct?'

I like her use of the word 'correct'. The way she doesn't say it is true. I wonder what Ben has told the police.

'We knew each other when we were young, then we parted,' I say and add with sudden candour, 'It was not so much a failed love affair as one that was never finished.'

Margaret's eyes are a bright, formidable blue. She nods, satisfied. I can see that she is pleased that her instincts have been proved right. It is always pleasing to be right.

I feel anxious not to cast Ben in too harsh a light. 'We hadn't intended it to start over again. It was my fault, really. I was so feeble after Beattie and Ben came to my rescue.'

The eyes glitter. 'On his shining white charger?'

'It wasn't quite like that.'

'It never is quite like that,' Margaret says crisply, enunciating each word carefully.

I have always thought that love affairs should be kept secret, tucked away in the dimness of privacy. They look so tawdry held up to the clear light of day.

Margaret sighs. 'Well, better you than anyone else. I never thought Rebecca was right for him. I never understood why he married her.'

'She was very beautiful.'

Margaret lets out a small snort of derision but I know that beauty is not to be underestimated. It pulls fiercely at the blood, making the heart beat faster, sending blood scurrying to the brain until reason, even intelligence, are clouded. Everyone who met Rebecca was enraptured by her. Even Margaret, whatever she says, succumbed to Rebecca's spell. And so did I. Yes, even me.

Rebecca made a point of seeking me out, appeared at my door clutching small gifts, a bunch of flowers for me, a packet of sweets for Beattie. The first she brought were chocolate dragees coated in hard silver shells and wrapped in layers of pink and lilac net, tied with a gauzy ribbon. 'I couldn't resist them,' she said. 'They looked so like fairy sweets that I thought immediately of Beattie.'

This was long before Ben and I became lovers, but I was jealous of her none the less. I wanted her nowhere near me. I glanced at my watch. It was two thirty. My working day was circumscribed by Beattie's school hours and I wanted to finish the manuscript I had promised to George, and post it on my way to school. I had only thirty minutes before I needed to leave and some marking up still to do.

But I could refuse Beattie nothing so I allowed Rebecca to come in, despite my irritation at being disturbed. I suppose, too, that I felt intrigued by her, wanted to examine the woman with whom Ben had chosen to make his life, so I accepted the flowers and the chocolates gratefully enough and led the way through the narrow house.

She drifted after me, stepping noiselessly in velvet slippers. 'What a marvellous room,' she said, when we entered the kitchen, 'and how clever of you to use that particular shade of paint. I would never think to put lavender in a kitchen.'

I glanced sharply at her, expecting to find some mockery in her face but seeing none, looked around the kitchen. It was a pleasing room and I was contented with it but disinclined to discuss it with Rebecca. My house is my joy, but it is a fierce, private joy born, I suppose, of years of being forced to trail after my parents from one bleak rented house to another.

'Would you like some tea?' I asked, reaching to fill the kettle.

'I wouldn't want to put you to any trouble.'

I was tempted to abandon the kettle with the rejoinder that if that was the way she felt, then I shouldn't be bothered at all but, as I say, in those early days I was still intrigued by Rebecca so I smiled and murmured something facile about it being no trouble at all, and made the tea.

Rebecca sat at the table or, rather, she arranged herself. She never slouched or lounged in the ungainly way that some people do but composed her limbs in a way that always reminded me of a person arranging flowers in a vase. It was impossible not to admire the resulting composition, however one might dislike the arranger herself.

I sat down, feeling large and awkward beside her.

'May I ask you something?' she said, her voice hesitant.

I shrugged, resenting the way that Rebecca's grace had quite the opposite effect on me. 'If you like.'

'Is it very difficult being a single mother?'

I took a sip of tea, wondering where this was leading. 'I wouldn't know, never having been anything else.'

'Don't you get very lonely? I mean – I'm not sure how I would cope.'

I think she wanted me to tell her that she would cope admirably, as do thousands of women every day, but I refused her even that scrap of comfort. 'It's hardly likely that you're ever going to have to.'

'No, I suppose not.' This was uttered on a note of wistfulness, accompanied by a tiny sigh and while nowadays I might have thought that Rebecca was trying to tell me something else entirely, at the time I thought she was deliberately pointing out my joyless single state and comparing it with her own.

'You don't seem the type to want children,' I said, with

infinite cruelty. Rebecca said nothing, simply hung her lovely head. It made me despise her all the more.

After a while, she lifted her head. Colour faintly stained her cheeks, as if they bore the sharp imprints of my hand. I blush for myself now, but then I only marvelled that Ben could possibly have fallen in love with this milksop.

Sensing that I was not to be drawn into any further conversation on the subject of children, Rebecca tried another tack. 'It's lovely for Margaret to have you and Beattie upstairs. She adores Beattie, of course.'

I wondered why she needed to qualify Margaret's adoration, but I had not to wait long to find out. 'She's the grandchild she longs for,' Rebecca said and for a moment I caught the suspicion of a tear. I said nothing. 'She doesn't say so,' Rebecca went on, 'but I know it's what she feels.'

I thought how like Rebecca it was to apply motive. It did not seem to occur to her that Beattie and Margaret might have found simple pleasure in each other's company.

'It's not that we haven't tried to make a baby,' Rebecca exclaimed. 'We've tried and tried, but nothing seems to work –'

I forced a smile, pushing it past the image of Ben lying between Rebecca's pale thighs, his eyes closed in ecstasy.

'But of course you understand,' she went on, 'being a mother yourself.'

I could bear it no longer. 'I must go and collect Beattie.'

'May I come with you?'

'Oh, I don't think so,' I said abruptly. 'She's not used to other people meeting her from school.'

'Just to say hello and give her the sweets,' Rebecca begged. 'I won't stay long, I promise. I understand how precious time is spent with one's children.' Her voice caught and I felt a brief sympathy. What must it be like to long and long for a child and not be able to conceive?

'Oh, very well.'

As we left the kitchen I saw her glance fall on the bunch

of flowers, still in their wrapper of paper. I had forgotten about them entirely. Had it been anybody else, I would have apologised and rushed to put them in water, but Rebecca's delicate reproach made me feel so awkward and humiliated that I pretended, by my silence, not to have noticed. She was always capable of making me behave badly in small but important ways.

Ben says that the autopsy report is straightforward. Death by overdose of a prescribed drug. The time of death is established as somewhere between two and three o'clock in the morning.

He recounts these facts over a glass of wine, his face impassive.

I think of the clock, sitting on my bedside table. Ben left my bed at eleven o'clock. The journey takes thirty minutes. Rebecca died three hours later. Feeling a sudden restlessness, I get to my feet, turn on the tap to fill the sink with water to peel potatoes. I go to the basket, pick some out, carry them back to the sink. Ben does not move, just stares into his glass, his face brooding and sullen. *Three hours.* I pick up a potato, slice away the tattered skin to reveal the pale waxy flesh beneath but my head is filled with blue flashing lights, the scream of sirens, white-tiled hospital floors, coiled silver wires attached to Rebecca's heart, pumping massive volts of electricity.

I glance at Ben. He meets my eye. I give a quick, reassuring smile. He looks away but not before I see something in his face, something dark and malevolent. I stare down at the potatoes, shimmering under the water, their flesh as pale and waxy as Rebecca's face. *Three hours.* Another picture flashes into my mind, a woman lying in a bed and me hunched over her, shivering uncontrollably. Best not to think about these things. I say nothing.

I finish peeling the potatoes, put them in a pan of clean water.

Ben watches my progress from sink to oven. 'Sorry,' he says. 'It's all rather difficult to take in.' His smile is weary, the tension of the past few days gathered in shadows beneath his pale eyes. There is no trace of malevolence. I lean towards him, ashamed of my previous imaginings, and take his face in my hands, lay a kiss on each tired eye.

'There was a letter,' he says, catching my hands in his, lifting them to his shoulders. I relax against him, lay my cheek against his bright, silky hair. 'It was hidden in her bag, stuffed down into a pocket inside the lining.'

I wonder why Rebecca did not leave the letter out for him to find immediately, but then I remember Ben telling me that the last time she had attempted suicide she had reproached him later with the letter, handing it wordlessly to him while she was recovering in hospital. I imagine those large eyes fixed on his face as he read it. Or perhaps it was just another of her guessing games. Rebecca loved games. The longer you took to guess, the longer she was at the centre of attention.

I do not tell him that I know about the letter, that the police have already informed me. I ask instead, 'What does it say?' He pushes my hands from his shoulders, turns away from me. Allowing him time to compose himself, I occupy myself by drizzling oil on the lamb chops, massaging it into the bloody flesh, sprinkling it with dried thyme and salt and pepper.

'I blame my husband and Jane Rose for my death.' I look up at Ben, startled. He shrugs. 'That's what it said.' I knew Rebecca was aware of our affair, for Ben had said he had told her, but nothing prepared me for the shock of hearing myself accused of her death.

Best not to think about it. My hands are shaking. I force them to deal with practical matters, slicing the tender florets of broccoli from their woody stalks. Research indicates that a daily helping of broccoli helps to avoid cancer. Lamb is also one of the healthiest meats, used widely in elimination diets when ascertaining potential food allergies. I learned all this when Beattie was small and suffered from weeping patches of eczema on the backs of her legs. I wonder, now, why I am cooking those particular foods. Am I trying to eliminate the poisons I can feel seeping into our lives?

'*J'accuse*,' Ben says.

His voice makes me jump. 'What?'

'Her final act of malice.'

I don't want to talk about Rebecca so I turn away, slice a chunk of cold butter from the block, flip it into the pan of hot potatoes. The chops are doing nicely, the fat darkening to a good crisp brown. I have already shaken the potatoes over a low heat, to steam off any excess water. Now I mash them gently with a fork. Too much agitation and they dissolve to a sticky glue. The butter runs through the cloudy landscape like rivers. I mash it in, spoiling the effect. 'Shall we eat?' I say.

After supper I do the washing up. A sink full of boiling soapy water, another of warm, clean water. I start with the glasses, then the silver, the plates and finally the pans. There is a dishwasher, but I never use it. I don't believe it gets things clean. The glasses are already sparkling on the rack to my right when Ben comes up behind me, presses his body against mine. I can feel his erection as he rubs himself against me, lifting my jumper, sliding his hands over my back, around to my stomach and clasping my breasts in his fingers. I feel the rasp of a callus against my nipple and wonder what manual work he has been doing to get it. He takes me like that, my hands in the hot, soapy water. I think about Rebecca refusing to make love to him.

Afterwards, he pulls down my jumper, smoothing it back in place, pulls down my skirt and carefully brushes out the creases. He did not bother to remove my pants, just pushed the leg elastic to one side. I am still wearing rubber gloves, hot and dripping, and stand there like a small child as he dresses me.

'There,' he says, giving me an appraising glance.

I think of Beattie. 'Done?' she always said, when I had finished dressing her.

'All done,' I say.

I think about the first time I put my hands on his skin.

We were eating fish and chips in St James's Park. Ben is a great one for talking, but that evening he was uncharacteristically quiet. I suppose it was that that warned me what was coming.

'May I kiss you?' he asked, shifting towards me until I could smell the vinegar on his breath.

I didn't move at first. The sharp wing of his shoulder jutted into my upper arm. It felt surprisingly hot, almost burning. Thin people always look as though they should feel cold to the touch. His mouth nuzzled against my neck. I kept looking straight ahead. My skin prickled with alarm. I wanted to kiss him so badly that I felt physically sick, but I knew that once I held him I should never want to let him go. 'No thank you,' I said eventually, 'but it's kind of you to ask.'

Ben slumped backwards and was silent. For weeks, that kiss had been buzzing about our heads like an insistent fly. After a while he yawned and swivelled round to lay his head on my lap.

I felt the heavy warmth pressed against my stomach and thighs, and laid my hands on his shoulders, feeling the sharp bones moving under them. This means nothing to him, I told myself. He would lay his head on the lap of a perfect stranger if she sat down next to him.

His feet were propped up on the top of the bench. There were holes in his shoes where the leather had come unstitched from the sole. 'Don't they leak?' I asked, trying to move the subject onto something neutral.

He settled his head more comfortably in my lap. 'I'll get some more when the rain comes. No point spending money now. Are you a virgin, Janey?'

I started slightly. Not simply because of the question, but because it was a long time since anybody had called me Janey. 'No.' This was a lie but I was embarrassed. I find I often lie when I am embarrassed.

Ben yawned again. 'Why is it that people make such a fuss about sex? It's not as if it's all it's cracked up to be.'

'No, it's not,' I said, wondering how many women he had made love to. Two? Five? Ten? A hundred?

'You're a comfortable woman,' Ben murmured, turning his face into my stomach. 'A man could get used to that.' At least, I think that's what he said. His voice was so muffled that I couldn't be entirely sure.

I stared down at the fragile bones of his skull, feeling a sudden violent longing to put my hands to his head and crush it like an eggshell, to clamp my jaws around it and ingest him slowly, feel the sharp contours of his skeleton ease past my stretched jaws down to the strong, efficient muscles of my throat; down, down into the black hole of my stomach. To consume him, subsume him like a boa constrictor. Sweet Jesus, I thought. *Sweet Jesus*. It was an expression of my father's.

We sat in the gathering gloom, Ben sleeping, my hands resting on the ridged bones of his chest and skull. I watched the ghostly shapes of the swans gliding across the lake, their necks swaying and arching above the dark water.

Ben sighed in his sleep. I looked down at his peaceful face, put my hand under his shirt and ran it across the smooth, satiny skin of his chest, bumping my fingers over his ribs, his nipples, and the few sparse hairs that prickled around them. I trembled, astonished by my own daring. He stirred suddenly. I pulled my hand away sharply, as if it had been burned. His voice rose up in the still night air, warm and sleepy. 'What were you doing?'

I glanced down, abashed, to see the pale triangle of his face floating in my lap, a smile moving across it. He caught my hand, pulled it towards him until it hovered over his heart. I swear I could feel the beat of it, like the soft fluttering of a moth's wing through the cotton of his shirt.

I pulled my hand away roughly, urgent to distance myself from the moment – from him. 'If we don't hurry, we'll miss the last bus home.'

The light is beginning to fade but still I am idle, dreaming through the day, just as my mother used to do. The doorbell rings. Shaking the memories from my head, I go to answer it.

It is a policeman, the Detective Inspector from the station. At first, I don't recognise him. He looks like any tired middle-aged man, his features bunched as if somebody has snagged them with a thread and pulled them tight. 'I'm sorry,' he says. 'Do you mind?'

He has more questions about Rebecca; what she was like, what her state of mind was the week before she killed herself, what her relationship was with Ben.

'She depended on him for everything. Even for keeping her alive.'

'I don't quite follow.'

He is playing dumb. I can see the intelligence lurking behind his eyes. 'She scarcely ate, unless he was there, encouraging her.' I think of her pale-pink tongue, curling out to receive the morsels of cheese or fruit that Ben dropped in her mouth. And then, in less indulgent moments, his face thunderous with frustration as he watched her push food around the plate. How disempowering it is to have a life put into your hands. 'Then, of course, there were the suicide attempts – she planned each of them so that Ben would find her. Save her, as she put it.'

'A hard burden to carry.'

'And a cruel one to impose.'

'Some people might think it was desperation.'

'Yes, they might.'

'But you don't?'

'No.'

I see nothing in his face now. No surprise or distaste, just an attentive blankness. 'You feel no sympathy for her?'

'She is dead. She hardly needs it.'

'One might feel sympathy for the dead.'

'I think it is the living who require it most.'

'You feel sympathy for her husband?'

'Of course.'

'What time did you say Mr Robinson left here?'

'Just after eleven. It's in my statement.'

He ignores this, affects a false confusion. 'Yet he did not call the ambulance until later. Three o'clock in the morning, according to our records.'

This is news to me but I compose my face to reveal nothing. 'If he says so.'

'Do you know what time he reached his house? What he did when he got there?'

'No.'

'You did not ask?'

I wish he would go. 'No.'

'Would you say that you and Rebecca Robinson were friendly at one time?'

For a moment I am tempted to laugh. 'Not in the sense of being intimates. But if you mean, did we see a great deal of each other, then yes. She made sure of that.'

'You don't sound as if you liked her.'

'Rebecca did not wish to be liked. She wished to be adored.'

No, not adored, worshipped. Adoration was too insipid an emotion for Rebecca. But what she hated more than

66

anything was indifference. The first time I realised this with any clarity was the occasion when I had flu, which developed into a mild form of pneumonia. Nothing serious, but it laid me very low.

Dear, kind Margaret had taken Beattie to school and I was lying in bed, hovering in that feverish state between sleeping and wakefulness, when the doorbell rang. Groping my way downstairs I found Rebecca, her arms filled with bundles of fresh flowers.

'I got up early and went to Covent Garden market,' she said, sweeping past me. 'Next time, I'll take you with me. It's such fun. I know you'd adore it.'

'Rebecca –'

'No, don't thank me.' She bundled the piles of flowers onto the table and switched on the kettle. 'I've brought croissants, too,' she said, emptying the straw bag that swung on her shoulder. 'And oranges to make us fresh juice. And coffee from that little place in Soho.' She looked at me uncertainly. 'You do like coffee, don't you?'

The fog in my head was too great to fight so I sank down onto the nearest chair and watched her. She was wearing a blue dress, with flowers embroidered at the hem. Her hair was swept back into plaits, caught behind, and left to tumble down her back. It amuses me now to think of the effort she must have gone to, how carefully she dressed to play her part but at the time I felt ill and ugly, caught at a disadvantage. I ran my tongue over furry teeth and watched her.

She looked at me with concern. 'I was worried about you.'

'I'm over the worst.'

'You don't look it.' Before I knew it, her hand was pressed to my forehead. It felt cool and light but I was conscious only of the sour smell of sickness that rose from me. I had not bathed in days. 'Burning up. Just as I thought. I'll just get these in water, then we'll get you upstairs to bed.'

'I'm fine.'

'If somebody had only told me how ill you were I'd have come straight away. It was only by chance that Margaret mentioned it. I don't know what you must think of me.'

'I don't think of you at all.' The words came out of my mouth before I could stop them but even through the mist in my head I saw the sudden stillness that took her. I could not have wounded her more effectively if I had stood up and plunged a knife into her back.

The Inspector's voice cuts in: 'But you did not bear her any malice?'

I smile faintly. 'No, not malice. Impatience, perhaps. She was a very persistent woman.' It had not occurred to me before, but I thought then how at odds that persistence seemed with Rebecca's nature, which was subdued – timid even.

'The pills that you gave her – did you believe that she would take them?'

It was a question I had turned over in my head a hundred times. 'I don't know.'

The Inspector stares at me for a moment. 'Miss Rose, you are not helping your case.'

I am genuinely shocked. 'My case?'

He gets to his feet. 'A woman has died. She was registered as being at risk, a danger to herself. You were aware of that. Yet you supplied her with the pills that killed her.'

'I didn't administer them.'

He looks at me wearily. 'Intent, Miss Rose. It all comes down to the question of intent.'

'I did not intend her to die,' I say, but even as I say it I am not certain it is true. My intention may not have been

68

that she would die, but the reality is that I knew she was at risk and I knew she had a bottle of sleeping pills in her possession. You might say that I gave her permission.

His gaze goes down to the carpet, to a faint pink stain near the armchair, where Beattie once knocked over a cup of Ribena. Nothing will remove that stain, although I have tried. The inspector pokes at it with his foot. 'Ribena. Nothing shifts it.' He has children, then. The knowledge adds a new dimension to his character. I wonder how old they are, when he finds the time to see them. He looks at me, his expression almost apologetic. 'The first thing you learn in my job', he says, 'is how few people intend that somebody should die. Even when they're holding a knife in their hands.'

After he has gone, I sit by the window. The laburnum and the lilac are just coming into flower. Another spring. Once, it was my favourite time of year but that was before it marked the date when Beattie went. Last time the lilac bloomed Beattie was still with me. I feel a sudden anger with Rebecca for spoiling another spring. And with Ben for allowing her to.

Six

Soon after we met, Ben invited me to a party.

'A party?' I said in astonishment. I was not the sort of girl who went to parties. Who got invited to them. I couldn't remember the last party I had been to.

Ben grinned. 'You know, where too many people crowd together in a small hot room, shout at each other over loud music, drink too much and go home weeping.'

'OK.'

'I promise not to kiss you.'

My heart turned somersaults. 'I promise not to weep.'

Ben grinned. 'Wonder who'll crack first.'

I hadn't thought to buy a dress especially for the party, but when I saw it, poised in the window of a small, narrow shop tucked between a launderette and an ironmonger, I knew I had to have it. It was a curious window for a fashion shop, entirely bare other than the dress, which was suspended on some sort of headless mannequin fashioned out of wire and lit by a single brutal spotlight.

The interior was no more comforting. I had a fleeting impression of a polished wood floor, white walls and a series of spindly but elegant wooden tables. A woman was arranging folded sweaters in neat piles, according to colour. She was small, but had a dancer's deportment, enhanced by a plain black sweater, black trousers and flat shoes like ballet slippers. Huge gold rings gleamed at her ears, her dark hair was swept back in a tight chignon. She was the most elegant thing I had ever seen. I vowed immediately to hunt down a pair of the slippers.

'The dress in the window,' I said.

She looked at me carefully, her dark eyes sweeping the length of my body. I am not beautiful but nor am I without vanity and one of the things I am vain about is my body, which is long and slender, and surprisingly well suited to good clothes. 'I'd like to try it on,' I said firmly.

The eyes gleamed approvingly. 'Ah, yes,' she said, 'the Muir.'

This meant nothing to me, so I simply smiled and nodded. A faint accent chipped away at the edges of her voice, although I could not immediately place it. French, perhaps, or Spanish?

'A fine designer.' She gave a little amazed shrug. 'English but one of the very best.'

The woman slipped the dress from the wire mannequin, leaving it gleaming austerely under the bright spotlight. I wondered what passers-by might think. Perhaps that it was a gallery of modern art or some such thing.

She beckoned me to follow her to a surprisingly large, comfortable changing room in the back of the shop and handed me the dress. 'It is the last one,' she explained, smoothing the fabric reverently before leaving me to commune with it in private.

I slid the dress over my head and stared at myself in the mirror, feeling a sudden clutching excitement in my throat. The fabric was a heavy, matte jersey of blue as dense and dark as ink, the only decoration three fine lines of topstitching at the neckline and the cuffs. Otherwise it was quite plain, almost brutally so. But it was a thing of extraordinary beauty, in it I approached something like elegance.

I stepped out into the shop where the woman was still bent over her task of folding sweaters. She looked up, frowning, then her expression cleared and she hurried towards me, her hands darting like small birds. 'But you must have it!' she exclaimed. 'It is like a small miracle.'

I did not take offence at this. I had already witnessed the miracle. 'Is it very expensive?'

The hands fluttered apologetically. 'Yes.' Something like regret appeared in her face.

She saw my expression. 'You would have worn it for ever,' she said sadly.

It was this that decided me; that use of the words *'would have'*, as if the miracle had passed me by, touching me just with the beat of its wings. 'I'll take it.'

She put her head to one side, slid a smile in my direction. 'Not so much for a miracle?'

As she wrapped the dress in tissue and wrote out a receipt, I asked her where she came from. She smiled. 'You cannot guess?'

'Paris?'

She shook her head delightedly, her eyes disappearing into wrinkles of pleasure.

I saw then that she was older than I had at first thought. 'Spain?'

She let out a small explosion of disgust. 'Oh, no.' Her head came up proudly. 'Poland,' she said. 'Warsaw.'

I murmured something non-committal about London being a nice place to live but her eyes took on a distant, dreaming quality and she said that, one day, she would return to Warsaw. 'Home,' she said, her face filled with bright yearning. *'Home.'*

I felt a momentary pang of envy, the completeness of which took me by surprise. Much later, I was to recall the woman's expression of dazzled longing. But I was older then and more inclined to fret over my torn and dangling roots. On that warm, bright afternoon, I was filled only with pleasure at the prospect of embarking on my new life.

We arranged to meet at the Tube station. I was wearing the navy dress. Ben walked straight past me, shirt-tails flying beneath the buckled hem of an old tweed jacket.

I called his name.

'Wow!' he said, revolving around me. 'Wow, you look so grown-up. Is it really you?'

'Yes,' I said and something of my disappointment must have showed in my face for he put a finger to my nose, pressing it gently. 'What are you *doing*?' I exclaimed, stepping away from him.

'Turning you on, Janey, turning you on. It was like the lights went out.'

'I'm fine,' I said, walking away from him towards the ticket office. My hands were shaking. I heard the slap of his broken shoe as he ran after me.

'You look amazing,' he said. 'It's an amazing dress. It's just that you look different, older.'

'Thanks. I suppose you mean I look like your mother.' I could not resist saying it, although it hurt only me.

Ben found this hilarious. 'No, not like Mum. She wears embroidered coats and weird patchwork skirts, looks like a sort of mad bohemian. After Dad walked out on her she took off on her travels.'

'Is your father still alive?'

His face changed. 'In a manner of speaking.'

I wanted to soothe him but could find no comfort so all I said was, 'I'm sorry.'

He shrugged, was silent for a time as we negotiated the ticket barrier and made our way down the escalator.

'You'd get on really well with Mum,' he shouted above the noise of the machinery. 'It would be like a meeting out of *National Geographic*, you two going on about your travels.'

I hate it when people call me a traveller; it reduces my life to a tourist map. 'They were not travels. They were my life.'

Ben looked at me oddly. 'Sure, sure. Whatever.'

I felt ashamed. How could he know?

He was quiet after that. We sat opposite each other on

the Tube, in the seats arranged in a low row facing each other. It was a long journey, out to Essex, on the fringes of the Central Line. It is the red line. There seemed to me some significance in that. I counted the stops. Sixteen. I wished I had not asked about his father. It was too noisy in the train to talk, to make amends. The chasm of silence deepened between us. Ben's eyes were fixed on a point above my head and I wondered if he was reading the Underground map too, calculating the time before he could escape, diving into the hot cocoon of noise and talk at the party. His eyes flickered across to me and I tried to smile, but it came out stiff and awkward, and he looked away. The next time I was ready for him and handed back a smile that was filled with warmth. Things eased between us. He stretched out his legs, poking the toe of his boot towards my feet. I looked down at his frayed boots, the sole of one hanging off, the steel caps nudging my neat, pointy-toed stilettos, and thought that they looked like married feet, imagined them naked, lined up next to each other in an orderly row at the foot of a bed.

The train stopped at a station. When the last few people got out, Ben glanced over at me, a thoughtful expression on his face. As it began to move off, he got to his feet and stood over me, hanging on a strap, his body looping like India rubber with the motion. I felt my body stiffen with alarm and willed it to relax. His crotch was parallel with my face, I could see the mound of his balls and penis through the soft, aged denim of his jeans. Every time the train jerked him towards me, the mound swelled and hardened until his penis jutted out, a long mysterious bulge under the fabric of his jeans. He looked down at my burning cheeks, his expression solemn and closed.

When, finally, the train stopped, we were overground again. We stepped out onto a deserted platform lit by sulphurous yellow light and walked through the silent ticket office, out into a dimly lit street. I blinked, trying to get my bearings but Ben was already a hundred yards ahead of me, moving with the swift assurance of the seasoned commuter. My pointy shoes clicked on the wet street and he stopped suddenly, turning to me.

His face looked jagged and angry under the neon street light. 'That dress,' he said. 'It makes you look so different.'

I stared down at the dress, my hands clutching at the dense, heavy jersey of the skirt. I wanted to rip it off. 'I thought it was lovely when I bought it,' I said sorrowfully.

His hand moved to my face, cupped my cheek. 'It is lovely. You're lovely.'

I thought he was going to kiss me but he didn't, and I remembered our promise. He wouldn't kiss me and I wouldn't cry.

We walked through the dark suburban streets, our hands stuck together with sweat and desire. I felt then how it was between us, how it would always be, and my heart skittered with fear and happiness. The blue light of a television flickered in every window. I could see the shadowy figures of people hunched on sofas, the yellow and blue flames of gas fires distorted by the bottle glass that gleamed in each tiny frame of window.

Ben's grip tightened until he was holding my hand so hard it hurt. 'Look at it,' he said savagely. 'Purgatory. The place where they send people too cautious to be truly good, too frightened to be truly bad.' He kicked a loose stone with his boot, sent it crashing into a metal dustbin. The noise was enormous in the empty street. I looked up, half expecting lights to flick on, angry voices to berate us.

We walked on in silence. I could feel the tension running through him; his hands felt like wire. I wondered what it was that had made him so angry and stumbled a little in my shoes, trying to keep up with his violent pace. When he stopped suddenly, I virtually cannoned into him. He was staring at a house on the opposite side of the street. It looked like all the others.

'Whose house is that?' I said in a loud whisper.

'My father's. It's where I grew up.'

I looked around at the smug, faceless houses. 'Here?'

'Sometimes, but mainly on the Central line.'

I waited, expecting sarcasm.

'I was trying to get away.'

The next morning, I get up early, make a cup of coffee and take it into the sitting-room, where I have my desk. The manuscript I have been working on is in a neat pile. I like my work, enjoy the faint smugness that comes with finishing something. It suits my secretive nature to labour over something, yet leave no trace.

I still work on a casual basis for George Curtis, my old editor at Allen Marshall Goodheart, but the company is failing, its dry solemnity is unfashionable and the work these days is all too casual. Sometimes I accept jobs on magazines too, stepping in when a sub-editor is sick, or on holiday. On the monthlies the atmosphere is relaxed, chatty even, a group of us clustered around a desk like housewives on a step, topping and tailing pieces of writing as if they are no more than runner beans. The money is good, but it's not editing I enjoy. I prefer the hushed, disciplined world of book publishing where the trick is to be sly, approach the thing from the side, slicing off a word here, a phrase there, cutting into the body of the piece with the delicacy of a surgeon removing a tiny but bothersome cyst. The stitches should never show.

I lay everything down before I start; a piece of plain white paper folded over to form a thick ruler so that I can move it down the page, line by line. If you try and look at too many words at once, your head begins to swim and you miss things. It is my job to catch every tiny mistake. Sometimes I miss one, only see it when the book is in my hand, handsome and crisp but marred by one tiny error.

Then I mourn my contribution to yet another imperfection in this world.

A set of HB pencils lies by the manuscript, not too soft a lead or they will smudge on the page, and a sharpener. Before I start, I sharpen all the pencils, six of them, starting with the shortest and finishing with the longest. I try to keep them all the same length but sometimes that is not possible.

I work happily for two hours, immersed in another world. I use my work like opiates but sometimes the effect wears off unexpectedly and I find myself beached on the shore. This is one of those times. Something else is nudging through the haze, another time, another place. It is unpleasant and I try to force it down but it will not be still. Even so, I can't figure out what it is. I think it must concern Ben, the missing hours. I try not to think about those hours. Ben did what he thought he had to do and it is not up to me to sit in judgement on him. I sense that he wants to talk about it, but he can't. I can see it in the stiffness around his eyes, the skin puckering with the tension of keeping something in. As for me, I'm not sure I really want to know. I have enough in the way of knowledge to deal with already.

He is drinking too much too – a bottle of red wine last night all to himself and a couple of brandies before bed. Then there's the sex. When he thrusts into me, I can feel him trying to connect, struggling to remove himself from the nightmare by fixing himself to the fleshy reality of another place. Try as he does, he cannot escape. I know the feeling and there is no drug on earth that will take it away.

When my mother became ill, we returned to England. It was soon obvious, even to my father, that we would never return to that other life. He took early retirement, used his savings to buy a cottage in Cornwall, close to the cool breezes and the chill sea spray that my mother had missed so much during the dry, burning days of their chosen exile. I was nineteen and not ready to let her go but she faded quickly, melting like a beached jellyfish in the sun. When I went in to her in the mornings, I half expected to see puddles of flesh on the sheets where she had lain. It was a horrible death, weary and agonising. My father relentlessly spooned sieved soup and liquid morphine to her mouth, refusing to admit that she was dying. Sometimes she held her face to him, like a baby bird, her parched lips curved like a beak. Other times she beat at him with feeble hands, berating him in a strange hoarse voice that was not her own. 'Let me go!'

The first time I heard her call, I ran on urgent feet to discover my father slumped on the bed, my mother lying half on top of him, her agonised face yearning to me, the stiff claw of her hand reaching out. How she had the strength to move I shall never know, but I didn't wait to find out. As the days passed, hiding from my mother's agony became less and less easy.

After she died, my father built a shrine over the mantelpiece, clumsily scissoring her image from photographs, sticking them to the peeling paint with Sellotape. A lock of her hair faded quietly in a screw of Cellophane; a vase of flowers, picked by my father from the garden, pink peonies, blue delphiniums, acid-green Lady's Mantle, burst with life beneath her smiling face.

There was precious little other life in that house. Neither of us thought of it as home. It was simply the place where we laid our heads, where my mother died. We both wanted to leave. Neither of us knew where to go.

'Take care of each other.' It was her final command; perhaps the only one we truly heeded. We were obedient. We cooked and cleaned for each other, although we rarely ate, and offered solace in mugs of sweet, steaming tea. We didn't speak much. We both knew there was nothing to say.

My father went on living, but grudgingly, his face turned towards the past. Stories were his only consolation. One of the stories he told, each time as if it were new, was about me as a child, and my amah, a God-fearing young Chinese woman called Mildred. Every afternoon, Mildred took me for a walk. 'You'd come home,' said my father, 'laughing fit to burst.' He was smiling. It was the only time that he did smile, when he was talking about the past. 'You were a serious child and not much given to laughing. So one day I decided to follow you both, to see what it was that amused you. Well, you know the Coopers' old house?'

I nodded, to please him. How could I know? I was three years old.

My father's eyes gleamed. He was enjoying the story. 'Mildred took you up the road that led to the Coopers' house – you remember, Frank Baxter and his wife took it over after the Coopers were transferred; Nigeria, I think it was. Not a happy place. What was Frank's wife called?'

He appealed to me, but I shook my head ruefully. His eyes clouded over. My mother would have remembered. He frowned, searching for her name. 'Mary, I think. I don't exactly recall. Anyway, I followed you up the road, keeping well out of sight. The next minute you were gone, vanished as if into thin air.'

To please him, I urged him to go on with the story, although I knew it by heart.

'I could still hear you laughing so I searched around until I spotted a dirt track, half hidden in the undergrowth. I followed it round to the back of the house and up, over a slight incline, and there you both were, sitting on a low stone wall, laughing your heads off.'

My father laughed until tears spilled from his faded eyes. I waited patiently. 'Headless chickens.' He was laughing so hard, he could scarcely get the words out.

I laughed too – my father's mirth was contagious – but my mouth ached with the effort.

He went on with the story of Mildred and me sitting on the wall, our feet dangling in the bloody dust of the local slaughterhouse yard. We looked, he said, as if we were in the front row of the theatre stalls. A thin man darted among the chickens, swiping off their heads with a machete. Soon, the yard was filled with headless birds running in furious circles as blood spurted from their scrawny necks and their scaly feet slipped in the dust as they scrabbled to escape their destiny.

It was always at this point that I stopped laughing. He looked at me reproachfully. 'Your mother found it funny.'

I stayed for six months, clinging like a limpet to the unreliable rock of my father. I irritated him, I knew, but I could not let him go. My parents were the only fixed point in my sky; when they changed orbit so did I. I was their satellite, revolving endlessly around their lives.

Once I thought that I had lost them for ever. I was very young, perhaps four or five and already onto my third country where I was sent to a kindergarten school. I spoke only English; the teachers and children spoke something else entirely. I forget what, but it was unintelligible to me. We managed well enough with hand signals and smiles, and there were toys to play with so I was happy.

Once school hours were over, the children lined the bench outside the low concrete bungalow that housed us. A teacher stood in attendance to hand us to our parents when they arrived to collect us.

One day, my mother did not come.

All the other children left. The teacher and I sat in silence. Gradually, her reassuring smile dimmed, gave way to anxious glances. I was desperate to pee, but did not have the language to tell her and anyway was terrified to move, in case my mother arrived and, not finding me there, went away again. It did not occur to me that she would wait.

I clamped my legs together, and my mouth, staring straight ahead at the dusty road down which nobody came. I knew in my heart that my mother had gone for ever, was lost somewhere in the bewildering chaos of strange countries and houses. The teacher took my arm, spoke to me urgently in her strange tongue. I hit her as hard as I could.

We waited for an hour.

When eventually my mother appeared, her face was distorted by fear and crying. The car had broken down and, knowing nothing of the language, she had tried, with gestures and words plucked from a phrase book, to get on a bus. It took her in the wrong direction.

As her arms went to circle me I pissed as hard as I could. Yellow liquid slowly seeped around us, warm and sour in the mid-day heat.

Years later, it was my father who made me go; plucked me from him like the limpet that I was and hurled me out to sea.

We were facing each other, sitting on either side of the shrine. It took up the whole mantelpiece and adjoining walls so there was nothing for it but to sit in contemplation of my mother, who peered down on us with anxious blue eyes. My father shuffled his feet as he did when he was about to say something uncomfortable. He was wearing slippers. The ends were frayed. I could see a yellow toe-nail peeking through. He never bothered to cut his toe-nails at that time.

'It's time for you to go, Janey.'

I roused myself. 'Go? But where?'

'I've booked you into a secretarial course in London. There's a hall of residence attached. You can live there.' He was smiling but the smile didn't reach his eyes. 'You'll meet girls of your own age.'

81

I would go, of course, just as I always had when my father said it was time to leave.

His voice was loud. 'It'll be fun.'

'Great fun,' I agreed. We did not look at each other. I could not face what I had done, nor could I tell him.

It was time to leave.

Seven

I feel hemmed in, the air thick around me. Every so often I glance up at the four walls, challenging them to move towards me, but they stay firmly in place. Beattie's room is directly above my head, malignant and threatening. I run up the stairs, bouncing lightly off the awkward turns in the staircase. I have it down to a fine art. Practice makes perfect. Beattie raced me up to bed every night. She always won. I stop in the doorway to her room. The Noddy duvet is back in place, the blue-cloud curtains drawn. I keep promising myself to turn it into a spare room, cream walls, tastefully neutral bedcover, a pleated silk lampshade on the table, but I find difficulties for myself everywhere I turn. I haven't the time to make new curtains, to find the right shade of paint, to hunt down a lampshade. The room stays as it is.

The cupboard and drawers, at least, are empty. Margaret did that for me, while I took myself off to the pictures. The film was *Women in Love*, the one with Oliver Reed in it. It was the only thing showing at the local cinema, which is one of those art house places. I thought Lawrence would suit my mood, but when it came to it, all I could think was, why are these people making such a fuss about nothing? Well, that's Lawrence for you. Not everyone agrees with me, of course, and towards the end of the film, during that scene when Oliver Reed walks off into the glaring landscape of snow by himself, a man in the audience got to his feet and shouted, 'No, don't do it. It's only a film.' You could have heard a pin drop. Then people started laughing. Out of relief, I suppose. I didn't laugh. I just thought, what an idiot.

I didn't ask Margaret what she had done with Beattie's clothes and she never mentioned them. I suppose she must have given them to a charity. She's been through a war, years of make do and mend. There's no way she's going to chuck away perfectly good clothes. She even has a special sponge thing in her bathroom, where you slot old slivers of soap, when they get worn down to the size of those things you find in budgie cages. Margaret says they lather up very well.

I wish she had thrown the clothes away. I get nervous every time I see a kid in the street, just in case she's wearing Beattie's old blue jumper, or her favourite dungarees. Her toys are still in the house, packed up in boxes and piled in my bedroom. I look at them now and again, thinking I should do something about them. Beattie was convinced the toys came to life at night, had themselves a great big party. Sometimes I'd find her lying awake when I went up to bed, her fingers prising her eyes open. 'Any sign of life?' she'd ask, burying her head in her pillow, then bouncing up, trying to catch them off their guard.

She loved parties.

There's no use moping around the house like this so I decide to walk up to the market. On the way, I stop by at Margaret's to ask if she needs anything. I find her hunched over a battered cardboard box, its corners butted together with yellowing Sellotape. As I move closer, her arm curls protectively around the contents.

'I'm going up to the market,' I say. 'Do you need anything?'

The colour is high in her face. 'I was just doing a spot of tidying.' Her eyes are bright. I wonder if it is the unaccustomed colour in her face that makes them seem so, or if she is upset about something. She says, as if in answer, 'It's nothing important.'

I see corners of photographs jutting sharply between the swollen knuckles of her hand. They can't be recent because they are in black and white, from what Beattie used to call 'the olden times.' A true child of her age, Beattie believed that any image not in colour must be old. The photographs surprise me. Margaret always claims she has no need of them, that all the images she could ever want are stored inside her head. She answers the earlier question now, as she often does. She says it's something to do with age, the past being clearer than the present. 'A banana. I was just thinking I could fancy a banana.'

'Just one?'

'Two, but no more. They spoil so quickly.'

I nod in understanding. Those of us who live on our own only ever buy in ones or twos. After Beattie went I could scarcely be bothered to shop at all, but gradually my cupboards are filling up again. I wonder if this is a good sign, like blood returning to a deadened limb. It's easy to shop for one up at the market, they're used to elderly women demanding a single chop or a quarter of beans. Not that I'm old. I just feel it sometimes. I suppose, now that Ben's going to be around, I'll have to get used to shopping for two again.

Margaret says, 'I was just thinking about Ben. What he must be going through.' Her hands crab into claws and she lifts them with a sigh, presses them against her breast to warm them. She suffers from arthritis, each joint a shiny red carbuncle on her thin, bloodless fingers.

As she moves her hands away from the box, I see Ben's eyes smiling up at me. The rest of the face is unfamiliar, round, scarcely formed, the nose not yet made, nor the mouth. His hair was very blond then, almost white, but with that same cowlick flipping over his forehead. 'He looks a happy child,' I say.

'Oh, he was, although he was always happiest when he

got his own way. Had a dreadful temper on him. But I dare say one could say that about most children.'

I leave her staring at the contents of the box, her old crabbed hands moving gently through the contents. I see now why she has got the photographs out. She wants to see if the boy she has in her head is the same one who once existed.

As I make my way up to the market, I wonder the same thing. That Ben that I hold in my head, that I've held in my heart these past eight years. Does he exist? Did he ever?

In those first few weeks of our relationship it was as though Ben and I were stuck in limbo, unable to move towards each other, unable to move away.

When people asked we said we were best friends. It wasn't true, but we liked the childish ring of it, the air of innocence and fun. There was nothing innocent between us. Instead, it was dark and complicated. There is the potential for destruction rooted in both of us.

We always went to parties together. We arrived together and we left together. What we did in the intervening hours was our business. It confused everybody, but most of all us.

'You won't kiss me.'

'And you won't cry.'

We laughed as we said it but we both knew that we wanted the opposite to be true.

I kept my side of the bargain. I never cried, not even when Ben had sex with other girls. It astonishes me to think of it now, but in those days sex was everywhere. It was pre-AIDS (but only just, we got in by a whisker) when desire still crackled like electricity and turned the air blue with lust, when hormones sang out like cicadas after dark. People did it in the garden, in the bath, in the bedrooms, on top of the coats. I even saw a couple making out on the dance floor, her skirt hooped up around her thighs, one white-knuckled hand clutching the waistband of his trousers as they gyrated to the floor. Dance floor is too grand a word for the dim, carpeted front rooms in which we jerked like jumping beans, jostling the occasional tables whose once polished surfaces were patterned like spirographs with sticky rings from spilled drinks, covered with cereal bowls filched from kitchen cupboards that slowly piled high with cigarette butts.

It was always me who emptied the ashtrays, creeping around the room with a cloth in my hand, mopping up stale beer. When I wasn't cleaning, I kept myself on the move, smiling a lot, looking pleasant. I even talked to the shy men who lined the walls, beer cans in hand, staring forlornly at the couples sliding their tongues in and out of each other's mouths. As the evening wore on, their smiles sagged with disappointment and their bodies with beer, and they slid quietly down the wall to join the other bodies littering the floor.

Ben and I always went home together, swaying against each other on the empty Tube or, if we were too late for that, propped together on the night bus, up high on the seat right at the front where the noisy heater belched out lukewarm, diesel-scented air. That was the part I liked best. I felt completely safe, as if I were on some magic ship, sailing over the dark, sleepy streets, Ben slumped against me, drink-sodden and satiated, his thin, sinewy arms limp as cooked spaghetti. He never alarmed me on those long journeys home.

I buy Margaret's bananas and choose something for myself, a mango, the orange skin scorched with red. It is oozing slightly, the soft skin tearing away from the root of the stem. It is overripe but better that than the hard fibrous green ones you so often find in this country. I lift it to my nose and sniff hard. Its cloying sweetness brings back memories of my mother packing up a picnic for Sunday lunch, my father driving our old Ford, white with a soft top that crunched down into a concertina at the back.

We felt we were the most glamorous people alive as we drove through the desert roads to the beach, the wind in our hair and the sand stinging our bare arms. We swam first and then we ate, the taste of sea salt mingling with canned sausages stuffed inside soft, sweet bread rolls, or a chicken leg, the roast skin flabby but sticky and delicious with jelly. Afterwards we sat in the shallows, the waves lapping at our waists as we ate mangoes, the sweet juice running down our arms into the salt water and the hot sun beating on our heads. I was perfectly happy then. Perfectly.

I pack away the memories together with the bananas and the mango, and set off towards the library. The man on the desk has a nose ring, a shaved head and a soft, high voice. 'What can I do you for, love?' he says, then gives me a mock serious frown when I ask where to find the Law section.

Placing a gentle hand on my back as if I were one of the pensioners who squat like crumpled packages on the long, low plastic sofas, he steers me to the back of the room and heaves a fat volume off a shelf. 'This should do you. No, don't you worry, I'll do it.' Carrying it to an empty table, he pulls out a chair for me and smiles. Above the black leather jacket and T-shirt his face is young and plump, and his eyes as blue and guileless as Beattie's. I picture him in the morning, standing before the bathroom mirror pulling fierce faces as he screws rings into his nose and ear. I want to tell him not to bother, that he will always look like somebody's son.

The entry for suicide is relatively short. Suicide, also known as self-murder, ceased to be a crime in 1961. The Act introduced a new offence. A person who aids, abets, counsels or procures the suicide of another, or an attempt to commit suicide, shall be liable on conviction to imprisonment for a term not exceeding fourteen years.

I turn the words over in my head. Is failing to prevent a suicide the same as aiding and abetting one? Has a person technically committed suicide after they have taken drugs, or after they are dead? If somebody has taken pills and you fail to get them medical help, are you aiding and abetting suicide or are you only guilty if you procure and administer the pills? I don't know.

Intent, the Inspector said. It is all a question of intent.

Somebody walks past. I sense eyes focused on the book that lies open in front of me. Guiltily, I slide my hand to cover the heading at the top of the page. The word seems to burn into my fingers. Homicide. In plain language, murder.

I look around. There is nobody there. My hand steals back to the index. I have one more entry to check. Euthanasia. The text, this time, is unequivocal. *Illegal and not distinguishable from murder.*

I leave the library and walk home. My legs are shaking slightly.

I'm still shaky when Ben comes round after work. The way he lets himself in, dropping his bag on the floor and leaving his jacket higgledy-piggledy on the stairs, you'd think he lived here. I'm about to ask him not to dump his stuff all over the floor but keep my mouth shut when I catch the heavy, clouded expression on his face.

'Hi,' I say.

He doesn't even say hello, just pushes past me. 'I've been at the police station for the past two hours. I need a drink.'

Picking up his jacket and hanging it on the hooks by the door, I wonder what it is that makes me more resentful – my tidiness or his lack of it. I leave the bag where he dropped it. I am training myself in the fine art of neglect.

I find him crouched over the cupboard in the sitting-room, tugging at the handle. 'Do you have to keep this damn thing locked? Even now?' His face is thunderous.

I lift the key out of the blue pot on the shelf and hand it to him. I always kept the drink cupboard locked when Beattie was around. I haven't got out of the habit of it yet. 'Yes.' My voice is tight.

He sighs, fumbles with the tiny silver key. 'Sorry.' The bottles clink as he pulls out the whisky. I put two glasses on the low table in the middle of the room. It is Indian and antique, bought by my father from one of the countries in which we lived. I forget which.

Ben looks at me. 'I said I'm sorry.'

I keep my face averted, conscious that I am behaving badly. Still, I will not relent. The yellow liquid looks like pee in the glasses. I sniff it tentatively. It's whisky all right. 'What did the police want?'

Ben tilts the glass to his mouth, swallows in one gulp. 'They won't leave Rebecca's letter alone. That and the fact that it was you who gave her the pills.'

'I didn't give them to her. She took them.'

'But you knew she had them.'

'Yes.'

'Why didn't you tell me?'

'I don't know. I suppose it just never occurred to me that she would actually take them.'

'She was on the At Risk register, for God's sake. Every doctor and chemist for miles around had her name on a list.'

He leans forward to pour himself another whisky but doesn't drink it. The glass dangles loosely from his hand. His fingers are long and tapered, with pearly nails and healthy pink cuticles. They are beautiful, unlike mine which are short and stubby, with square nails set in pads of flesh. I bite my nails too when I am concentrating, which makes them uglier than they need to be. It used to worry me, putting those jagged nails on his tender skin.

'OK. It's your turn now for some questions.'

'Janey, please. I've just spent two hours with the police.'

'What did you do after you left that night?'

He leans back against the chair, closes his eyes. 'I went home, of course.'

'Was she dead by then?'

'I don't know. I didn't look,' he says in a dull voice.

I try to feel indignant but can't. Indignation seems inappropriate around death. I think of Rebecca standing in my bedroom, the bottle of pills in her hand. She is smiling. I wonder if it is that or the whisky that's making me feel nauseous.

'What time did you call the ambulance?'

He opens his eyes, looks at me oddly. 'What?'

'What time did you call?'

His voice is cold. 'I don't know. I wasn't exactly watching the clock.' A muscle twitches slowly in his cheek. Once, it would have made me horny. Sometimes I think Ben and I have begun dislike each other. I desire him too much. He needs me too much. These things make people irritable. I look over at him. His beautiful mouth is clamped in a hard, mutinous line. I'm not sure whether I want to hit him or fuck him. Maybe both. Now he's hunching down in the chair, his arms folded protectively across his chest.

I think about the first man I kissed, more out of curiosity than desire. Afterwards, I put away my tongue and closed my lips and thought that I would not do that again, not for a long time. It was a mistake I did not learn from. There is an enervating quality to sex without desire. It makes you feel tired and sad. Or at least it does me and I can only speak for myself. The first time it happened, I thought I was doing something wrong or, rather, that I was doing something not quite right. What that was I didn't know and I've always thought that's rather the trouble with sex. Everything else, we learn as a part of mimicry. Even facial expressions are learned; the faces of anger, joy, fear are all received information. Sex is the only physical action that we see no one else engaged in. We never know if we have it right or wrong. No wonder people get in such a state about it.

I've never had that trouble with Ben. We're sex junkies, can't keep our hands off each other. Except that night when he came to tell me about Rebecca. I must have had an instinct that something was wrong. I remember his expression, how closed off and heavy he looked. It wasn't me he wanted but a body to bury himself in, to forget if only for a few moments about Rebecca. Perhaps I should have let him. Is it better or worse to fuck a man when his wife is lying dead in their bed? I don't know.

I don't have any of the answers to Rebecca's death. I don't know why she wanted to die, or even if she did. Was it an act of faith, to believe that Ben would save her, as he had done before? Or a monumental act of arrogance. Whatever, she calculated it all wrong. Or maybe not. She is more present between us now than when she was alive.

Ben sighs, stretches out his hand. 'I'm sorry, Janey. Come here.'

I go to him and he presses his face to the puckered roll of fat between the waistband of my trousers and my T-shirt. Baby fat, I call it. It has never gone away. My baby left, but the fat is still with me. I feel the rasp of bristles against the tender flesh and pull away. 'No,' I say. 'Not now.' He looks up at me with that same heavy, closed expression he wears so often these days.

The first time we make love is at a party. One minute I'm cleaning ashtrays, the next I'm lying on a pile of coats, a button digging into the small of my back, Ben's bony jaw jutting into the soft part of my neck. There is whisky on his breath, the smell of dope clinging to his hair. It flops over his forehead, brushes against my face with tiny feathery strokes. His eyes are closed. Mine are open, watching him. It's my first time, so I have no comparisons to make. All I know is that my body's been open to him for weeks. Perhaps he knows that too. We don't undress, just move bits of clothing aside and plug into each other. I am wearing the navy dress, the one that makes me look like a grown-up. Perhaps he mistakes me for someone else. But no, there's his voice, shouting my name as he comes. He comes fast. I know enough. I've read the magazines. It hurts a bit, but his voice calling my name makes up for everything.

When it's over, he will not look at me. He buttons himself up, covering the tender blue-white flesh, and ducks from the room with an awkward wave of his hand. I sit on the bed for a while, then go downstairs. My body is singing. I pick up a cloth, bend over a table to hide my burning cheeks. If anyone were to look at me, they would know.

I sense a movement, look up to see Ben frowning over me. 'Are you all right?'

I can see from his eyes that he's been at the whisky again. Tiny beads of sweat decorate his upper lip. He is nervous of me. Sex changes everything. I stand awkwardly, the dirty cloth dangling from my hand. 'Fine.' I try a smile, but my mouth is dry with fear and desire. My lips stick to my teeth.

'Yeah, well, just thought I'd check. See ya.'

He fades into the mass of bodies writhing in the centre of the room. I watch him go, wrap my arms round my body to warm myself. I realised that I am shivering uncontrollably.

'Are you all right?' A man I haven't noticed before is standing next to me. His face is smooth, his hair sleek and dark. He looks as if he has been well cared for. He hands me a glass. 'This will make you feel better.'

I take it gratefully, feeling the red wine puckering at my dry mouth, glowing down my throat. 'Thanks.'

'I saw you earlier. I like your dress.'

I smile. I had noticed him earlier too, because of his leather jacket, which is new. Among the crowd of faded denim and ripped surplus, it makes him look remarkable, as if he is wearing fancy dress. Behind him I can see Ben on the dance floor, his alarming hips gyrating wildly. I feel a warmth between my legs.

I drag my gaze away, turn back to my companion. 'Are you from round here?'

He grins, his eyes taking in the mass of tangled bodies. 'I was at school with this lot but I went out to work, while they were all bumming around at college.' His smile conveys the world of men and work.

Ben's hands are sliding up and down a smooth, golden back. I feel jealousy rise like bile.

'And you?'

'I'm a friend of Ben Robinson.'

'I understand he's trying to be a writer.' He looks as if the thought amuses him.

I can find nothing to say, so say nothing.

'The name's Alan. Alan Roberts. I'm in real estate.' I must look confused for he laughs suddenly, his whole face relaxing. 'I'm an estate agent. I always think real estate sounds more interesting.'

I realise that he is younger than I had at first thought.

I catch a glimpse of Ben weaving through the heaving bodies, leading the girl with the golden back. She is laughing. I take a gulp of red wine, my teeth chattering against the glass.

Alan looks at me with concern. 'You really are cold. Let me get you something hot. There's some mulled wine in the kitchen.'

'Thank you. I think I'll go and get my coat. It might warm me up,' I say, knowing that nothing will warm me now but Ben.

'Right-oh. Meet you back here then.'

I go upstairs, groping my way into the darkened room. A noise like a sob echoes in the room and I stiffen. A girl tumbles to the floor. I move towards her but then I see that she is laughing and very drunk. A face looms up from the pile of coats, white and glittering with sweat.

'Janey.'

'I came to get my coat.'

'You're not leaving?'

'I'm cold.'

Ben springs from the bed, flings coats and jackets around like a madman. 'It's brown, isn't it? With gold buttons.'

'Navy blue.'

He picks up a coat, hands it to me. Even with the wild glitter of whisky in his eyes, there is a pleading quality to his gaze. 'You said you weren't a virgin.'

'I lied.'

'Why?'

I shake my head.

'You shouldn't lie to me, Janey.'

I find my coat, retreat to the door. Ben comes after me, shirt unbuttoned, trousers sliding off his skinny hips. The light from the hall glances off his blue-white skin. 'You shouldn't fucking lie to me, Janey.'

From the bedroom, the girl starts laughing hysterically. Ben picks up a coat and chucks it at her. 'Cover yourself up, will you?'

I put my coat on and walk slowly down the stairs. I am on my way to the front door when Alan appears in front of me, holding two glasses of red wine. I had forgotten about him. 'Here,' he says, thrusting the glass into my hand. It shakes violently, wine spills down my blue dress. 'You look terrible.'

'I'll be all right.'

'Look, why don't I take you home?'

'I'm fine,' I say again.

'Well, I'm not. I thought it would be all right, coming back into the old crowd. But it's not all right. Not all right at all.' He smiles, to show that it doesn't matter, but I can see that it matters a great deal. There is something endearing in his discomfort. I pay him better attention, look at him more closely. His smile is kind.

I look away, finding sympathy unbearable. 'Well, if you really don't mind . . .'

'Not at all. My car's outside. Just hang on for a minute while I go upstairs and get my coat.'

I wonder if it was his coat we were lying on earlier, imagine semen drying in white crusts on the soft pile. Ben's semen. Wrapping my coat more securely around myself, I lean against the wall and close my eyes.

A hand touches my cheek, tracing a line across my lips. It's Ben. 'Bad idea, Janey. Dreadfully, savagely bad.' The laughing blonde is draped over his shoulder, chewing drunkenly on his ear and making small whimpering sounds, like a kitten.

'What?'

Ben jerks his head in the direction of the stairs and Alan's retreating back. 'Him.'

I stare at the blonde. 'Speak for yourself.'

Ben shrugs. The sharp movement dislodges the blonde, who slides noiselessly to the floor. He looks faintly surprised, then steps carefully over her recumbent body, puts his hands on my shoulders. 'Let me take you home.'

'No.'

'Why not?'

'Because –'

'Because what?' Exasperation is edging through the

alcohol. He moves forward again so his body is almost touching mine. I want to open his shirt, put my hands on his skin. I want to kiss him.

My body starts to shake again. I drop my head, cross my arms protectively over my chest. 'I don't feel well.'

'Poor baby.' Ben leans towards me, trapping me against the wall. His breath is hot in my ear, slowly he puts out his tongue, pressing its hot length against the tender spot just below my ear, licks gently along the line of my jaw, circling up to my mouth. The sensation is so intense, I think I am going to faint. I pull away my mouth, sobbing for breath. 'Stop it, please stop it.'

'Jane?'

Alan's face looms over Ben's shoulder. Ben is so close that half of Alan's face is obliterated by Ben's ear. His ears stick out slightly and are on the large side. When the light is behind him, they glow pink. I have never seen such a beautiful ears.

'She's fine.' Ben answers for me.

'Are you coming, Jane?'

Ben turns, stares him down. 'I told you, she's fine.'

I step between them, look at Ben. 'I need to go home. I need to get away.'

He thinks I mean, away from him. He doesn't know about the alarming sensations in my body, the claws of jealousy stuck fast in my heart. 'Please, Ben, I really –'.

He steps back, his arm lifting. For a minute I think he is going to hit me, but then I see he is trying to ward off my words, as if they were hard objects. 'Well, fuck you.'

I say, 'He has a car outside.'

Alan says firmly, 'I think that's quite enough,' then asks, 'Are you all right, Jane?'

I nod, too numbed to speak. Ben moves away, still watching us. His eyes look very dark from where I am standing, although they are pale blue. His mouth is an ugly oval.

'Don't forget your girlfriend,' Alan says, indicating the blonde girl on the floor.

Ben stares down at her sleeping body, then his mouth curves in a grin. 'Plenty more where she came from,' he says, lifting his hand in an exaggerated, childlike wave. 'See you around, Janey.'

My hand goes up automatically, as if we were lovers, saying farewell at a railway station. Then he is gone and I am left standing, my arm hovering in mid-air. I think, I will not weep. He kissed me but I will not weep.

I scarcely notice Alan on the journey home. He concentrates on driving, which he does well, easing the powerful car through the empty suburban streets. It is soothing, like being driven by my father who also handles cars well. After a while I am sufficiently collected to murmur an apology, to say truthfully that I am very tired.

It is only as we approach my house that it occurs to me that he might think that I was asking for something more than a lift home. But when we pull up outside, he puts his arm round me and hugs me awkwardly. 'You go and get a good night's sleep,' he says. 'Soon have you right as rain.'

It is his clumsy tenderness that undoes me. I have always been susceptible to the kindness of strangers. I lean forward and kiss him. Had I not done so, it might have saved us all a great deal of trouble.

Eight

The first time that Alan and I made love, his face took on the awful sentimental look that some men get after sex. 'That was good, little one,' he said, dropping a kiss on my forehead, as if I were a small child. He had never called me that before but I noticed that once we started to have sex, Alan increasingly addressed me as 'little one' – and not just in the intimacy of our bed but in quite public places too – even though there is nothing about me that could remotely be described as little. I suppose, really, that it was just his way of staking his claim as the dominant male; as if, through language, I could be reduced to something small and shoved in his pocket like a possession.

I had not intended to end up with Alan. It just happened. Or perhaps I just let it happen.

Ben says now that I ran off, but it wasn't that way at all. The day after the party he wouldn't speak to me. I tried a few times but he averted his face or stared past my shoulder, his expression as mutinous as a child's. I suppose that in my own way I was as bad as him. I thought at the time it was pride that would not allow me to pursue him, but now I see that it was fear. We had only made love once, but it was enough. Ben alarmed me in a way that he never had before. My body became an alien place, tropical where it had been temperate, stormy where once all had been calm. The nights were the worst, the dreary small hours of crying, and tossing and turning, as I recalled my face squashed against the bluish-white skin on his chest and his penis plugged into me, making me feel that, at last, I had connected to life.

We went on like this for about a week, then my father telephoned. We had not been in touch for a few months, but he had never been a communicative man and after my mother died he withdrew into himself. It was unusual for him to telephone. He still had his generation's irrational terror of long-distance calls and, while Cornwall is not another country, in those days it seemed far enough away from London to feel like one. He wanted me to go and see him.

I went, of course.

When I arrived he was sitting in front of my mother's shrine, the television roaring. He seemed older and shabbier. The photographs of my mother had begun to curl at the edges. I pushed at them with my fingers, trying to stick them back. His eyes flickered resentfully at the intrusion, but he said nothing.

I told him something about my life while we drank mugs of sweet tea. I had got out of the habit of taking sugar but did not mention it. Any change of routine upset him in those days. I think that even my news upset him, it was so unfamiliar. We tried, for a while, to talk about the past, but my memories had faded, like the yellowing photographs stuck above the mantelpiece, and my father became irritable when I got things wrong. I had my reasons for not wanting to talk about my mother so I maintained a steady resistance to his talk of 'do you remember?' until the conversation between us slowed to a trickle until it was as dry as the gullies of the desert where we used to live.

Eventually, he got up and shuffled off to his bedroom, returned carrying an old Sainsbury plastic carrier into which he had bundled the family silver, a selection of mismatched knives and forks and spoons. 'You'll be wanting to get yourself a place of your own soon,' he said awkwardly. 'I thought you might find these useful.'

At the time, I had a room in a house in Fulham. I found it when I finished the secretarial course and began to earn some money of my own. It was advertised in the evening paper: 'Quiet, tidy person to share. Own room'. There were four of us in the house, although you would not have known it. We were a colony of mice, scurrying in and out of our rooms, clearing up the mess of our droppings in the kitchen with deft and tidy movements, uttering tiny morning greetings before we hurried off to work. We were all young women, embarking on our lives. I remember none of their names now, although I do recall their faces; soft, round English faces with shining cheeks and eager smiles.

I started to tell him something of it but then I noticed his expression, which was attentive but focused on some other time, far from that house in Fulham. 'Thank you,' I said. 'They'll be useful.'

He added that there would be some money too. 'But you'll not be getting it until I'm dead,' he said, wagging his finger at me in mock fury.

I smiled.

I went back to London. Ben continued to ignore me, Alan to deluge me with flowers and telephone calls. The week passed slowly. On the Friday evening there was a telephone call to say that my father had been admitted to hospital. A slight case of pneumonia. Nothing to worry about. I said I would make arrangements to travel down.

The voice – it was female, a nurse I suppose – said there was no need, he was on the mend. The cardiogram was clear; he was a fine, strong man. I packed anyway, booked a ticket on the early-morning train. The phone call came at six, just as I was folding my dressing-gown to put in the suitcase. It was saffron-coloured silk, embroidered with flowers and had belonged to my mother, collected on some distant duty-free stop. The call was from the hospital. My father's heart had stopped. A dreadful shock, they said, dreadful.

I gazed at my mother's robe.

My father's heart didn't stop, I said. It broke.

I took the train anyway and telephoned George when I reached the cottage. I told her that I needed to take a week off work, but not why. I was not being precious. My defence in difficult situations has always been silence. I spent the time attending to arrangements for the funeral and packing up my father's stuff. And my mother's, too. He had kept everything, every tiny scrap of her life.

When I got back to work, Ben had gone.

He left without telling anyone. It caused little ruffles of consternation throughout the office but quite quickly he was replaced by a dull young man with a tide of acne ebbing down his throat. After a while, it was as if he had never existed.

Unfamiliar with myself, as are most people in their twenties, I mistook emptiness for loneliness. Foolishly, I tried to fill it with Alan. Although not an original man, he was kind to me and persistent, too, and with both my parents dead and Ben gone I was in no state to resist him. Roses, dinners, tickets to the theatre, declarations of love, it was heady stuff and I was not used to it. At the time I believed I was in love, but I see now that the only feeling I felt towards Alan was gratitude. It is pleasing to find somebody waiting to give you a lift home after work, to have notes pushed through your letter-box, to receive late-night telephone calls checking to see that you got home all right. Those small kindnesses are not to be underestimated and nor is gratitude, which is a very powerful emotion indeed and one that is often mistaken for love.

It was a pleasant enough existence. I enjoyed my work and slowly became better at it under George's expert tutelage. George, or Georgina Katherine Curtis, to give her

her proper name, was a paragon among women, a monument to sweetness and cleverness. Authors loved her and so they should, not least for her ability to peer into the unpromising lining of a sow's ear and fetch out a silk purse. There were times when I felt I should drown under the weight of words that daily poured over us, weeks when the new James Joyce could have walked up to me and spat in my eye, and I would have sent him away with a few sharp words for his pains. Not so George, who read every unsolicited manuscript that passed through the doors of one Albion Mews – perhaps not the whole thing, but the first two chapters at the very least and more if the book seemed promising.

I began to emerge as an editor of sorts, although I despaired of ever achieving George's subtlety of touch or her tone, half martinet, half comforting nanny, which writers found so encouraging. From those early days of filing, I graduated to writing the occasional blurb for a book jacket (for the less important authors; George always guarded her own like a lioness brooding over her cubs) and finally to editing manuscripts. My speciality, as I explained, is costume history, so it was useful to have the Victoria & Albert Museum just up the road for checking facts and dates. I spent a lot of time there, not for any high-minded reason but because I found its marbled halls and ancient artefacts soothing, reassured, I suppose, by the slow contemplative tide of history.

I put Ben away, bundled him up with my mother's scented good-night kisses, my father's gentle teasing and the blue skies and hot suns of my childhood. And there he stayed, up in the attic of my memories, for two long years.

It was George who first noticed his name, edging into the very bottom of the best-seller list. The Egg has finally hatched, she said. I cut out the list from the newspaper and put it in the wooden box that I keep by my bed, together with my mother's ring. I need not have bothered. By the time the book went to number one, Ben was staring out of the pages of every newspaper in the country. You could not get away from him. Or so it seemed to me. It was then that I first saw Rebecca. She was gazing out of the page of newsprint, her smile tilted towards the camera. Ben was slightly behind her, his eyes fixed on her face with a look of unmistakable, hungry yearning. ROMANTIC FICTION, the headline said. Rebecca Carter, as she then was, was a poet. Or, rather, she had published a slim volume of poems that had been moderately well received. Clever, beautiful and well-connected, she had left Oxford with a second class degree and a trail of broken hearts. It was irresistible stuff for the media. Much was made of Ben's career stacking books for a small publishing house who were blithely unaware of the shining talent housed under their own roof. George smiled when she read that bit. It was she who had set Ben up with his present publisher, encouraging him to go elsewhere because she knew he would get a better deal.

I went out and bought a copy of Rebecca's poems which were, as I suspected they would be, written in the sub-Sylvia Plath style to which so many young female graduates are attached. Even so, they slid into my head and I discovered that, once there, I could not shake them off. Nor could I shake off the image of her face, smiling out at the world while Ben hovered behind in lost adoration.

I still have that scrap of newsprint. At the time, I read and reread it, pictured Ben roaring around the circuit of parties like a young literary lion while Rebecca stood on the sidelines, patiently biding her time. I saw her face, pale and glittering, swinging in and out of Ben's vision, and imagined her pressing her long, slender body against his during the formal exchange of kisses, lingering just slightly longer than is correct. I knew it would not be enough for Ben, his pale eyes, feverish with success, watching her as she moved about the room, tossing her hair back, smiling into every face. Rebecca always smiled. Was it only me who saw how her smile never reached her eyes?

The day Ben married Rebecca, I moved in with Alan, to a small flat in West Kensington. Alan was not making a lot of money. Estate agents didn't in those days and publishing scarcely paid a living wage, so I was not bringing much in. My father had left me some money. It seemed to me a considerable amount, but I did not tell Alan about it. At the time, it felt like too intimate a secret to share but I think now that I kept quiet because I knew that Alan would insist I invest it for our future. I had no thought about the future and wanted none. I simply lived from day to day.

The flat, as Alan was careful to point out, was in a good address and part of a handsome row of Georgian terraces. It was cheap because Alan had done a deal on it through his work, but mainly because it overlooked the railway line. But it had a beautiful large sitting-room with tall, elegant windows, a small but comfortable bedroom, a tiny kitchen and bathroom, partitioned off from the rest by a thin wall surmounted by a fringe of frosted glass. There was no central heating but although we noticed the cold, we never thought to complain about it.

Anyway, we were happy. Or at least we thought we were. When I look back at that time I can scarcely make out Alan's features, his face is a white smudge with two darker smudges for eyes, as if I am seeing it from a long way off. Try as I might, I can't get it into focus. I rarely see Alan these days, not since Beattie left. There is no longer any reason to. But even when I do, I cannot fit him into the years that we spent together. He does not seem like a man whom I had ever known intimately, more like a casual acquaintance one meets occasionally, then thinks no more about.

I was a good little housewife. After a while, I even began to take a ridiculous pride in my ability to cook and clean, to iron shirts and unplug lavatories, and went on in this way for about a year. Then Alan proposed. I was feeling rather sick at the time, flushed and nauseous although all I had eaten was a small helping of a modest supper of cauliflower-cheese. I sat at the table in a daze while Alan lowered himself, somewhat laboriously, to his knees and presented me with a small diamond solitaire. I remember his words exactly. 'Will you do me the honour of becoming my wife?'

I looked at him, still feeling rather sick. His eyes were moist with emotion but it is an emotional moment, persuading a free woman to enter a life of servitude. He jerked the ring at me, still entombed in its stout leather box. 'Well?' he demanded, a thread of irritation drawing through his voice.

The nausea began to surface and my eyes to water with the effort of repressing it. I believe Alan thought I was about to cry with gratitude, for his face softened and he rose to his feet, dropping a tender kiss on my forehead. 'I'm sorry, I've taken you by surprise.' As he moved back to his chair, I took my chance and bolted for the lavatory where I was prodigiously sick.

By the end of the week, I was certain of two things: I could not marry Alan and I was pregnant.

I told no one about the pregnancy, not even him. It was not difficult to keep it from him. He was too busy sulking at my lack of grace at his proposal and refused to communicate further than a query as to the whereabouts of his shirt/shoes/car keys. I felt too sick and tired to do anything other than drag myself to work where I explained away my unaccustomed lassitude with a story about a gastric bug. Nobody questioned it.

About two weeks after I discovered I was pregnant I returned home from work to find the door of the flat unlocked and the smell of boiled fish hanging heavy in the air. Alan appeared, arms held wide, a shy smile sliding across his face.

I bolted for the lavatory. When I had finished retching, I opened the door and found him standing outside. I am not sure whether it was the smile or the fish, but another bout of nausea felled me and I stumbled weakly against him. Alan put an arm round my shoulders and led me to a chair in the sitting-room. I watched in astonishment as he raised my feet and slipped a cushion under them.

'Better, little one?'

I said nothing.

He cleared his throat. The smile still had not left his face. 'Well,' he said. 'Here's a turn-up for the books.'

A wave of tiredness rolled over me, smoothing out all the kinks and awkward, knotted parts of my muscles. I leaned my head against the back of the chair and felt my eyelids closing.

Dimly, I heard Alan say again, 'Well!'

When I woke, he was standing over me holding a tray. 'I've made you some supper,' he said, laying the tray clumsily on my lap. The ammoniac smell of slightly stale fish coiled its way around my neck. I felt my throat tighten in protest.

'Haddock,' Alan explained unnecessarily, returning to the kitchen to fetch another tray of food which he perched precariously on his lap. 'We'll have to move, of course,' he said, his mouth full of food.

I poked listlessly at my fish.

He glanced over at me. 'Well, perhaps not yet but one mustn't leave these things too long. The wedding neither,' he added with a meaningful look at my stomach.

Getting up, I carried the tray of uneaten food into the kitchen. 'I'm sorry,' I said, apologising for not eating the food that he had so clumsily and lovingly prepared. I meant more than that, of course. I meant to say that I could not marry him but I had not the energy, that evening, for a fight.

When, at last, I emerged from the fog of sickness, I began to make plans. My state of pregnancy didn't show. I had lost a great deal of weight during my weeks of sickness and was now so pale I looked almost translucent. Even so, I was filled with sudden energy. Every morning, I bought the evening papers and spent my lunch-hours tramping the streets looking for a flat. At last I found one, in a downtrodden area just off a busy street.

'You planning to share?' the estate agent asked, showing me a small second bedroom, scarcely large enough to fit a bed.

I looked at the room with satisfaction. It was perfect for my needs. 'Eventually,' I said.

I paid the deposit and went home armed with a small silver Yale key that I kept hidden in my bag. The next day, during my lunch-hour, I went out and bought a bed; the day after a table and the day after that a chair. They were delivered to the flat the following Saturday afternoon. I told Alan I was going shopping, to find myself a new dress. When I returned empty-handed he was not surprised. It is my habit to shop, but not necessarily to buy.

Every evening after work I returned to our flat and cleaned. I wiped down the walls with soap and water, polished the windows until they shone, shampooed the carpets and waxed the wood. It took me four days. 'Nesting,' Alan said, with satisfaction.

On the fifth day Friday, I took the afternoon off work and went home and packed my bags. By the time Alan returned I was ready. The silver key was in my pocket, a suitcase and a clutch of plastic shopping bags were gathered at my feet.

'What's all this?' Alan said.

I put my hand in my pocket and rubbed the silver key for comfort. 'I'm moving out.'

'But you're pregnant.'

I said nothing.

His head swung in heavy bewilderment. 'We're getting married.'

I rose to my feet to put my arms round him, then, thinking better of it, sat down heavily again. 'I'm sorry.'

'It's my baby too,' he said, and the sadness and confusion in his voice made me flinch, but I was decided and held my ground.

'I'm sorry,' I said again.

Alan looked down at the bags clustered around my feet, then up at my face. 'You've nowhere to go.'

'I'll manage.'

I think he saw then that my mind was made up for he said nothing else. We were young and our child was not yet real to us. Had she been, I don't believe he would ever have let me go.

When I slotted the silver key into the front door of the new flat, I felt an unaccustomed emotion. It took me some time to realise it was joy.

Nine

Ben is still a writer, although these days his words rarely add up to more than two lines. He works as a copywriter for an advertising agency but is described, rather more grandly, as creative director. They pay him well and are pleased to have him.

After his novel shot to the top of the best-seller list, it dazzled for a few brief weeks then went out, as surely as if a hand had snuffed out a candle flame. He wrote a second book but carelessly, hooked into his own myth and magic. He thought it would come easy. It didn't.

I suppose you could say that he still writes best-sellers, although these days they are about lavatory paper and nuclear fuel, published in bold type on Supersite posters. There's one at Cromwell Road, where the road heaves up to a bridge, then drops down sharply on its way to Hammersmith.

The advertising job is an interlude, a diversion that keeps him amused. Or so he likes to say. It feeds into his real work, the words kept safely locked in a drawer of his desk at home. Novels are a work in progress, like life. That's the other thing he likes to say, particularly after a glass or two of good red wine. And what is life made up of but love and death, and death and love – the great blueprint for art? Ben's looking for the universal story – not just a slice of life but the pie itself. One day soon, he says, he'll find it. Dream on, I think, but without malice. Sometimes dreams are the best thing in life.

I put some baked potatoes in the oven for supper. Ben is

coming over after work. He said, 'I'll be home about eight,' when he called earlier. I wonder if it is a slip of the tongue or whether Ben really has started to think of this house as his home. I'm not sure how I feel about that. Once, it was all I longed for. Rebecca's death has changed everything, even Rebecca.

Margaret telephoned earlier to say she needed help moving some of her beloved plants. 'I've already unwrapped the tender ones,' she said, sounding as excited as a kid at Christmas, although Christmas for Margaret is probably an infinitely duller time of the year than the shy unfolding days of summer. 'They've all come safely through the winter, bless them.'

I let myself into her flat, which I do when she is expecting me because it's less bother than making her get up and answer the door. She says the dullest thing about old age is all the advance planning required; how to get up out of a chair, how long it will take to walk to the shops, the half hour it takes in the morning to get her fingers to unstiffen before she can make a cup of tea.

I find her eating supper, or it may be her lunch. A lifetime of teaching has given her a distaste for timetables. They make no sense to her any more. She eats when she is hungry and sleeps when she is tired. Life, she says, is much more restful that way. She is wearing a red velvet turban, a new acquisition purchased from the local charity shop. Her hair is still thick, but she has recently discovered a bald patch at the crown of her scalp, the size of an old penny and shiny as the surface of a hard-boiled egg. 'Age,' she says fretfully, 'is singularly lacking in grace.'

The turban has slipped slightly, giving her a roguish look. A boiled egg, brown with a speckled shell, sits on a tray on her lap. 'Would you like one, dear?' she says. 'It won't take a minute and these are frightfully good, from that man who runs the farm stall at the market.'

I tell her I'll wait and eat with Ben.

'How is he, do you think?'

I say that he sounded much happier on the telephone.

'And what about you, dear?'

'I'm fine.'

'I see,' she says, attacking her egg with greater vigour. 'And if you were not fine, then how would you be?'

I think about this for a moment. 'Disconcerted.'

'This Rebecca business?'

'Yes.'

'And other than death, which is always disconcerting, what is it that's making you so unsettled?'

I think for a moment, although there is nothing I can tell her. It is, I later recall, a moment of epiphany, when my relationship with Ben changed irrevocably. I still hold in my mind the sight of Margaret's face that evening, the trusting expectation slowly dimming to disappointment. Secrets are corrosive, they eat into trust with first one lie, then another. How can I tell Margaret what I know? Only Ben and I know the truth: that he found his wife dying and did nothing to help her. Only one of us knows whether Rebecca could have been saved. Can I love a man in possession of such knowledge?

'Nothing,' I say.

Margaret watches me intently, but when I keep my silence she drops her head with a sigh and scoops the rest of the yolk out of her egg, leaving the white peeking out of the brown of the shell like a ragged lace collar. Lifting the tray off her lap she says, 'Will you come into the garden? I'd like to get everything rearranged before the light goes.'

I follow her out through the french windows, watch as she stoops over a clay pot and pokes tenderly at some emerging green shoots. 'Agapanthus,' she says. 'It means, literally, love flower.' Beattie and I gave her the pot for her birthday. I had not known its meaning. Although it is nearly seven o'clock, it is not yet dark. The air is filled with the lovely lightness of an emerging summer. I imagine it uncurling from the cold hardness of winter, like the plant in the pot.

'Will you put it over there for me, dear?' Margaret says, pointing a swollen forefinger to a patch of brick below a low stone wall. I pick up the pot and heft it over, place it on the mossy ring that marks the scar of its last summer outing. I work for half an hour, lifting pots onto the terrace and shifting others into the shade of the old apple tree, while Margaret moves silently through the garden, her crabbed hands tenderly hooking emerging green shoots over a trellis, nipping out dead leaves, tucking earth among roots as gently as she would tuck a child into bed. The peaceful rhythm of our work begins to dispel some of the awkwardness between us and when, finally, she declares our task finished, she moves towards me, slipping an arm through mine. We stand, watching the light fade.

'It is a great comforter, nature,' Margaret says. 'Although it can be dreadfully cruel too. I've wondered recently whether, if Ben and Rebecca had been able to have children, things might have been different.'

'I never knew how serious she was about that.'

'Oh, much of the time I think she felt quite desperate.'

I think of Ben and how he said, in that terrible howling voice, that she refused to fuck him. For seven years, she refused to fuck him.

'She wanted to try IVF but Ben wouldn't. Not that I'm saying he's to blame. It takes some men like that. They can't bear the idea.'

I go upstairs to prepare the supper. Just as I am getting the potatoes out of the oven, Ben telephones to say that he has been held up at work and won't be coming over after all. His voice sounds light, almost carefree. The coroner has released the body. The funeral is to be the day after tomorrow. He says that now we can bury the past together with Rebecca.

*

113

Beattie was a summer baby, which might account for her sunny nature. She was pleased about life, right from the start.

Alan came to visit us in the hospital when she was a day old. I blinked at the fleshy reality of his face, the nose and eyebrows so fiercely defined after the smudgy blur of Beattie's features. His clothes carried the scent of the outdoors with them, strong and sharp in the warm, milky haze of the maternity ward.

We were in touch fitfully via letter and telephone during the months of my pregnancy. As the time approached for the birth, he sounded both preoccupied and hesitant so it was something of a surprise to find him, so solid and substantial, by our bed. I found I had a hard time connecting him to Beattie. So, I think, did he, but he is at heart a kind man, determined to do right by his child. He brought with him to the hospital a young woman with large, solemn eyes and neat hair.

She stood behind him, half hidden by his bulk until he reached out a hand and pulled her forward. 'This is Barbara.' Small and fine-boned, I might have thought her fragile had I not noticed the determined set of her jaw. 'We have some news for you,' Alan said, and a faint flush crept over the starched white collar of his shirt.

I thought, so that accounts for his hesitancy on the telephone. He's found his little one at last. Even in heels she would scarcely have come up to my shoulder. Barbara said nothing but Alan pulled her forward as if she had been resisting. 'We must tell her now. It's only fair.'

Seeing that he was preoccupied with some small but important drama, I looked at him with greater interest. He phrased the news carefully. 'We are to be married.'

Barbara did not seem the least bit impressed by this announcement of her future. She scarcely glanced at the two of us, her interest reserved exclusively for Beattie who lay in a cot by the side of the bed, wrapped up like a small white sausage. I rather admired her. It was as if Alan slipped over her sleek dark head as water does off a duck's back. I knew from experience that it is the only way to behave around Alan. He is an overwhelming man, if you allow him to be.

'You can pick her up if you like,' I said. 'She's due for a feed anyway.'

As I watched Barbara's small nose sniff sensuously against the baby's skin, I imagined a parade of children with large, solemn eyes and neat hair, and felt a stab of envy at her certainty of her place in the world.

Alan was somewhat put out by my lukewarm reception of his news. 'Aren't you pleased?' he asked with a slight but telling belligerence. I could see that he had hoped that I would – if not cry – at least show some strong emotion.

The only feeling I had was pleasure and told him so. 'I'm delighted,' I said truthfully.

'I know it's rather sudden, but the moment we met, we knew we were destined to spend our lives together.'

I looked over at Barbara. Her gaze was inscrutable.

'What's your baby called?' She had a small, clear voice, like a bell.

'Beattie.'

Barbara smiled. 'Pretty name.'

'Short for Beatrice. It was my mother's second name.'

Alan bridled. 'Beattie, is it? I don't recall being consulted.' He peered down at the smudge of Beattie's face. 'It could be worse, I suppose.'

I smiled, thinking of the list of names Alan had sent me before she was born. They were all boys. 'Beattie Rose,' I said with satisfaction.

Alan's mouth opened in protest, but after a glance at Barbara he closed it again, perhaps remembering that soon enough there would be plenty of children in the world bearing his name. And wanting his money.

*

Beattie and I went home, and slipped into an easy routine of sleeping and eating. The world passed us by. And good riddance to it, I thought, gazing out from our warm, snug flat into a rain-grey morning. The pavement was filled with commuters. They scuttled along like beetles, legs emerging from under the shiny black shells of umbrellas.

Beattie whimpered gently in her sleep, her mouth working at the memory of a breast. She did not stir again, so I went into the kitchen to make myself a piece of toast. For days I had lived on toast slathered with butter and honey. The oozing yellow sweetness suited my mood. I sat listening to the radio, not really concentrating on the disembodied voices but watching Beattie as she slept. I was pleased with her. We were comfortable together.

It was only when the doorbell rang that I realised that it was almost midday, and I was still in my dressing-gown, which was none too clean. I opened the door to discover Ben standing outside it.

'So it's true what they say about new mothers never getting dressed,' he said, wearing his boy's smile, both impudent and charming.

I did not smile back. 'As you can see,' I murmured, going to sit down before my legs buckled under me.

He moved easily about the small flat, taking off his raincoat and hanging it on the row of hooks on the back of the door. He pushed his hair off his forehead in the old familiar way but I noticed he wore new leather shoes, shiny and expensive. Smiling down into the straw Moses basket where Beattie lay, her small bottom gently humping under a blanket, he said, 'She looks nice.'

'I like her.'

Beattie let out a series of snuffling noises, her mouth working against the sheet, her bottom moving in agitation, then the snuffles turned to whimpers which I knew would, at any moment, rise to a crescendo. Gazing at her helplessly, I prayed that she would stop. I did not want to put her to the breast with Ben there.

The cries increased in volume until Ben scooped her up, holding her easily, fingers curled loosely around her downy head, her feet tucked into the crook of his arm. Depositing her gently on my lap, he fetched a blanket from the cot and arranged it tenderly around my shoulders, so it fell across my breasts. Beattie's head butted me as she searched for the nipple. 'She's hungry,' he said and turned away while I fumbled with my dressing-gown. As Beattie found the nipple and began to suck, a fierce hot pain welled up inside me, while milk spurted from my other breast in sympathy. I put my hand to the dampness that spread across my dressing-gown and felt a hot rushing warmth hit the pit of my stomach as Ben turned to smile at me. I sat, helpless and open under his gaze.

'Is it nice being a mother?'

'I'm not sure I know yet.'

'I'd like it.'

'I expect you'll be a father one day.'

'I'd rather be a mother.' His gaze was fierce. 'To be . . . oh, attached I suppose, to know with certainty my place in the universe.'

'I'm not sure that babies give you that.'

'Of course they do. That's why men stumble around while women look on smiling serenely, knowing them for the fools they are.'

'You are too harsh on yourself.'

'Am I?' His expression was unreadable.

I try to picture his face as it was then, wonder if he knew that he and Rebecca would never have children. I wonder why he married her, if she would never make love to him. *She never fucking fucked me.* What did he mean by that? It is hardly the action of a woman desperate for a child. Perhaps he exaggerates, means that she never connected with him, just laid her long, cool, pale body by his side and allowed him to pleasure her.

'What did you mean', I say, 'when you said that Rebecca never fucked you?'

Ben has taken the day off in preparation for the funeral, which is tomorrow. We lunched in the local Italian restaurant and now we are walking in the park. The cherry blossom is out, the lilac well into flower. It seems a day to defuse any difficulty.

He hunches his shoulders and stares over at the pond. 'What did you think I meant?'

'Did she refuse to make love at all, or refuse to participate when you did?'

'Delicately phrased.' He sounds amused.

'I want to know.'

'Surely it doesn't matter now?'

I can see his point. When Rebecca was alive, I never asked about that side of things. I thought about it, of course, but I never asked. May as well hand him a stick and ask him to beat me with it.

'I thought she wanted children?'

His expression is comical. 'Who told you that?'

'She did.'

'First I've heard of it.'

'She said she wanted to go for IVF but you refused.'

He turns to me, his face screwed up with anger. 'Get off my fucking back, will you?'

'Very well.' I turn and walk away, just as I always do when things get difficult. I am good at leaving.

I walk for a long time, crossing the bridge, circling the rose garden, climbing the grassy slope near the Open Air Theatre where Beattie and I played hide and seek while we waited for a play to start. It was *Watership Down*. I was more frightened than Beattie when the Fascist rabbits took over. She leaned over and patted my hand. 'The goodies always win in the end,' she said, her face radiant with certainty.

It is getting cold. My shoes are thin and so is my jacket. I walk faster, trying to warm up, and before long I find myself crossing the Outer Circle of the park and heading up St John's Wood High Street. It's full of shoe shops and tea-rooms, the sort where they sell fragile pastries filled with confectioner's custard. A woman, blowsy with a surfeit of unoccupied time, walks towards me, fat ankles sagging over polished leather shoes, a fox fur strangling at her neck. Her mouth tugs down at the corners. As she passes I notice her lipstick. It has bled into the downward lines. I wonder what she has done to deserve such a face.

A blast of musty beery air hits me, together with the tinny noise of a jukebox. It is later than I thought and I wonder where Ben is now, if he has let himself into my flat with his key and is waiting for me, or whether he has taken himself to his own house, removing his presence as punishment.

He did that a lot when Rebecca was alive, whenever he believed that I had behaved badly in some way – not paying him enough attention, making too many demands, or simply not smiling enough on him. He sometimes took himself away from me for days, knowing that I could not telephone him at home and then, when I had reached a nadir of despair and self-reproach, would reappear, full of life and charm, to kiss away my miserable tears. He played me like a violin.

I am not feeling so easily played these days and the reproach that I feel is no longer directed at myself but at the lie in which he has us enmeshed as tightly as flies within a spider's web. Before I met Ben I took great joy in solitude, in the luxurious sensation of anonymity that all big cities bring. It is a freedom like no other, although it can be a prison too for those with nowhere to turn to relieve their solitude. But all pleasures have their price.

I push open the door of the pub. It is early yet so there's hardly anybody about, save a lone man drinking at the bar and an old woman enthroned behind a table with a small glass of barley wine. I can tell, from the easy familiarity with which she has flung her coat on the seat beside her, that this early-evening drink is part of a pleasant daily ritual. I understand that. Those of us who live alone must impose an order on the day, if it is not to impose its chaos on us.

She looks away at my glance, refusing to acknowledge me. There is still some stigma attached to women drinking alone. Perhaps, after all, the coat on the chair is a camouflage, suggesting a seat saved for a friend. The small deception suddenly depresses me and I hurry to the bar and order myself a vodka and tonic.

The publican is one of those men whose duty it is to force his fellows into a sense of cheer, however false. 'Might never happen, love,' he says, dishing up a fingerful of vodka in a smeary glass, plonking a small bottle of tonic at its side. I smile in cowardly fashion, thinking resentfully, what does he know what's happened to me, and swallow the drink in two gulps. His expression shifts into neutral and I can see by the way he's watching me that he thinks I might be trouble. When I order another, a double this time, he serves me, but doesn't say a word. 'Cheers,' I say. I am always absurdly pleased by such tiny triumphs.

The only other drinker in the bar is standing some way off but he's somehow managed to position his pint of beer so it stands midway between the two of us. I've never understood why it is that men, even small ones, take up so much space, leaving their belongings strewn all around the place – not to mention their arms and legs. If a man is sitting next to you on the Underground, you can bet anything that he's got his legs stretched wide as they will go and there's not an inch of arm rest left but for the spill of his arms. But if it's a woman, there seems to be plenty of room for everyone, and some spare, on account of the way she'll keep her knees pressed together and her body shrunk into the seat so it doesn't take up one more inch than is officially allowed. You could tuck three women quite neatly in the space that two men take up.

'It's a crying shame,' I hear the publican tell the man. There's an impassioned retort and suddenly a pint's worth of beer hits me smack on the chest and cascades down my front.

The man stares at his arm in bewilderment, then turns slowly towards me. We regard each other in astonished silence. 'Oh my God,' he says, 'don't move.'

The beer is very wet. I can feel it soaking through my jacket and trousers, the foam lets off little bubbling squeaks as it settles. This seems to galvanise the two men into action, for suddenly they break free from their astonished immobility and run round gathering up cloths and sponging me down. Two sets of hands rub at my breasts, at my stomach, at my thighs.

The man who knocked over the glass is down on his knees, rubbing at two dark stains spreading across my legs. After a while he sits back on his heels and stares up at me. He has curly black hair and brown eyes, and reminds me of a dog I once stole. He had a kind face too. 'You really are very wet,' he says.

'It doesn't matter.'

He looks faintly angry, in the way you do when somebody refuses your help. 'Of course it matters.'

I pick up my glass from the bar, drain it quickly.

'Where do you live?'

'Not so far.'

Picking up a bundle of keys from the bar, he says, 'You'll catch your death like that. Let me at least drive you home.'

'I'm fine.'

'Well, I'm not.' His grin is rueful. 'Or I would be if only you would let me help you in some way.'

I relent and smile back at him. 'It's very close. I'd rather walk.'

'At least let me pay for the dry-cleaning.' He pulls out a battered wallet, shuffles through it with impatient fingers. 'Damn. Not enough money. I tell you what, I'll send it to you.'

I am anxious now to be gone. 'It won't be much. It really doesn't matter.'

He hands me a small white card. 'Here's my number. Call me and let me know how much it is and I'll send you a cheque.' I look at the card, held in his hand. His finger-nails are bitten, like mine. 'And please don't say again that it doesn't matter.'

I take the card, just to shut him up, and shove it in the pocket of my jacket.

His eyes follow the movement of my hand. 'I'll be expecting your call,' he says, and I see then that I have amused him in some way.

'Don't count on it,' I say, just to rile him because he sounds like a person used to getting his way. Then I notice that his face has fallen, not in a big way, just a tiny collapse around the eyes and mouth, and I feel sorry immediately and say, 'But it's kind of you anyway.'

'They're your clothes,' he says, with a shrug that tells me I have hurt him in some small but remarkable way and I think how easy it is to give unkindness, even to strangers. Still, I'm not in the mood to hang around and discover what it is that pleases or hurts a man who has just thrown beer all over me. So all I say is goodbye and walk quickly out of the pub.

Ben is not there when I get home. I should call him. It's his wife's funeral tomorrow, after all. And I should apologise for flouncing out on him in that childish way but I know that my anger with him goes deeper than the silly argument we had in the park and that, in some ill-defined way, it is my forgiveness I believe he should crave.

I go upstairs to change out of my damp, beer-stained clothes, dumping them on the floor in the bedroom and changing into a T-shirt and a dressing-gown before going downstairs to make myself a cup of tea. When I have changed, I go into Beattie's room and switch on the night-light, turn down the duvet and arrange the teddy bears carefully on the pillow.

Downstairs, I find a note on the kitchen table, written in Margaret's crabbed hand. She finds it difficult to hold a pen these days. It says that the cars will collect us at twenty past ten, to take us to the funeral, and that the police called round again. They didn't say why.

Ten

Rebecca's coffin looks absurdly small in the cavernous gloom of the church, its polished wood surface half hidden under an extravagant bunch of white lilies. It seems impossible that it is Rebecca lying so quiet and harmless beneath it. Propped against the lilies is a stiff cream card bordered in black. It says, 'I love you. For ever. Ben.' I avert my gaze from the card. Its intimacy seems unseemly in this cold, hollow place. Ben, Margaret and I are the only people present. We huddle together like guests at a party to which nobody has turned up. None of Rebecca's friends are here. Ben says he isn't up to facing them. At least, not yet. He placed an announcement in the newspapers, explaining that the funeral was to be just family and promising a grand memorial service. He'll enjoy that.

We scarcely speak. When we met at the entrance to the church, he looked at me warily, asked if I was feeling better today. Better than what, I wanted to say but he put a hand to my cheek, as if to brush away a tear. His fingers were cold.

Once we are seated, he hunches forward as if he is nursing a nagging pain. I can feel the tension gathered in him and fancy that if I touch him, his back will be as unyielding as metal. I keep my hands folded in my lap. Margaret sighs, settles a gloved hand on his shoulder. It looks like a small brown mouse curled on the black wool of his suit.

The vicar leads us in the opening hymn. The space swallows our voices until they are no more than a whisper, rustling the thin pages of the scruffy leather-bound hymn books. When he talks about Rebecca I wonder who this stranger is. A wonderful wife. A talented poet. A tragic loss. Greatly missed. Ben stares ahead, glassy-eyed.

After the service we return to Margaret's flat, wander aimlessly through the rooms, unable to settle. Ben opens a bottle of wine. He raises a glass, smiles. For a terrible moment I think he intends to propose a toast. To what? To the future, perhaps. I remember how he said that we could bury the past along with Rebecca. I'm not so sure. Memories don't decompose as easily as bodies. But he says nothing, just tilts the glass to his mouth, swallows the wine in hungry gulps.

Margaret has disappeared. I look out of the window, see her bent over her beloved plants, scooping up a handful of earth, patting it tenderly around the stem of a plant. I wonder if she is thinking of Rebecca, who is also tucked up snugly in the ground, and envy her that simple relationship with the earth, its direct line to the pattern of life.

I turn to Ben, tell him the police have been round to see me again. 'What do you want me to say to them?'

He sighs. 'Do we have to talk about this now?'

'They may come back again today.'

'So tell them what you've already told them.'

'I told them you left here at eleven o'clock but I don't know where you went after that.'

He looks at me with astonishment. 'I went home, of course. Where did you think I'd gone?'

I sit down wearily. 'I don't know.' I feel I don't know anything about him any more. 'But what did you do when you got home?' My voice is pleading, conciliatory. I want him to tell me that Rebecca was already dead, that she'd been dead for hours, that there was nothing he could have done to save her.

'I read a book.'

'You read a book.' I struggle to find an ordinary tone. 'Is that what you told the police?'

'I told them exactly what happened. I went home and I wasn't sleepy, so I sat and read a book. Then I went upstairs to bed and found Rebecca dead.'

The way he tells it, it's the most normal thing in the world.

Margaret is at the door, brushing earth from her hands. She smiles at us both, says she thinks we could all do with a cup of tea, but Ben is out of his chair, moving towards the door. 'I've got to go.'

'Go?' I say. 'Where?'

He kisses me tenderly on the mouth. 'To meet some people from work.' At the door he turns to smile at us. 'Life must go on.'

Margaret says she is tired after the morning's ordeal and will sleep. 'Get some rest too,' she says, patting me on the arm. 'You look all in.'

Margaret's right. I am all in. Upstairs, I start to tidy the house, hoping it will soothe me, restore some equilibrium. The place is a mess. I straighten cushions, push the heavy Hoover up and down the treacherous stairs, wipe surfaces, clean windows. As I work, I wonder whether I made the whole thing up, about Ben coming to see me that night and telling me about Rebecca. Maybe it was a joke. No, not that, a test of the depth of my love for him. He often used to ask me what I would feel if suddenly there were no Rebecca. Imagine if it were just the two of us, he would whisper tenderly into my eager ear. And I imagined. Most fervently, I imagined.

Rebecca threatened suicide so often that her future absence became a permanent fixture in our play-acting. Not *if*, we thought, but *when*. When she's gone we'll make love all night. When she's gone we'll buy a house by the sea. When she's gone we'll be happy ever after.

Perhaps Ben got carried away by the game. Perhaps, when he came to me that night, he was just pretending. It was only afterwards that he went home and, most horrible of ironies, discovered her dead.

Perhaps he killed her.

This is no good. I am getting too solitary. My imagination is running away with me. From me. It's moving to another dimension in the game we used to play, a complexity that we never considered.

When she's gone we'll hate each other.

I must get out of this house. It's a week since I spoke to anybody other than Ben and Margaret, apart from that bloke in the pub who chucked his beer all over me. And it was he who did most of the talking. I wonder if he is like that all the time, speaking when other people are silent, and think for a moment about his eyes, how mournful they looked in his smiling face. He gave me a card. Where did I put it? Then I remember. It was in the pocket of my jacket, which I delivered to the dry-cleaners early this morning, before the funeral.

I suppose that's the end of it, then.

As I clean my desk, I discover the two manuscripts I have been working on. On impulse, I pick up the telephone and call George. Would she like me to deliver them that evening? She sounds pleased to hear from me, asks if I have time for a drink. A drink with a friend. How ordinary that sounds, how pleasing.

Slamming the door behind me, I hurry down the road and clamber onto the bus.

George looks so much the same that I want to hug her. 'That's nice,' she says, when I yield to the impulse.

I sit down, accept the glass of wine she pours for me. 'Bad business about Rebecca. Fulsome obituaries, though. I suppose you saw them?'

I shake my head, startled. It occurs to me then how hermetically sealed my world has become. For a week I have not looked at a newspaper. I have forgotten that Rebecca was celebrated enough to deserve an obituary. She has shrunk to the size of my life.

'The funeral was this morning.'

'Was it well attended?'

I say that Ben wanted it kept very small but that there was to be a memorial service later, when he was feeling more up to it.

'I suppose that's to be expected. Suicide is dreadfully difficult for the living to come to terms with. Even now, it carries an element of shame.'

It is an emotive word. It is then that I realise it's what I have been feeling these past few days.

George asks if Ben has taken it badly.

'He doesn't seem able to grasp the truth,' I say, accurately enough.

'They were so close I expect it'll be some time before he does.' She broods over her wine. 'I know she was fragile but somehow I thought she'd get through it in the end. We all did.'

This is a new, intriguing version of Rebecca. 'I always thought she was the strong one in that marriage.'

George dips her head. 'Oh, no. She deferred completely to Ben. Did everything he said.'

I think of Rebecca's unborn babies. 'I didn't know.'

'He stopped her writing. When he couldn't any longer, he hated her doing it.'

'Is that what she said?' I cannot keep the cynicism from my tone.

George looks at me with mild surprise. 'Oh, no. It was Ben who told me. He had the grace, at least, to look a little ashamed.'

I absorb this news silently, then ask, because startling aspects of Rebecca are revealed to me every day, 'Was she talented?'

'Very, although it was a raw talent. I always thought

she'd come to it later.' George sighs. 'Well, now we'll never know.'

When I get home, I find a typed letter on the doormat. It's from the police, asking me to go down to the station again. There's a message from Ben on the answer machine to say that he's sorry not to be with me this evening, but he's very tired. 'Sorry I lost my rag yesterday, it was the strain of everything.'

I think of his face, ugly with anger. But it was more than anger. It was a child's face, furious at being thwarted. I wonder how often Rebecca saw that face.

She'd imply, sometimes, that Ben was very demanding, liked things done in a certain way. I dismissed it at the time, thought it was Rebecca being feeble or, in an obscure way, boasting.

I remember one afternoon when she had come to see Beattie. I'd promised tea, entirely forgetting that Beattie was over at a friend's house. Or maybe I had chosen not to remember. It occurs to me now that I was often capable of such small deliberate cruelties to Rebecca. I was capable of compunction too and offered her tea, saying that Beattie would not be long. As it grew later and still Beattie had not appeared, Rebecca grew more and more agitated. I tried to calm her, saying that surely there was nothing to rush home for. There were only the two of them (oh, yes, I could never resist the opportunity to needle her) and Ben often worked late. But she would not be soothed, kept checking her watch as the minutes moved on, torn between a desire to see Beattie and – what seems to me now – fear of what Ben would do should he return home to find the house empty.

'Oh, it's no use,' she cried, almost running to the door as the clock struck six.

I let her go. At the time I thought she was merely taunting me, trying to prove how much Ben needed her.

Now I am not so sure. I go to bed, still wondering.

The next morning I present myself at the police station.

The Inspector asks me cheerfully how the funeral went.

'Much as they usually go,' I say and then feel sorry for being snappy. He was probably trying to be nice. 'It was fine. Quiet.'

He looks marginally surprised at this. 'Mrs Robinson was something of a celebrity, I understand.'

'Ben ... Mr Robinson didn't want anyone there but family. There is to be a memorial service at a later date.'

His mouth works thoughtfully as he stores away this information. 'In here,' he says.

We go into a room, different from the one I was in before, inasmuch as the table is set at a sharper angle to the wall. Otherwise it is almost the same, impregnated with that lingering, sour smell you find in rooms that don't get a lot of air.

'I'm sorry to ask you this again, Miss Rose, but I wonder if you could just go over, once more, the events of that night.'

I tell him what Ben has told me, that he went home and read a book.

'Is that usual for him?'

'To read a book? Oh, yes.'

The Inspector's eyes shift away. He is not pleased by my attempt at humour. 'To stay up so late reading.'

'He is a writer. He once wrote a best-selling novel.' I sound like a child, boasting.

'I am aware of that, Miss Rose. I've read the cuttings.'

It takes me aback. How foolish of me not to realise that the police would have access to all the newspaper libraries. I look at him, wondering what he's read of Ben's and Rebecca's lives.

'You say that Mr Robinson arrived at your house at

around ten that evening. Do you know where he was before that?'

I offer no suggestions. Lying by omission is one thing, offering a downright deceit is quite another.

'And when Mr Robinson arrived at your house, how did he seem? Did he behave quite normally?'

I say he did, which is true. It was only later, when we went upstairs to bed, that he grew agitated about Rebecca. 'We drank a cup of tea.'

'Tea?' The Inspector looks disappointed. Perhaps he expects people written up in newspapers to lead more glamorous lives. 'And that was all you did?'

'Yes,' I say, remembering the flicker of anger in Ben's eyes when I refused to make love. I wonder idly if the police have theories about this, whether wanting sex is a sign of guilt in a man. Or not wanting it. Ben always wants sex these days.

As I leave the station I think, I am Ben's alibi. I am Ben's lie. The phrase hammers through my head. What will happen to him if I tell the truth? What will happen to me if I don't?

On the way home I meet Helen, the mother of a friend of Beattie's. She gives me the guilty look of a mother who has a child to kiss at night and asks me how I am.

We have not seen each other since Beattie went.

I say that I am fine, all things considered, but when she glances away with a mute plea for rescue in her eyes I see that she thinks I'm referring to Beattie. I consider distracting her with the story of my lover, who has recently murdered his wife, except of course, that it's not murder, it's the very opposite. Murder is active, whereas what Ben did is passive. I wonder if there is a term for it, for not stopping somebody from dying.

Instead, I say that I'm busy, so snowed under with work that I haven't a moment to think and roll my eyes in that

131

mock-exasperated way that people do when they're pretending irritation but are secretly excited by their own importance.

Helen smiles, relieved, and we talk easily until the inevitable moment when she mentions Sophie, her daughter. She could hardly do anything else as we are talking about work and the business of life, and Sophie and her two brothers are Helen's work. You can't expect a woman not to mention her daily reason for being because another has been deprived of it but a shamed, furtive expression gradually closes down her animation until she is stumbling and apologetic.

When neither of us can bear it any longer, she says tearfully, 'I'm sorry about Beattie.' Her hand reaches out to my arm and grips it, and through her fingers I feel the full force of her terror. 'Time will heal.'

I want to tell her that hell has no respect for time. I think instead of Philip Larkin's line, that being brave means not frightening other people. 'Thank you,' I say.

We part and I walk slowly home, allowing myself a soothing burst of hatred for her healthy children. Nobody should be expected to be an angel in the privacy of their own mind.

Eleven

Ben wants to take me out for dinner. Choose somewhere smart, he says, as if we have something to celebrate. The telephone line crackles and fades, making him seem very far away. I can only just hear him when he tells me, 'It's about time we resumed normal life.' I don't know what he's thinking of. Our life has never been normal.

At the dry-cleaner, a young woman hands me a small card. Her nails are painted red except for the moons, which she has left unvarnished. The unpainted bits look white and dead against the crimson polish. 'Found this in the pocket of your jacket.'

She watches while I turn over the card. 'It's a solicitor, see. Thought it might be important.' Her eyes search my face for clues. Perhaps she feels she has some claim on the card, being the one who rescued it from the machine.

For a moment, I think she has made a mistake, that the card does not belong to me. Then I remember the man in the pub. I pocket it quickly. 'Thanks.'

She looks disappointed, as if I had started telling a story and stopped without finishing it.

When I'm safely out of sight, I get the card out of my pocket. His name is Richard. Richard Gardiner.

Well.

I put it back in my pocket.

It is a glorious sunny day, the way it so often is in May, as if the weather gods have decided to tease us by sneaking in a snatch of summer, only to haul it back in readiness for June. You'd think, by now, that we wouldn't be fooled but there's no stopping the English when it comes to a bit of heat. For an inhibited nation, we are joyously unashamed by bare flesh. Everywhere I turn there are naked arms larded with winter white, legs mottled like pale-blue marble, stomachs peeking shyly over the waistbands of cotton shorts. The sun makes everyone smile, their faces turning to the sky like flowers to the sun.

The market is packed this morning, a good-natured press of bodies, fruit and vegetables. There are women in bright saris, men in soft cotton robes and Londoners shouting their wares in loud guttural voices.

I make my way through the market, past the old council blocks with their fretwork of iron staircases and balconies, and down to the street where I live.

I bought the house when Beattie was five. My father's money was still sitting in the bank. It was time for us to put down roots, find somewhere with a bit more space and a patch of green.

We looked at hundreds of houses, but none of them felt to us like home until we found this one, pale pink and a little dilapidated, in a noisy, colourful community of Indians from whose houses drifted the smells of spices and garlic, and a constant babble of voices and music. I stood in the street, breathing deeply of the cooking smells carried on the hot summer air and imagined I was a child again.

There was one drawback – a big one, according to the agent. A sitting tenant occupied the basement of the house. She was not, he said, anywhere near to dying but added, his smile sharp, something to the effect that you never knew your luck. Mrs Vale, he said her name was, and she owned the garden – or at least had sole right to its use.

'Mind you,' he added, 'you won't get a four-storey house for less.' He looked around and muttered something about an up-and-coming neighbourhood, but even his salesman's patter faltered at the lines of brightly coloured washing flapping from the open windows of the houses around us and the communal chatter that ebbed and flowed as tiny half-naked children scampered in and out of the peeling front doors.

Alan was appalled. 'Surely, you're not serious,' he exclaimed, staring out at scraps of litter bowling down the windy street. 'This is not a place to bring up a small child.'

'And where would you suggest?' My tone was icy, perhaps unforgivably so, but I always had difficulty equating the idea of Alan as Beattie's father. This is unfair to Alan, and perhaps to Beattie too, but when I looked at her small, serious face I found I could not join her to that time when Alan and I lived – and, I suppose, loved – together.

Alan sighed. 'Where will she play? There are no parks. A child needs fresh air.' I looked at him, stolid in a suit and tie, his language peppered with cosy aphorisms. It had taken him just a few short years to reach middle age, a place that seemed his natural habitat. Barbara was his 'lovely lady', his children his 'little bundles of joy'. He had two children by then. The eldest, Rosie, was scarcely a year younger than Beattie and the other, 'my fine boy', was two.

Barbara was pregnant again and they had just bought a house in the suburbs, in Acton, where there are plenty of parks and fine open spaces. What seemed to be lacking – at least to me – was any feeling of life. They say that an Englishman's home is his castle and I judge that to be an admirable description, except that the true Englishman surrounds his castle with a moat and a drawbridge too, which is hoisted at the merest suggestion of movement. I may be solitary, but it is a state in which I can only take pleasure if life is teeming all around my silent cocoon. To be solitary in the suburbs, with only the blank doors and manicured lawns for company, would reduce me to a gibbering wreck. There is a difference between being solitary and being lonely although most people, being frightened by both, seem unable to distinguish between the two.

'There's a park up the road,' I said. It was not strictly true, the small square of green faced on all sides by buildings could hardly be described as a park but there was grass in its square perimeters and a few surprisingly sturdy trees. 'Anyway, there's always the garden.'

'The garden does not belong to you. It's the old woman's and I don't suppose she'll welcome a small child causing havoc.' He glanced outside. 'She obviously takes great pride in it.'

Alan went on – he was a persistent man – 'For the price you've paid, you'd have got somewhere very decent, and in a better area too.'

'I like it here,' I said mutinously.

Alan's gaze took in the washing lines outside the window, fluttering with brightly coloured sari cloths. 'I suppose you feel at home.'

I remembered fat Claire from my first English school: 'Dirty aay-rab, dirty aay-rab.'

'Yes, I do,' I said stiffly, although I don't believe he meant to be unkind. He thinks of me as an exotic. It is his way of explaining away my difference – and my difficulty.

Once Alan had gone, I took Beattie by the hand and led her to the playground. A few mothers stood around smoking and idly chatting while their children shrieked on the rusting iron frames. After a cursory glance, they took no notice of us. I was just another young mother seeking refuge from the confining walls of a small child's world. I pushed Beattie gently on the swing. The movement made her eyes grow rounder, but she uttered no sound, her head moving with the tilt and lurch of a world made unfamiliar. I felt depressed by all that Alan had said and skulked around the streets feeling restless and dispirited. Beattie, as if catching my mood, remained silent, staring at the shabby streets with solemn and critical interest. At least, I felt it was critical. Perhaps Alan was right, I thought, watching two thin boys clamber up and down a discarded mattress. Perhaps this was no place for a child.

As Beattie and I climbed the chipped stone steps to our front door, the old woman from downstairs rounded the corner from her basement entrance. I opened my mouth to greet her but, before I could speak, she had turned away and hurried past us, face averted.

I had tried, on various occasions, to arrange an introduction, but she had refused all my efforts. 'Nothing personal,' the estate agent said. 'She just likes to keep herself to herself.' It is a state I understand, so I did not take offence, but on that first afternoon I could not help but wish it could be otherwise. I felt I recognised a kindred spirit in her and would have liked to get to know her better. As she hurried past, I saw that her face had a closed look to it that I immediately knew, having seen it in my own mirror. It is an expression that causes acquaintances and colleagues at work to describe me as devious, although there is no deviousness in me other than a desire to avoid contact with anyone with whom I do not instinctively feel at ease.

Further depressed, I boiled an egg for Beattie's tea. I ate toast, standing by the old butler's sink while I stared down into the garden below us. It was certainly beautiful, glowing with roses and honeysuckle, and I wondered if Alan was right. Perhaps the old woman would never welcome a child into that garden. For a brief moment I echoed the estate agent's sentiments and wished her dead so that the whole house and garden would rightfully be ours.

The following week I lost the front-door keys. Well, I didn't actually lose them. I knew perfectly well where they were, hanging on the hook, just inside the door that I had so eagerly slammed. Sitting down on the top step, I offered up a prayer to Saint Anthony, patron saint of lost causes.

Beattie took my bag from me and searched through it. She was an optimistic child. I think she thought if she looked hard enough the missing keys would turn up. 'Bother,' she said, having turned the entire contents of the bag out, and took off down the steps.

I called after her, 'Where are you going?'

She pointed at the flat below and disappeared. Beattie did not have my trouble with strangers. Reluctantly, I followed her. As I rounded the corner, I discovered the peeling door standing ajar. I could hear Beattie's clear, confident voice. It is a constant amazement to me that I could have produced such a child. '*I* know where they are,' Beattie said, 'they're hanging on the hook by the front door.'

I heard the reply. It was a deep voice and melodious. 'It seems as good a place as any.'

'Unless you're outside the house,' Beattie pointed out.

'Yes. That does make things more difficult.'

I pushed the door and went inside. Margaret, as I now know her name to be, gave me a brief smile. 'It seems you've locked yourself out.'

'We're sorry to bother you,' I said quickly, conscious of her earlier hostility, 'but we wondered if by any chance you had a spare set.'

Margaret studied my face carefully. After a while she said, 'As a matter of fact I do.' She paused, as if sizing me up. 'But now you're here, we may as well have a cup of tea.'

It was months before she told me why she had been so hostile. She'd had a hard time of it after her husband died. He'd spent his last few years gambling on the Stock Exchange, leaving her with a barrow-load of debts. 'I sold everything, including our beautiful house, and found this flat to rent. The previous owners, who were elderly, and I co-existed very peacefully for eighteen years but when I heard you were buying it – a young woman with a child –

I thought you were going to try and drive me away. One hears such stories.'

I remembered my thoughts, that first night we moved in, and blushed.

'But then, of course,' said Margaret, smiling, 'I met the irresistible Beattie. And you too,' she added, patting my hand.

I don't know what I would do without Margaret.

After the noise and colour of the streets outside, the house has a waiting air, as if it's holding its breath. Everything is in the exact same place I left it, a dirty mug in the sink, a carton of milk on the kitchen table. I pick it up, lodge it in the shelf in the fridge door. In this heat it might spoil.

A manuscript sits on my desk, waiting for my attention. It is a biography of a famous designer. I skim-read the first chapter, to get a feeling for the writer's style. I find it bores me. It doesn't seem much of a life. Perhaps it will improve, as lives sometimes do. Or not.

The thought sends me into a panic. Who am I to judge another life when I have managed my own so badly – as the mistress of a man whom I no longer trust? Do I love him? I find the question difficult. I am in the habit of loving him. For eight years he has consumed my world. I don't know how to look outside it. Without him I would feel dispossessed.

Funny how often it is that people ask, where do you come from? As a child, I felt a passionate envy for the girls who had lived in the same town, the same house, all their lives. I thought, how soothing that familiarity must be, how beautifully ordinary to walk down a street and think, this is where I belong. Home, they say, is where the heart is. Where is my heart now? My mother, my father, Beattie are all gone. There's Margaret, of course, a good caretaker of hearts. And Ben, but he grows less familiar by the day; he is a stranger in possession of my heart. I think of his voice on the telephone, how small and far away it sounded. He seems so sure of me. Why, when I am not sure of myself?

I go downstairs to see Margaret. She is bent over the Hoover, her face red with exertion. 'How I hate machines,' she grumbles when she sees me.

I take it from her, turn it upside down and peer into the dusty bottom. 'It's the fan belt.'

'How clever you are,' she marvels.

I shrug. 'It's always the fan belt. I'll take it into the repair shop for you later. Would you like to borrow mine, in the meantime?'

'God no. Any excuse to give up housework is welcome.'

I laugh but think of my flat upstairs, obsessively neat, every speck of dust chased to oblivion. I cannot rest unless everything is in its place. It is my way of controlling a world that feels increasingly chaotic.

'Each to her own,' Margaret says, reading my mind.

Beattie cured me of it a little. 'OK, Mum,' she'd say, rolling her eyes but bending obediently to pick up her toys, because she knew it pleased me. As if it mattered. What I would give now to have plastic littered across the sitting-room floor. Even those tiny specks of plastic that populate the miniature worlds of Polly Pocket and Lucy Somebody-or-other. I have forgotten the names now. Once I knew them better than my own. Only the other day, the Hoover spat one out in disgust. I picked it up, thinking it was a piece of grit or a bead from a broken necklace. It was a tiny doll. Painstakingly, I searched through Beattie's collection of Lilliputian houses – the Magic Castle, the Wedding Chapel, the Country Cottage, the Musical Dingly Dell – and found the place where it should live, a pink pock mark in the plastic floor of the Wedding Chapel. When I looked carefully at the speck in my hand I saw that it was the bride.

My obsessive tidiness has grown worse again. When I

come back up the stairs from Margaret's, I find everything oppressively in its place. It looks so sterile that I can bear it no longer. I pull Richard Gardiner's card out of my pocket, dial the number before I can change my mind.

The woman on the switchboard asks for my name. 'It won't mean anything to him,' I say. 'Just tell him it's the woman from the pub.'

Maybe solicitors have people ringing up all the time who say they're from the pub, or the launderette or the greengrocer, because she doesn't say a word. There's a clicking sound and, the next thing I know, his voice is saying, 'Have you dried out yet?'

I say I'm as good as new. He laughs, says he didn't know there was so much liquid in a one-pint mug.

After that, there's silence.

'Well,' he says after a while, 'where shall we meet?'

'Meet?' I hadn't thought as far ahead as that.

'So I can pay for the dry-cleaning.'

I'm about to say that I don't want his money, when I realise he thinks that's why I've called. As I don't know why I have called, I say nothing.

'How about the pub where we met before?' he asks. 'Or would that bring back too many awful memories?'

It's only after I've put the phone down that I realise I am supposed to meet Ben that evening. I call him to tell him I can't make it, that I'm having a drink with a friend.

'What friend?' he says.

It's true that I have few friends. I got out of the habit of them when I was young. We moved so often that scarcely had I made some than they had to be abandoned again. It hardly seemed worth the bother. I have many acquaintances, of course. I am good at riding the surface of people's lives without ever dipping into their centres.

When Beattie came along she was all I needed and when she left I had Ben. Ben does not like me to have friends. They take up the time I could spend with him. When

Rebecca was alive, it was always assumed that I would make myself available, however inconvenient it might be. It occurs to me now that Rebecca did not have many friends either, although Margaret says when they first married there were always other people around. They seemed to fall away with the years.

I tell Ben I am meeting somebody from work, in connection with a free-lance editing job. That satisfies him, because he wishes me luck before he says goodbye.

I put down the telephone, conscious of the lie, but somehow happier for the small moment of rebellion.

It seems like a long time since I worried about the way I look and I dress carefully, in a striped navy-and-white T-shirt, navy trousers and sandals. I even put gold hoops in my ears. It's a fine evening, so I decide to walk, cut through the park and up that way. I feel happy and for a minute I can't work out why, then I realise it's because I feel like I'm taking a holiday from the claustrophobia my life has become. The sun is shining and for the past hour I have not given Rebecca or Ben a thought.

I feel fine in my clothes, imagine I look like I've just stepped out of a holiday ad, a poster for a Mediterranean cruise or some such thing. I smile benevolently at the world, even at the young guy who's hanging around on the corner by the pub. He's always there, hand outstretched, hoping to cadge some loose change off somebody. He moves towards me, encouraged, I suppose, by my smile, although I have never given him anything before. Then his gaze flickers past, settles on likelier prey.

It's an old bloke, tottering slightly on the uneven paving slabs. He's wearing a good tweed overcoat, buttoned all the way up and a shirt and tie, and his old face is kind, with shining blue eyes. The young guy edges towards him, voice rising in a beseeching whine.

'Fucking bastard,' the old bloke says. 'Fucking poncing off other people. You should be ashamed of yourself.'

For a moment the young guy looks shocked. So do I. Then he grins. 'What's the matter, grand-dad? Fucking fought in two world wars, did you, for the likes of me? Well, I'll fucking tell you what you were doing. You were fucking wasting your time, that's what.'

The old boy quivers, and for a minute I think he's going to have a heart attack and drop down dead on the pavement, right in front of our eyes. Then he turns and marches towards me, one leg dragging slightly. I see the effort in the set of his shoulders but, as he passes, I see it's not anger that's making him shake but tears.

I catch sight of myself in a shop window and realise I look like a sailor, escaped from a third-rate pantomime.

Richard is standing by the bar, a glass of whisky at his elbow. 'Less chance of drowning you,' he says, lifting the glass.

We smile awkwardly and Richard makes a great show about remembering what I was drinking that night, a vodka and tonic. It is then that I realise he is nervous.

While he orders the drinks I study him. He has the look of a frog about him. A very nice frog, to be sure, but a frog none the less. It's something to do with his mouth, the way it stretches across his whole face so when he smiles, his whole face smiles too. Then there are his eyebrows, which peak like circumflexes above large, shiny brown eyes that bulge a little, and a squashed nose, with a skewed bump to its centre as if he has been in one fight too many.

Turning, he hands me a drink. 'Easy now,' he says, holding it with elaborate care.

He's wearing a suit, straight from the office, I suppose. It's wrinkled and shiny on the shoulders, and his tie has a stain on it. Soup, by the look of it. He notices it too and tries to hide it by holding his arm across it. It looks awkward, as if he's wearing a sling. I want to tell him that it doesn't matter.

'It's soup,' he says, giving up.

'What flavour?'

'Tomato. They only do tomato, chicken or beef in the local sandwich bar. Tomato's my favourite.'

We stand in silence for a moment, then he says, 'I suppose I should give you your money. I've got it all ready for you.' He pulls out a battered brown envelope, the sort with a shiny transparent window in the front. 'Stolen from office stationery, I'm afraid. Millions are lost by companies every year because of people like me.'

He hands me the envelope. It feels heavy. I can detect the shape of different coins through the flimsy paper. 'It contains exactly the amount you told me on the telephone,' he says, looking worried. 'Are you sure it's enough? It seems very little.'

'I have a very cheap dry-cleaner.'

'Ah. Well you must tell me where it is. I'm always on the look-out for cheap dry-cleaning.'

That explains the shine on his suit. 'Yes,' I say. 'I know. I mean – I'm sure.'

He brushes furiously at the shoulders of his suit. 'Oh dear. Is it that obvious?'

'I'm afraid that while cheap dry-cleaners are very good for certain things, they are inclined to ruin good suits.'

Why am I telling him this?

'And I'm afraid this wasn't a good suit in the first place.' He looks anxious for a moment. 'I never know where to find them – without paying a fortune, that is.' His face lights up. 'Perhaps you could help me. You seem to know a lot about the subject.'

I laugh. 'Not much, but my father was obsessive about his suits. He always said you get what you pay for.'

'Maybe I could ask his advice.'

'I'm afraid that wouldn't be possible. He's dead.'

'God, what an idiot I am. First I pour beer all over you, then I upset you by asking about your dead father.'

He looks so anxious that I laugh. 'It's all right. He's been dead for some time. It no longer . . .'

'It's just that I talk too much when I'm nervous. Look, I've gone and done it again. Cut you off when you were right in the middle of a sentence.'

I wonder how he copes with clients. A solicitor's job is to listen. Maybe he doesn't get nervous at work. Why is he nervous with me? The idea is novel. It gives me a new perspective on myself. For a moment I see myself with different eyes. *Look at that interesting, frightening woman standing at the bar.*

He is fishing in his pocket for his wallet. 'Let me get you another.'

'No.'

'No?' he says, looking so crestfallen that I add quickly, 'What I meant is, let me buy you a drink. Look, I have plenty of money.' I do, too. I went to the bank earlier, just in case Richard and I went to round two.

He holds out his hand. 'No, I insist. I have a diabolical plan. If I buy two drinks, then you'll feel so beholden to me that you'll have to meet me again.' He pays for the drinks, hands one to me and says, 'Actually, I thought you wouldn't ring.'

I have disappointed him, then. 'Did you?'

'Yes, but I'm very pleased that you did.'

So am I.

Richard talks on, about his work, his flat, his separation from his wife. The phrase gives me a sharp jolt of pleasure. Then I wonder what I think I'm up to, letting myself get excited about a man I scarcely know. It's not as if my life isn't complicated enough already.

It's just that there's something familiar about his face. I

don't mean that I've seen it before, just that it's the kind of face you could get to feel at home with.

Twelve

Ben says, 'There's something I should tell you about Rebecca. She was sterile. A botched abortion when she was young. She was never going to have children. All that stuff about IVF was a total fiction.'

I wish he hadn't said that. The thought's in my head now, its roots sinking through the layers of my mind. Words are powerful things – we should treat them more carefully. It's like a man I once met who said he'd never read a book in his life. 'I don't like having other people's thoughts in my head.' I didn't ask him if he refused to listen to what people say as well. Perhaps I should have done. I occupy my hands with a wineglass, although the temptation to raise them to my ears and block out everything Ben is saying is formidable.

He drains his glass of wine, leans back in his chair. There is something complacent in his gaze. 'She knew I desperately wanted children. In the end, I think that's what drove her to despair.'

'Did you consider adoption?'

'With Rebecca's mental history?' His voice is heavy with contempt. 'I don't think so. Anyway, she said she felt unworthy.'

Of what? Of Ben? Of life?

'Do we have to talk about Rebecca?'

Ben looks taken aback. As well he might. We have spoken of nothing else for the past two weeks. I wonder if we have anything left to say. 'Not if you don't want to.'

'A new beginning, you said. Resume normal service.' I

am almost pleading. For what? For things to be the way they were between us. But how were they? Without Rebecca to fill it, the distance between us feels huge. That's the trouble with triangles. Take away one corner and the thing collapses.

We are dining out, eating in a smart restaurant. Ben chose it, as I knew he would.

'Well what shall we talk about?' His voice is sulky.

'I don't know. Work, perhaps. What did you get up to today?'

'I had twenty-five meetings and wrote a sparkling couplet about dog food.'

He is not going to help me out.

'That the sort of thing you want to hear?'

I shake my head. It is hopeless. Nature abhors a vacuum and we have created one. Oh, I don't regard myself as innocent in Rebecca's death. Perhaps that's why I let Ben off so lightly. Ben knows that. He has me in his power, just as I have him. We are welded together by shared guilt. I think of something the Inspector said. It's all a question of intent. Ben reaches out a hand, curls it round my wrist. His skin feels cold and unfamiliar. I force my fingers up, stroke the skin on the inner palm of his hand. It used to be our secret message when Rebecca was around, that quick hidden pressure.

Ben smiles at me. 'I'm sorry.' His smile still has the power to disarm me. His eyes are fixed on my face. It is a knack he has, of blocking everything out around him and concentrating on the person he is speaking to. It is a useful talent.

The waiter is saying, 'Some more wine, sir?'

Ben turns his smile upwards. 'What a good idea.' His hand reaches for mine. 'Shall we, Janey? Would you like that? Shall we just forget everything else and have a good time?'

I don't want another bottle, I want to go home but, as I

say, Ben still has the power to disarm me. Grinning awkwardly, I say in a stilted voice, 'That would be nice.'

We make love when we get home. Or rather, we start to but it's as if neither of us can connect. Ben puts his cock inside me and I circle my hips, moaning slightly. Sometimes a bit of play-acting helps reality along. I am still moaning when I realise that he is lying still, his eyes boring into my face. 'Oh, for God's sake,' he says, wrenching himself off me.

'What's the matter?'

'What do you think?'

'Ben, I didn't mean –'

'I could see precisely what you meant.' He is scrabbling around under the bed. 'Now where the fuck are my trousers?'

'They're over there, by the door.'

He strides across the room, retrieves his trousers from the top of a pile of boxes stacked by the door. They're Beattie's toys, each box carefully labelled. *Soft Animals. Polly Pocket. Barbie and Other Dolls. Farm. Train Set. Assorted Plastic.* Ben drags on his trousers, stubbing his toe. 'Oh, for fuck's sake. There's so much stuff in here. Why don't you get rid of it?'

'Nowhere to put it.'

'It's not as if you need this stuff any more. Anyway, there's plenty of room in this house.'

Don't say it, I pray. Please don't say it.

'There's a room across the hallway. Why don't you clear that out?'

'You know why.'

'No, I don't.'

Why is he doing this?

'I just didn't feel like it after Beattie left.'

'She didn't leave, Janey. Leaving implies that she might come back.'

My voice is cold. 'I don't want to hear.'

'Well, it's about time you did. She's not coming back and the sooner you face up to that, the better.'

'For whom?'

We stare at each other, white-faced. This is not about Beattie. This is about something else.

'Beattie's dead, Janey. She's fucking dead.'

He's right. She's dead. She is fucking dead.

'Whee,' Beattie said and took off down the road like an aeroplane. By the time I got there it was too late – for all of us. The driver was out of the car, his face as white as Beattie's school shirt. He held his hands out to me, clasped as if in prayer. 'Ran straight out in front of me,' he said. 'Nothing I could do.'

I lay down on the wet road next to Beattie, pressed my face to her warm cheek, to her small, puzzled smile. A scarlet worm of blood wriggled out of her ear.

'Shouldn't be doing that,' said one woman indignantly. 'It's dangerous to touch them.'

A small crowd gathered around us.

'It's the mother,' said another voice. 'Poor soul.'

I thought of Johnny Johnson and of Mrs Johnson and her poor, lost soul.

Margaret turned up at the hospital, regal in a black velvet turban and wool cape. Pale crescents of skin showed below her eyes, as if the colour had been washed away. 'Hurry up,' she said. 'The taxi's waiting outside and you know how they charge.'

She wasn't being unkind. It was just Margaret's way of getting me out of that place as fast as she could. She was right.

There was nothing left to stay for.

Beattie was down in the mortuary. They let me go with her, walking beside the trolley. I held her cooling hand, her poor, broken body making scarcely a hump under the green sheet. When we got to the scratched aluminium doors that closed with a dull thud, they wouldn't let me go any further. A nurse escorted me back upstairs and sat with me for a while. I could see she wanted a smoke and a cup of tea but I wanted the company, so I said nothing. In the end they called Margaret. I couldn't think of anyone else.

I gathered my things obediently and followed Margaret to the lifts.

'I've made up the spare bed,' she said.

I opened my mouth to protest but she silenced me with an imperious look. 'It's just for a few days, until you feel more settled.'

When I said it was hardly likely that I would ever feel settled again, she sighed. It wasn't a sigh of impatience, more like the kind you let out when language ceases to have any meaning.

The next day Alan came and wept over me, while I sat pale and unbending in a chair, and thought about his healthy, living children. The way he carried on, you'd have thought Beattie was his child. Well, she was I suppose, but only on account of one stray sperm. I wonder if he'd have let it loose so carelessly if he'd known what was to follow. It wasn't even as if Beattie liked him much. I hug the knowledge to me like a present, allow myself a small smile. I was all the world to her, the only one she truly loved. Odd how the clichés tumble through your head at a time like that. After a while I couldn't stand Alan's crying any longer, told him to pull himself together.

He dashed clumsy fingers at his reddened face while I gazed at him dry-eyed. 'Don't you care about anything?' he asked as he left. 'Anything at all?'

He was upset, that's all, but Margaret shooed him out of the door like an unpleasant smell. 'Ridiculous little man,' she said.

Everyone whom Margaret dislikes is little to her,

although she stands only five feet tall in her stockinged feet.

She went and made some tea, appeared with it on a tray with a starched linen mat and a small vase of flowers, as if we were both invalids. I noticed she hadn't offered Alan any. 'We'll have to organise the funeral,' she said gently. 'What would you prefer, do you think, a burial or a cremation?'

I have always rather fancied a cremation for myself, imagined my ashes floating in the air, getting up people's noses. Ashes would be no good for Beattie. Or, perhaps what I meant was that they'd be no good for me. In the end, it is the living who matter and I knew I needed somewhere that I could go to be with her. 'A burial,' I said absently, 'and something lovely to stand over her, an angel, perhaps.'

Margaret bent her head to her tea. 'I think that would be appropriate,' she said.

We sat there for a while in silence, then Margaret got up and went away. She reappeared a little later, holding a notepad with a blurred posy of pale yellow primroses in one corner and a Bic biro. 'We need something for the headstone. Some words.'

I gazed at the primroses blankly, realising that I knew nothing of words after all, that there were no words to convey the piercing sweetness of Beattie's short life. Even so, knowing that words are wandering, elusive creatures who only come when you charge at them, herd them together like a dog rounding up sheep, I bent my head and wrote down any that sprang into my mind. I spent hours writing and crossing out. When Margaret appeared at six o'clock with a glass of wine, the paper was covered with dense biro scratches. Only two words stood out clearly, inked over and over until they leaped from the page. One was Beattie. The other was love.

Margaret took the notepad from me and gazed at it for a while. Finally she murmured, 'I think that says it all.'

And that was how it was:

Beattie Rose
Love

The man who had been driving the car that killed Beattie was standing in the churchyard, a little away from the group of mourners. I went and took one of his cold red hands, pulled him into the circle. 'Thank you,' he said.

Afterwards, he laid a small bunch of violets, tied with a black velvet ribbon, on top of the bunches of hothouse flowers crackling in their Cellophane prisons. I liked him for that, for not choosing an elaborate wreath. 'My wife picked them,' he said, 'in the garden this morning.' He nodded towards the plot of freshly dug earth. 'Got a kid of my own,' he said. 'Two, actually.' Then hung his head in shame, appalled by his own riches.

I nodded abruptly, terrified by my anger, and went to find Margaret. She was standing by the grave looking small and frail, her velvet-flocked veil trembling slightly with the movement of her head. She took my arm and clung to me for support. 'Shall we go home now, dear?'

Ben was waiting by the car. Rebecca was not with him. He said it would have been too much for her. This was before Ben and I started the affair, when I had no real reason to dislike her. Except that she had Ben. And I did not.

A reply, sharp and venomous, was forming on my lips but before I could speak, Ben held out his arms and I went into them. We stood like that for a moment, clamped together, then he began to shift restlessly and pulled away, but not before I felt the hard bulge of his erection against my thigh.

Without a word, I got into the front seat of the car and took Rebecca's place.

For weeks after Beattie's death, Rebecca did not come near me. The fear of death was too great in her. Odd, that, for a person who tried to commit suicide with such regularity, but we often flirt with things we fear. I used to drive myself mad when Beattie was tiny, imagining every sort of accident that could befall her. I wondered how I would survive. Now I know.

When, eventually, Rebecca did come, her gaze was anxious. She arrived with flowers, not thinking, I suppose, that I'd seen enough to last me for a lifetime, that all flowers did was remind me of misery.

I hadn't seen Ben since the funeral, there was nothing going on between us, so there was no reason to blush. But I did. I knew the inevitability of the next few weeks as well as if I'd written it with my own hand.

Rebecca looked at my burning cheeks. 'Are you all right?' She mistook my awkwardness for sadness and I was grateful for it, although I knew her anxiety was not for me. It was for herself. She didn't want to have to confront my pain. Even in her moments of blackest depression, Rebecca liked to pretend that the world was a happy place, liked to surround herself with loveliness. That's why she wrapped satin ribbons round her wrists, to hide the ugly truth that life is never as pleasing as we would like it to be. I wondered what she would do if I said that, no, I was not all right. For a moment I was tempted to weep but I had become too used to protecting others from Beattie's death. I said that I was fine. She was so pathetically grateful that I wished I had been able to squeeze some tears from my eyes.

It's an odd thing, being intimate with death. It makes you feel guilty, as if somehow you have done something you shouldn't. People crossed the road to avoid me and if they could not, addressed the air above my head. It was as if I had ceased, with Beattie, to exist. After a while I grew used to it, diverted myself with how quickly I could bring the slow suffusing spread of relief to their faces. I won when I could speak normally, as if nothing had happened. Except that it had. I was damaged beyond repair, I would never be the same person again. But I kept the change to myself, hugged it like a secret as if, by protecting it, I could protect Beattie too, keep her fast by my side.

It was then that I started to behave in peculiar ways although, at first, they weren't peculiar enough to warrant attention.

Every evening, at six o'clock, I ran a bath. It was the bath that Beattie would have had if she had been alive. Then, at seven fifteen precisely, at the time she used to go to bed, I went into her room, turned down the duvet, plumped up the pillow and drew the curtains. I went out and bought a night-light, although Beattie never used one. She hated light at night when she was trying to sleep. It was the only time she ever really quarrelled with her friends, when they came for a sleep-over and it was time for bed. Beattie insisted on the door being completely shut so no crack of light showed. Her friends wanted the door left open. Although she was a meticulously polite child and believed that guests should always be allowed their way, on this point Beattie was obdurate. She usually ended up with me, while her friend slept in her bed, the door safely ajar and the light from the landing streaming in.

After she died, I kept the night-light on all night in case Beattie should wake from her cold sleep and wonder where she is. She won't, I know, so it is foolish of me to keep it there but I feel superstitious about it, like those Catholics who cannot walk past a church without offering up lighted candles to the dead.

When Ben and I became intimate and he began to spend some time at the house, I expected him to say something about the nightly ritual of the running of the bath and the drawing of the curtains in Beattie's room.

He didn't, nor did he comment on the turned-down covers on Beattie's bed. He accepted it as naturally as the nightly locking of the front door. I was grateful to him for that.

The first time I stepped out of the natural but crazed derangement of grief and crossed over the invisible line that divides the sane from the insane, I took a dog.

It was an appealing dog, coal black with velvet eyes and ears that twitched like scanners, so I couldn't have been all that mad.

It was sitting outside the newsagent, its lead looped through an iron ring that clips the padlock to the steel night shutter. Fancying it had a kind face, I bent to pat it but, before I knew it, my hands were fumbling for the knot on its leash, then it was looped over my wrist and I was walking away, the dog trotting obediently at my heels.

Occasionally, its eager step faltered and it craned its head back over its shoulder, making soft whimpering sounds at the distant newsagent shop, but I walked briskly and it abandoned its yearning with a quiet snuffle and followed me home.

When we got into the house I realised I had nothing to feed it on so I rummaged through the deep freeze looking for possible dog delicacies. I found a half-empty bag of Beattie's chicken nuggets at the back and thrust them into the microwave, blinking away tears.

The dog whimpered softly in sympathy. Crouching down, I pressed my cheek to its silky head, felt the bones moving smoothly under the surface of the skin and smelled its hot, doggy breath. It lifted its paw and scrabbled at my knee. I took the hard, callused pad in my hand and held it, feeling comforted, until my knees began to crack under the pressure of crouching down.

The microwave popped off with a ping, and I shook the steaming nuggets into a china bowl and set them before the dog. It snuffled at them, screwing up its nose against the rising steam. Realising that they were too hot, I doused them quickly under cold running water and offered them back. The dog sniffed them quickly, then slid down to the floor, dipping its head to its paws and gazing at the bottom of the kitchen cabinets with sorrowful resignation. I decided to call it Newcastle, on account of its coal-black coat.

I made a cup of tea and sat at the table drinking it, the dog at my feet. Its hot breath warmed my bare toes and I felt almost happy. It seemed a long time since there had been another living presence in that room. By myself, I didn't seem able to fill the place. I tried whistling and singing but the sound got sucked into the air, in the way that an extractor fan gulps smoke from an oven. I no longer listened for noise, for the shouts of children out in the street, or of car engines. I listened only for the hard, unforgiving sound of silence.

The dog snuffled gently at my feet, poking out its tongue and licking delicately at my toes. It tickled, which made me laugh and wriggle my toes. The dog gave me a reproachful look and buried its face in its paws. I wondered what to do with it. It seemed unkind to have brought it all that way for a bowl of soggy chicken nuggets.

A key turned in the lock and Margaret appeared, framed in the kitchen door. 'Oh, I'm sorry,' she said. 'I thought I saw you go out. I came to steal a tea-bag. I've run out and was desperate for a cup. I hadn't the energy to get down to the shops.'

The dog lifted its head, one ear cocked at the sound of this new voice, then slumped back down with a sigh.

A tiny perplexed frown appeared between Margaret's eyes. 'Where did he come from?'

Was it a he? I had imagined it was a female dog. A worm of guilt wriggled into my conscious mind. I stamped on it firmly. 'It's a stray.'

Margaret bent to pat its head, then her fingers flashed down, circling its neck. A silver disc appeared between them. 'It's wearing a collar,' she said. 'Its name is Tramp.'

I let out a small sound of contempt. Imagine calling a dog like that Tramp.

'The address is written here,' Margaret said gently. 'Look.'

I turned my face away, stared out of the window.

'It's a local address. Quite close to here.'

We walked the dog back to its owner together. Margaret had the red leash wound firmly round her gloved hand. Perhaps she imagined I would bolt, dragging Newcastle after me.

We reached a small estate, not far from the street where the newsagent was. The address was a flat on the ground floor. As we drew near, the dog's tail began to wag until its whole body quivered with anticipation. The front door opened and the dog let out small excited yelps. An elderly man with reddened eyes looked at us suspiciously and the dog leaped forward, pushing at his knees with its pointed snout.

His face cracked into a smile. 'Thank you,' he said. 'You found him. Oh, thank you.'

'He was wandering around,' Margaret said firmly, 'up near the market.' She sounded so disapproving, that I stared at her, taken aback.

'He wanted to go for a walk,' his owner said, 'but I wanted to get the paper first.' He stared down fondly at his dog. 'He's a mind of his own.'

'I'm sorry,' I said.

He looked at me kindly. 'It's me who should be sorry, love. He's done it before. That's why I put the collar on him.'

'No harm done,' Margaret said and put her lips together, as if she might say something accusing. It was me that she wanted to accuse, but she daren't. I had suffered too much already.

We stood awkwardly on the doorstep for a few minutes more, reluctant to let the small drama go unrecognised, then the dog owner mumbled something about a kettle on the go inside and we took our leave.

'I know. It was stupid,' I said.

Margaret relented. I was being normal now. 'I think we could both do with a nice cup of tea.'

Thirteen

Later, when I was feeling better, I began to refer to that time as 'my dog days'. It made me laugh, although nobody else saw the joke.

Margaret must have told Ben about the dog because he turned up on my doorstep, holding a bunch of flowers.

'What are those for?' I said. In the other hand he was holding a bottle of wine.

'I thought you might need cheering up.'

'No more than usual.' He shouldn't have been standing there, holding flowers and wine like a lover. He had no right.

'Heard you took a dog for a walk.'

'It was a nice dog.'

'I'm sure it was.' He wore a soothing voice, the one that people used around me all the time after Beattie died. He took a step towards me. 'I can't bear to see you suffer like this.'

I moved away. I don't know why, but I did not want him near me. 'There's very little you can do about it.'

'I could help you. I know I could. Better than anyone.'

'Only time can help me, Ben. That's what everyone tells me.'

He put his hand on my arm. 'Don't,' he said. 'Please.'

I turned slightly, dislodging his hand. 'How's Rebecca?' I wanted him to remember that he was the one who left.

'It's not Rebecca I'm concerned about.'

I said nothing.

'You haven't forgotten, Janey. I know you haven't. The

way things were between us.' He let a long silence follow. 'The way things are.'

Then he put his arms round me.

It sounds so corny, looking back, but when I felt the warmth of his body against mine, I knew I couldn't resist him. Nobody had touched me since Beattie died. Except for a clumsy pat at my hand, an arm fumbled round my shoulders, I hadn't felt flesh for months. It undid me, that simple touch. I fell on him like a woman starving, ravening for the feel of skin on skin, for that warmth peculiar to other bodies.

I missed Beattie in so many ways but, more than anything, I missed the feel of her. When she was alive I never wanted anyone else, never thought about taking a lover. She was all the love I needed. Just the feel of her skin against mine was enough. Like satin, it was, but warm. They say we shouldn't desire our children, that it's unnatural. It's rubbish, of course. What we've forgotten is the innocence of desire.

When she was a baby, Beattie used to turn her cheek and press it against my neck so it fitted exactly into the indent between my jaw-bone and shoulder. When she did that, I'd feel a tiny squiggle of desire in my belly. Not sexual desire, something far deeper than that. Our skin would stick together so you couldn't feel where hers ended and mine began, and it was then I'd think how some people who aren't too well versed in affection might confuse the two.

After that first touch from Ben there was no going back. I was like an addict, craving my next fix. At first, I think he was a bit taken aback by my hunger for him. He liked it, though, I could tell. In the twilight days after Beattie died I limped after him like a dog, terrified to let him out of my sight. He liked me best like that. I know, because once I started to feel better and stopped craving him so badly, he'd casually drop Beattie's name into the conversation, or use an expression of hers, or just remind me about some little way she had. When he did that I'd be all over him again, grabbing at his arms like a person drowning.

I didn't notice how he'd use Beattie's name deliberately, not at first. It's only lately, now I've begun to see more clearly, that I'm beginning to realise what he was up to. He's like a kid himself, the way he craves attention. Rebecca was that way too. I sometimes wonder how they managed together. It must have been stifling in that house, like being locked in a windowless room with the central heating full on.

The morning after the argument about Beattie, Ben comes round early, before work. He's holding a brown paper bag filled with croissants although he says he can't stop and eat them with me. He'll be late. He stands on the doorstep while I watch the buttery grease form dark patches on the paper bag. Ben says he's sorry about the night before, and I can see he really is because his hands are shaking and there's a white line of a frown across his forehead as if somebody's scored the skin with a blunt pen. He says he feels as if his skin's been turned inside out so his nerves are on the outside.

I say I'm sorry too, that I feel terrible. It's true, I do feel terrible. After the argument I was up half the night, thinking about Beattie lying in the road and how I should have been right next to her, grabbing at her arm to stop her running out like that. There's any number of ways I can torture myself if I put my mind to it. Or even if I don't put my mind to it. When I finally fell asleep, I dived headlong into one of those drugged stupors that leaves you shaky and vulnerable. I woke at six, in a panic, wondering what I'd do if Ben really had left me.

I tell him all this. He smiles, presses his face against mine, his blue eyes filling my gaze like a patch of sky. When he pulls back I see the smile has changed, gone from relief to a sort of triumphant pleasure. While Rebecca was alive, I never noticed its particular quality. I suppose I was just grateful that Ben smiled on me at all.

Ben's smile reminds me of a game my father and I used to play when I was a kid. We lived in a house on stilts. They weren't stilts really, but great stone pillars flagged around with marble. It was cool down there, perfect for bike riding and long, complicated games of hide and seek. Gotcha was a game of hide and seek. First you hid, then you stalked your prey as they tried to find you. Sometimes it went the other way and the hunter became the hunted. It always ended the same way, both of you yelling at once. It was the tension, I suppose. Even as we yelled, we smiled and smiled, to see the terror and excitement in the other person's face.

There's that smile again, Gotcha, then he's gone, telling me he loves me and leaving me with the bag of warm croissants leaking grease all over my newly washed T-shirt.

I watch him go, but it's not him I'm thinking about but Rebecca and how her smile never touched her eyes.

Sometimes she wouldn't bother to cover the scars on her wrists, would wave her hands around, using them at every possible opportunity, as if she was showing them off. It was always at times like those that she and Ben seemed particularly close, cooing endearments at each other, exchanging secret glances across the room. I used to think that she did it to annoy me, to show me that Ben loved her best. Now I'm not so sure. Sometimes I think Rebecca showed her scars like badges of love, to please Ben. He likes women who are wounded in some way.

I go into the house, make myself a cup of coffee. May as well eat the croissants, now that I've got them.

At the first flaky mouthful I am back with my mother. She loved croissants. She loved them so much that a special delivery from a London bakery would arrive at my boarding-school on the last day of each term. Those and a packet of bacon. I carried them with me, hand baggage on the aeroplane, to whichever country my parents were living in. After she'd kissed me she always said the same thing, her face lit with pleasure: 'Have you got them? Did they arrive?' When we got home we made pigs of ourselves, licking the buttery grease from our fingers as we exchanged all our latest news.

I still love croissants. They are my madeleine. That's why Ben bought them, to make up for our argument.

As I sit, eating, a memory springs unbidden into my mind. I try to push it back down into the depths but it bursts up to the surface, like a plastic ball in water. It is of my mother's face in death, her expression serene, cleansed of pain.

I wanted to talk to her so badly, fill in the gaps from the weeks of hiding from her, wanted to see her smile, her eyes softening as they met my gaze. I wanted it even as I knew she would not smile again.

When the doctor came I stood by the bed, stiff with terror. In his presence I dared not look at my mother's face, in case my expression should give away our secret. So I fixed my gaze on the base of her neck, on the square of skin just showing above the clean white lace of her night-gown. I had prepared it myself, smoothing it down with a hot iron, longing to spray the ruffles with starch, to get them to lie just right. But I knew the starch would be as painful to her as a necklace of fish bones, so I left it. The lace looked fine. A little limp perhaps, but pretty.

My eyes ached with the effort of not looking at my mother's face. The doctor's smooth white hands flashed in and out of my vision. When I looked again, her face was gone, blanked out by the sheet he had pulled up to cover her head. I wondered if that little touch of melodrama was necessary.

'A merciful release,' the doctor said. He was not talking to me.

I looked over at my father, saw his shoulders stiffen at the fatuous expression.

The doctor patted the broad, rigid shoulders with an awkward hand. 'She was in terrible pain,' he said gently, 'and now she is free of it.'

My father did not move. The pain was all his now.

George has sent over two new manuscripts for me to work on. They arrived on a bike, just after Ben left.

I unpack them gratefully, happy to have some work to do, to keep my mind off Ben. I make a mug of tea, settle myself at my desk, sharpen all my pencils until they're the same length and fold a piece of plain white paper until it makes a ruler. Just as I finish the telephone rings. I look at it in irritation, wondering whether to leave it to the machine. Then, thinking it might be Margaret needing something, I pick it up.

It is Richard. 'I wondered if you'd like to have dinner with me.'

A jolt of pleasure takes me by surprise. I grip the receiver hard but say nothing.

'Not if you don't want to,' he says, so quickly that I know he has braced himself for rejection. 'We could have lunch instead. That always sounds so harmless, although I can't think why.' His voice sounds bemused, as if he is puzzling it out. 'I'd say most affairs are started over lunch, wouldn't you? A harmless business arrangement, an innocent hour plucked out of the day.'

He is talking too much.

'I want,' I say.

Surprise makes him silent.

I say it again, just in case he hasn't understood: 'I want to have dinner.'

'Good.'

That's all he says. I wonder if he's one of those people who, when they get something they thought they really wanted, don't know quite what to do with it. I know a lot of people like that.

'Where?'

'What?'

'Where shall we go?'

He says there's a half-way decent Italian, near to the pub we met in before. He gives me the name of the street then rings off. But his voice, as he says goodbye, is light. I can tell he's pleased.

Fourteen

Richard has a child, a boy called Sam. There are so many things about him I don't know, a whole other world inside his head. Sam lives with his mother. He is seven. Richard is very proud of him. I can tell by the way the light shows behind his eyes when he talks about him.

'Do you have children?' he asks.

'No,' I say, after a moment.

'Then I won't bore you with mine.'

I want him to bore me, want to hear every mundane domestic detail of his life, but I say, my voice sounding lame, 'I don't mind.'

He picks up my hand and kisses it, as if it were the most normal thing in the world. I want him to go on holding my hand but he doesn't, puts it back down on the table as carefully as if it is made of some fragile sort of glass. Maybe he does that to lots of women, maybe it's part of his repertoire of charm, like Ben's way of fixing his eyes on you and blocking out the rest of the world.

Then I see that our food has arrived and he's given me back my hand so I can eat. The people at the other tables drop away, our glasses fill and empty, plates are cleared and replaced by new ones, and we go on asking each other questions, as if we're the most interesting people in the world. I tell him something of my childhood, which surprises me. I don't usually like to talk about it. It is so alien to most people, there is no shared memory to link you into the paths and winding roads that most conversations follow.

Richard asks where I feel I belong.

There is no easy answer to that question, so I don't give him one.

'There are advantages to being an outsider,' he says. 'You see things more clearly.'

If only that were true.

Richard drives me home and then, because we don't seem able to finish the conversation we are having, he comes inside.

When I return from making mugs of coffee, he is holding a photograph of Beattie. He looks sad. I see then how much he minds about Sam not being with him.

'What a beautiful child.' It's true. Beattie was a beautiful child. When she was tiny, people stopped us in the street so they could gaze on her. 'Who is she?'

'My daughter.'

He looks baffled. 'You told me you didn't have children.'

'I don't. She died.'

Richard's face is white. I turn away, unable to bear the shocked misery on it as he contemplates the death of his own child. People can't help but make that leap of imagination. It happens every time.

He says nothing. I am grateful to him for not offering platitudes. Most people can't resist it. There is nothing to say, but they say it anyway. I feel his hands on my shoulders. Then his arms go round me and he is rocking me, as if I were a child in distress. Only my mother and Margaret have ever held me like that. I suppose that's why I start to cry. I cry until his shirt and jacket are soaked with tears.

'I'm sorry,' I say, when it is over.

He does not take his arms away. 'For what?'

That's when I tell him a story. It concerns my dog days, that time when I was still half crazed over Beattie. Or fully crazed, depending on how you look at it. Anyway, I know

I felt I should shatter like a badly cracked vase if anyone handled me too roughly.

What happened was this. I kidnapped Alan's child.

The afternoon it happened I was driving around. I used to do that a lot after Beattie died, just climb into the car and drift aimlessly through the faceless suburbs. I hate cars and I hate driving but I liked to drive through streets where men tinkered with motor bikes and women hung out washing, where kids played on the tiny green patch in front of their houses where their mums could keep an eye on them. Nothing's safe any more, not even kids.

Anyway, that's how I came to find myself outside Alan's house. Rosie answered the door. She is Beattie's half-sister, although you wouldn't know it to look at her. She is a plump, placid child with sandy hair cut in a short straight fringe that bobs over her round obliging face.

I hadn't meant to take her. It was a spur-of-the-moment thing. I regretted it almost as soon as I had done it. Not because I was worried about Alan but because I quickly discovered that I disliked his child intensely. The more I disliked her, the longer I kept her with me, as if to unlock the part of her that would make me like her. It didn't happen, of course. It never does.

'Hello, Rosie,' I said. 'Where's Mummy?'

'Out in the garden, doing something with her roses.' Rosie stepped aside politely. 'Would you like to come in?'

The noise of boys' voices, shouting, floated down from the top of the stairs. Suddenly I couldn't bear the idea of stepping into that hot, crowded house. 'I've a better idea,' I said. 'Would you like an ice-cream?'

Rosie eyes travelled to my hands, half expecting to see them clutching a handful of lollies. 'Yes, please.'

I stretched out my hand. 'Let's go, then.'

'Where?'

I clamped down on my impatience. All at once, there

169

was nothing so important to me in the world as getting Rosie out of that house. 'To the shops.'

Rosie looked behind her doubtfully. 'What about Mummy?'

'Oh, Mummy knows all about it. I telephoned her earlier. We'll have to go quickly or they'll shut before we get there.'

Rosie's round eyes blinked in alarm but she held out an unwilling hand. 'Mummy didn't say anything to me.' There is nothing so affecting in this world as the trust of small children, but I steeled my heart against it.

'That's because it's a surprise.' The feel of her small hot fingers in mine made my heart leap painfully. I stopped, momentarily winded.

'What's the matter?' Rosie asked, tugging her hand away in alarm.

I captured her fingers in mine again. 'Nothing,' I said, feeling them squirm. The texture was all wrong. They weren't like Beattie's hands at all. But I held onto them and led her to the car.

'Belt up,' I said cheerfully, revving the engine.

Rosie blinked, confused. 'What?'

'Put your seat-belt on.' Beattie would have understood.

'Mummy always does it for me,' the child whined.

Leaning over, I snapped the silver clip into its buckle.

We set off, Rosie's round, placid face set towards the windscreen. Beattie would never have sat so quietly, staring at the road ahead with mute indifference. I pressed my foot down hard on the accelerator and watched the needle climb to seventy. We flashed through the quiet suburban streets like a silver fish spinning through warm currents of water.

I laughed, feeling the road jump beneath the car, looked down at Rosie to share my pleasure. It was then that I saw tears running down her plump cheeks. I took my foot off the accelerator.

'You're going very fast.' Her eyes were round with fear.

'It's late. I don't want to miss the shop.'

She whimpered quietly as I swung the car through its final journey.

As we got out to walk to the sweet-shop, Rosie looked up at me, still snivelling, then slipped her hand into mine. I felt her damp, warm flesh press in mine and hated her.

She dithered endlessly beside the ice-cream counter.

'A Rocket.'

I pulled back the sliding top. It was stiff. I tugged harder and caught my hand on the metal rim. The cold made it hurt. I swore softly. 'Shit.'

Rosie gazed up at me with reproachful eyes.

'Sorry.'

'I'll have a Fab.'

The ache in my hand and the soft eyes made me irritable. 'I thought you said you wanted a Rocket.'

'We–ell –'

The freezing air rose like steam in the hot stuffy shop. I saw the owner's eyes narrow, seeing the precious cold escaping.

'Hurry up, Rosie.'

'A Rocket. No, a Fab.' Her voice escalated to a wail. 'I don't know what I want.'

I reached into the cabinet, grabbed two frozen sticks. 'Have both, then.' I meant it kindly, but my voice came out sharply. Her face crumpled. I glanced over at the shop-keeper but I could tell that he saw nothing amiss, only another irritable mother and a tired, fretful child.

I paid for the lollies and swung out of the shop, Rosie trailing behind me. 'I can't get the wrapper off.'

'Here.' I tore off the flimsy paper, sucked cold sugary water from my hand.

We climbed back into the car. I slotted the key into the ignition and the engine fired into life.

'Are we going home now?' Rosie's eyes were blue above

171

a clown's mouth of red syrup. She sucked noisily on the lolly.

I smiled down at her. 'How would you like to come back to my house?'

Her eyes widened with alarm.

'I've got something for you. A present.'

She took the lolly out of her mouth. 'But it's not my birthday.'

'Consider it an un-birthday present then. I'd like to give you some toys.' The toys were Beattie's. Who better to give them to than Beattie's half-sister? Feeling pleased with myself, I pointed the car towards home.

The present was not a success. 'They're all broken,' Rosie said, her eyes round with astonishment.

I picked up a Barbie. It had a faint black scuff across one perfect plastic breast. Perhaps Ken's a wife-beater, I thought, rubbing the black mark against my T-shirt. The bruised breast looked livid in the fading light. I tossed the doll back into the box. 'Please yourself,' I said stiffly and walked into the kitchen where my hands felt automatically for the kettle switch.

A scuffling noise made me turn round.

'This one's all right.'

Rosie was holding up a different Barbie, dressed in absurd yellow, pink and white frills. Flower Barbie. I remembered buying it for Beattie, on the Saturday before she died. She was very proud of it. My eyes filled with tears. I gripped the edge of the sink, to stop myself from snatching it from Rosie. 'Have it, then. That can be your present.'

'Can we go home now?'

'How about some supper first? I can do you some chicken nuggets,' I said, wondering if there were any left in the freezer within their eat-by date. It wouldn't do to poison Alan's child, as well as kidnapping her.

'I don't like nuggets.'

'A boiled egg, then, with soldiers.'

'I want to go home.'

I smiled brightly. 'Or some pasta? Beattie used to like it with lots of grated cheese on top.'

'I don't like cheese and I want to go home.' Rosie's face was flushed, her breath coming in long, drawn-out gasps. I recognised the symptoms and moved quickly to the fridge. 'Coca-Cola then? I bet you like that?'

The doorbell rang. I ignored it. It rang again.

'Fuck off,' I muttered.

Rosie's eyes expanded like saucers.

The doorbell rang again. 'Oh, for God's sake,' I exclaimed and threw open the door to discover Rebecca standing outside.

'Is this a bad time?' she asked, edging one velvet-slippered foot into the flat.

'Slightly.'

'I knew you must be here. I saw you arriving earlier.'

Her eyes darted past my body, which was blocking the view into the rest of the flat. 'Margaret's run out of sugar. I came up to see if we could borrow some.' She slid past me, her slender form flickering like sunlight moving across a wall. 'You know what a passionately sweet tooth I have.'

I trudged after her, saw her hesitate as she spied Rosie, curled up on the sofa. She recognised her at once. I used to have Rosie over from time to time to play with Beattie. Well, it was only right, they were half-sisters.

'Hello, Rosie. What are you doing here with Auntie Jane?'

Rosie burst into fresh sobs. 'She took me, she told me we were just going to buy an ice-cream, then she made me come here.' The words came out in a strangled flood of tears. Her nostrils were flooded with yellow snot. I looked at her, marvelling that what she said could be true.

Rebecca turned slowly. 'You took her?'

'To buy an ice-cream.'

'She didn't, she didn't. She said I was to come home with her and have a present but all she gave me was that old doll.' A small accusing hand pointed at Beattie's Flower Barbie, which had been discarded on the floor, the petals of its skirt twisted around the golden head. I picked it up, stared at the child with distaste.

Her gaze was defiant. She felt safe with Rebecca there. I tried to feel some guilt, a flicker of remorse, but couldn't. I turned away.

Rosie's voice rose, playing to the audience. 'I want to go home to my mummy.'

Rebecca sank to her knees, twining long white arms around the child's chubby back. The sobs increased in volume.

'Really, Jane, I don't know what you were thinking of.'

'I wasn't thinking.' My tone was sulky.

'Come on, Rosie,' Rebecca said. 'I'm taking you home.'

'She hasn't finished her Coca-Cola.' I didn't want Rebecca taking her. I wanted to do it myself.

'I hardly think that matters.' Rebecca's voice was exasperated. She took the child by the hand, helped her up off the sofa.

I went and stood in front of the door. 'I said I'll take her.'

'Jane, you need help.' Rebecca's grey eyes were slanted. 'At least let me call Alan.'

'There's no need for that. I'm taking her back now.'

'I'm calling anyway,' she said, moving towards the telephone. 'They must be out of their minds with worry.'

In the end, of course, Rebecca drove Rosie home. I followed behind, in my car. I wasn't about to let Rebecca give her version of events without me there. Anyway, I believe in facing the music. I like things over and done with.

We had hardly covered a mile when a police panda car pulled up behind me and followed us at a careful distance all the way to Acton. I suppose Alan called them. I'd have done the same myself. We must have made an odd sight, proceeding through the quiet suburban streets at a stately pace.

When we got to the house, another marked Panda car was slewn up across the drive and Alan was standing by the front gate, his body stiff with anticipation. The minute he saw the cars he swung towards them although we were still some way off.

Rebecca deposited Rosie, now sobbing furiously, into Alan's arms.

Sitting in my car, waiting for some of the drama to subside, I could see their faces turning towards me, Alan's a stark white triangle, Rebecca's a softer, fuzzy oval, but both jerking above their bodies with the swift angular movements of excitement.

The door of the house flew open and I caught a glimpse of a uniformed policewoman standing in the shadows, then Barbara emerged. She didn't run, as I'd expected her to, but walked slowly up the path and held her arms out to her child. Alan stopped talking long enough to put her into them. Barbara buried her face in the child's neck. I was too far away to hear anything so I must have sensed rather than heard the sharp inhalation as her nose sought out her little girl's familiar, comforting smell. I bowed my head, remembering how I used to do that with Beattie, how I'd kiss her sleeping face, press my mouth to her satin cheek, inhaling the warm, familiar smell of her. I will never smell that smell again, however many children I kiss. No child ever has the same scent as another.

The next thing I knew, Alan was pulling open the door of the car and thrusting his face into mine. 'Are you mad?' he shouted. I moved to get out of the car to talk to him but he was on me before I'd even got my legs from under me. His fingers jabbed into my arm. I knew there would be bruises on my skin the next day, but I couldn't blame him.

175

I felt the fear in his hand. 'No, you don't. The police are inside. They want to talk to you.'

Pulling me out of the car, he pushed me up the path, his fingers still digging into my arm. About half-way up I stopped and half turned. 'Please let go of my arm.'

His grip tightened, but then he looked at me fully for the first time. I suppose my face must have been as white as his, for he dropped my arm and followed me up the path.

Barbara watched me over her child's head. Her gaze was black, unreadable.

Alan and I moved into the sitting-room where a policewoman sat gazing into space. I wondered how many hours she had to sit like that, unable to pick up a magazine or flick on the television switch. Unable to do anything, except look attentive.

'This is the woman,' Alan said.

The policewoman got to her feet and introduced herself. Then she asked me if I had taken Rosie from the house earlier.

'Of course she bloody took her. She just bloody drove up the road, cool as you like. If it hadn't been for Rebecca – for Mrs Robinson, I dread to think what she'd have done.'

The policewoman did not look at Alan. She said, 'You realise that this is a serious offence?'

I nodded. I of all people realise that taking a child is a serious offence. But at least they were getting theirs back.

Alan was shifting from foot to foot, in the way he does when he is angry or excited. 'I want to press charges.'

The policewoman turned to look at him then. 'That's up to you, sir, but it seems to me that the matter –'

'I don't bloody care how it seems to you, I want to press charges against this woman.'

'That won't be necessary.' We turned to see Barbara in the doorway, her face strained but composed. 'Rosie's fine,' she said. 'She's asleep.'

'Barbara,' Alan said. 'I think it's best if you leave this to me.'

Barbara's gaze went to her husband's face, then flicked away, dismissing him. 'Jane's child died three months ago,' she said, addressing the policewoman. 'She is obviously still distraught.'

'Obviously,' Alan said.

The policewoman looked at me, a brief glance of pity, and turned back to Barbara. 'It's up to you both, of course.'

Alan interrupted. 'I'll say it's up to us —'

'If you'll excuse us,' Barbara said, 'I'll take Jane into the kitchen and make her a cup of tea. She doesn't look like she's in any sort of state to drive herself home.'

I opened my mouth to refuse, but some quality in Barbara's gaze impelled me to follow her. I looked out of the window. Rebecca's car had gone.

Barbara said nothing but her movements were deft and efficient, as if she was determined to spend the least possible energy on a task as mundane as making tea. I wondered if she lived her life like that, patting the days briskly into shape.

It was only when she had put a cup of tea in front of me that she spoke. 'You should get some help.' There was no anger in her voice, just a brisk sympathy.

I took a sip of the tea. It was hot and very sweet. 'There is no help.'

The briskness went from her, then. She slumped back in a chair and gave a sigh, a faint hissing release of air. 'No,' she said, after a while. 'I can quite see that there isn't.'

When I finish the story, Richard says nothing. I don't know if his silence is a retreat, or a soundless communing of sympathy. He just sits there, looking sad and displaced, as if the world he knows has shifted slightly on its axis and he hasn't found his balance again, but he never takes his eyes off me. 'Would you like another child?'

I wonder why nobody has ever asked me that question before. Perhaps they lacked the courage. 'There is no other child,' I say, my voice stiff.

'There is no other Beattie but there is another child, if you want one.' He lays his hand across my belly. 'Here.'

I feel the shock of it, like a burn. His hand is brown against the blue of my skirt. 'No,' I say and shift away. It has never occurred to me that I could have another child.

Richard says, 'Anything is possible.'

I look at him and for a moment I believe that it might be.

Richard has only been gone half an hour when Ben turns up, his face flushed with wine. He says he has been drinking alone, sitting in the house that he and Rebecca used to share. 'I couldn't bear it,' he says. 'I had to come and see you.'

I haven't the heart to turn him away. There is too much shared history between us. It's that, more than desire or pity, which makes me reach out to him.

We go upstairs, undress in silence.

'Aren't you pleased to see me?'

'You know I am.'

He lies down on the bed, spread-eagled across it so I have to bunch my legs up, tuck myself into a corner. He looks up at me through slitted eyes. 'You know you're very hard to love.'

I sip camomile tea, pondering on his remark. There was a time when I would have believed him, would have clung to him for reassurance. Now I know better. We are all of us hard to love.

'I expect so,' I say, after a while.

This is not what he wants. He's on me like a flash, lifting the cup from my hands, pushing me into the bed, his face pressed to mine. I see the glare of blue eyes, the flash of white teeth and I know he's wooing me with his boy's face.

'But *I* love you. I love you like nobody else ever could.' He presses his mouth to mine. I know what he means, although he does not say it. He means that he is the only one who can save me. No one else would take the trouble.

We fuck. It is the only word for it. I am on top of him, forcing him down. He bucks underneath me, his bony hips grazing my thighs. Neither of us will relent. We ride each other like that, right to the end. There are no winners here.

Fifteen

Ben has been down to the police station again.

'Why won't they leave me alone?' he says. 'My wife has committed suicide. Isn't that enough?'

He stomps around in heavy boots, black, with steel-capped toes. Everyone wears them in advertising. It creates the illusion they've got their feet on the ground.

'I've told them everything that happened that night.'

His face is flushed with anger and I wonder what other illusions Ben has created for himself.

'No, you haven't.'

There, it's out.

He looks at me, then away. I can tell from the set of his shoulders that this is a conversation he doesn't want to engage in.

'It's what she wanted,' he says stubbornly.

'How do you know?'

'Because she told me. How do you bloody think I know?'

'She told you that if she tried to kill herself again you weren't to help her? Is that what you mean?'

He looks me full in the face. 'She told me she wanted to die.' His expression says, *satisfied now*?

'People sometimes say those things. They don't necessarily mean them.'

'She did.'

I notice how he never uses Rebecca's name any more. There is no intimacy in his voice when he talks about her. Perhaps it's the only way he can cope with what he's done.

'How do you know?'

His face shifts. I am letting him down. It is not supposed to be like this. He moves forward, puts a hand to my breast. My belly jumps at his touch. I can see what he's up to, using his body to block out words. 'No,' I say.

Anger tightens the lovely curve of his mouth. When I refuse him he says it's because I don't love him, not in the way he loves me. Ben uses love like a weapon. I wonder if he used it to bludgeon Rebecca too.

The silence lengthens between us. I let it stretch. It's amazing how people will talk into nothing. It's words that keep us from the truth.

Eventually, Ben says 'She was a sad woman, Janey. She had a history of depression. The world was an intolerable place to her. And you know I could never refuse her anything.'

He smiles – a brave, regretful smile. In his head he has created himself as the hero of the piece. It is what he tells everyone: That Rebecca was impossible, wounded and neurotic. He tried to save her from herself. And that last time he failed.

I almost believe him myself. Almost.

I don't know what Rebecca did all day, except shop and wait for Ben to come home. She spent quite a lot of time with Margaret, and with me, although neither of us wanted her. It was just that she was the kind of person whom it is difficult to get rid of.

She'd turn up at the house unannounced and just slide into the kitchen. It was no use trying to stop her. She was like mercury in your hands. Unless you came right out and said, look, it's about time you went or, I need to work, she'd sit around in the kitchen, drinking endless cups of tea. She never looked hurt when you said it, just sort of resigned – as if she'd been expecting it.

The first time she turned up like that I slammed around

the place in silence, making my breath loud with disapproval. She took so little notice that after a while I began to feel foolish, as if I was putting on a show of temperament in front of a vase of flowers. After a while it got so I scarcely noticed she was there. I didn't even bother to make tea for her, just left her to get on with it while I went into the sitting-room and sat at my desk to work. Sometimes it gave me a shock when I walked back into the kitchen and found her still there.

The strange thing was that the Rebecca who sat around in my kitchen came to seem quite different from the Rebecca who was married to Ben. I even felt sorry for her. Sometimes, after she'd left, I'd notice signs of fumbling, apologetic attempts to help out – a plant saucer swimming with water, the faint scummy marks of detergent on a surface where she hadn't rinsed the cloth out properly.

She was fond of Beattie, though, and kind to her too. That made up for a lot. 'I *adore* that child,' she'd say, in that false over-expressive way she had. It used to irritate me, the way she could never say anything without turning it into a drama, but in a funny way I miss it now.

She let Beattie brush her hair and braid it, or coil it at the back of her long neck. She even let her dress her up sometimes, as if she was a life-sized doll. She didn't seem to mind Beattie touching her; in fact, it was almost embarrassing the way she encouraged it.

It never seemed to occur to Rebecca that Beattie didn't adore her back but treated her much in the way that the rest of us did – like a lovely decorative object that required no other attention except admiration. I think it was Beattie's simple acceptance of her that Rebecca loved. She didn't have to be anyone but herself.

After Beattie died Rebecca still came to visit, but less frequently. By then, the affair with Ben had started so I had reason to hate her. I didn't, though, not when she was sitting in my house. It was when she wasn't there that

Rebecca got on my nerves. Then she became Ben's Rebecca, the woman whose every habit I knew because Ben had described them in careful detail.

Most of all I knew the way she held Ben back, criticising everything he did, not in a loud, shouty way but by silence. Ben says nobody could create silence like Rebecca; it hung over their house like a low, enveloping cloud. And although she didn't like to be touched, she had to be near him at all times, even pulling her chair right up to his at the table when they were eating, so he'd have to sit with his elbow pressed right into his side. If he got up to do anything, even go and have a pee, she'd have to know where he was going. He said it drove him mad and I believe it did but only during the times when he didn't feel like it. The rest of the time, I think he was secretly pleased. She made him feel wanted.

We often gathered at Margaret's place for Sunday lunch. In company, Ben was always after Rebecca to sit right near him; he'd even feed her at mealtimes, taking the fork out of her hand as if she was a kid. It was I who felt mad then, but it didn't stop me noticing that when Ben wasn't in the mood for Rebecca and she'd sit next to him, as she usually did, he'd shift away sharply leaving her staring around in bewilderment as if she'd suddenly found herself in a place she didn't recognise.

Worse than that was the look on her face. A sort of baffled hurt, plain as a neon light that stayed right there until he relented and moved back towards her again. Sometimes I think her problems were less about the way she was made than the person Ben made of her.

Once, when she seemed more than usually bored and lonely, I asked him why she didn't go out and get a job. He laughed. 'Work? She can hardly get herself to the shops. How's she going to hold down a job?'

I think he was wrong about that. One day, when Rebecca was round at my house, she asked me if I thought she could do a job like mine. At the time, my head was filled with Ben's version of Rebecca so I didn't say anything, just stared at her with a sort of contempt. Then, when she blushed and murmured something about liking words, I got a bit sharp with her. I think I murmured about people who liked reading books always thinking they could write one. At the time I thought her poetry – long abandoned – was just a childish dalliance.

I feel quite sorry about that now, especially after what George said about her talent and how it was Ben who stopped her writing.

Rebecca needed Ben. I know that. But, looking back, I suppose that after Beattie died I thought I needed him more. Or perhaps that I deserved him more. Anyway, all I know is that just lately I've started to see Rebecca in a new light. I don't mean I've started to like her. That would be the most blatant hypocrisy. I couldn't do that. If I did, I'd have to hate myself.

Even so, it makes me no better than Ben. Perhaps it's that that stops me from going to the police and telling the truth. I think Ben knows it too. He's taken to wooing me again, sending reminders of his presence when he's away. A bunch of flowers arrived this morning: cream roses, white lilies and papery blue scabious. All my favourites. He knows me well. The message said, 'Love, Always. Ben.'

Does it mean, I'll love you always? Or, I'll always be there? Or, I'll always be Ben? I don't know. I just know that for some reason I do not like the word. It rouses a small cold feeling somewhere in the pit of my belly.

Richard calls and asks if I'd like to go on a picnic. The forecast is good, he says. I immediately say yes, even though it's on Saturday and I know there'll be some explaining to do to Ben.

'I thought maybe Hampstead Heath,' Richard says. 'I've got a kite.' As if that's all the explanation that's needed.

'Well, a kite would be wonderful.'

'The thing is –' his voice goes up a register and I know he's nervous of saying something.

'Yes?'

'Well, I hope you don't mind, but the thing is, it's Sam's day with me.'

'Oh.' At least that explains the kite. Still, I can't think of a thing to say. I haven't spent any time with a child since Beattie left. I don't know how I'll cope. Richard's voice breaks in: 'Well, if you'd rather not –'

It's true. I'd rather not, but I know that I've spent too long hiding from life, seeking sanctuary in Ben. It's time I got out, put some perspective between us. Maybe then I'd understand what this business with Rebecca is all about.

And, of course, Richard will be there, which will make everything OK. 'I'd love to.'

In the past week Ben's become more demanding than ever. It's as if, now Rebecca's left, he's beginning to assume some of her characteristics. If I even so much as go into another room, his face assumes that hurt expression I've come to dread.

'We don't have to be *glued* together to show we love each other,' I say, after he's asked me for the eighteenth time where I'm going.

A tiny smile of triumph steals across his face. I so rarely talk of love and this, at least, is an admission of the state we're in. Seeing no answering smile in my face he says resentfully, 'You used to like it.'

'That was then.'

'What do you mean, *then*?' he asks, and his voice is so quiet I know we're in for some sort of confrontation.

I consider walking out of the room, putting some distance between us until we've both cooled down, but I know he'll come after me and things will be, if anything, worse. 'You know.'

'No, I don't know. Before Rebecca died? After Beattie died? Before we fucked? When exactly is *then*?'

Before you let your wife die. I don't say it, of course. Words are not objects to be thrown around carelessly and anyway, I'm not even sure it's true. Perhaps it was exactly as Ben says. Perhaps it really was Rebecca's final wish that if he found her dying he should let her go. I think of my mother, hammering frantically on my father's chest and shouting, 'let me go', her face contorted with humiliation and frustration. It's a sight I shall never forget.

It's not up to me to say what went on between Ben and Rebecca, to judge what is the truth. It's just I can't bear the secret. It sits on my shoulders like a weight. 'Please let me go to the police,' I say.

Ben looks genuinely startled. 'What for?'

'Let me tell them the truth – that you came to see me after you'd been home. That you knew Rebecca had already taken the pills.'

Ben looks suddenly exhausted. 'They'll never understand.'

'They will if you explain, in the way that you've explained it to me. With her history –'

'No.'

'But *I* don't understand.'

He stares at me for a long time. 'No. I can quite see how difficult it must be for you. I'm sorry, I should never have got you involved.'

I say nothing. What is there to say?

Ben says in a low voice, 'She really did want to die, you know. She made me promise that the next time she tried to kill herself I wasn't to stop her, no matter how hard it was. And it wasn't just once that she asked me, but a hundred times. In the end I gave in and promised. I never believed she would actually do it, even though she'd tried before. So, when I got home that night and found her I panicked.

186

That's why I came to you. I thought if there was anybody in the world I could turn to – '

He breaks off, gets wearily to his feet. 'I suppose I ought to go. I can quite see that you don't want me here.'

For a moment I am tempted to laugh. He looks so much the tragic hero that I forget the horror of the reality. 'I'll go to the police,' he says, 'if that's what you really want.'

I shake my head. 'I don't know.' I am uncertain now. I think of the law book in the library. *A sentence not exceeding fourteen years.*

I put my hands to my face. 'I'm sorry. I just feel so confused.'

Ben pulls me to him, kisses me gently on the forehead. 'I know you do. So do I. The only reason I dragged you into this in the first place is that, knowing your history with your mother, I thought that you of all people would understand what a promise means, however far it puts you outside the law.'

'What do you mean?'

It is years since I told him about my mother. He's the only person I've ever told and he's never mentioned it before. I thought he'd forgotten all about it.

Ben smiles. 'I think you know exactly what I mean.'

Sixteen

I have lived my mother's death a thousand times, perhaps more. In the weeks when she lay dying, I felt her eyes on me wherever I went. Beattie had her eyes: guileless, trusting blue eyes; eyes as wide and open as a summer sky.

My father couldn't bear to let her go. He was relentless, demanding – a new medicine, a new diet, another expensive specialist summoned from London. Neither of us could talk to him. If we tried he turned away, but not before we saw on his face an expression of such relentless agony it knocked the breath from our lungs.

Then the day came when my mother stopped crying out with the pain, stopped doing anything at all except lying with her eyes clamped shut, her beautiful hands balled into crabbed fists by her side. I knew she was willing herself to die. It was then that I said I'd help her.

We planned it carefully. I fed my father sleeping pills, ground up in his nightly cup of cocoa. Then I washed her, using cotton wool pads soaked in warm water and her favourite scent. She couldn't bear anything coarser on her poor skin. A clean white night-gown, the pillows pummelled to fresh volume, one beneath her head, one to her side. I combed what was left of her hair, rubbed sweet lavender oil into her temples. Her eyes moved gratefully, following me. I knew I was putting off the moment. Eventually, I could find nothing else to do and sank down slowly onto the chair by the side of her bed. I took her desiccated hand. It felt unpleasant. I would not look at her, wanted to sit for a while in silence, but she was anxious to get on.

'One more minute.'

She moved her head fretfully. 'What if he wakes up?'

'He won't.'

'*Please.*'

I picked up a pillow, carefully gripping it on either side, measuring its centre over the tip of her nose. Balance is everything.

She gazed at my face, locking the memory of it with her remaining good eye. 'Promise me you'll go through with it, whatever happens.'

I found myself unable to speak.

Her tone grew urgent. 'Promise me.'

'I promise.'

She smiled, then, a young, almost carefree smile. I lowered the pillow. As it drew nearer to her face, I saw her expression change to one of terror. I stopped, the pillow hovering above her face.

'No!' she cried.

I snatched the pillow away, staring down at her in confusion.

Her face screwed up in frustration. 'Get on with it.' She sounded almost angry.

I pressed down, pushing the soft, dense weight tight on either side of her face. She made no sound. I leaned a little harder. It was not so bad after all.

Her arms began to twitch, then her legs. Suddenly, her arms were flailing in the air, the claws of her hands grabbing for my hair. I looked at her, screwing my head round to gaze down the length of her body. Her legs kicked convulsively, cycling in the air as if she was doing exercises. They humped up and down under the soft white sheet. I could not believe the strength of her. My arms weakened, but I remembered the promise I had made.

Suddenly she was quiet. Her legs gave a final convulsive

twitch and collapsed flat, scarcely making a bump in the sheet. I slumped down, the full weight of my body pressed across her face. Minutes passed before I raised my body from hers. But I dared not lift the pillow. What would she look like? Would her face be trapped in the same rictus of horror?

Eventually curiosity got the better of me. I lifted a corner of the pillow, peeked under it. I could see nothing, only the sharp curve of her jaw-bone. How thin she was. Her face was once round, the flesh swooping in a lovely curve across her cheeks and jaw.

My whole body was shaking violently. I ripped the pillow from her face and discovered that she was smiling. How dare she smile at a time like this. Her eyes were open. I longed to close them, to slide my fingers across the pale crescents traced with faint blue veins and veil her gaze. I dared not. Whoever heard of a sleeping corpse? Dead eyes are always open. Aren't they? I tried to remember little Johnny Johnson, to recall whether his eyes were open or closed. He was the only dead person I had ever seen. The rest were fakes, in the movies. Dead people always have their eyes open in the movies. But all I could remember of little Johnny Johnson was his white Aertex shirt, the black tyre track decorating his chest.

I gazed down at my mother. She looked peaceful, her eyes wide and unblinking, as if she was preparing her face for the camera, for the sudden flash of white before the shutter clicks.

Was she dead? My hands were shaking too much to feel for a pulse. Grabbing the old silver-backed mirror from her dressing-table, I held it close to her mouth. Was that a faint mist in the centre? I stared down at her in alarm, heard my own breath coming in great heaving gasps. Perhaps I breathed on the mirror inadvertently. I scrubbed the smooth cold surface on the sheet, held it against her nose and mouth. A shadow still seemed to form on it.

'Mummy,' I whispered. 'Mummy, I don't know what to do.'

It was a long time since I had called her mummy, but the smile did not move. Closing my eyes, I picked up the pillow and put it back over her face. Then I lay down on top of it, my body straddling her face and shoulders. I don't know how long I stayed there, jerking convulsively at every tiny sound. It was an old house and loudly protested its advanced age.

I pulled myself off her but didn't use the mirror again. Nobody could survive that. Could they?

After carefully rearranging the bedclothes, I went and sat in the armchair in the corner and watched over her sleeping face. I still did not believe that she was dead, although I killed her myself. No, not killed. Assisted. Helped her find death. *Mother's little helper*. She had not called me that in years.

I sat in the chair by her bed, laid my head back and thought about the morning. I had planned it carefully. My father would come in, find me asleep, my mother dead in the bed. Would he shake me, violent in his anger that I slept peacefully while my mother died? Or would he cry out, making the terrible animal moaning that I heard him make some nights? In any event I must be prepared to wake with a cry of surprise and shock, to hurry over to her bed and cast myself down, sobbing over her body. I tried to imagine what it would be like to find my mother dead. How would I behave? Would I cry out or weep silently. Would I weep at all? I acted out the responses in my head, knowing that I would not sleep, too agitated by the knowledge that I must mime the terrible reality of death. My father must never know. My mother made me promise. I swore that to her, but I promised it less for her than for myself. What would he do to me if he found out? He was not a violent man, except in the depth of his love for my mother, which was awesome.

The first thing I heard was the sound of crying. The noise woke me with a jolt. I opened my eyes and stared around the dim room. My father was sitting cross-legged on the floor, his head in his hands, crying as helplessly as a child.

I went and kneeled beside him, my arms around his shoulders. He scrabbled at me, pulling me down. Thinking he had discovered our secret and would strangle me for it, I struggled briefly as the sobs intensified. He clambered over me, pushing with stiff fingers. His eyes were closed, his face a screw of agony running with tears. A rope of snot slid down to his chin and hung there. He lowered his head, butting me with his chin in a movement that was familiar although I could not immediately place it. My father was trying to climb onto my lap.

The next morning, flowers arrive from Ben. Red roses with a card attached: 'Never forget that I love you.'

Never.

I stuff them haphazardly into a vase, grab my bag and leave the house. Richard is waiting.

Margaret is in the front garden, attending to her pots of geraniums. 'Going out, dear?'

'To a picnic.'

'With Ben?' She sounds surprised.

'No.' I explain that I am meeting friends.

The words come out too fast and I blush slightly as if I am caught out in some wrongdoing, but she says mildly, 'That's good. It's about time you got out more.'

I go to her, press my lips to her cheek. The old skin is fine as rice paper, but her hands squeeze my arm with surprising strength. 'You enjoy yourself,' she says almost fiercely.

Richard was right. It is a beautiful day. He and Sam are waiting by the pond. As I approach, I see Sam nudge Richard fiercely, then stare away as if unconcerned. On the way from the Tube I'd stopped at a shop and bought a giant-sized bar of Cadbury's Milk Chocolate and a large bottle of Coke. I hand these to Richard. They are cumbersome. By the time he has fumbled them from my hands, some of the awkwardness is dispelled.

'My contribution.'

I don't look at Sam, not directly, although I already have some measure of him: small, sturdy, with the same curly brown hair and quick, engaging smile as his father. He has plasters on both knees and an egg-sized bruise on one shin.

Richard grins down at him. 'He's not allowed them at home.'

'Neither am I but that's the point of a picnic, isn't it? Out here, we're not at home.'

Sam edges a little closer, looks up at me curiously. 'Why aren't you allowed Coke and sweets? My mum says it's because they're not good for children but you're not a child.'

'That's true.'

'So?'

I stare down at him innocently, knowing that if he gets exasperated enough with me he'll relax. 'So what?'

He lets out a small explosion of disgust. 'So – why aren't you allowed them?'

'Because they're bad for grown-ups too, except that grown-ups don't have other people telling them what to do – or at least not most of the time.'

'Wish I was a grown-up. People are always telling me what to do.'

'I know how you feel.'

'But you *are* a grown-up.'

'I know, but just lately everybody seems to have taken it into their heads to tell me what to do.'

'Tell them to mind their own bloody business.'

I look down at Sam, startled, but his face is perfectly

calm. 'It's what my nanny tells me when I ask her who she was talking to on the phone.'

Richard says quietly, 'She does what?'

He has sneaked up behind us on noiseless feet.

Sam flushes. 'She's a real pain,' he mutters.

Later, I apologise to Richard.

'On the contrary, I'm grateful. He'd never have mentioned it to me, or his mother. He thinks we need protecting.'

'Do you?'

Richard grins. 'Yes, probably.'

We walk on a while in silence.

'He's certainly good with strangers.'

'He's had a lot of practice. We separated when he was four. He's had to learn to fend for himself.'

I want to ask Richard if he too has learned to fend for himself, but I don't, just smile into the summer morning.

'How old was Beattie?'

Most people won't talk to me about Beattie for fear of upsetting me. Or themselves. But I know how much courage it takes to ask about a dead child so I say, 'She was six years old. And nine months.'

Richard's gaze is fixed on Sam, who is practising backward running on the path ahead, a small, sturdy speck of blue and red in shorts and T-shirt.

'And it never gets better,' I say, because I know that's the question he wants to ask.

Richard has packed a very good lunch. There's roast chicken, runny cheese, a baguette, cherry tomatoes, apples and a treacle tart. 'Sam's favourite,' Richard says, looking down fondly at his son's curly head.

Sam looks up at me. 'Are you Daddy's girlfriend?'

There is an awkward silence. Richard and I glance at each other and away.

'Well, I'm a friend of your father's and I'm a girl,' I say after a while.

'But you're not an actual girlfriend?'

'No.'

Sam shrugs, then chews on a chicken drumstick.

Richard busies himself with opening the wine. When it is safely poured, he says, 'Sam, would it matter if Jane were my girlfriend?'

'Well, Mummy keeps saying you need a girlfriend. She says maybe it would stop you being so grumpy.'

Richard frowns, embarrassed.

'So I was sort of hoping', Sam went on, 'that maybe she *was* one.' He looks at me doubtfully. 'Because not all girls are girlfriends, are they?'

I shake my head.

'Let's play football,' Richard says, getting to his feet and running off without a backward glance.

We drop Sam off at his mother's house. Richard walks him to the door, his hand curled lovingly round his son's neck. As the door opens, I catch sight of a woman, long blonde hair, slim figure, black trousers and top. I look away, stare straight ahead out of the windscreen of the car, although there is nothing to see in the empty street. She's pretty, I think. The thought alarms me and I begin to scrabble in my bag, not because I'm looking for anything, but because I need something to do. Just then I hear a shout. Somebody is calling my name. I look up, startled, to see Sam waving and yelling. I lean forward, absurdly grateful to be remembered, press my face to the window. 'Bye,' I mouth. 'Bye-bye.'

I see blonde hair retreating, Sam turning on his heel and slipping through the door. It slams shut violently. I imagine Sam leaning against it with both arms to push it, as you do when you're small, and his mother calling, 'Don't slam the door!' irritable to have the peace of her day shattered by her noisy, intrusive child. Or maybe she's smiling at him, asking him how his day went. Or maybe she's both, irritated and at the same time happy. Children get you like that.

I sometimes wonder, if Beattie came home, how I'd be with her. I know it's not possible, but I imagine it none the less, have in my head this picture of me as some sort of a saint, endlessly smiling and patient. I don't suppose it would be that way at all, not once I'd got over the gratitude. Joy doesn't last long. Life has a way of butting in on it, toning it down to a respectable shade of grey, so before you know it you're coasting along in neutral again. Which, I suppose, is the way it should be, otherwise you wouldn't notice the sudden uplifting surge of happiness.

Richard climbs into the car. He is smiling but I notice the knuckles on his hands are white when he grips the steering wheel.

We drive for a while, then he says, 'Would you mind if I didn't drop you at home quite yet? It's just I always feel a bit down after Sam's gone.'

'No,' I say. 'I'd like that.'

'Where shall we go?'

I don't mind, but I don't say so. Indifference is almost always unhelpful. That's what Beattie always said. 'It doesn't help,' she'd cry, when I said I didn't mind what particular game we played and she buckled under the weight of choice. So these days I always come out and suggest something, even if it's only to provoke a discussion.

'The pub?'

'I'd take you to my place, only it's such a mess it would feel like ritual humiliation. See the bachelor living alone. See how badly he copes.'

I laugh but don't offer to go to my house. Suddenly I want to keep him away from it, as though there's something bad there, something nasty and infectious he might catch. I feel his eyes on my face, but say nothing.

'The pub it is, then,' he says after a pause.

*

Ben's at my place when I get back, stretched out on the sofa watching TV.

I stand in the doorway looking at him. An empty bottle of red wine and a glass are on the floor next to him. He doesn't take his eyes off the screen, although I know he's conscious of my presence.

'Hi.'

'So you're finally back.'

'Seems like it.'

He looks up at me. 'Pretty late, for a picnic.'

'It was a lovely evening. We stayed to have a few drinks.'

'We?'

'Some friends ... Ben, I didn't actually expect to find you here.'

'Ah, but I expected to find you here.'

'Well, I'm sorry about that –'

'I had plans for us for the evening.'

'Oh.'

'Is that it? Is that all I get? Just, oh?'

'I'm sorry, but you didn't actually say you had plans. You left last night without a word about what we were doing today, or even when we might be seeing each other again.'

'I just assumed we would be together.' He holds his hand out to me. 'Come here.'

I move over to him, take his hand. He pulls me down onto the sofa next to him, draws my head to his shoulder. His hand comes up and strokes my face. 'There, that's better, isn't it?'

He feels hot and I remember that first night I touched him, how warm he felt to the touch and how his skin seemed invested with magic, as if a live charge ran through it.

'Just us together,' he murmurs softly into my hair, 'like we always planned.'

His hand moves under my T-shirt and I feel the old familiar drag of desire. My anger begins to evaporate. It was what Rebecca wanted, I think. He was doing it for her. He told me because he trusts me, because I'm the one he runs to.

As he pushes up my T-shirt, his mouth working to please me, I look down at his blond head.

Something has changed. The picture I have always had of the two of us has lost its sharp, bright focus.

Briefly, I mourn the loss.

Seventeen

The Inspector is closing the case.

'It seems we've gone as far as we can.'

His expression is watchful. I say nothing. He doesn't like Ben. I know that much, not from anything he says but from his voice, the way it becomes so guardedly polite when he talks about him.

'And you have no more to add to your original statement, Miss Rose?' He says it lightly, almost teasingly, but I can see he is waiting for me to falter.

'No.'

He sighs. 'Very well.' Some sixth sense tells him that he has missed a vital piece of information, but policemen are not paid to deal in intuition. 'Well, if ever you feel you need to come and talk to me,' he says, 'then please don't hesitate.'

When he stands and holds out his hand, his tired face creasing into a smile, he looks so familiar that I want to say something like, it was nice knowing you, or see you again some time, and the effort of repressing both phrases makes me silent. I wonder once more when he finds the time to see his children.

When I get home, I peer through the windows of Margaret's flat.

A shadowy figure slips across the hallway. Tapping on the window I call 'it's only me' and Margaret comes to the door, her hands thick with dirt. 'I've just been doing a spot of tidying up in the garden, but it was so hot I decided to come in and have a cold drink. Will you join me?'

She pours glasses of orange squash from a bottle so old the squash has turned the colour of dirty rust water, then struggles to evict the ice from its plastic chamber. Not fancying having half of Margaret's garden in my drink, I take it from her, prise the cubes out and drop them in the glasses. 'That's better,' she says, drinking the sugary liquid and smacking her lips like a child.

I tell her the police have closed the case on Rebecca.

Margaret looks mournful. 'Poor creature. I never thought we did right by her.'

'Did you like her?'

'She was rather a sad little thing but I believe I should have done, had she not been married to Ben. He brought out the worst in her.'

'I thought you said that you couldn't understand why he married her?'

'Well, I couldn't,' Margaret says, a touch of impatience in her tone. 'It was obvious that he would grow bored of her soon enough and boredom's a very difficult thing. It can make people behave in unpredictable ways, most of them destructive.'

There was a time I would have leaped to Ben's defence. Margaret notices my silence. 'How are you two getting along?'

'Fine,' I say, but there is a dullness to my voice.

Margaret fixes her eyes on the window. A wreath of pale-pink roses frames the splintered wood frame. 'Pretty, aren't they?' she murmurs. 'Take a lot of care, though. A little fertiliser dug in around the roots, a good drink every day. It's a thirsty thing, needs lots of water so I give it the remains out of the washing-up bowl. You'd hardly credit such beauty springing from a few bowls of dirty water and a handful of blood and bone.'

'No.'

'Living things need a great deal of care if they are to thrive. And encouragement. Ben is a very bad gardener,'

Margaret goes on. She sounds almost fierce although her eyes are still fixed on the pink blooms nodding outside the window. 'One minute he lavishes a thing with attention and the next he neglects it completely. Both actions are inclined to be unhelpful. While you can kill a plant by neglect, by far the most common method is overwatering. Love by drowning, you might say.'

She smiles, pleased by the joke but I sense, underneath, a deep distress. Margaret's loyalty to Ben is intense and has been severely tried of late. 'He's a good boy, really, but he can be rather overwhelming. It doesn't do to allow oneself to be sucked in. All living things need space to grow.'

I think of Ben's eyes, how he presses his face to mine until his blue gaze fills my world. 'Yes,' I say, feeling suddenly tired. 'I can quite see that.'

I don't suppose that most of us mean to do harm. Not really. We just, most of the time, fail to connect cause with effect. Like those kids in America who shot their class-mates and killed five of them. They meant, they said at the trial, to fire over their heads. When they said it they were crying. They wanted to take back every single one of those bullets. They looked bewildered that they couldn't.

I first saw that bewilderment as a child. It was on the face of Mohammed, our family servant. He was a kind man – although I suppose at the time he was really not much more than a boy. We played together whenever I could persuade him to take time off his duties. I thought of him as my friend although probably he just tolerated me in order to keep my parents happy and hold on to his job.

One of the games I taught him to play was Gotcha. Right from the start he seemed to like it. We played it every day when I got home from school. Even when I grew tired of it, he'd beg and plead, shouting 'Gotcha, Gotcha!' in broken

English, until I gave up trying to persuade him to play anything else.

He almost always won and, when he did, he'd snatch me up and hug me hard, his laughter filling the dim, cavernous space under the house where nobody else went. He hugged me so hard it hurt – wouldn't stop even though I struggled and squirmed, trying to get away from the hard thing he kept in his robe, right under his belly. It got so it dug into me so painfully, and he held me for so long, that I refused to play any more, no matter how much he begged. For days after that he followed me around, his big liquid eyes staring at me mournfully. 'Gotcha?' he whispered hopefully. 'Gotcha?'

One day, when I was home from school and bored in the long dusty hours of the afternoon, I went to find Mohammed to see if he would play.

'Gotcha?' he said, his eyes lighting up.

'Something else. Football.'

He shook his head, said he had work to do, but all the time I could see his eyes on me, checking my reaction.

'One,' I said, holding up a finger to be sure he understood. 'One game of Gotcha, and then we play football.'

We played and he hugged me more fiercely than ever that afternoon. When the hard thing jabbed into my belly, I started to cry. He dropped me and ran off, leaving me sprawling on the ground in bewilderment. Once I'd got over my tears, I ran after him, demanding he keep his side of the bargain and come and play football, but he kept his head turned away so I couldn't see his face and flapped his hand, shooing me away.

That evening, as my parents sat listening to the BBC World Service news and quietly sipping their gin and ice, I told them about the hard thing that Mohammed kept in his robe. 'When he hugs me,' I said, 'it sticks into my tummy and hurts.'

I could tell by their sharp stillness that they were listening. My mother's blue eyes were pale with anxiety. 'Are you quite sure, darling?' she said, after a long silence.

'Quite sure.'

Her eyes searched out my father's, then she asked whether I had ever seen the hard thing in Mohammed's robe, or if he had ever asked me to do anything like taking off my clothes.

I was astonished. 'Why would he do that?'

That seemed to calm her but my father got to his feet and walked slowly across the veranda and into the house. A door slammed violently, then there was silence. It was then I knew that Mohammed had done something bad. My father never slammed doors.

Later, my father told me that Mohammed was leaving, that he had done something unforgivable, but that I was not to make him feel any worse than he already did, which was quite bad enough.

Mohammed left our house that night, but not before he sought me out. His eyes were red from crying and he would not look at me but stood some distance away, fumbling in his white robe so that I thought, at last, I would discover the secret of the thing he kept in there. He drew a long thin object from his pocket, wrapped in a screw of newspaper. 'Sorry,' he said, using one of the few English words that I had taught him.

Reaching across the distance that separated us, I took the screw of newspaper. 'Friends?' I said hopefully.

'Salam al ekum.' Peace be with you.

'El ekum salam.' And with you.

When I unwrapped the newspaper I discovered that he had given me his biro. The cylinder of its body was filled with pale-blue liquid and a tiny boat that bobbed up and down each time you turned the pen. Mohammed was very proud of that pen. I think it was the only thing he owned of any value.

The house is hot and still, the only life the red message light flashing on the answer machine. The first is from Ben, saying he's managed to get tickets for a play I want to see. He'll meet me at the theatre at seven. The second is from a magazine, asking if I have two spare weeks available to fill in on the sub-desk.

And the third is Richard. He is thinking of me, he says. His voice is awkward, as if the last thing he wants to do is think about me. He sounds so enraged with embarrassment that it makes me smile.

'Are you still thinking of me,' I say, when I get through to him, 'or has the moment passed?'

'Passed, but it would return if you had a drink with me this evening.'

'I can't,' I say regretfully. 'We have tickets for a new play. We were lucky to get them.'

That *we* slides in so furtively that at first I don't notice. When I do, I could happily cut out my own tongue.

All I can hear is silence.

'Richard,' I say. 'Richard?'

I could lie, say I'm going to the theatre with a girlfriend but I've used the plural too carelessly, in the way you do when you're hooked up permanently with somebody.

'Tomorrow, then,' he says, but his voice is heavy, as it is when somebody has disappointed you.

Sighing, I pick up the telephone again and call the magazine. They want me to start work the following Monday. I agree and ring off. Even the promise of work and money fails to lighten my mood.

I go through to the kitchen to make some tea. When the kettle clicks off I pour boiling water over the tea-bag and watch it rise to the surface, its papery skin fizzing with bubbles.

It reminds me of the tea I made the night Rebecca died. I must have drunk ten cups while I waited for Ben to call.

He never did. He handed Rebecca's life to me as if it was no more than an old discarded coat. An image haunts me – of Ben reading a book while Rebecca lay dying. I shake my head as if to dislodge it, wander into the sitting-room and sit at my desk, staring at a manuscript, but the type shifts in front of my eyes. *I made her a promise. I thought that you of all people would understand what a promise means, however far it puts you outside the law.*

I should understand. Ben read a book. I slept – right next to my mother's dead body. I kept my promise and I slept like a baby. Later, her absence filled the house. It was then that sleep came fitfully, in death she took up more space than she ever had in life.

Poor mother. Poor Rebecca. The two are becoming tangled in my mind, the same drooping grace, the same pale, anxious eyes.

'I've never thought that I belong,' Rebecca said. 'I suppose you think that's silly.'

'No.' I, of all people, understand about not belonging. 'I think we all feel like that sometimes.'

She bit her lip, white pearls denting the pink flesh. 'I suppose so. Does it frighten you?'

'No,' I said, my voice abrupt.

It frightens me more than anything else. I think that's why Rebecca longed for a child, to anchor her to the world. I despised her for it at the time. No child should be made to suffer the weight of a parent's failings. But I believe that's why I saw Rebecca so little after Beattie died. She couldn't bear to see me adrift, cast loose from the home that Beattie and I made together. It terrified her, perhaps even more than it terrified me.

'I can't bear it,' she said, when a toy of Beattie's appeared one day in the crack between the dishwasher and the wall. It was a curved grey loop of plastic, for blowing bubbles. It's not as if I don't clean the house almost daily, but mementoes of Beattie still find their way to the surface of my life, as buried stones will in a patch of earth. Rebecca wept as I threw it away. 'I just can't bear it.' I turned my back on her, resentful of her claim on my grief. I kept it turned until she left. It was then that I stopped feeling any compunction about taking her husband. In claiming my grief, she had tried to take my child. I would have Ben in return.

It sounds harsh, I know, but Beattie made sense of the world for me. When she died, all certainty went with her. All certainty but Ben. That's why I felt I had more claim to him than Rebecca. I suppose that's why he is still so precious to me, the only familiar landmark left from that place I used to know. But even he is less familiar now, his image grows more cracked and distorted by the day.

The centre of town is busy. It's just before seven, business is over for the day. I walk fast through the crowd, dodging men in suits, their faces coloured grey by the day's work then tap-dance impatiently behind a young bloke lost in a book.

A group of French kids, fresh off a coach, suck on cans of Coke and admire each other's hair, coloured in fuzzy patches of pink and blue. They pull threatening faces, trying to look like Punks, but even the faces and the crazy hair can't disguise how well-laundered they are.

On the corner, a small gaggle of bewildered tourists turn their street map round and round until they're dizzy.

I see Ben's head over the crowd. He brushes his hair back in that old familiar way that still makes my heart leap. Ducking behind a large middle-aged woman, I try to see him through a stranger's eyes. His hair has a new dullness to it, that tarnished patina that affects the fair, and the corners of his mouth pull down in a droop. But then he sees me and his face lights up, all the features perking up at the corners, and I see by the sudden turning of women's heads that he's just as handsome as he always was.

He's in a good mood. I move towards him, my spirits lifting. I'm so susceptible to him, it's like a contagion. He wraps his arms around me and kisses me hard on the mouth. The people around us stare. Some smile. I grin back, infected by their pleasure.

'I hear the police have closed the case,' I say. 'You must be pleased.'

Ben shrugs. 'A routine suicide.'

It's almost as if he believes it himself.

At the interval we stand in the bar, Ben's arm looped round my shoulders. One of the women who smiled at us earlier as we kissed outside the theatre nudges her husband. He turns a hard stare in our direction, then looks away, leaving his wife blinking sadly into the middle distance.

The play is by a young writer, hailed as the new Osborne. 'They're all the new fucking Osborne,' Ben says, but his tone is good-natured. He doesn't even get riled when the bloke standing next to us says there are no young writers of any talent any more. He's so close, we can see the patch of stubble on his cheek where the razor missed that morning. When he says it, his voice loud and objectionable, I feel that helpless dip in my stomach, like when you're going down in a fast lift, or swooping downhill on a roller-coaster, but Ben just smiles. There was a time he'd have joined in a conversation like that, wading in, metaphorically rolling up his sleeves, but tonight he does nothing.

After the play we go to a Chinese restaurant. Wind-dried ducks hang in the window like giant bats, their skins glazed a dark mahogany brown. Inside it's small and steamy, filled with the chatter of Chinese families. I wonder what it is they're talking about, leaning intently across the tables at each other as they scoop rice into their mouths. There's a rhythm to eating rice, fluid and sensuous. Westerners are bad at it, inhibited by the clack-

clack noise of chopsticks against the bowl, the rude smack of lips. The first food I ever ate was rice. Mabel fed me rice before each meal, concerned that the vegetable mush my mother spooned out of jars wouldn't make me grow. My mother, fretting over my poor appetite, took me on an endless round of doctors. One day, alerted by the flecks of rice around my mouth, she followed me to Mabel's room, found me squatting on the floor, a bowl tucked between my sturdy thighs, heaped with steamed rice studded with fragments of chicken and prawn, with flecks of egg and spring onion.

We order food and a bottle of wine. The waiter hovers impatiently, anxious to get the order into the kitchens. The salt and pepper pots are shaped like pagodas.

The wine arrives and two glasses, one still smeared with the last diner's lipstick. I wipe it on my napkin.

Ben leans back in his chair, smiling. 'I've got some news.' It's a deal for a new book. He had lunch with the publishers that day. 'They loved the story so much, they biked a contract over this afternoon just on the basis of a two-page synopsis.'

Steaming bowls of rice appear and a dish of chicken, grey shreds in a glutinous sauce. Ben shovels food into his mouth, scarcely noticing in his excitement what he's eating. 'I thought they'd want pages of the stuff, some sample chapters at the very least but they said, no, it was fine as it was.'

I am pleased for him and say so. He smiles and raises his glass. A bead of rice trembles on his upper lip. As he talks about the lunch meeting – no expense spared, all the big guns lined up from publisher to senior editor to marketing director – his eyes shine and there's a hectic flush to his cheeks. He looks more connected than I've seen him for a long time. I wonder if this is how he was when he first met Rebecca, the excitement radiating from him. He is a surfer, riding the world like a wave.

'What's the book about?' I say.

'Love and death.'

Love and death. What else are books about?

A chill creeps over me. 'Whose death?'

His face closes up. 'Let's not talk about work any more,' he says in a hard, bright voice, the one he uses for people he doesn't have time for. 'Tell me about your day. And let's have another bottle.'

Before I can say anything, his arm is up and he's turning away, trying to summon a waiter. I can't see the expression in his face, but a muscle flickers in his jaw. It's then I understand. The book he's going to write is about Rebecca. And me.

I'm beginning to wonder if Rebecca really did know about Ben and me. He said often enough that she did. He told her himself. 'It's better that way.'

I didn't question it. I thought that telling her meant he loved me. How foolish love makes us. It probably meant he loved himself.

Because of Rebecca knowing about us, I always thought she was really clever – devious too – the way she sought out my company when she knew I was fucking her husband. The first time she did it I complained to Ben, who got really angry with me. Said it was her way of keeping an eye on me. 'Better a mistress you know than a lover you don't,' he said. That way, she would stay calm about us. 'She's clever. It's just like Rebecca to come up with an idea like that.' Weird, more like, I replied, but if there was anybody who was being weird, I'm beginning to think it was Ben.

What if he is lying? What if she didn't know about us at all? It makes her seem far less calculating, innocent even. And I think with a terrible wrenching of the spirits that it wasn't that she sought me out to gloat over me, but simply because she was after a little company, friendship even.

She told me once that Ben didn't really like her to have any friends, that he wanted to keep her all for himself. At the time, of course, I thought she was bragging, telling me that Ben thought she was the most important person in the world, but maybe it was just a tiny plea, a small cry for help. Looked at that way, it's obvious why he encouraged her to see me so often: because he knew there was no way I was going to be her friend, not when she was the very last person on earth I wanted to have around. He allowed her to see Margaret too, of course, but then who wouldn't? There's no denying he loves her, won't have a word said against her, not even some teasing remark about her not being so steady on her pins any more. He'll jump down your throat if you so much as dare to breathe such a thing.

Still, it must have been nice and cosy for him, having the three people he loves most in the world locked together in an unwitting eternal triangle, all depending in one way or another on each other. I depended on Rebecca. I see that now. She fed my passion for Ben.

It's always been Ben; the sight of him, the feel of him, the thought of him. He says sometimes that I don't need him. It's not need, this feeling. It's something far more primal than that. I don't know how to leave him. I just know I have to. I used to think that I was good at leaving. But how do you walk away from yourself?

In the paper this morning there was a story about a man who got his hand trapped in a piece of farm machinery. It sucked him in, inch by inch. He survived, but only because he took a knife and hacked off his hand, just above the wrist.

That's the way I'm beginning to feel about Ben. That's how bad it is.

Eighteen

Richard doesn't say anything about me being a plural of a person, but I notice how intently he stares at my left hand, as if checking for a ring. I don't say anything either because I know if he asks about Ben I'm going to tell the truth, even though I don't want to. And that, I suppose, will be that.

I wonder why his wife let him go. He seems too precious to be allowed out on his own. Perhaps he went of his own accord although I find that hard to believe. He's so devoted to Sam, the sort of man who'd put up with any amount of trouble just to be with his son full-time.

'You really are away with the fairies tonight,' Richard says. He's looking at me with that lopsided grin that breaks your heart. Or would, if you allowed it to. He has a tiny cast in one eye so that sometimes, when he's tired or anxious, his bad eye wanders and you're not sure whether he's looking at you at all.

Well, I'll miss that.

'Something on your mind?'

'Nothing much,' I say. Only that I think my lover killed his wife. Only that I have a lover at all.

'Are you involved with somebody?'

'Is it important?' I am trying to put off the moment but I can see by his face that it's not going to work.

'Yes.'

'I've been having an affair with somebody. His wife just died.'

Richard looks a bit startled at that. 'How?'

211

'She committed suicide.'

'Nasty.'

'Yes, it was. It is.'

'And is it a serious affair?'

For a while I don't speak but he's got his eyes hooked into me so I can't look away. 'It was.'

Now it's Richard's turn to be silent. 'So you have to let him down gently. Is that what you're saying?'

It wasn't what I was saying, but I realise with piercing clarity that it's what I want. When I'm with Ben I can't see straight. When I'm away from him I see how bad we are for each other. I want no more secrets and lies, I want us both to go gently into the night.

I smile. 'Yes. That's what I'm saying.'

Richard leans back in his chair and his face takes on a sort of settled, peaceful look. 'Well that's all right, then.'

My hand steals out to his. For a moment, he doesn't realise what I'm doing and his fingers fumble against mine awkwardly, so I feel a fool and I'm just about to take my hand away when they swoop down on mine and he holds them in a strong, warm clasp. It feels so good it takes my breath away.

I say, once I've got it back again, 'It *is* all right.' At that moment, I truly believe it's going to be.

The next evening I meet George for a drink. She is waiting in a wine bar near her office, comfortably ensconced at a small wooden table, her bulk spilling over an uncomfortable bentwood chair. If you did not know her you would assume she was a farmer's wife, up to London for the day and just taking the weight off her feet after an exhausting day's shopping. She is dressed in her usual manner – a long gathered skirt, big cotton man's shirt and a knitted waistcoat but today she has added a pair of grey woollen socks that peek out from brown open-toed sandals. It is a sensible decision. The day is chilly, as it sometimes is in June.

She waits until I am in earshot, her blue eyes narrowing as she examines my face. 'You look better,' she says in her forthright way. 'Less secretive and closed off.'

'And you look exactly the same.'

She laughs. On the table are a bottle of wine, two glasses and a yellow pack of the brand of small cigarillos she smokes. 'I got us a bottle. I decided for some obscure reason that we deserve it.'

I can think of many reasons, none of them obscure. 'Lovely,' I say, sliding into a chair.

We talk for a while about work, then George says, 'I hear Ben's signed up with a publisher.' Naming a young editor who's barnstorming the literary establishment, she adds, 'I'm not sure he'd be my first choice but Ben seems pleased. I had lunch with him today.'

I am never quite sure how much George knows of what goes on between Ben and me, and I'm not going to be the one to tell her. It's not that I think she would disapprove exactly. It's more that I believe it would disappoint her and she's not a person you want to do that to.

'He was full of the book, said at last he felt like writing again, as if some sort of block had shifted.'

'Did he mention what it was about?' I ask, keeping my voice carefully casual. Or at least, I try to.

'He wouldn't say. Well, you know how writers are, always panicking that if they so much as breathe a word of the story it'll disappear in a puff of smoke.' George's expression is thoughtful. 'My theory is that it's in some way connected with Rebecca's death. Do you remember me saying that he couldn't bear Rebecca to write? He was consumed with jealousy. Very nasty it was too. Some weeks back we were all at a party and some chap asked Rebecca when we could expect her next volume of poems. Before Rebecca could even utter, Ben said something to the effect that it was better if the world was protected from her tiny talent. He laughed, of course, as if it was a joke.' George looks reflective. 'Nobody laughed with him.'

I feel sick. How often Ben and I had laughed over Rebecca's poetry. I remember Ben's words exactly: 'She gave up in the end, poor darling. Realised it was a losing battle.'

'I believe he feels badly about that now. Perhaps the shock of Rebecca's death has jolted him in to writing again. Or maybe it's just that he's got a story to tell.'

Yes, I say, maybe he has.

Ben's first book, The Egg, was a coming-of-age novel. That wasn't its real title of course. Ben called it *Suburbia*, because that's where it was based, on the last stop on the Central line, the place where people live who are too cautious to be truly good, too frightened to be truly bad. I remember him using that line when we first met. It gave me quite a shock to see it splashed all over the jacket of his novel but then I thought there's no reason why you shouldn't repeat a thought just because it's been used before.

Anyway, it was about a kid who hates his dad. Not just hates him, despises him with a dark, considered loathing. In the book you never quite work out why this kid despises his dad so much. He's a regular sort of a bloke, a bit boring perhaps, a bit scared. That bit rang true anyway. We're all in our own ways a bit boring and a bit scared. The dad's a tax inspector, which I thought was the most obvious cliché but nobody else seemed to mind. 'A parasite,' Ben calls him. Ben's real dad is a dentist, which I think might have worked better: 'A giver of pain' you might say. Anyway, Ben claimed that while the book came from his life, it wasn't his life at all, so he couldn't go around using straight facts and claiming them as fiction. I can quite see that.

The kid does everything he can to make his dad's life miserable. I'll say something for Ben, he doesn't make out the kid to be the hero. Quite the opposite. He's a vile little piece, a lot nastier than his dad could ever be. He starts playing around with his parents' lives. At first he does small things, sneaky stuff to make his dad look stupid. Soon, it gets so his mum calls him stupid out loud, not just in the privacy of her own thoughts. Her contempt grows as fast as the dad's bewilderment. Then the kid starts planting all sorts of ideas in his mother's head, about how undervalued she is and how his dad just uses her as a sort of domestic slave. He makes her see everybody, not just his dad, in a new way. Then there's the neighbour, Mrs Thomas, Doreen she's called, who was his mum's best friend until the kid starts working his nastiness on them. The friendship crumbles away until it's just a tiny bit of rock on which the two of them can't stand comfortably together. In the end, the kid convinces his mum that his dad's having an affair with Doreen, so his mum packs her bags and off she goes, leaving her sad, bewildered husband behind. He isn't having an affair with Doreen, of course. Never was.

Ben's mum did go off in true life. True life. That was one of Beattie's expressions. I don't know how Ben's father felt about that. He never talks about him.

When I asked Ben about the book, he went off into a long-winded explanation of how it was his psyche dealing with his own feelings of helplessness as he watched his parents' dead-end marriage and the ruinous effect it had on his mother. It was Ben who encouraged her to leave. 'Best thing I ever did,' he says. According to Ben, his dad's the coldest man around. 'Nobody could reach him, he never let you close. I made myself active in the story,' he said, 'and that way I got rid of the anger.'

When the book was published, Ben gave lots of interviews to that effect. The newspapers were over Ben's dad like a rash, camping outside his house, taking his picture, desperate to get quotes on how he felt about his brilliant son's success. I thought he was remarkably sanguine, all things considered.

I don't think Ben has, though. I don't think he has got rid of his anger. When he talks about writing, he goes red in the face as if he's been sitting too close to the fire. Very fair skin does that, of course. His voice gets fractionally too loud, too. According to him, writing is a purely selfish act, which is a convenient way of saying that the artist has a right to plunder life in any way he chooses.

He's right, of course. Life is the primary source. There just isn't any substitute. Even the imagination feeds on reality, distorts it and convolutes it until it's unrecognisable from its raw form. But still it's there. The essence of all things is life itself.

But you wouldn't take a life in return for a book.

Would you?

When I get home, I discover a message from Barbara on the answer machine. She would like to meet as soon as possible. 'I have something for you,' she says.

Her voice sounds strained, as if she's been swallowing secrets.

Nineteen

We meet in Peter Jones, in the café at the top of the building. Barbara is there when I arrive, sitting calmly on an orange plastic chair with a pot of tea, two cups and a round of cucumber sandwiches on the table in front of her. 'I didn't know if you'd be hungry,' she says, 'so I got these just in case. Eleven thirty is such an in-between time, neither breakfast nor lunch.' She is used to feeding people.

I sit down and wait in silence as she rearranges the crockery on the table, pushing it away from my side as if to make space for me. After a while she says, 'Do you take milk or lemon? I wasn't sure so I got both.'

'Milk, please.'

She pours milk and tea, her movements quick and deft. Everything about Barbara is so neat it's as if she's been stamped out of a piece of shiny white paper. 'Have you ever noticed how a slice of lemon turns tea paler?' she says, peering into the cup. 'Now why do you suppose that is? Some chemical perhaps?' She appears relaxed but she is talking too much and her expression when she looks at me is bright, as if she's slid a protective coating over her true feelings. I wonder what it is she's hiding. After she's poured a cup of tea for me and taken a sip from her own, she picks up a hefty brown manila envelope and passes it across the table. 'This is for you.'

'For me?' I say stupidly, although my name is written out on the brown paper in large, rounded letters.

Barbara says, 'She was most insistent that I deliver it to you in person. I'm sorry it's taken me rather a time but what with half-term and Johnny starting at a new school, everything's been rather hectic recently. Anyway, a couple of weeks aren't going to make a difference.' She pauses, says briskly, 'Well, not to Rebecca, at any rate.'

I have the impression that I am underwater. Sound seems to take a long time to reach me. When I find my voice, the volume swims in and out of focus. 'Did you say Rebecca?'

'Yes.' Barbara sips at her tea, making tiny blowing sounds because it is too hot. 'She told me that if anything were to happen to her, then this must go straight to you.'

The envelope is cold and heavy on my lap. I say in bewilderment, 'I didn't even know you two were friends.'

'We met at Margaret's when I came to collect Rosie who'd been playing with Beattie. Anyway, Rebecca was there and we just got talking.' She looks at me, her gaze direct. Her eyes are a dark, uncomplicated brown. 'I liked her.'

So Rebecca did have a friend. I wonder if Ben knows.

'She came over for tea, then she started to visit quite often, maybe once or twice a week in the past year.'

After Beattie died, I thought. After I took her husband from her.

Barbara picks up a cucumber sandwich and takes neat bites out of an edge. 'Not enough butter,' she says, frowning in disapproval. 'Actually, I think she was lonely, with Ben at work all day. And she enjoyed being with the children. She liked to go and meet them from school.'

I stare down at the envelope. I see then that my name is written in Rebecca's clear, childish hand. 'Do you know what's in here?'

'Poems. Hundreds of them.' She abandons the half-eaten cucumber sandwich. The rounded, even bites are half-moons, edging the bread like scalloped embroidery. 'Every poem she's ever written.'

Pulling open the flap of the envelope, I peer inside. All I

can see is a thick sheaf of paper. 'These can't be for me. There must be some mistake.'

Barbara frowns. 'No mistake. If you look, you'll see there's a letter addressed to you.'

Fishing my hand into the dark interior, I pull out a long white envelope. 'Jane Rose' is written in thick black ink. I don't open it. 'When did she give the poems to you?'

'She gave me a whole batch about a year ago, then brought them to me as she wrote them.'

I say quietly, 'Do you know why?'

'I understand that Ben didn't like her to write. She seemed to think it was best that he didn't know.'

Her face is a studious blank. I see that she knows more about Rebecca's relationship with Ben than she is letting on. I imagine Rebecca sitting writing after Ben left for work in the morning, or filling the long evenings when he was with me. 'But the letter? When did she give you that?'

'Months ago, soon after you –' Barbara fiddles with a teaspoon. 'Soon after that incident with Rosie. Rebecca was very affected by Beattie's death. Well, we all were, particularly Alan.' She gives me a quick, embarrassed glance. 'I know he doesn't say so, but he does desperately mind.'

Grief is such a selfish emotion. I never think about Alan or how he must be feeling. 'I'm sorry.'

'Oh, well, he's much better now,' Barbara says, as though he's recovered from a nasty bout of flu. 'Much more his old self. It was you we were worried about. Rebecca kept saying that we should do something. We wanted to help but none of us quite knew how.' Her smile reveals small, even white teeth. 'So in the usual way, we did nothing. Anyway, soon after that Rebecca gave me the letter and told me to keep it with the poems. I was to give them to you if anything happened to her.'

I think of the other letter that Rebecca left when she died. 'Did you believe she would kill herself?'

Barbara sighs. 'I still can't believe it, even now. But I don't think it was anything specific, if that's what you mean. Rebecca found the world unbearably uncomfortable, she couldn't seem to find her right place in it. She once told me the only person who would truly understand was you. It was something to do with feeling you don't belong anywhere?' She looks at me questioningly.

I nod, although I say nothing.

'She tried to explain it to me but I'm afraid I wasn't much help. I know my place in the world only too intimately.'

I imagine Rebecca, sitting in Barbara's sunny kitchen, soothed by the ebb and flow of daily life and Barbara's brisk certainty.

'Did she say what she wanted me to do with the poems?'

'Publish them. And protect them, of course.' Her tone is brisk but she reveals her feelings with a quick sideways glance.

Of course. Protect them from Ben.

'I see.'

Barbara is gathering up her handbag and a clutch of plastic carrier bags. 'School uniform,' she says with a grimace. 'The children grow like weeds, in seasonal bursts. It's just unfortunate they don't hibernate in the winter.'

I wait for her to falter, remembering that I no longer have a child to buy school uniform for, but she doesn't, just chatters on about how they're growing and the prize Rosie won for spelling. I find myself smiling. It's a long time since somebody treated me as if I were normal. 'Now I really must go,' she says, dropping a kiss on my cheek. 'Do let me know about the poems. I'm longing to read them in published form. Oh, and Alan sends his love.'

I watch her neat navy back until it is swallowed up in the crowded store. Rebecca may have put the poems into my care, but Barbara is their guardian angel. She will not rest until they are published.

I carry the heavy envelope home carefully on the Tube, clutching it to my breast like a baby. A man jogs me. My arms tighten in alarm. If the poems were to be lost or damaged, they would be gone forever. Like my child. The responsibility brings me out in a hot flush. I feel my cheeks burn with it. Why did Rebecca choose me? Why not Ben? But I know the answer to that already.

When, at last, I am home, I carefully unseal the flap of the envelope and pull out a thick sheaf of paper. It is divided into sections, each marked with a piece of coloured paper. There are hundreds of poems, years of work.

I open the letter.

Dear Jane,

I am entrusting these poems to your care.

As you can see, I have divided them into three volumes.

Each volume is dedicated to Beattie Rose.

When they are published, the dedication must be used on each volume and continued in perpetuity.

I have made you the executor of my literary estate and have lodged a letter with my solicitor to that effect. The decision cannot be contested. The various drafts of all the poems and my notebooks are also with my solicitor, should they be of interest in the future.

Thank you for looking after them for me,

Rebecca.

The words are carefully drawn, evenly spaced as if this is the final draft of a letter she has composed many times until she was satisfied with it. The only mention of Ben is implicit. The decision cannot be contested. He will try, I know.

The name and number of the solicitor are carefully written out on a separate sheet of paper. I call and make an appointment for early the next morning. Then I settle down with the poems.

I sit and read all afternoon, and into the evening.

Some of them are about Beattie. Some are about Rebecca's unborn children. Some are about love. Many are about death.

None of them is about Ben, unless you count the ones about love, but I recognise nothing of Ben in them. It is as if he never existed in Rebecca's life.

After I have finished reading, I pack them away and call George. If there's a better woman to publish these, I don't know her.

The next morning I take a taxi to the solicitor's office. It is in Lincoln's Inn Fields and I enter the building, reassured by the air of solid respectability. I am to meet a Mrs Johnson.

She is in her forties with a quick, intelligent face and a mass of auburn hair threaded with grey. Her name is Mary. 'Miss Carter said you might be surprised, shocked even, by her request.' I am surprised, but more by the use of Rebecca's maiden name. It is as if she has dissociated herself completely from Ben. Mary Johnson's eyebrows quirk in a frown. 'Are you?'

'I was, but I can understand her reasons.'

'Miss Carter appeared to think that her husband would attempt to contest the decision.'

'Yes, I believe he will.'

'And how do you feel about that?'

'I would rather he didn't know.'

'And if he were to find out?'

'He would probably kill me.'

It is a colloquialism. Of course. Mary Johnson regards me in silence for a moment. 'Well, in that case we must do everything we can to avoid him knowing. All the business of the estate will have to be directed through this office, of course. In that way we can guarantee complete anonymity.'

'Good.'

'It will mean quite hefty legal fees.'

'I can manage.'

We finish the legal business of signing forms and letters, and I get up to go. I say that there is only one person who will know my identity.

'Is that wise?'

'She is the only person I would trust to publish them in the way that Rebecca would want. Have you read the poems?'

Mary Johnson's quick, clever face softens in a wide smile. 'Oh, yes.'

I take a taxi home and collect the envelope of poems, which I have hidden under the mattress in Beattie's room for safe-keeping. Ben never goes into that room. He says it gives him the creeps.

Then I go to the print shop and have two sets of copies made, sealing each set inside a heavy brown envelope. The originals I take to the bank and lodge in a safety deposit box. I fill out forms in triplicate and depart, clutching a small silver key.

I consider leaving one set of copies with Margaret but decide that it is the first place Ben will look, so I call Richard and ask him to meet me for lunch. Carrying two sets of copies, I set off for my appointment with George.

'Where did you get them?' George peers at me through steel bifocals.

'She left them with Barbara, Alan's wife, to give to me. There's a letter, making me literary executor.'

'I see. Does Ben know about this?'

'No, and he must never know. Nobody must. Let him believe that Rebecca sent them to you herself, before she died.'

'As her husband, he will claim her estate.'

'He can't. It's in her will. I went to see her solicitor this morning. Nor am I named. Everything is to be done through her solicitors in order to protect my identity. You're the only person, other than Barbara of course, who knows. And she won't say anything. She gave Rebecca her word.'

'She must have trusted you a great deal. I had no idea she was so fond of you.'

'It was not me she was fond of. All the poems are dedicated to Beattie. I am merely her protector.'

George is silent for a while. 'In that case she understood you very well,' she says, after a while.

'Yes,' I say sadly. 'It seems that she did.' She understood Ben even better. She knew he would destroy the poems, just as she knew I would protect them. It was a risk, leaving them to me. What if I had given them to Ben or destroyed them myself, out of jealousy? How could she know that I wouldn't?

George is saying, 'Now, do you mind if I have a read, just to get the sense of them?'

I return to my musings. Perhaps Rebecca believed that Ben would contest the will and discover she had left the poems to me. He would be furious, of course. That knowledge would destroy our relationship faster than anything. Is this what she wanted?

Somehow I don't believe so, although I have no reason to think otherwise. Rebecca understood that I know Ben as well as she did, the dark side of his nature, his obsessive need to control. She knew I would protect the innocence of

224

her art, as passionately as I had longed to protect my innocent child. And failed. I will not fail again. Perhaps Rebecca instinctively knew that I yearn for a second chance. Dedicating the poems to Beattie was a masterstroke, of course. She knew I would allow nothing destructive to happen in her name. And she loved Beattie. I see that now. At the time, jealousy blinded me to any genuine feeling on Rebecca's part.

Why didn't she leave Ben? I know the answer to that even as I say it. She was too weak, too powerless in his presence. Perhaps she believed I have the strength to escape and this is her way of helping, of throwing a lifeline to anchor me to a better place. Only Rebecca truly understood the dark night of Ben's soul.

George reads silently, her fingers drumming on the desk. I recognise the sign from long ago, when we worked together. If a book was good, or even just showed promise, she would begin to fidget, rhythmically pushing up the sleeves of her cotton blouse as if her fingers itched to get down to business. George discovered a fair number of new authors in that way. Well, she discovered at least two a year, which is a fair number indeed.

'How many poems are there?'

'Three hundred, but a good percentage of those are rough. The rest are divided into three volumes, each with a title and a dedication.'

'These are copies, I take it?'

'The originals are in a bank.'

'Good. Well, I'll see what I can do.'

It is a formality. We both know what she can do.

As I leave, George calls out to me, 'Thank you for bringing these to me.'

The offices where Richard works are in a Georgian house near to the British Museum. The reception is a tall, thin block chopped out of the original drawing-room. A woman with thick glasses and a wide centre parting in her brown hair regards me with a bored expression. There's a poster for a Picasso exhibition framed behind her head. You'd think, with the prices they charge in these places, that they could afford a bit of decent art. She tells me to take a seat.

I go and sit in one of the upright wooden chairs with mock leather seats and backs lined up against a wall like a railway carriage. The woman and I stare at each other in silence. 'He'll be down shortly,' she says and turns back to her magazine.

I've hardly had time to pick up a newspaper before Richard comes bounding down the stairs, taking them two at a time. He lands in front of me, rumpled and out of breath. 'I was so pleased when you called,' he says, his hands outstretched. I go to take them but only manage one, what with the newspaper being in the way and the heavy envelope of poems in my lap pinning me to the chair. We end in a flurry of awkwardness. It takes us a few minutes to sort ourselves out and when, finally, I'm standing, I want to take his hand back in mine but don't, conscious of the women's curious stare. We shuffle in the narrow hallway, grinning like idiots, until Richard says, 'Come on, I've booked a table round the corner.'

The day is benevolent, shimmering with the promise, at last, of summer. I want to take Richard's arm but it's awkward with the parcel I'm carrying and anyway, I suddenly feel shy with him so I content myself with walking too close, my arm pressed to his as we stroll along the crowded pavements. I glance up at him. He is smiling. The worn fabric on the shoulders of his suit glitters in the sunshine. It makes me feel fonder of him than ever.

'In here,' he says, taking my arm and steering me into a small Italian restaurant. We crowd together in the entrance as we wait for somebody to notice us. I'm standing a bit in front of him but a group of people come in behind and jostle us closer together so his body moves warm against my back. Just for a moment I think I feel his mouth against my hair but I can't swear to it, because right then a waiter tells us our table is ready and we are marched over to the far corner of the room.

I can't get over how pleased I am just to look at his face.

We order a glass of wine each, and some pasta and salad, then I tell him that I need a favour. His eye droops for a moment and I realise how disappointed I have made him feel, as if the sole reason I want to see him is for a favour. 'You're the only person I can trust.'

'Surely not,' he says, but I can tell he's pleased.

I pick up the heavy envelope. 'I need you to put this somewhere safe and keep it for me.'

'What is it?'

'Please don't ask me that because I can't tell you.'

'You're a mysterious woman.' He smiles as he says it but I can see disappointment in his face. It is always disappointing not to be trusted. For the first time, I regret my secretive nature. I think how good it would be to have my whole life laid out before this man, all the peaks and dark valleys of it stretching out before his kind, forgiving gaze. When I fell in the darkness he'd know just where to reach out his hand to find me and pull me up again.

'I wish I could tell you,' I say. 'Truly I do but I made a promise.'

'Well, then you must keep it.' His voice sounds heavy. He doesn't like secrets between us any more than I do. 'I just hope it's a good promise.'

I puzzle over this for a moment. Are there bad promises? Why, yes, I suppose there are, although a promise always sounds as if it should be a good thing. But perhaps that's just because the breaking of them is considered bad. Good and bad. Black and white. Night and day. Things never work out like that, of course.

There's grey and off-white, there's dawn and dusk and there's dark, rain-filled days.

Then I think of Rebecca's poems, of what Ben would have done with them had she left them unattended in the house. 'Yes,' I say. 'It's a good promise.'

Richard takes my hand. 'Will you come to Paris with me?'

I couldn't have been more surprised if the flowers on the table had sat up and sung.

Twenty

By the weekend the news of Rebecca's poems is all around town. George had the great good sense to call Ben as soon as they decided to publish, spinning him a line about the manuscript suddenly appearing on her desk, delivered via her solicitor.

Then she called me, knowing I'd be worried. 'I gave nothing away. He was a little difficult at first but nothing to be concerned about.'

This is George at her tactful best. Ben has a reputation for being impossible. I used to say in his defence that it was only that he speaks his mind. I suppose you could say it's taken me a while to realise that his is the only mind he's interested in, which doesn't seem quite right for a writer. Not that Ben's alone in that. There are plenty more where he comes from.

'He claimed it was his idea all along. Then, of course, he realised that the publicity over Rebecca's lost poems will do him nothing but good when his own book is published.'

Of course.

I am not surprised to find Ben sitting in my kitchen when I get back from doing the Saturday morning shopping. Not that I need to these days. It's just something I enjoy – pretending I'm one of the regular people.

I've hardly got through the door, weighed down by four bulging plastic carriers, before he's scooping me up in his arms and saying, 'I realise I've been neglecting you.' I let the shopping bags go, they're so heavy they're almost touching the floor anyway, and stand with my arms stiff at my sides as he kisses me. He pulls his head back, stares into my eyes. That blue compelling gaze of his. 'I'm sorry. It's the book,' he says, letting me go. 'It's possessing me.' Writers never bother with more elaborate excuses. The book is sacred. Everybody knows that. It's written all over Ben, the way he stands, so arrogant and sure, or strides around the kitchen. He flings himself into a chair, legs thrust out so they're right in my way. 'It takes up all my time.' He pushes the hair out of his eyes, smiles up at me. 'Forgive me?'

'Of course.'

There are times when he likes my independence. He dislikes it only when it doesn't suit him. Once he's finished the book and finds me gone, that's when he'll mind. Will I be gone? I hope so but even thinking the thought, having it in my head, scares me. I discover I am still standing where he left me, arms rigid to my sides like a sentry. I shake the tension from my limbs, move across the room to put the kettle on, stepping over shopping bags and legs.

'I'm glad it's going so well,' I say. 'Would you like tea? Or coffee perhaps.'

'Tea.' No please, or anything. No, I'm sorry if I'm disturbing you. He acts like he owns the place. What's got into me? I don't know. I feel as if I'm seeing him through somebody else's eyes. Rebecca's perhaps. How did she see him? She always seemed so adoring, besotted even. But then there's the matter of the poems. The way she wrote them in hiding and left them to me. Then there are the poems themselves. There's loathing in there as well as love.

'My time's been taken up with something else too,' Ben says. I look down at him. His eyes are closed as if he's in some sort of pain. I know that expression. It's the one that

makes women drop to their knees to soothe away the hurt.
I've seen Rebecca do it. Me too.

I wait.

His eyes open, his hands come up to his face, push away
the hair in an expression of rueful defeat. 'It's Rebecca.'

The name hangs in the silent kitchen.

'Rebecca?' I turn away from him so he won't see my
face. I feel his gaze fixed on my back.

'I'm sorry. I know she's the last person you want to talk
about but this is the last time we'll have to, I promise. Then
it'll just be you and me.'

I busy myself unpacking the shopping. 'What's happened?'

'A manuscript of her poems has turned up at Allen
Marshall Goodheart. Three volumes in all.'

'I see,' I say stiffly. 'Well, I'm very pleased for you.'

'No, you're not, you're furious and I can't say I blame
you. The last thing either of us wants is Rebecca coming
back into our lives. I wouldn't have told you except that
this does, in some way, concern you too.'

I look at him then, full in the face. 'How?'

'The poems are dedicated to Beattie.'

My eyes fill with tears. Sometimes even the mention of
Beattie's name can do that to me.

Ben's on his feet, his arms round me. 'Shh. I'm sorry, I'm
sorry.'

I move away, pluck a bunch of tissues from the box I
keep on the window-sill. It's a habit I started when Beattie
was small. It's extraordinary how many tissues a child can
get through. 'Why?' I say. I really am upset now.

'All I know is that she was incredibly distressed by
Beattie's death. I didn't realise how distressed until I heard
about the dedication.'

'You never mentioned it before.'

'Oh, for God's sake, Janey. What am I supposed to say?

That my wife is mourning my lover's dead child? How weird is that going to sound, especially to you?'

Blowing my nose I say, 'A child's death affects everyone and Rebecca desperately wanted children, didn't she?'

Ben slumps down in a chair, an arm across his eyes. He scrubs at his face in exasperation. 'She knew she couldn't have them but she just carried on as if one day, she would. It was pure fantasy,' he says bitterly. 'A place she rarely left.'

'I thought you said she never fucked you.'

His eyes are brilliant blue. 'Do we have to go into that now?'

'I just don't see how she could believe she could have a child if she wouldn't fuck.'

Ben closes his eyes. 'She would only fuck at the right time of the month. The rest of the time she refused. She didn't give a toss about me, or how I might feel about that.'

'Did you want children?'

'God, no.' The answer's out before he realises it. He says quickly, 'I mean, not with Rebecca in that state. How the hell was she going to look after them?'

'You once told me you wanted to be a mother.'

He looks at me in disbelief. 'Did I?'

'You said you wanted to be connected.' It was one of the things that had charmed me about him, all those years ago.

'Oh, *connected*, yes. Everybody wants that.'

I had it all wrong. I have so much about Ben wrong. When he came to see me when Beattie was a tiny baby, I thought it was because he empathised, took genuine delight in a new life. But I see now that all he was doing was weaving a picture around himself, leaching away our emotion to pass off as his own. Beattie and I had nothing to do with it. It was just a sentimental notion; just words.

'Do you want more children? Is that was this is all about?' His voice is hard. It comes out as an accusation.

I realise then that Ben and I could never have children together. We could never make that step into the real world. Our passion for each other is both simple and claustrophobic. There is no room in it for anyone else.

Ben says, 'Janey, we don't need anybody else. Not when we have each other.'

I smile at the sheer predictability of him. 'No.' Let him figure out what that means. 'Did you know about Rebecca's poems?'

'Well of course I did. It was me who encouraged her to keep writing.'

I say nothing.

'I've been searching for them since she died. Turns out she lodged them with her solicitor. I should have realised, of course. I kept telling her to put them somewhere safe. They sent them straight to George, on Rebecca's instructions. I was pissed off they hadn't sent them to me first but they had to act on her instructions. That's Rebecca for you, neurotic to the end.'

'Are they good poems?'

Ben smiles, gets to his feet. 'That's enough about Rebecca. Let's pretend she never existed.' He holds out a hand. 'Come to bed. I've missed you.'

Let's pretend. The story of my life. I'm as bad in my own way as Ben is. Perhaps we deserve each other.

On Monday morning I start two weeks' work on one of the big women's monthlies. I'm taking over from Vicki, a sub-editor, who's on holiday.

'We're so pleased you've agreed to help us out. I can't tell you how desperate I was feeling.' That's what Tessa, the chief-sub, says when I show up at her desk. A big-boned woman with a settled expression, there's no air of desperation about her unless you count the raw red ridge on the bridge of her nose that comes from her habit of banging her glasses back in place when she's under pressure. Which, I discover later, is most of the time. It is June, the time when magazines are preparing their huge autumn issues. 'If only people would take their holidays in the autumn when we're working on the January issue. It's so tiny, I could turn out the whole thing single-handed.' She has the look about her of a woman telling the truth.

Tessa tells me to sit in Vicki's place, then gets distracted by a production schedule and forgets about me completely. So engrossed is she that she never quite manages to sit down properly and spills over the desk, her bitten fingers hovering over columns of dates and figures. I rearrange the few pens on the desk, clear away balls of crumpled paper, then grab a paper off the stack delivered that morning. That's the good part about working in a magazine office: you get all the newspapers for free.

I flick idly through the pages, loiter over a story about a woman who'd discovered her long-lost twin forty years later. Didn't even know she had one but, wouldn't you believe it, they're identical right down to the fat-sausage perm of their hair.

When I see the photograph on the top of the facing page it takes me a while to register the shock of familiarity. Like seeing your own face reflected in a shop window when you least expect it. Except that this is not my face. It is Rebecca, her hair loose around her shoulders, her wrists tied with black satin ribbons. DEAD POET'S LEGACY, says the headline. Suspended below it, in the centre column, is a blurry postage-stamp photograph of Ben. There's only one word beneath it, *Distraught*. He's not going to like that, being upstaged by his dead wife. He's grabbed all the copy, though. There's quote after quote from Ben. The story's a gift to a journalist, of course, and this one can't disguise her glee in unwrapping it. The two were *inseparable*. Rebecca was a *famous beauty*. The recently discovered poems are *remarkable*. Ben is *distraught with grief*. Not so distraught that he forgets to give his book a healthy plug.

A tribute to his wife, a fictionalised account of their life together, her huge talent, their passionate love and the terrible legacy of her suicide.

I can bear no more and stop reading. The subs desk is filling up. There's Jeremy, long and pale as a bean sprout, who gives me a shy smile, then ducks his head, blushing, so he doesn't see how I smile back. Next to him sits Evie, who's got so many studs in her she looks like a walking hardware store. There's two in her nose, one in her eyebrow, six in each ear, running in a glittery curve from the crinkly bit at top of the ear right down the soft pink lobes. She must weigh sixteen stone. The lightest thing about her is her voice. 'Pleased to meet you,' she whispers.

Across from Evie is Heather who's small and studious-looking. Her thick black hair is cut short as a boy's, clipped high at the nape of the neck and in a wide band around the ears so the pale skin of her scalp shows through. Her passion is football. She wants to work on the sports desk of a national newspaper but complains that nobody takes her seriously. Tom, her boyfriend, writes and edits the Manchester United fanzine ('the unofficial publication,' says Heather proudly. 'Otherwise he couldn't tell the truth.'). They spend all their money trailing the team round the country, even went to Europe by coach. It took thirty-six hours and the man behind vomited all over the back of their green plush seats. 'The smell was something hideous,' says Heather.

Tessa hands me a stack of proofs, says they were needed yesterday. 'Last week, actually, but lunch-time would do. And don't take any notice of Eddy when he starts shouting. It just makes him feel better.'

Heather never draws breath, although her head is bent to a set of proofs and a neat trail of blue printer's symbols creeps down the column, following her pen like an invisible spider. Watching her gives me a giddy feeling, like seeing somebody patting their head and circling their stomach at the same time. Nobody else seems to notice. Perhaps it wears off after a time, like visiting a house next to a railway line where all the occupants say, 'Noise? What noise?'

Somebody goes out for coffee. 'Jane?' whispers Evie. 'Cappuccino?' I hand over the money. When Jeremy returns bearing white plastic cups of coffee, pale-brown liquid oozing from the lids, I dip my tongue in the sweet, chocolate-flecked foam and begin to relax into the rhythm of the place. It feels good to be out among people again, but the best thing about it is that I realise I haven't thought about Ben, or Rebecca, in hours.

A man sidles up to my desk and introduces himself. He has soft brown hair and one of those faces that look young until you get up close. This is the famous Eddy. 'Don't want to rush you,' he says, 'but any chance we'll see those proofs by lunch-time?' I say I don't think it'll be any problem and after he's gone Evie whispers that he only does this job to fund his habit. I arrange my face in an urbane, sophisticated way but it turns out that Evie's talking about Eddy's jazz habit. He's a genius with a trombone, plays lots of private parties and small esoteric clubs. He's even played Ronnie Scott's, says Evie, but he hasn't got a date this week so we're in for a quiet time. Heather says it's the late nights and the drinking that make him shout. She doesn't touch alcohol herself, not even beer. 'Well, it's ruined the game, hasn't it?' she says, her face taking on a dark, troubled look.

Jeremy doesn't speak, but every so often he pushes his supply of Maltesers across the desk at me; they're in the low flat box that you only ever seem to see in cinema foyers. I wonder if he's saved them from his last trip to the movies, or whether he has a secret source of supply. I take one, put it on my tongue and let it dissolve until it sticks to the roof of my mouth.

I finish the set of proofs, start on another batch.

'You're fast,' Tessa says, although she hardly glances up. Her pen moves methodically. Small white plastic cups of espressos gradually form a neat line in front of her.

After lunch the editor, Maggie, comes over to the table. 'These are fine,' she says, dumping a pile of proofs in front of Tessa. 'Have we got a headline for the Eating Disorders piece yet?'

'Jane's working on it,' Tessa says. 'She's standing in for Vicki for a couple of weeks.'

'Welcome,' Maggie says, but her smile skitters over me in a way that suggests she'd never be able to pick me out in a line-up. 'Who's in the profile slot for October?' Tessa names a young English actor, about to star in a major Hollywood movie. 'Move him to November, will you? I've got a bit of a coup for October but I need a tight deadline on it. Can we juggle the flat plan to move that section into late pages?'

Tessa bends obediently to the production schedule, her pen moving rapidly. 'If you're prepared to run it against facing pages with no double opener.'

'No can do,' Maggie says crisply. 'He's gorgeous. And he's got a great story.' She chucks a newspaper on the desk, folded to indicate the page. I glance over at it, feel a blush creeping up my cheeks and bend my head to my work.

Now, of course, she has everybody's attention. 'He's a writer but we mustn't hold that against him. Chap by the name of Ben Robinson. He wrote a best seller about five years ago, hailed as a major new talent, then he seemed to lose it altogether. Anyway, I had lunch with his publisher today. They've just signed him up on a major deal.'

I glance up to see Tessa looking faintly bored. 'So what's the story?'

'He was married to the poet, Rebecca Carter. You remember her, heart-breakingly beautiful. They were always in the papers together. It was the great literary love story. Anyway, she committed suicide three weeks ago. She'd tried twice before, apparently, but he'd always been able to rescue her. Anyway, this time she succeeded and he's devastated. This new book's a tribute to her, his way of coming to terms with the loss. Then, last week, a whole set of her unpublished poems turned up. I just found out at lunch today. Everybody's talking about them. They're being hailed as a literary masterpiece.' Maggie is almost rubbing her hands together in glee. 'It's irresistible.'

'Love and death,' Tessa supplies helpfully. She knows the stuff of which mass-circulation magazines are made.

'Precisely. And I want a box on the facing page. Facts, figures, help-lines, photographs of famous suicides ... He's agreed to an interview. The newspapers are all running with the story, of course, and *The Times* are doing a big feature, but Ben's agreed to give us the exclusive magazine interview.'

I start slightly at the familiar use of his name and my pen jerks. A thin line of red runs the length of a column. I move my hand across the paper to hide it, then take a pot of Tipp-Ex and paint out the red streak with tiny dots of white.

'Sue's working on a writer for the piece,' Maggie goes on, 'and the picture desk are checking availability on photographers. I want somebody really classy, the dreamy close-up, anguished writer as pin-up. You know the sort of thing.'

I bend back to my work. Maggie's high heels click gently on the industrial carpet as she walks away.

Tessa sighs and begins to write over her production schedule, which is already covered in thick cross-hatching and amendments. 'Three weeks,' she says. 'He must be really devastated if he's up for publicity already.'

'Maybe it's his way of dealing with it,' Evie whispers.

Tessa shoots her a look. 'Maybe.'

*

As soon as I leave the office I call Richard. I don't like to make personal calls on work time. Not until I've got some measure of the place.

The same bored receptionist answers the phone.

'You sound tired,' Richard says, when I get through.

'A bit. Can we meet for a drink?'

'Sure. Give me half an hour. Our usual place?'

'Our usual place.' The words sound so sweet on my tongue, I can almost taste them.

When I get there, Richard is sitting a table in the corner, two drinks lined up in front of him. His head is bent over the evening paper. I stand over him, my hand hovering just above the curve of his neck, where his hair curls over the collar. If I dropped my hands just two inches I'd feel the hair springing under my fingers, the warm heat of his skin rising to greet them.

Richard looks up. 'Is this him?' I follow the track of his finger across the black-and-white newsprint and see Ben and Rebecca smiling up at me. Above Rebecca's head is a dark halo left by the damp imprint of the bottom of a glass.

I sit down with a graceless clump. 'Yes, that's him.'

I can't get over how young Ben looks.

Richard looks over at me, his expression casual. He is trying not to make too much of it. 'It seemed such a coincidence.' His eyes scan the story beneath the photograph. 'No mention of you here.'

'Nobody knows about me.'

'Except Ben.' The name sounds ugly in his mouth. I want him to spit it out again.

'Except him.'

Richard is quiet for a time.

'It says here that they've discovered some of his wife's unpublished poems. She had left them with her solicitor, which suggests to me that she didn't want the husband to get his hands on them.'

I say nothing.

239

'The poems are dedicated to Beattie Rose. Nobody knows who she is and her husband refuses to say.'

Well, at least Ben's done that much for me.

Richard is watching me, his gaze careful. 'Jane, why are the poems dedicated to Beattie?'

'Rebecca was fond of her. I suppose she loved her. She couldn't have children of her own.' I shake my head. 'It's all so terribly complicated.'

'So you knew her?'

My voice is a whisper. 'Yes.'

Richard's voice is steady. 'Did you like her?'

'Not back then.'

'What changed your mind?'

Richard is so direct, so pure and uncomplicated. I feel grubby beside him. 'I began to see her through different eyes.'

He waits.

'My own,' I say, 'instead of Ben's.'

'The envelope you gave me the other day to keep safe. Were those her poems?'

'Yes.'

'Like Rebecca, you're also hiding them from Ben?'

Me and Rebecca. Both hiding from Ben. 'Stop it,' I say. 'Please stop it.'

Richard picks up my hand, kisses the cracked and dirty nails, presses his mouth to the palm. He never takes his eyes off my face as his tongue seeks out my skin, and I feel the tiny rasp of his teeth against my fingers. When he gives it back to me, with a sudden abrupt gesture, I feel the absence of it like a chill. I press my hand to my cheek, trapping the memory of his kiss. It feels cold.

'There's something badly wrong here,' he says, 'and very soon you're going to tell me all about it.'

'It's nearly over.'

He does not believe me. And nor do I.

Twenty-one

The next day at the magazine is uneventful. I slide into the routine just as if I have always been there. Even Heather's chatter feels familiar; I have learned to ignore it as the others do, punctuating a long pause as she draws breath with an interested sounding *oh*? or a guttural, inattentive grunt of assent. We take turns, play it as a team, coming in solo, as a duet or – sometimes – as a full chorus. The noise rising from our table is measured so carefully to the beat of Heather's chatter that people passing might take us for a voice percussion choir.

There is no mention of the feature on Ben and I wonder if it has been dropped, but as I am going out at lunch-time to get a sandwich, I notice a sheaf of press cuttings on Sue's desk. Ben smiles out at me, but it is not this that makes me pull up short but the sight of Rebecca. I am not familiar with the photograph and I notice how Rebecca is pushed to the background, her image shadowy and wavering. Her shoulders are slightly hunched, her lovely face caught in an uncertain smile and her gaze is fixed, not on the camera, but on the back of Ben's head. I stare at the photograph for a long time. Is this the real Rebecca, forever in Ben's shadow, pushed back into the background of his life? It is so at odds with the image I have of Rebecca in my mind – Ben's image, the one he gave me – that I find myself wondering which is the truer of the two. They say that photographs do not lie. I never thought that was true. To my mind, photography is the most deceitful of media.

'Are you an admirer?'

I jump, find Sue standing at my elbow. She touches me gently on the arm. 'Sorry, didn't mean to startle you. Maggie's mad about him,' she says, dumping a Diet Coke and a greaseproof package on the desk. 'Can't abide him myself. Mad as a snake. Don't think much of his work either.'

'You know him?'

'Vaguely. He was the year above me at Oxford. Thought he was God's gift.' She unwraps the package, chews noisily on a sandwich. 'I mean, look at the way he's elbowed his wife into the background like she was some sort of prop. She was the one with talent, if you ask me.'

I find my voice. 'Apparently the new poems are very good.'

Sue shrugs. 'Of course.'

Her eyes fix on me. I wait for her to fill the silence with words. She has secrets to tell. 'Friend of mine was her editor. Said she stopping writing, like that –' a crisp snap of fingers – 'made some feeble excuse but Janet always reckoned it was him. Jealous of her. Well, it's the old story, isn't it? All those women who fall for lesser talent, then end up washing their socks.'

She takes another bite of sandwich, examines the bitten part carefully. 'God knows what they put in these.' Turning back to the news cutting, she jabs a mayonnaise-covered finger on Ben's face, leaving a grey stain of grease. 'Anyway, that's the photograph I'm after using. Speaks volumes, particularly because our esteemed leader –' she jerks her head in the direction of Maggie's office '– wants a whitewash on this. Tragic hero, that sort of thing.' She peers down at Rebecca's face, her mouth working over the remains of the sandwich. 'Hers was the tragedy, that's what I reckon.'

I look over Sue's bent head at the watery image of Rebecca hunched in the shadows and wonder if that's how I appear when I'm with Ben. Or would appear, if anybody were to see us together. I wonder what it is he wants with me. I have no particular talent and no beauty to speak of. I have only one thing that Ben wants. Worship. I have worshipped Ben all my adult life. It is then that I see it all quite clearly. It was never Rebecca who wanted to be worshipped but Ben. I had it wrong all along. I remember again the time when I had pneumonia and she brought me flowers, how I said to her that I never thought of her at all and the way she recoiled as if I had struck her. It wasn't her need for adoration that made her flinch, it was my cruelty, following so closely in the footsteps of Ben's. It was always Ben's version of her that I saw. I never saw Rebecca at all.

Reaching out a finger I run it gently across her face.

'Beautiful, wasn't she?' Sue says, a note of longing in her voice. As I said, Rebecca's beauty got everybody that way. They couldn't resist her. They all wanted to make her their own.

'Yes,' I say, 'she was.'

When I get home, I am dog-tired, unused to being so much among people. Or perhaps it is the burdens of the secrets I am carrying. I shrug my shoulders as if to shake off the weight of them and stare up at the blank windows, thinking of Beattie as I always do when I get to the house. Home, I used to call it. *Home*. That's when Beattie was alive. No use thinking about such things. I try to empty my head of memories, the sound of her shout when she heard the bang of the front door, hurling herself down the stairs to greet me, her face incandescent with joy. It would not have lasted, I remind myself, staring up at the empty house. She would have grown and separated herself from me, as all children must. The flare of delight would have dimmed to a glimmer. I, at least, can still hold Beattie's face in my mind, unsullied by adolescent ill humour, innocent of my human frailty.

'Dreaming your days away,' says a voice.

I blink off my thoughts, turn to find Margaret emerging from the passageway that runs down to her flat. She is bearing a large tatty black vinyl handbag and a purposeful air. On her head is her favoured cherry-red velvet turban and her sparrow body is swathed in a black knitted cape with a frilled edge that has seen better days. Moths have pricked tiny holes in the fabric. The old white skin of her neck shines through like faint stars. It makes me smile to see her, as delighted with herself as a child. 'You're looking very sprauncy tonight.'

Margaret chuckles. 'Yes, I feel rather splendid. I'm going to a concert at the Wigmore Hall. An old friend called me this morning to say she had a spare ticket. Wasn't that kind.'

It is not a question. More an afterthought.

'Wonderfully.' I have neglected her recently. There was a time when I spent all my days with Margaret.

She settles her cape at a jaunty angle. 'Well, I must be off, dear. You know how unreliable the buses are these days.'

'I'll drive you.' I say it on the spur of the moment, half hoping that she'll refuse. When she does, I want to take her more than I want to do anything else. Funny how rejection gets you like that.

She sits bolt upright in the car, peering eagerly through the windscreen. Wisps of grey hair have freed themselves from the turban to float about her shoulders like moulting feathers. Her long, pointed nose darts forward like a beak, capturing the moment with quick, precise movements like an eager but shabby bird. 'Did you see that?' she exclaims, or 'Isn't that interesting?' but they are questions that demand no reply, signifying some deep, private pleasure. Sometimes Margaret behaves as if she's been in solitary for years, although she gets out and about as much as the next person. She is just one of those people for whom life is a source of constant – and mostly pleasurable – astonishment.

Soothed by her eager presence, I am unprepared when she swivels in her seat and fixes me with her bright bird's eyes. 'Now, who's this new young man you're seeing?'

There's no point trying to shrug it off. Nothing escapes Margaret. 'Richard.'

'I knew it.' Her expression is triumphant. 'You have the look about you of a person on the brink of something.'

'You don't mind?'

Her old hand reaches over, pats my arm. I stare down at the red knuckles. 'If you mean do I mind about Ben, then the answer is no. I know I'm besotted by my great-nephew but he can be difficult. Telling him might be a little unpleasant at first, but once he's got used to the idea he'll be perfectly fine. He's the sort of man that women like to devote themselves to.'

A little unpleasant. There's that English understatement again. Ben's face looms up, blocking out the London traffic. *I'm the only one who truly loves you.*

There is silence, broken only by the sound of Margaret bustling around in her seat, a streamer of black wool flashing across my eyes as she rearranges her cape. 'That didn't come out quite as I intended. What I mean is he won't be lonely for long so you don't need to worry. Anyway, he'll be holed up for months writing this absurd book he's set his heart on.'

'Absurd?'

'He'd be better advised to leave well alone.' Margaret's voice is crisp with disapproval and I think what an admirable headmistress she must have made. Even the most boisterous fifteen-year-old must have quailed under that tone. 'No good will come of it. But he won't be told.'

'What did you mean when you said it might be unpleasant to begin with?'

'He takes these things badly. Rebecca tried to leave him once. It was not a success.'

Sometimes I wonder what I have been doing for the past year. Walking underwater? Wearing a very tight cap that blocked my ears and shaded my eyes? How can I have got Rebecca so utterly wrong? I think hard, try to remember dates and places. All I see is Ben's face, blocking out all the rest of my life. 'When was this?' the words come out badly, as if my voice has not been used for a while. The feeling that I have been absent these past twelve months persists. I wonder if I have spoken at all, if I even exist. Perhaps I have become like Rebecca, a figure hunched in the shadows. I stare down at my hands on the steering wheel, the bones of my knuckles showing white.

Margaret says, 'Well, it must have been a year or so after they married. I don't exactly recall. It can't have been that long after they got together. It was before the miscarriage, certainly.'

'The miscarriage?'

'Why, yes, dear. She had three. Didn't you know? I had assumed Ben must have told you all this. You two have always been so close.'

I say nothing. There is nothing to say.

'After that, she couldn't seem to conceive at all but I told you all about the IVF treatment. Well, I believe I did.' She is looking at me doubtfully, a spasm of alarm in her eyes.

If there's one thing Margaret fears it is Alzheimer's so I say quickly, 'Yes, you told me all about that. I remember it distinctly.'

Margaret's face perks up. The alarm vanishes. 'I thought I had. Anyway, Ben wouldn't hear of it, just as he wouldn't hear of her leaving.'

'What did he do?'

'Well, nothing much.' Margaret sounds doubtful. 'Rebecca said it was as if she had been struck dumb. She

246

spoke and words came out of her mouth, but they made no sound.'

'She told you about it?'

'Why, yes. She came to me for help. I don't believe she had anywhere else to go.' Margaret's voice rises on a note of distress. 'There was very little I could do, of course. I couldn't intercede between her and Ben, so I just listened. It went on for weeks and then I suppose they were reconciled. I did mention it, *en passant*, to Ben but he dismissed it rather, said she'd just been going through a bad patch.'

I stop the car outside the Wigmore Hall. Margaret gazes at me anxiously. 'She was rather a neurotic creature, you know.'

I lean over and kiss her. 'I'm sure you did everything you possibly could.' The old face brightens. I get out of the car and go to help her out of the door, deliver her to her friend who is waiting by the entrance of the handsome red-brick building. The friend is stout and greying, packaged in a neat brown coat with a patterned silk scarf tied at her neck. Respectability hangs around her like scent. 'Here's my date,' she exclaims loudly, after introductions have been effected. 'All set?'

'All set,' says Margaret, then turns to me, a look almost of exasperation on her face. 'Really, these things are better left unsaid. It does no good to go over the past but as we've broken that most important rule, I'd like you to remember one thing. *You are not Rebecca.*'

I press my mouth to her cheek, soft as a week-old balloon. Margaret pats my shoulder. 'Thank you for the lift. It does one good to arrive by carriage.'

'Do come along, dear, or we shall miss the start,' says her friend, scooping Margaret into her path with a shooing motion of her hands until the tiny figure is swept before her like a leaf in the wind.

*

When I get home I pull out all my old recipe books.

I have decided to cook dinner for Richard. Nothing special. At least, that's what I tell myself. It doesn't do to make too much of something. That way, you are never disappointed. I want to make him something good, that will warm him. I don't bother to work out what this means.

I know already.

When I told Richard I was going to prepare a meal for him he said nothing, just smiled, but the pleasure in his face made my heart turn over. He is not a communicative man, he uses words as if they are valuable, doesn't shower them around in that spendthrift way Ben has. Richard's silences are like soothing blankets of comfort. With Ben, the silences are filled with movement, the unspoken words tumbling about like animals trapped in a sack.

When I'm with Richard my body yearns towards him, struggling for expression. There is an answering pull in him too, but he says nothing, just thrusts his hands deep in his trouser pockets, imprisoning them as if they are something unreliable that need containing. When we left the pub last night we parted in the street, turning from each other abruptly – as if there was some urgent business that we each needed to attend to. I hurried to the bus-stop, although there was no need, a bus in these parts is a frequent sighting and, at that time of night, usually empty.

I didn't hear him call until he was nearly upon me so, when I turned, I almost crashed into him, emerging from the gloom, heavy with intent.

When he spoke he gulped in the air, as if he couldn't get enough to push the words out of his mouth. The sky darkened around us. Thunder was on the way. Or perhaps it was just in my head. Thinking he was about to call the whole thing off, I bowed my head, unwilling to hear what he had to say. He took another gulp of air. 'There's something I forgot to tell you.'

'What?'

He was silent for a minute. 'This dinner you're going to cook. I don't like cheese. In fact, I really rather hate it.'

I came up smiling, his face close enough to mine to kiss. 'Well, I won't buy any, then.'

If he had touched me then, my legs would have collapsed under me. Maybe that would have been good. We could have fucked right there, on the pavement, in the middle of the queue.

'Good.'

The heat was overwhelming. I felt my cheeks redden with it. 'Is there anything else?'

For a moment he looked confused.

'That you don't like to eat?'

'Oh. No. Nothing else.'

A bus rumbled down the road, its lights appearing from the gloom until it loomed over us. I like buses at night, the snug, steamy warmth of them, that feeling of sailing high, cutting through the dark swell of the city like a ship moving through water.

'That's my bus.'

Our stillness was broken by the sudden commotion of activity as people stepped from the deck, others emerging from the shelter of dim hedges where they had been silently waiting. There's a sort of panic that affects people as they are about to board a bus. The everyday action takes on a sudden urgency. A woman pushed past me, elbows working, fingers scrabbling to gain purchase on the boarding handles, wound with greying plastic tape. I hung back until they were all safely aboard, then turned to say goodbye, the words snatched out of my mouth by the loud snort of the engine.

Richard's hand came up to my neck, the heat of it travelling down into my legs until they buckled under me as the bus jerked into motion, ripping his hand away. I hung on to the hand-rail, staring back into the night but all

I could see of his face was a white blur and the dark patches of his eyes and mouth.

Why do I feel as if I will never see him again?

Shaking the image from my head, I sit down to plan the food that Richard and I will eat together. Perhaps a lemon tart for pudding with a featherlight crust; lemons, eggs and sugar whisked to a pale yellow cloud of sweetness. Something light before that – a risotto, the soft oval grains of rice cut by the saltiness of parmesan. Oh, but he doesn't like cheese. Does that mean all cheese? Perhaps a roast then – chicken with its skin crisp and salty, filled with a stuffing of chanterelle mushrooms and spikes of rosemary. Some thin green beans to go with it, a salad to follow.

I go to bed, hover on the fuzzy edges of sleep, dreaming about food and Richard. I allow nothing else to intrude and fall asleep, my mind filled with sweetness.

Twenty-two

Early morning, on my way to work at the magazine, I catch the bus to Berwick Street Market where there is a butcher who stocks maize-fed chickens from France, plump and yellow as butter. It is a warm day, but the sun only struggles fitfully through the low grey clouds.

The bus is crowded. I climb up to the top deck, wedge myself into a seat towards the front. The conductor doesn't bother to make the long trek upstairs, perhaps conserving his energy for the day ahead, so the coins for my fare grow sticky in my hand. A man in the seat in front whistles tunelessly. The woman next to him, plump and elderly in a tight flowered dress, jerks her head irritably in his direction. He doesn't seem to notice or, at least, to pay any mind. You wouldn't have to if you were in the habit of inflicting that sort of noise on the world.

I get off at Oxford Street and thread my way through the market, past displays of vegetables and flowers, past luminous pink plastic brushes and sage-green sta-pressed pillowcases.

The butcher calls me *Madame*, which makes me feel serious and secure, as if I were somebody else altogether and not a woman preparing a meal for a new lover when she has not yet discarded the old. The irresponsibility of it thrills me. For the first time, oh, *ever*, I feel I am as entitled to a share of the richness of life as the next person. Carried away by this vision of myself, I order garlicky sausages studded with raisins of fat and a rack of lamb, each delicate rib crowned by a white paper fringe, like a row of party hats. 'Lovely,' I say gaily, as the butcher deftly rolls the meat into paper parcels and tucks them into a plastic carrier bag. I don't know when I'm going to eat them. Nor do I care. Sharing is an extravagance. A wonderful luxury denied me since Beattie left.

Ben and I rarely eat together. He is not interested in food, although he has strong views on it. Rebecca was a wonderful cook, but people who are afraid to eat often are. She cooked a meal once in Margaret's flat, invited me along. I went, I am ashamed to say.

Ben and I had just got together, so it was a chance to gaze at him, breathe the same air. The meal was delicious, although you would not have known it to hear Ben. Too much cream, too much spice, too fussed around. Rebecca deflated slowly, like a souffl left too long out of the oven but I was delighted by Ben's cruelty, thinking it showed how much he cared for me. Throughout the meal I would look up, find his eyes on me, shining with shared secrets. Looking back, I see that I was less his accomplice than his audience.

I wonder, now, how Rebecca could have stood it for so long.

Tessa and Jeremy are already at their desks, although it is still early. Jeremy gives me a shy smile, then ducks his head; Tessa flips a silent salute, her eyes never leaving the set of proofs she's working on. I carry the bag of meat to the small kitchen, set back behind the loos. It's scarcely more than a broom cupboard containing a sink, a kettle, a catering-sized box of tea-bags and a huge, rusting tin of instant coffee. Set under the sink is a small fridge. I open it to discover pots of diet yoghurt, an open carton of decaying cottage cheese and an assortment of half-used cardboard packs of milk. I push the meat to the back, hoping the garlic in the sausage will not infect everything with its smell.

Heather arrives, late and indignant. 'Some stupid bastard jumped in front of a train. *Chaos*. We were stuck outside Earls Court for half an hour. In this heat, too. I don't see why people can't be more considerate. Why kill yourself in rush hour. Why not wait until eleven when it's quiet?'

'I don't suppose you're thinking about other people if you're about to kill yourself,' Jeremy says. His cheeks dull to a painful red under the focus of three pairs of eyes. 'Or maybe they just slipped.'

'Oh God,' whispers Evie, shuddering.

'I don't believe in suicide,' Heather says, sliding into a chair.

Tessa looks interested. 'How can you not believe in something that exists?'

'I mean, I don't believe it should be an option,' Heather says crossly, 'giving up like that.'

'Oh, that –' Tessa says, losing interest.

'Despair isn't an option,' Jeremy says. There's something defiant in the set of his mouth. 'For some people it's a fact.'

Heather is scrabbling in her bag, still out of sorts from her journey. She doesn't look up at Jeremy. 'How would you know?'

'My brother chucked himself off a motorway bridge.' His mouth quivers, then settles. 'He was a manic depressive but my mum still thinks he slipped.'

Heather stares at him, appalled, her arm half submerged in her bag. 'I'm sorry,' she says on a little gulping sound.

Jeremy looks away. 'You talk too much.'

There is silence on our desk for the rest of the morning. Everyone tiptoes around Jeremy until he announces that he is going out to get coffee.

'Why didn't anybody tell me?' Heather asks tearfully.

'Nobody knew,' Tessa says briskly.

'But *Jeremy*. He looks so ordinary –'

'There's no such thing as ordinary. Everybody feels

different in some way.' Tessa's settled expression becomes almost fierce. 'For Christ's sake, we make a living out of it.'

We cast furtive glances at each other, wondering what secrets we have to tell, then Jeremy returns with the coffees and a semblance of normality is slowly restored.

Ben telephones in the afternoon. 'Somebody called Ben for you,' Evie says, handing me the receiver. Heather lifts the instrument so it will reach my desk more easily. We are all being unnaturally polite with each other.

'Hi,' I say, grateful that Ben didn't give his surname.

'I want to take you out to dinner to celebrate,' he says. 'Those poems of Rebecca's have upped the ante on my book considerably. The last offer was sixty thousand.'

In the circumstances, well done seems inappropriate so I say mildly, 'That's good.'

'Damn right it is. And I've just discovered that you're working on the magazine that's doing a profile on me. You can make sure they treat me kind.'

'I don't think you need to worry about that.'

'Have you told them about us?' There is an edge to his voice.

'Of course not.'

'Better not. Not while all this business with Rebecca is going on. I meant to say it before –' he pauses delicately.

I feel very tired suddenly. 'Don't worry about it.'

'Good girl. Now, where would you like to go tonight? Just name the place. No expense spared.'

'I can't, not tonight.'

Irritation surfaces in his voice. 'Why not?'

'I'm busy.'

'Doing what?' Just recently, Ben's voice has taken on a loud, bullying quality. Or maybe it was always there.

'Something to do with work.'

He sighs impatiently. 'Oh, very well. It'll have to be tomorrow, then.'

I say, 'I'll call you in the morning,' but he has already gone. I replace the receiver quietly.

I ask Tessa if I can leave a bit early.

'Having people round?' Heather says, when she sees the bulging carrier bag.

I am so much alone that I have forgotten the habit of people in offices of trying to share in other lives. 'Yes.'

'Cooking something nice?'

'Chicken.'

'I do a nice chicken casserole. We like to have something hot after a match. I cook it ahead, then just pop it in one of those foil containers to keep warm. Works a treat. Well, it's nice to have proper food when you're on the road. All those burgers and stuff get you down after a while.'

Jeremy's right. Heather talks too much.

'Goodbye,' I say. 'See you all tomorrow.'

I can see I have offended Heather by my silence, but I'm not in a mood to care. Another week and I'll be gone. I am good at leaving.

Richard says, 'Delicious smell.'

'It's only chicken.'

'Chicken', he says firmly, 'is my favourite.'

The way he says it gives me a lift of happiness. How easy I have become to please.

He hands me a yellow plastic carrier. 'I bought wine, red and white.' A faint awkwardness colours his voice. 'I didn't know which you preferred.'

His fingers touch mine as I take the bag and we start slightly, suddenly shy with each other. Richard clears his throat. 'It's a long time since somebody cooked for me.'

'Can you cook?' I ask. I am at the stage where everything about Richard interests me. It is a novel experience after Ben, who was always more alarming than interesting.

'As a matter of fact, I can. My wife says I am astonishingly competent.' His voice slides into awkwardness again. 'I mean, that's what she used to say.'

I try to imagine Richard when he was married, standing in the kitchen, a glass of wine in one hand, a chopping board piled with vegetables in the other. His wife would be sitting at the table, a drink in front of her, laughing as they discussed the events of the day. Dismayed, I realise I have imagined it too well. The thought makes me nauseous. 'Let's have a drink,' I say, leading him into the kitchen and producing a corkscrew.

I watch Richard's dark head bent over the bottle of wine. He pours two glasses. His hands are shaking slightly. I wonder if it is me that's making him shake, or something else.

'You're making me shake,' he says.

I hold up my hand and he lifts his to meet it, laying our fingers together, one by one. They tremble against each other, sending out tiny sparks of static. We quiver like leaves. 'My God,' Richard says, his voice filled with wonder.

That's when Ben walks in.

'I'm so sorry. I didn't expect to find anyone in. I just came to collect some books.' I can tell by his smile that he is lying.

Richard and I are standing side by side. Neither of us moves. Ben's eyes narrow above his smile. He expects me to step across the floor, stand next to him so that Richard becomes the intruder.

I stay where I am.

'Ben Robinson,' says Ben, moving forward, his hand outstretched to Richard. 'I'm delighted to meet you at last. Jane's told me so much about you.'

I see Richard's glance flick uncertainly to me and back to Ben. 'Richard Gardiner,' he says, taking Ben's hand.

Ben drops his hand, strides around the room as if

searching for something. 'Darling, do you know where I left those books? I could have sworn I put them on this table here yesterday morning.'

I say nothing. There are no books.

Ben smiles over at Richard. 'I'm so sorry. I know I'm interrupting. Janey said you were helping her out with some advice on something. I forget what.'

I say, 'Richard is a solicitor.'

If Ben is surprised, he conceals it well. Then, something sly tiptoes into his expression and settles itself comfortably. 'How very useful. We were saying only the other night that Jane ought to get some legal advice.'

Richard says nothing, just stares right through Ben as if he hasn't spoken. I could kiss him for that. I could kiss him. Full stop. Ben goes on talking but I'm so concentrated on the idea of kissing Richard I don't hear a word he says.

He brings me back, though. 'Have you told Richard about your mother yet, darling?'

'Oh, he doesn't want to hear all that old stuff,' I say, making my voice airy although my heart's thundering fit to burst. 'And those books that you're looking for are on the shelf over there.'

Ben does not move. 'I'm sure he does, darling.'

'I don't, actually,' Richard says politely. He moves across to the bookshelf, picks up a pile of books. 'Are these them? Interesting choice, I must say.'

Ben grabs the books, shoves them gracelessly in his black rucksack and holds out his hand to Richard. 'Pleasure to meet you.'

Richard takes the proffered hand but says nothing about pleasure. He doesn't say anything at all, an omission that somehow contrives to leave Ben stranded in the middle of the beige carpet.

He shuffles his feet. It's a long time since I saw him looking awkward. Forcing a smile, he says, 'Well, I won't disturb you any longer. I can see you have business to discuss. Bye, darling. I'll call you later.'

We gaze on him, silent but smiling, until the force of our smiles propels him from the room.

The front door bangs faintly.

'My God,' Richard says again.

Neither of us moves.

I begin to shake, this time from fear. I remember what Margaret told me about the time Rebecca tried to leave Ben. *Rebecca said it was as if she had been struck dumb. She spoke and words came out of her mouth, but they made no sound.*

Turning to Richard I say, 'I'm sorry.'

'He is rather alarming.'

'Yes. I know. I'm sorry, I should never have got you involved. Please don't feel you have to stay.'

'Do you want me to?'

Sweet Jesus.

'Yes.'

It's then that we start kissing. Sweet, sweet Jesus.

Twenty-three

Flowers begin to arrive at the magazine every day. Great, ostentatious, vulgar bunches. I am hounded by flowers. Stalked by scent. Every day the card is the same. *Love Always.* I slide it out of a white envelope and straight into my bag, pretending not to notice the curious stares.

The man who delivers the flowers does not look as if he enjoys his work. He has fat, pale cheeks and dun-brown threads of hair pulled tight across his greasy scalp, and wanders the corridors calling my name in a depressed voice. 'Flowers for Jane Rose,' he says mournfully, dumping the bunch in front of me, spraying orange lily pollen and stray leaves across pristine white paper proofs.

The extravagance of the floral tributes has turned me into something of a celebrity. Pens are stilled, conversations halt as they arrive, the most recent bunch so monumental it appears to be moving through the office unaided. Heather bunches her lips in a silent whistle. 'He must have raided the entire shop,' she says wonderingly.

'Whoever it is is certainly determined to make an impression,' says Tessa, when the fourth bunch arrives.

I take the first bunch home. The second I arrange in vases in the office. When there are no more vases, I give the flowers away. Heather takes the third bunch ('don't mind if I do') and Evie the fourth. 'Really? Are you sure? Well, I don't know what to say.' I don't know how she gets them home on the bus, they are almost the same size as her and Evie is a person of considerable bulk.

This is not the action of a sane man.

I can stand it no longer. I call Ben. 'Stop it. Please stop it.'
'I love you,' he says. 'It's just my way of showing it.'
'It's embarrassing me.'
'How can a bunch of flowers be embarrassing?'
'It's the extravagance. The surfeit.'
'Like my love for you,' he says cheerfully and puts
down the phone. He does not mention Richard. Nor do I.

It takes Richard a week to ask me about my mother. He is
round at my house. This time, I have put the chain on the
door. He says, 'What did Ben say about finding me here
the other night?'
'He didn't.' I do not mention the flowers or the notes.
Love always.
'He said nothing at all?' Richard looks startled.
'It's Ben's way of dealing with it.'
'I see. Have you told him anything about us?'
What is there to say? I met a man. I kissed him. I like
him very much. We have not been to bed together yet. We
will, though. Soon. The knowledge crackles between us
like static. I must tell Ben. I must. The familiar panic grips
me. What will he do? And what will I do without him?
Who will I be without Ben?
Richard is sitting on the sofa. I am standing by my desk,
over by the window. There is so much space between us.
The beige carpet looks like acres, stretching away from me
to Richard, who is a dot in the distance. I wrap my arms
around myself, feeling the cold. It is cold today. Summer
never seems to come. A tiny Richard shifts his head, looks
over at me, a frown tugging between his eyes. He smiles,
reaches out for a mug. His hand shakes, spilling tea.
'Shit.' We stare down at the brown stains, seeping into
the carpet. 'I'm sorry. I'll go and get a cloth.'
I move over to him quickly. 'No. It doesn't matter.' I
take his shaking hands in mine, hold them until the
trembling subsides. We lean back against the sofa, my

head on his shoulder. His hand moves across my arm, up and down, up and down, as if he is stroking a cat.

Richard says, 'What did Ben mean, the other night, about your mother? About needing legal advice?'

I am silent.

Richard glances down at my face and says, 'You don't have to tell me if you don't want to. It just seemed that he believes it gives him some sort of hold over you.'

He is asking too much. I want to push him away. 'And will it give you some sort of hold over me too?'

Out of the corner of my eye I see his face curve into a smile, a protection against the cruelty of my reply. But I feel the hurt leap in him, in the tightening of the muscles in his arm. His hand stops its stroking. After a while, it begins again. He says, 'It might. It depends what it is.'

'I killed my mother.'

Richard becomes very still. The air seems to crowd against us, the particles clogging to a solid mass. I can hear nothing, just the beat of blood in my ears. The only movement in the room is the hands of the clock on the mantelpiece. I count one, two.

'How?'

The air is moving again. I take a shuddering gulp. Only then do I realise that I have been holding my breath. 'I put a pillow over her face and held it down.'

'I take it she was ill.'

'Yes, very.'

My mother's legs were so wasted by illness they were scarcely more than twigs. She hadn't the strength to move when she was living. Facing death, she had the kick of a mule.

'It's still murder. I looked it up in the library.' I recite the sentence, which I have committed to heart. *Euthanasia. Illegal and not distinguishable from murder.*

Richard's hand tightens on my arm. He pushes it up and down in a long, slow, soothing movement. 'Technically, that's correct but it depends on the circumstances. What was the cause of death given on the death certificate?'

'Cancer.'

'Issued by the doctor who treated her?'

I nod.

'And he saw no reason to believe that she might have lived longer?'

He said he was surprised she hung on for so long. Those were the doctor's words exactly. Richard's face turns towards me and I realise I have not spoken. I try again. This time the words emerge and hang in the air, slowly revolving between us.

'Did she ask you to help her?'

I like the way he uses the word help.

'Yes.'

'And do you mind about that now?'

I consider this carefully. I have always assumed that I mind. You should mind about killing your own mother. You should mind about killing. Death seems an awful thing to hang over a person's head.

'I minded when my father was alive. He didn't want to let her go.'

'Did he know?'

I feel nausea rise at the thought and swallow hard.

Perhaps Richard mistakes this for tears for he says, 'I'm sorry. I'm asking too many questions. Bad habit.'

I shift away from him, reach out for my mug of tea. 'But useful for a solicitor.'

Richard does not smile. He hunches forward, his brow creased in a perplexed frown. 'I still don't really understand why Ben believes this gives him some sort of hold over you.'

I don't look at him. 'It binds us together, as secrets do. I've never told anyone else about it.'

'It doesn't seem so bad a secret.'

It used to. It felt like a terrible secret but it seems almost benign laid out under Richard's forgiving gaze.

Richard glances over at me. 'Is there something else?'

I think of Rebecca. An eye for an eye. A death for a death. I cannot tell Richard about Rebecca. Not simply because of some deep, residual loyalty to Ben but also because Richard is a deeply moral man. It would be unfair to burden him with such knowledge. I say, 'There is shared history. We go back a long way. It's . . . complicated.'

Richard sighs. 'All relationships are complicated.'

I think of his wife and Sam, and wonder if I can explain to him about Ben and me. I wonder if I can even explain it to myself.

'The real question', Richard is saying in a low voice, 'is whether there's any room amid all these complications for us.'

'*Yes*'.

The vehemence of my reply startles us both. Richard laughs. 'I think that's the answer I was looking for.' He leans forward, wraps me in his arms. 'Let's go to Paris and see what we find there, away from all this.' We still have not been to bed together. Thoughts of it rise through my mind like bubbles, bursting on the surface of consciousness in sharp, fizzing sounds. Richard stretches out his legs. *Pop, pop*. Richard puts his hand to his mouth. *Pop, pop, pop*.

Shy suddenly, I move away from him. 'Will you stay for dinner?'

That smile again. 'That would be nice.' *Pop, pop, pop, pop*.

'There are lamb chops. And frozen peas. And potatoes. I could mash them with butter and cream. Put some spring onions in them.' There's a stillness to his smile now, a concentrated quality as if he's listening beyond my words to some faint, distant sound. Help me out here, I think. For God's sake, help me out. 'Or there's some spaghetti, if you prefer. I think there's a jar of pesto somewhere. Margaret made it. She grows basil every year. We could have it with a green salad, some good olive oil. No cheese, I promise.' I am talking too much. I can think of no other way of expressing this urgent physical need.

Richard holds out his hand. 'Shall we go to bed now?'

'Yes, please.'

It is my last day at the magazine.

The article about Ben arrives in a brown manila envelope marked 'Urgent'.

A bunch of flowers appears. *Love Always*.

I put them on the floor, under my desk.

Heather eyes them. 'Aren't you going to put those in water?'

'No.'

'Suit yourself,' she says, shrugging.

'I'll do it for you,' Evie whispers and bears them off to the kitchen, cradling them gently in her arms. When she comes back she says, 'I put them in the art department. They never get flowers in there, poor things.'

An inferno of delphiniums and orange tiger lilies towers over a blown-up photograph of Ben and Rebecca. Another, of Rebecca looking luminous, lies on the desk next to it. She stares up at the ceiling with wide, lovely eyes as a young assistant, Mark, picks up a scalpel and slices off a wide border of paper just above her head. He turns the photograph round and round, trying to get it to fit to layout. 'She's a blinder,' he says, smoothing a thumb gently over Rebecca's golden hair. *Mummy, there's a lady with fairy hair in the house*.

'She isn't any longer. She topped herself,' somebody says.

Mark looks startled. 'Silly mare,' he says, but his voice is gentle. He turns back to the photograph, the blade of the knife flashing as he reduces Rebecca's face to fit the page.

She gazes back, blindly lovely, as he steps back, checking his work. 'Shame,' he says.

I go back to my desk, finish tidying up some copy, keeping an eye on Tessa's in-tray.

'May I read it?' I ask, when the interview with Ben is sent through from Maggie for marking up.

Tessa shrugs. 'Sure. Do me a headline while you're at it, would you. We're on late with this. It needs to go down by the end of the day.'

I take the pages from her and start to read.

The interviewer is a woman. I imagine Ben's pale eyes fixed on her face. I read on. She is helpless under that gaze.

'Rebecca was my great love,' says Ben Robinson. His voice catches slightly in his throat, then he recovers himself. 'Sorry,' he says with a smile, but even that cannot disguise the glitter of tears.

I flick through the pages impatiently.

'She was dead when I found her. There was a stillness about her. I don't mean death. I mean a strange aura of calm, as if she had at last made peace with herself. She looked very beautiful. I don't know when I finally called the ambulance, but it was very late. I couldn't bring myself to give her up.'

I try to picture the Inspector's face as he reads the article.

'She was a depressive of course. I believe that's common knowledge. Everybody knows that Rebecca had attempted suicide before.'

I roll a clean sheet of paper into a typewriter, type out a headline, rip the paper out of the typewriter and clip it to the text.

FAREWELL MY LOVELY.

Heather looks at it lying on the desk. 'I see what you're getting at but do you think it's quite appropriate in the circumstances? After all, it is the title of a novel about a crime.'

'I know,' I say.

*

265

Richard and I are leaving for Paris the next morning, Saturday. We are returning on Monday night.

I pack a suitcase, taking care with my clothes, then go downstairs to see Margaret. I ring the doorbell once and wait. If she does not answer, I will use the key. I am just about slot it into the lock when I hear a faint scuffling sound behind the door. It inches slowly open and Margaret's face appears. She is pale, her crabbed hands clutching at the door frame.

I put a hand under her arm, feel the sparrow bones beneath my fingers. 'You look tired.'

'Just a little dizziness. Nothing to worry about.' But I notice that she leans on me as we make our way down the narrow passage to the kitchen.

'Have you seen a doctor?'

'Don't be silly, dear. Dizziness is nothing unusual at my age.' She is not wearing her turban tonight. As I settle her into a chair, I notice the pink bald spot on her head peeking shyly from the grey hair and feel a flood of tenderness. 'How long has this been going on?' I say.

'Jane, will you stop this at once. I really can't bear people fussing.'

Colour is slowly flooding back into her cheeks.

'I'll put the kettle on, and make us some tea.'

'Oh, tea, tea. I'm flooded with the stuff,' she says, suddenly irritable. 'Open a bottle of wine, there's a dear. There's one in the fridge. It's good wine. Ben bought it for me.' She smiles with something of her old mischief. 'At least then I'll have an excuse for dizziness.'

I open the bottle, pour two small glasses.

'A little more, dear. No rations in this house.' She takes a sip. 'Very nice. I must say, Ben doesn't stint on decent wine. He was in a high old mood when he brought it over. He's been offered *millions* for the book, you know.' I smile at the exaggeration. 'Something about some poems of Rebecca's turning up. According to Ben, they've got everybody very excited.' She pauses, says thoughtfully, 'I had no idea she was so talented.'

I think of George, of Ben refusing to allow Rebecca to write. 'Few people did.'

'And I hear they're dedicated to Beattie. That was kind, wasn't it? She was always very fond of her. She often said to me that if she ever had a daughter, she'd like her to be just like Beattie.'

I feel absurdly touched. 'I didn't know that.'

'Beattie always showed her great kindness, of course. She was that sort of child. Always had a good word for everyone.'

I have a sudden clear vision of Beattie standing in this kitchen by the table. She had two purple bruises on her arm where Mary, the class bully, pinched her. 'Right, that's it,' I said, threatening to go in and talk to her teacher the next morning. Beattie patted my arm gently. 'Don't worry, Mummy. She'll come right in the end, you'll see.'

Where did such charity come from? Not from me. I blame her father.

Margaret is saying, 'The concert was very pleasant. Nora and I popped into a nice little wine bar afterwards and had supper. The young man looking after us was charming. Gay, of course. He became quite attached to my red velvet turban.'

Her voice trails off and she stares meaningfully at the bottle of wine. 'Lovely wine, dear.'

Looking down, I see that her glass is empty. I fill it with a generous hand. Her cheeks are now quite pink. 'And don't ask me if I should. I'm having a marvellous time and the dizziness has quite disappeared. I feel better than I have in days.'

I smile. 'Well, I must go and finish packing. I'm going away for the weekend. I came down to give you the telephone number, in case you need me.'

'That was kind, dear. Anywhere nice?'

'Paris.'

'How very splendid. Perhaps *you* should take my velvet turban. It's much admired in fashionable circles.'

Laughing, I kiss her, then stick the piece of paper with the Paris number on the pinboard by the telephone. 'Now, you're sure you'll be all right?'

'Run along, dear. I shall be perfectly happy finishing this delicious glass of wine. Anyway, Ben said he might pop by later. He likes to check up on me, make sure I'm not getting up to any mischief.'

I have not told Ben that I am going away. He is so preoccupied with the book, he'll scarcely notice anyway. Now the thought of him crowds in on me, like a chill on a lovely summer afternoon. I wonder at his intention in coming to see Margaret. Is he keeping an eye on me too? I am becoming paranoid. I push the thought from my mind.

'I think I'll have an early night,' I say pretending a yawn.

'You do that, dear. I'll send him your love.' There is an unspoken question in her voice.

I do not answer it.

Twenty-four

Richard is organised, efficient. He sorts tickets, changes money, shows the passports at immigration control, carries bags. I have travelled by myself since I was nine years old, taking long-haul flights to distant countries. The rituals of long habit are firmly in place but I abandon them gladly, trail after him as happy and carefree as a child in the charge of a loving parent.

There are trinkets to amuse me, a magazine, a bottle of scent in a gold box, fruit drops to suck to stop my ears popping. 'OK?' he says, smiling tenderly. I grin like a lunatic. It is a long time since anyone took care of me.

We march briskly to the flight departure gate, follow the blank walls of a passage zigzagging down to the plane. 'I'm sorry to rush you,' he says, holding out a hand as I lag behind. 'It's just I hate all the fuss. I like being there.'

My wish is not to travel, but to arrive.

'Me too,' I say, taking his hand. It gives off a regular, comforting warmth. I keep hold of it.

In the taxi leaving the airport we are silent, adjusting our internal rhythms to this unfamiliar situation. 'At least the traffic's not too bad,' Richard says as we make our way up one of the wide boulevards that mark the fringes of the city. It is not a remark that requires a response, but just his comfortable way of saying he is there.

The hotel is small and crowded, situated on a long, narrow street off the Boulevard St Germain. The first impression is of colour and pattern, covering the carpet, the curtains, the chair covers. Even the chandeliers are porcelain and picked out in flowers. A young man, wearing a well-cut navy jacket and an incurious stare, checks us in. We are early, the room is not prepared. He says this without regret. There are many things to do in Paris, even for lovers.

'Never mind,' Richard says, catching me by the hand. 'We can leave our bags here and go and get some lunch.'

We cross the wide sweep of Boulevard St Germain, wander through narrow streets until we stumble across the river, flowing grey and sluggish through the city. 'Come on,' Richard says, pulling me across the road and up some steps to a wooden footbridge. We lean against the railing, staring out at the extravagant silhouette of Paris, the buildings curved and voluptuous as well-fed women.

There's a bench, half-way across the bridge. Richard leads me to it. 'There's something I've always wanted to do.'

'What?'

His arms go round me. 'Kiss like a Parisian.'

We return to the hotel after lunch. The same young man is behind the reception desk, his jacket as pristine as if he had stepped into it at the dry-cleaner. I wonder for a moment whether the French give off some peculiar body heat that keeps their clothes pressed. Richard and I are crumpled and dishevelled, as much from wine and emotion as from travelling. I stand idly by, dreaming a little, as Richard takes charge, organising bags and keys. '*Mademoiselle*?' the young man says, handing me a folded piece of paper. It is a telegram.

I open it, stare at the brief message.

'Who's it from?' Richard asks, seeing my expression.

I hand it to him wordlessly.

'Fuck,' Richard says.

It says, *Love Always. Ben.*

'Fuck, and many more fucks.'

'Richard,' I say.

Richard doesn't look at me. He turns to the receptionist. *'Je m'excuse.'*

The young man bows gravely but he has lost his blank, incurious stare. *'Ce n'est pas grave.'*

'That's where you're wrong,' Richard says, dumping our bags in the tiny lift and flattening his body into a corner. I step in after him, folding myself between the bags and the wall. The metal door clangs shut. We rise through the air like sardines in a tin.

Richard sighs. 'How did he know where we were?'

'I left the number with Margaret. I thought she might need to get hold of me.'

'And this is just his way too, I suppose?' His voice is hard.

I bow my head. 'I'm sorry.'

We unpack in silence. I fold and hang clothes, arranging my few possessions to bring some semblance of homeliness to the room. It reminds me of my mother. She used to like to organise her belongings the moment she arrived in a new place. We are like cats, marking out our territory. Richard, who unpacks by the simple expediency of opening a drawer and tipping the contents of his bag into it, lies on the bed, watching me. His expression is morose. I imagine the two of us in this room for three days, each brooding in our different ways on Ben. I look over at him. 'He'll spoil this if we let him.'

Richard sighs, stares up at the ceiling. 'Yes, I'm sorry. You're right.'

I go into the bathroom, arrange toothpaste, shampoo and moisturiser on the narrow shelf. Everything I have brought with me is brand new, the dog-ends of my other life abandoned back at home. When everything is arranged to my satisfaction – the toothbrush in the glass provided, the little disc of soap unwrapped – I go out of the bathroom. A corner of Richard's blue shirt hangs from a drawer. My fingers itch to take it out and fold it carefully but I resist the impulse and pick up the empty bags, intending to store them on the top of the wardrobe, trying to smooth away nervousness with order.

'I love you,' Richard says.

I look over at him, startled. It is not what I expected. Not now. I duck my head, pleased.

Richard yawns, stretches his arms and legs like a starfish on the bed. 'I was watching you unpack. You looked so familiar that for a moment I couldn't work out what it was I was feeling.' His voice sounds warm and sleepy, as if it's coming from a long way off. 'Then I realised. You make everything seem so beautifully ordinary.'

I consider this for a moment, my arms filled with bags. *Beautifully ordinary*. Like home. Like coming home. I open my arms, let the bags tumble to the floor and climb on the bed next to him. 'Are you going to sleep?'

He reaches for me. 'What do you think?'

When we get up again it is late.

We wander the narrow streets, looking for somewhere to eat. Richard won't use a guidebook. 'I like happy accidents,' he says, kissing me. The first restaurant that we try, which looks charmingly French on the outside, is filled with loud American voices. We back quickly out of the door, apologising to the owner. At the second place there are no empty tables, but finally we stumble into a third. It looks no more than a wine bar from the exterior, but when they hand us the menu, handwritten in thick black ink, it is obvious that it is run by somebody who loves good food. We eat greedily and drink robust red wine, holding hands between courses and whispering like teenagers. The waiter indulges us, bringing thin slices of *tarte au citron* and two spoons, abandoning us with a fractional bow to huddle over armagnac and coffee. It is then that Richard asks if I have told Ben about us.

'He knows.' It is not a lie, exactly. I have not told Ben, not in so many words, but he knows. I know he knows.

Richard's expression is grim. 'Then why the telegram?'

'It's just his way.'

'You mean he will ignore the situation for ever?'

I think of Rebecca's suicide and reach for his hand. 'He'll grow bored soon enough and leave us alone. Please believe me.'

Richard frowns. 'And should I believe that there is nothing left between you?'

I hesitate too long. 'It's history,' I murmur, 'just history.'

'If we are to start anything, then you must put a stop to this thing with Ben as soon as you get back.'

I want to say to him that we have already started something, but I know from the tension in his muscles as he holds on to my hand, from the slight almost imperceptible hesitation as he bends to kiss me, that he is still holding a part of himself back. He does not trust me entirely. I can't blame him. I don't entirely trust myself. With an impatient gesture, he says, 'There is unfinished business there and there always will be unless you put an end to it.'

Richard does not know that I never say goodbye; I just turn my face away and leave. Countries, schools, houses, animals, friends, I never once said goodbye to any of them. I just left, without a word.

'I'm not much good at endings,' I say.

'Even happy ones?' he says and gives me that slow smile that makes me want to run round and round, the way kids do when they're too full of happiness. It's a huge emotion, happiness.

I don't say to Richard that I have never believed in happy endings, only happy beginnings. There's always a first time.

When we get back to the hotel, the young man behind the reception desk hands me another telegram, his expression apologetic. '*Il y a un autre.*'

I turn it over, pass it on to Richard to read.

Love always. Ben.

'Fuck?' supplies the young man gravely.

Richard smiles grimly. 'Mille fucks,' he says and tears the telegram to tiny pieces. After that, we tear them all up, scatter them like confetti in the hotel waste paper bin. It is tin, painted blue and white to approximate Wedgwood pottery. There are four telegrams the first day, six the next. It becomes a game. The young man holds up the waste-paper bin, as we rip up the paper and let it fall like petals.

For two days we eat, drink, walk, talk, make love. It feels good. It is good. I pretend not to notice the wariness that comes and goes in Richard's face like the sudden squalls of rain through which we run, shrieking like children. He does not mention love again.

Twenty-five

It is past midnight when Richard drops me at home. He carries my bag to the front door, kisses me searchingly.

'Go,' I say pushing him gently. 'You'll be a wreck tomorrow if you don't get some sleep.'

'Never,' he protests, but climbs back into the waiting taxi.

As soon as I open the door, I know that something is wrong. I couldn't see the light from outside but it's here now, spilling into the landing, bouncing softly off the stairs. I lower the bags gently to the floor, step softly, balancing all my weight on the balls of my feet.

A stair creaks. I hold my breath but nothing stirs.

Is it Ben up there? Or somebody else? You hear such stories these days. A woman alone, a man with a knife. Better not to think, better to keep moving, arching a leg over the awkward turn of the staircase.

The light is coming from the sitting-room, a blond head slumped forward on the desk, hands splayed like starfish. It is Ben. I let out a loud sigh, realise I have been holding my breath.

I move towards him, see Richard's business card, the corner just touching one of Ben's fingers. What is it doing here? He must have taken it from its place by the telephone where I left it. I no longer need it, the number is committed to heart.

'What took you so long?' he says.

I gasp, feeling the shock like cold water on warm skin. 'I thought you were asleep.'

He lifts his head, holds out both hands, fingers stiff. 'Ten telegrams,' he says, flexing his fingers to show the number. 'I sent you ten fucking telegrams and still you didn't come.' His expression is dazed, the way it is when you surface too fast from a deep sleep.

Thinking he is referring to Richard and the trip to Paris, I say, 'Look, Ben . . .'

'No, *you* look. I can't believe you didn't come.' It's then that I see how pale he is, his face bleached to that unhealthy pallor that's more grey than white, his eyes rimmed with red. I have known him so well and for so long that I understand immediately that this is not about Richard. Something bad has happened.

'What?' I say.

His face crumples. 'Margaret's is hospital, in intensive care. She fell and hit her head.'

I grope my way to a chair. 'The dizzy spells?'

'She's in a coma.' He drops his head to the desk so his voice comes out muffled. 'She looks so *small*, Janey, it's like she shrank overnight. They've taken her teeth out or something so her face is all caved in and there are tubes in her mouth and nose. It's enough to make you weep.' And he does. It's a horrible sound.

I honestly think that Margaret is the only human being Ben has ever truly loved.

The hospital is ablaze with light and sound, and an overpowering smell of bleach and microwaved sausages. Even at this hour, people clutch bunches of yellow chrysanthemums, children sit on chairs swinging their legs and looking bored. The noise and bustle is a shock after the dark stillness outside. In here, there's no telling whether it's night or day. It's darker in intensive care. The light here is ghostly, dimmed right down to the lower levels of sight, the gloom pricked by red stars glowing on hulking, forbidding machines.

Margaret is hunched down in bed, her skin yellow against the sharp bones of her face. Tubes protrude from her nose and mouth, a few wisps of grey hair escaping from the bandage that swaddles her head. Ben's right. It is enough to make you weep.

After a few minutes, while we stare down at Margaret, incapable of finding anything to say, incapable of any sort of speech at all, the nurse on duty tells us to go away. Her manner is kind but unyielding. You can tell she's used to dealing with any amount of awkwardness. 'The best thing you can do for her is go and get some sleep. We'll telephone you if there's any change.' The way she says it, you can tell she isn't expecting any. 'Come back in the morning. You can sit with her all day if you like.'

I turn away, take Ben by the arm.

We walk slowly through the darkened car-park to my car. I am driving. Ben is in no fit state, his movements slow as a sleep-walker's.

'Where shall we go?' I ask.

Neither of us wants to go back to my place, not with Margaret's flat so cold and lifeless below.

'Home,' he says. Just like that. After all this time, I have never been to his and Rebecca's house, although I have imagined it for long enough.

I start the engine. 'Off we go, then,' I say and realise I am talking to him as if he is a child.

The house is big. Even bigger than I thought it would be, four storeys painted cream and black, hidden away in a quiet cul-de-sac in Chiswick. Inside, it is discreet and expensive. And curiously sterile, as if each piece of furniture and object were allocated a place from which it has never dared stray.

Ben blunders up the stairs. I follow, up two flights to a room occupying the whole of the second floor. I have never known a master bedroom that better deserved its name. It is carpeted in cream and there is a four-poster that looks antique – Indian perhaps – with intricately embroidered muslin curtains hanging from each of the four corners. The bed, which is covered in pale-green linen and piled with green and gold embroidered pillows, looks as though nobody has ever slept in it.

Ben kicks off his shoes and lunges across the pillows. 'Come here,' he says, holding out his arms, his voice thick with exhaustion. Or perhaps it's emotion. We're both strung out about Margaret. His face is wet with tears. I put my hand up to brush them away and almost before I know it, we're making love, pushing away our clothes and tearing into each other with a violence that shakes me. Even so, I don't stop. I don't know what it is – fear, anger, lust – but it's like we're trying to climb into each other's bodies.

Then it's over.

'Jesus Christ,' Ben says, and falls into sleep like a stone.

I lie back on the pillow next to him, intending to rest for a moment before I go to the bathroom and rearrange my clothes. I must have fallen asleep too because when I wake all the lights are on but outside there's that charged stillness – almost as if the night is holding its breath – that tells you it's somewhere in the early hours of the morning. I look at the clock. It is five o'clock. Ben is sleeping. I watch his face for a while, the angelic curve of his mouth, the almost perfect planes of his face, blond hair flopping across the pillow. It is then that I understand something so clearly it knocks the breath out of me. I don't want this face. I want another one entirely. It is Richard's head I see on the pillow next to me, his dark hair tousled with sleep. Richard looks like a demented chicken in the morning, his hair springing at uncontrollable angles from his scalp. When he wakes, the first thing he does is smooth it down into shape. He sleeps with a smile on his face. He doesn't like to be hugged in the night. He wakes up talking. I am not the only woman to know these intimate details. I just feel that way.

Ben wakes, reaches for me.

His face is still dulled with sleep when I tell him it is over. 'Over?' he repeats, stumbling slightly over the word, as if it is in a foreign language, a shape unfamiliar to his mouth. He looks bewildered, as if he cannot connect the person in front of him with the woman he knows. It is then I realise that I have told him nothing of what has been in my head these past few weeks. I had expected anger. There is none, only a tender concern, as if I am a child, revealing to its mother an experience she has known nothing about. He puts his hand to my face, his touch light, as if I have been hurt in some way.

When I was a kid, I played a sliding game. We had marble floors scattered with Persian rugs, some of them no bigger than a hand towel. I'd run along on all fours, hands stretched on the carpet, feet scrabbling against the slippery stone; then, when I'd got enough speed, I'd do a frog jump onto the rug and whoosh, off I'd go.

It helped to pass the time.

Well, one afternoon when I did that frogjump, my arms somehow collapsed from under me and I landed hard on my face on the marble floor. I tasted the blood before I saw it, felt the gaping puncture my broken tooth had made in my bottom lip. They were new teeth, my grown-up ones, so I must have been about eight.

My mother always had a nap in the afternoon. The heat was blinding and besides, there wasn't much else to do, not when you've got three servants. I knocked on the door, then cupped my hands to my mouth, worried about dropping blood all over the clean floor. The door opened to my mother wearing the bewildered expression of a person who's been deeply asleep. When she saw me, her face changed.

It is that same expression, of love and terror, that Ben is

wearing now. It frightens me more than anger ever could. 'Over?' he says. 'No, it's not over. It will never be over between us.'

'Please understand, Ben,' I say fretfully. 'It's better this way. We can both start again, forget everything that's happened.'

Perhaps something of my fear shows in my face for Ben loops his arm round my neck, pulls my head to his chest. 'Shh,' he murmurs. 'It will be all right,' as if I am a child and have no idea what I am saying.

I leave Ben asleep and drive home. It is not yet six o'clock but already light. It is a beautiful morning. When I get home, I find six messages from Richard on the answer machine.

I dial his number, although it is early.

His voice comes on the line, dulled with sleep. 'Where were you? I've been calling all night.'

I hesitate, then say, 'I was at the hospital. You know those telegrams we tore up? Well, all the later ones were about Margaret. When I left for Paris she was having dizzy spells. She must have had a bad one because on Sunday morning she fell and hit her head. She's in a coma.'

Richard knows my relationship with Margaret. I talk about her often enough. He is awake now. 'Oh, God. What do they say at the hospital?'

'There's nothing to say. All we can do is wait.'

'Well, if there's anything I can do, just let me know.'

'Thank you, but there's nothing anyone can do, except sit with her. That's where I'm going now.'

'I could pick you up when I finish at work, take you out for something to eat.'

I'm at that exhausted stage when your head feels as if it might part company from your neck. So I'm not thinking particularly straight when I say, 'I think I'll go home. I need some sleep. I was up most of the night.'

I've hardly finished getting the words out when Richard says, 'Was Ben with you?'

'Well, of course he was. Margaret is family.'

'I'm only too aware of that.'

I don't want to get into this conversation so early in the morning so I promise to call him later.

It never occurs to me that Margaret will die. I have seen too much death in my life already. The bad part is over. Soon, there will be a new beginning. Soon, with Richard.

I sit with Margaret, holding her hand, watching the rise and fall of her bird-chest. Wires and tubes monitor her heart and breathing. Her breathing is faint, quick and shallow as a small child's, but her body still moves, which they say is a good sign. Imperceptibly, during the long day she curls into a foetus, only to be straightened out by brisk hands as night begins to fall.

'Must you?' I say, watching the nurse uncoil her brittle arms and legs, lifting the swollen knuckles one by one away from the thin, papery flesh of her palms.

The nurse, who is bending and straightening Margaret's limbs as if she were a doll, does not even look at me. 'Mustn't let her stiffen up, dear,' she says, rolling Margaret onto her side and rearranging the nappy in which her withered haunches are swathed. I look away. Margaret would hate me to see this.

'Talk to her,' the nurse says. 'It will help to bring her back.' Her voice is brisk, each sentence a command; her rubber-soled shoes squeak on the linoleum floor as she moves briskly among machines and silenced bodies, her fingers beating a staccato of distress.

I talk to Margaret, my mouth inches from her ear. There is a low chair by the bed on which I sit all day, crouching forward, my arms angled like frog legs on the sheets. I lean my chin on my hands and talk, on and on, my voice filling the long, empty hours. I talk about my childhood, about Beattie, about Ben.

I tell her about Richard, about how he makes me feel I've arrived, as if my travels are finally over. I tell her that I haven't told him yet, that just saying it to her is, for the moment, enough. I'll tell him, I say, once I've found the courage to say the words out loud.

I tell her about the heat of Richard's hand on my belly, how the warmth of it makes me understand that another child might be possible. Not to replace Beattie, I go on hurriedly, never to replace her. A different child, another future.

I talk like this until the early evening when Ben arrives, bringing the sharp, gritty smell of the city with him.

He puts his arms round me and we sway by the bed, pressed close together for comfort.

'No change.' There is nothing else to say.

On the first night of my vigil at the hospital there is a message from Richard. He is sorry, he says, about our conversation that morning and even sorrier about Margaret. 'I know it's hard, but try not to worry.' Then there's nothing, five beats of silence, then his voice again, coming very fast and breathless like he's nervous, telling me he misses me. That's all, he says, then a click and silence.

I telephone, but there is no reply and the answer machine is not turned on. There is nothing for it but to go to bed. I wrench off my clothes, dive into sleep. I do not dream. It's as if all the words and images have been emptied out at Margaret's side.

In the morning I call Richard again but still there is no reply. Puzzling over this, I play his message on my answer machine for comfort, pressing the replay button over and over again. Just the sound of his voice soothes me. He could be reading the weather report, for all I care. I hurry to the hospital, his voice clutched fast in my mind.

Every day I sit with Margaret. Every night I telephone

Richard. There is never any reply. During the day, I call his office from the pay phone in the hospital corridor. Richard is always in a meeting. I leave messages, but not my love. Love has no place at work. Sitting by Margaret's bed, I hold up my hands, count on my fingers the days since I heard Richard's voice. Five days. A handful of days.

On the sixth day I find Ben pacing the corridor outside intensive care, his expression agitated by excitement. Margaret has spoken her first word.

I must call Richard. He will want to know.

Hurrying to the pay phone, I slot in silver. Richard is in a meeting. He has been in a meeting for a week now. Or in Newcastle, Manchester, Leeds, Brighton. Is there any distance a solicitor will not travel?

'When will he be out of the meeting?' I ask.

'He won't,' says his secretary. She sounds slightly irritable, as if she is talking to a tiresome child. 'I'm afraid he's given instructions that he is not able to speak to you.' Why do people always say that they are afraid, when they mean quite the opposite?

The pain takes my legs from under me.

The nurse from intensive care – Maggie, she's called – finds me crouching by the telephone, the receiver still in my hand. 'You've been doing too much,' she says, helping me to my feet. 'It's always the way with people with loved ones in intensive care. They take too much on. Next thing we know, we're nursing them.'

I allow her to lead me back to Margaret.

Her eyes are closed.

'Margaret,' I whisper. 'Margaret, help me.'

She does not move.

'Can't hurry it, dear,' says Maggie. 'Not when the mind's finding its way back again.'

Twenty-six

Margaret is coming home.

I go to the hospital to collect her, find her dressed in her old outdoor coat, perched at the foot of her bed like a child waiting to be taken out of school. She has applied lopsided circles of rouge to her cheeks and put on her red velvet turban. It lurches drunkenly over her forehead.

'How do I look?' I say she looks fine. She never did get her turban to sit straight, anyway. It would be more of a worry if she'd got it on right. Still, I can't help noticing how she grips my hand as we negotiate the low steps down to the car-park. 'Don't go so fast,' she exclaims in a faint, querulous voice. I slow down. The last time we left this hospital together, it was Margaret who hurried me down these steps to the taxi waiting to take us away from Beattie's poor broken body. She led me as if I was blind.

I settle her in the car. She sinks back against the seat, eyes closed. As we inch our way through the morning traffic, I say, 'The agapanthus are in flower. Just ready for you coming home.'

'They'll be nearly over,' Margaret says fretfully. 'They would have been at their best two weeks ago.'

'They look lovely. The whole garden looks lovely.'

She eyes me accusingly. 'Have you been watering?'

'I have.'

Margaret tugs at her seat-belt as if it is that, not her injuries, which has been keeping her from her beloved garden. 'Doing it properly, I hope. Not just waving the can over their poor thirsty heads.'

'An under-gardener at Kew could not have fulfilled his duties better,' I say, laughing, but she turns from me with a sigh and gazes out of the window.

I have been in and cleaned up Margaret's flat, but there is still an air of neglect to the place. 'I feel as though I've been away for a year instead of a month,' Margaret says, rearranging the tea caddie and sugar bowl. I see then that I have put them in the wrong place and wonder how many other irritating kindnesses I have committed.

'I think I shall go and freshen up,' she says. I lift her suitcase, intending to follow her but she stands in the doorway, blocking the way to her bedroom. 'Do stop following me around, Jane, there's a dear. I can manage perfectly well on my own.' She turns away with an impatient shake of her head and I realise that it is not me she is angry with but the indignities of age.

'I'll do it later,' I say cheerfully. 'I'll go and get the kettle on instead.'

Margaret hesitates for a moment as if she wants to say something else, then gives a dismissive snort and makes her way slowly down the passageway to her bedroom.

The water is just coming to the boil when a wail of dismay emits, piercingly, from the direction of the bedroom. Hurrying down the passage, I find Margaret sitting at her dressing-table, dabbing at her cheeks with a powder puff. Her eyes seek out mine in the reflection of the mirror. 'How could you let me leave that place looking like a drunken clown?'

I smile. 'You look fine.'

It is then that I see the glitter of tears in her eyes but before I can speak she whirls round, almost losing her balance with the violence of the movement. 'I may have had a bang on the head,' she says furiously, 'but I have not been reduced to a simpleton.'

Turning back to the mirror, she mutters that the light in the bathroom in the hospital was so dim it was impossible to see anything. Not that I was to think that her eyes were going too, because they weren't, but because they kept the voltage particularly low to save on electricity. Her hands shake with distress. It takes her a long time to get the powder applied to her face.

I bow my head in shame. In my anxiety not to embarrass her – or was it myself that I was truly thinking of? – I have taken away the one thing that Margaret holds dear: her dignity.

A chair creaks, then Margaret's hand is on my shoulder. Her touch feels unusually heavy and with a shock I realise that she is leaning on me. She is frailer than she would have either of us believe. 'I'm so very sorry, my dear.' Her voice is subdued. 'They say head injuries are dreadful for one's temper. Shall we go and have that cup of tea?'

Margaret allows me to make the tea, even though I can see she is longing to be alone in her kitchen, freed from the hampering kindness of visitors. Letting me make the tea is her way of making up. 'Wonderful to be back among the lovely ordinary things,' she says with a sigh of pleasure, her bright eyes darting around the room.

I smile at her but cannot shake off the sudden chill that has descended on me. What is it? Something Margaret said. Then I remember. It is what Richard said when he told me he loved me. You make everything seem so beautifully ordinary. That's what love is, the thrill of recognition. Why had I never understood it before? In all the years I have know Ben I never felt that ordinariness.

'What is it, dear?' I turn to see Margaret watching me, her expression concerned.

'Oh – nothing,' I say with a sigh.

'And who, pray, is nothing when he's at home?'

'Remember I told you I met somebody I liked? Well, it turned out he didn't like me after all.'

'Richard, wasn't it?' Nothing wrong with her memory, then.

I nod, not trusting myself to speak. I have told no one else about Richard. I have no one else to tell.

'I am sorry, dear. You seemed so very excited about him.'

'I was, but it seems he doesn't feel the same way about me.'

'You've told him how you feel, I suppose?'

Not in so many words. 'Sort of.'

'Well, I'm not entirely sure what *sort of* means, but it sounds very unsatisfactory to me.'

'He doesn't return my phone calls.'

'No doubt there's a perfectly reasonable explanation. It may be that something untoward has happened.'

I smile, comforted by Margaret's briskness. 'I expect you're right.'

'Well, if I were you, I would go directly and see him. There's no point mourning something until it's dead.' Placing her hands on the table, she hauls herself painfully to her feet. 'Talking of which, I think I shall just go and have a peek at my poor neglected garden. It must wonder where I've been all this time.'

'Would you like some help?' I ask, watching her unsteady progress across the room.

'No thank you, dear. Afterwards, I shall lie down for an hour or two. Far too much excitement for one day.'

'I'll come and see you later, then. There's a cauliflower-cheese, just needs heating through when you're hungry.'

'Thank you. I shall enjoy that.' She pauses in the doorway, waits for me to leave. I cannot help but notice how she moves into the garden, groping with her hands, like a person moving through the dark.

I leave a note for Ben, jammed under a flowerpot on the doorstep: *Margaret's sleeping. Doesn't want to be disturbed. I'm upstairs.*

*

'How is she?'

'Fragile – but obstinate.'

Ben grins. 'A family trait. It's part of our charm.'

He has used the key to let himself in. Tossing it in the air, he catches it with one finger, loops it into the palm of his hand, thrusts it into his pocket. His smile is insufferable.

'Why don't I take you out to dinner? I think we could both do with a square meal after the last couple of weeks.'

'Thank you, but I'm not hungry.' Anyway, it seems wrong, going out to enjoy ourselves with Margaret being so ill.

'You must eat.' I hate it when people say that, as if the thought would never have occurred without their help.

'Really, I'm fine.'

'Well, let's have a drink, then.' Pouring two glasses of red wine, he hands one to me and raises the other to his mouth. 'To us.'

'To Margaret,' I say.

'To Margaret and to us. Did she tell you that I've organised a nurse for her? Well, she's not a nurse exactly, although she is medically trained. More of a companion, really, somebody to do the shopping and cook for her.'

'That's good of you,' I say, wondering how long it will take Margaret to see off this companion. I give her a week.

'Are you all right, Janey? You don't seem quite yourself tonight.'

'Not myself,' I say gaily. 'Well, of course I'm not myself. These past few months have been enough to turn us all into other people entirely.'

Then I start to cry. I don't often cry in front of other people so I have never managed to turn it into the elegant arrangement that some people seem to contrive. My nose turns scarlet and my mouth tugs down in an ugly curve, and the tears don't slip silently down my cheeks, they just sort of spurt, to be honest.

His arms go round me. 'What is it, darling. What's the matter?'

I had not intended to cry. I don't really know why I am doing it, except that Richard has gone and there seems a terrible inevitability to my life.

Twenty-seven

The days pass. Richard does not call.

I no longer expect him to, no longer tense when the telephone rings. Richard has left me, just as everyone has always done. It has never occurred to me to ask why. Ben is right. I am hard to love.

I go about my daily life, attending to the rituals it demands. Most of all, I try not to think about Richard. It is difficult. He appears at inconvenient times, but particularly when I am trying to sleep or eat. I have more or less abandoned both those activities now. Sleep goes unremarked, the knife and fork lie idle by the plate. I go up to bed every night in the pretence that I shall sleep, turn my head to the wall and my thoughts away from Richard. It is Beattie who visits me then, wrapping her silken arms round my neck or patting me gently on the back as she used to do when I was sad or tired. 'Better, Mummy. All better now.'

I am not better. I am worse than ever.

Ben telephones me every day. He is terrifyingly cheerful. The book is going well. He says it is nearly finished. Huge bunches of flowers arrive from him every morning, as regular as the post. I put them in the bin. If he notices their absence when he visits, he does not remark on it.

One morning, a woman telephones. 'Jane Rose?' she says. 'I understand you are Beattie's mother.'

Something in her tone alerts me. 'Who is this?'

She explains that she is a journalist, working on an article about the first volume of Rebecca's poetry, which is to be published the following week. She is writing what she calls a 'colour piece' to accompany the publication. I wonder what colour it will be. Purple, most likely.

'The dedication has been causing rather a stir,' she says. 'Particularly when it was revealed it is to be used on all three volumes.' Her voice drops. 'The publisher is very mysterious about the identity of this Beattie Rose which, of course, has got everyone talking. There was even a suggestion doing the rounds that she was a lesbian lover.' Her voice is light, amused.

I say nothing.

'I found it hard to believe, particularly considering Rebecca Carter's marriage.' The woman allows a delicate pause. So she has met Ben. I imagine her face, turned up to that blue gaze. 'Then I found out from an impeccable source that Beattie is a child.'

I know the source but feel too weary even for indignation.

The woman hesitates. 'I understand how difficult this is for you. It's never easy when a child dies . . .'

Easy? There it is again, that blithe, careless English understatement. I should not blame her. There are no words for a dead child. I say, 'Do you have children?'

Her voice sharpens. 'No, but that doesn't stop me understanding how you must feel. Look, all I'm trying to do is to get some background on Rebecca and it seems to me that the child is key to that.'

Is that all Beattie is now? Is her blithe, glorious presence diminished to just two words? *The child.*

'The person you need to speak to is not here,' I say.

Her voice rises in alarm. 'What? Who is this? Who am I speaking to?'

'Someone else entirely,' I say almost gaily as I put down the telephone. I go upstairs to Beattie's room and lie down, face pressed to the Noddy duvet. Just lately, I have taken to sleeping in this room, in Beattie's innocent, narrow bed.

Margaret is worried about me. 'Why don't you go and see him,' she says, almost with exasperation.

I can't. He does not want me.

'Or at least go and see a doctor and get some pills. Edna says the new ones are tremendously helpful.'

I don't want pills. I have enough problem keeping the world in focus as it is.

These days, I spend a lot of time thinking about Rebecca. Is this the way she felt, swamped by Ben but at the same time unloved and unlovable? *Nobody could love you like I do.*

Poor Rebecca, lying cold and unloved under the earth. Brave Rebecca, escaping Ben as she did. I have never thought badly of her for her suicide. It is perhaps the only thing I have never thought badly of her for. Sometimes I wish that she were here, so that we could swap notes. Have a laugh about Ben and his sly, controlling ways. He loves us both, of course. There's no question about that. His love is awesome, monumental. The biggest piece of love in the world. It's overwhelming. I feel myself sinking under the weight of it. Each day I recede further from the world. If only Rebecca were here. She would understand.

The doorbell rings. I am not expecting anyone. I wait, hands tensing around a mug of cold tea. It rings again, more insistently this time. I get up. Perhaps it is Margaret. She knows I am here.

'Margaret said you were here.'

It is Barbara.

Her eyes narrow as she takes in my appearance. I'm not looking good, although I say it myself. Too thin, too pale, my hair unwashed.

'May I come in?'

I stand aside to let her pass.

'I wanted to thank you for looking after Rebecca's poems,' she says, her neat figure brisk in the narrow passage. She climbs the stairs. There is nothing to do but follow.

'I merely put them in good hands,' I say. 'Better hands than mine.' It's true. Everything I touch withers and dies.

'You know, of course, that Rebecca didn't believe the poems were any good? She called them scribbles, because that's what Ben called them.' She enters the kitchen, her keen eyes taking everything in. It is tidy. Spotless, in fact. Well, I don't do much in it these days except make tea. She goes on, scarcely drawing breath as she puts down her bag and pushes back the immaculate white cuffs of her blouse, as if she is preparing to go into battle. 'I know it's un-Christian to throw stones but I hold that man entirely responsible for her death. Well, I must say,' she adds, looking around, 'it looks very tidy in here.'

I say, amused, 'Shouldn't it be?'

'I expect that sounded rather nosy,' she says, losing some of her briskness. 'It's just that Margaret telephoned yesterday to say she was worried about you. She seems to think you haven't been looking after yourself.'

I switch on the kettle. 'I'm fine.'

'Let me do that. You sit down.'

She looks so determined that I oblige, watch her pluck two mugs from their resting place on the draining board, find milk in the fridge, search in the cupboard for a bag of sugar. I don't like to say that I don't take sugar in tea. It seems ungrateful to interfere.

'It will give you energy.' She answers my unspoken thought. 'You look exhausted.'

'I don't sleep much.'

She turns away, busies herself with making tea. 'Is something worrying you?' I know that voice, that deter-minedly casual tone. It's the one you use around children when you want them to tell you something they're reluctant to reveal. It never worked on Beattie.

'I keep thinking about Beattie.'

She turns to face me, her eyes filling with tears. 'Oh, Jane, we all thought you were so much better.'

She looks so sad that I almost tell her it's not Beattie at all. Well, it is Beattie but only inasmuch as Beattie has become the focus of everything that is wrong in my life. I know it's cowardly to use my dead child so badly, worrying at the scab of her memory until the pain of it obliterates lesser hurts.

Barbara brings the mugs of tea to the table, sits down and regards me levelly. 'As a matter of fact,' she says, 'I thought it might be something to do with Ben.'

I can think of nothing to say so, in my usual way, I say nothing.

'Rebecca always said that you were in love with him, had been since you were very young.' Barbara looks away. 'She didn't blame you in any way, but it worried her. You see, Ben is a thoroughly destructive man.'

'Did she know?' I whisper.

'That you were having an affair?' Barbara says briskly. 'No, but I guessed as much. Rebecca was an innocent in many ways. She knew an affair of some sort was going on. Well, she could hardly avoid knowing, Ben took so little pains to hide it. But she never for a moment thought it was you. She tried to leave him once, but he convinced her she was so unlovable that nobody would ever want her.' Her tone is contemptuous.

All these secrets hidden away, layer upon layer of them, like onion skins. Shall I ever get to the centre. Do I want to?

'She did meet somebody. A kind man, she said, very gentle. Too gentle, by all accounts. Ben found out and put a stop to it.'

'How?' My voice is a whisper.

'Oh, he fed him some story about Rebecca being unstable and running after different men all the time. It was part of her sickness, he said, although if anybody was sick in that marriage I'd say it was Ben. That's when the first suicide attempt happened, when this chap stopped taking her calls. All her letters were sent back unopened. It was only by chance that Rebecca found out what Ben had done when she bumped into this chap years later at some publishing do. It was too late by then, of course. He was married to somebody else. Had a kid, I think. A daughter. Or maybe it was a son.'

'Are you sure?'

Barbara's tone is irritable. 'Of course I 'm sure. A child, she said, although it can't have been very old. No more than two or three.'

'About Ben being the one who broke them up?'

'Now, about that I can be quite definite. I distinctly remember Rebecca telling me that when she found out, she made her second suicide attempt.' Barbara sighs. 'After that, she turned the whole thing round in her head. Told the story again and again, almost as if it was a fairy-tale, except that the handsome prince was driven away. "He didn't want to go." That's what she kept saying. Those lovely eyes of hers would fill with tears and she'd say, "Babs..." She always called me Babs. "Babs," she'd say ...'

I am no longer listening, am gathering up my bag, searching for loose change and a jumper to throw round my shoulders, although the sun is showing signs of coming out. Yes, the sun is definitely coming out.

Barbara watches me, her eyes shrewd. 'Where are you going?'

'I have to see someone.'

'Would you mind very much if I gave you some advice?'

'Yes, I mean, no, I wouldn't mind,' I say, impatient to be gone.

'If I were you, I'd give your hair a good wash first.'

Richard is in a meeting, can't be disturbed.

'I'll wait,' I say.

The receptionist jabs at her thick glasses in agitation. 'He didn't say he could see you.'

I walk over to the hard wooden chairs arranged in a line by the wall. 'I don't mind how long it takes.'

Her voice rises. 'It's really not how we do things here. People must have an appointment.'

Smiling, I arrange my feet and knees in a neat line, clasp my hands purposefully in my lap. 'You won't even notice I'm here,' I say pleasantly, although something inside me is goggling in astonishment as if to say, I never knew you had the nerve.

She does notice that I'm there. At first, she tries to ignore me, then her gaze starts to jerk from me back to her work until her head is bobbing up and down like one of those artificial dogs you see in the backs of cars. I watch her out of the corner of my eye. Up and down, up and down she goes until, finally, she can bear it no longer. Reaching for the phone, she drops her voice, whispers urgently.

It doesn't take Richard long. Perhaps she pleaded with him to come and have me thrown off the premises, for he walks slowly down the stairs with a heavy, deliberate tread, head bent, each foot placed carefully on a step. He is a big man, an imposing presence. I am not fooled. I can see his reluctance in the very swing of his arms. He looks like a small boy, sent unwillingly off to school. It makes me smile to see him. I am still almost smiling when he reaches me.

'Jane,' he says heavily.

'Can we go somewhere and talk?'

He will not look at me. 'I don't think that's a good idea,' he says, his eyes searching some place far over my shoulder. I examine his face closely. It looks wonderfully familiar to me but there are deep lines etched under his eyes and a stiffness around the mouth. He submits to my scrutiny, his expression unchanging. He might just as well be carved from stone, so still is he, scarcely breathing. Only his lazy eye gives him away, wandering gently.

I say, 'None of what Ben told you is true.'

His eyes move to my face, a quick, startled glance filled with hope. Then some other thought seems to occur to him for his face shuts down, takes on the same blank and sombre cast. 'I don't know what you mean.'

I take him by the arm. 'Yes, you do. He telephoned you, didn't he? He took the number from your card. It was by the telephone. I found him with it that night we got back from Paris.'

Richard looks away, discomfited. 'Perhaps.'

'He told you that I'm disturbed in some way, that I like to play around with people's emotions and then bugger off again.' Tugging at his sleeve like a child, I urge him forward. I want to get out of this place. The receptionist stares unblinkingly, unable to take her eyes from us. I push at Richard. He shambles a little, then picks up speed until we are virtually running towards the huge oak doors. When we are outside, I say, 'In fact, he told you that I'd come back and try it on again.' As soon as I say it, I know it's true.

'Where are we going?' Richard asks, gazing up and down the street in bewilderment.

'I don't know. Anywhere,' I say, taking his arm. 'I can't say I blame you, of course. Not after all those stories about kidnapping dogs and children, and killing my mother.'

His gaze swings down to me like a searchlight. 'All true,' I say quickly. 'But I can see why you might think I really am disturbed. I don't blame you for believing Ben, truly, I don't. I'd have thought I was a lunatic if I were you. Then of course there were the telegrams in Paris and those ludicrous bunches of flowers –'

'What flowers?'

I am talking too much. It must be happiness. The very sight of him gladdens me. I always talk too much when I am happy. It's a family trait. My mother was the same, one moment silent and drooping, and the next, off like a train.

There were times you could almost see the steam coming out of her ears.

'What flowers?'

'Never mind.'

'It wasn't what Ben said,' Richard says, frowning. 'I dismissed all that as mischief-making. It was your letter that convinced me what he said was true.'

I stop dead. I couldn't have stopped more sharply if someone had dropped a brick wall right in my path. 'What letter?'

'The letter you wrote when Margaret was taken ill, after the night you spent with Ben. You know, the one where you said you'd discovered that you were still in love with him, that Ben is the only man for you.' His voice is caustic with anger. 'Or maybe you write so many letters you can't remember who you send them to?'

My voice is calm. Dead calm. Flat as a glassy pond. 'I don't know what you're talking about.'

Richard frowns. He is uncertain now. 'You did spend the night with him. I know because I rang you all that night and when I spoke to you in the morning you sounded sort of strange. At the time I thought it was just worry over Margaret.'

'Where's the letter?'

'I tore it up.'

'No, you didn't.' I grab at him, shake him in a fury of impatience. 'I know you didn't, just from your face. Where is it? What have you done with it?'

At first I think he is going to refuse me but the wildness of my behaviour seems to convince him of the importance of my question for his expression changes suddenly to one of sheepishness and he starts patting clumsily at his pockets. 'I've been meaning to throw it away. I can't think why I kept it.' He finds his wallet, beaten-up leather and bulging with money. His big fingers fumble helplessly through the stack of paper.

'Oh, give it to me,' I say, although my hands are shaking more than his. My fingers close on a thick square of paper, folded and refolded so many times it is splitting at the seams. Opening it up, I stare down at it. The words jumble in a snarl of letters. I don't care. I don't need to read them to know what they say. 'Give me a pen.'

'What?'

'A pen, quickly.'

Richard hands me a handsome black fountain pen, dull and scuffed with use. I fumble off the cap, point the nib at a clean square of paper, write, *I love you.*

He stares at the words, then at the letter I am supposed to have written. 'It's not your handwriting.'

'Of course it's not my handwriting.'

We must look a sight, crying in the middle of the street.

Twenty-eight

George and I are having supper in an Italian restaurant that she often frequents. The table-cloths are checked in red and white, and on each there is a dusty posy of dried flowers and candles forced into wine bottles, their shape scarcely visible under the carapace of wax that has accumulated over the years. But the food is good and the waiters are kind. Their hair is greyer than George's and they tread the well-worn path from kitchen to table at snail's pace. '*Bella*,' they say, solemnly presenting us each with a dark-red rose, its stem tipped with a screw of silver paper. '*Bella*.'

'They're dead by the next morning,' says George.

'The waiters or the roses?'

George laughs. 'The waiters, of course.' She shakes out a large linen napkin, smoothes it over her comfortable lap. 'Now, tell me what's happened. And don't say, *nothing*, because I can see something has, simply by looking at your face.'

'Next time I shall wear purdah,' I say, fiddling with the cutlery. I pick up a knife, trace the blade along the lines of red and white cotton. George says nothing. Long years of dealing with writers have taught her the art of listening. 'I have fallen in love. It may be a mistake.'

George's eyes are bright with enquiry. 'In what way?'

'I was in love with somebody quite different for years. Now, I've discovered that I no longer love him. I don't even like him. I'm frightened that I may be about to make the same mistake, all over again.'

'Ben.'

Am I so transparent? I glance at her warily, expecting regret, but her expression reveals nothing, only the same kindly attentiveness she has always shown me. I say, with a sigh, 'Yes, Ben. And now I'm about to do it all over again with somebody called Richard.'

'And why might poor Richard be a mistake?'

'He's not the mistake. I am. I've always rather despised women who jump from one man to the next without pausing for breath. And here I am, doing the very same thing.'

'It depends, really,' George says thoughtfully, 'on why you're doing it. Anyway, mistakes aren't necessarily a bad thing. Not if we use them wisely.'

I drink red wine, thick and soothing. 'There's a part of me that wants to run in the other direction, the way I always do if I sense any sort of difficulty. I am good at leaving.'

'Ah, well, on the theory that we all constantly make mistakes, and not only mistakes but the very *same* mistakes, there is something that's possible to change.'

'How?'

'Stop and look back over your shoulder. See what it is you're leaving.'

It's a thought.

'How does he make you feel, this Richard?'

'Like I've arrived at a safe haven.'

'And Ben?'

'Ben,' I say, and not without a sudden feeling of regret. 'Ben was the big dipper.'

The next day, Ben and I are sitting in a pub, feeling astonished. 'Why here?' he says, looking around. 'You know how I hate these places.'

'I think they hate you too,' I say, smiling because he looks so shiny and modern, like a sleek new car parked in a dusty yard. He is drinking vodka, which he dislikes but he dislikes the wine more. 'It's filthy in these places. Warm and sweet. Janey, why are we here?'

'Somewhere neutral.'

'How intriguing. We must have something serious to say to each other, then. Couples in bad movies always meet in places like this when they have something serious to say to each other.'

'Where's Rebecca's letter?' I say, refusing to be distracted. You can spend a whole day with Ben and never tell what you have come to say.

'What?'

'The letter Rebecca left when she died.'

He is momentarily taken aback. 'I threw it away, of course. It's hardly a memento to keep pressed in the family album.'

'You wrote it, didn't you?'

'Don't be absurd, Janey.'

'She didn't know about us at all.'

Ben looks at me wearily. 'How many times do I have to tell you. You're imagining things. It's the strain of the last few months –'

'Just as I imagined the letter you sent to Richard. Was that the strain as well?'

'I have no idea what you're talking about.'

He hasn't the grace even to look a tiny bit discomfited. I gaze at his handsome, impenetrable face and know that I will never understand why he did what he did. Maybe it's better this way.

Smiling, he says, 'Well, of course, it's right that we're here, after all. Remember when we first met? How we used to go to that dreadful pub and eat pie and beans. Or rather, I ate. You just watched. That's when I first realised you were in love with me. Sitting there staring at me with those great big eyes, unable to eat, while I demolished all your food.'

'I'm leaving you, Ben.'

'At last we've arrived at the serious bit.' He is grinning, his mouth curved in a mocking expression. 'I was wondering when we were going to come to it.'

'Don't laugh at me. I really am leaving you.'

He dashes the hair from his eyes, sighs faintly. 'No, you're not.'

I say nothing.

'You just *think* you're leaving me. You can't exist without me, Janey. You know that. It's been the same way ever since we met.' He leans across the table, chin resting on his hands, utterly relaxed. 'Are you frightened of me, Janey? Of what I'll do? Is that why we're meeting in this absurd place?' A smile plays around his mouth, his eyes are a bright, unsullied blue. An artist would paint him as an angel, a woman would clasp his head to her breast. 'Or are you frightened of what I might do to lover boy?'

That's when I decide. I had not, until that moment, known what I would do. When love turns to hate, it is like a glass dropped on stone. The pieces will never make a whole again, never reflect the same pure, uncorrupted image.

Ben leans back easily, dropping his hands to the table. 'He'll never love you as I do, Janey. Nobody will ever love you as I do.'

No. Thank God.

I mistook obsession for love. Or is it possession? It doesn't much matter. Both are interchangeable. Neither is good.

I should have learned that much as a child, the lonely witness to my parents' passionate marriage. I thought that sort of greedy, obsessive love was all I would ever want, just as I believed it was all my mother ever wanted. Now, I'm not so sure. There were times when her beautiful hands shook with agitation as she pinned a hat to her soft fair hair, fingers trembling as she painted her mouth a deep improbable scarlet. Those were the times she went out alone, leaving my father to pace the house until she returned. When she came home, she was gentle with him. I don't know where she went. She never spoke of it. She left him in the end, though. Died without permission. He hated that.

Ben loses his composure temporarily. 'Say something, dammit. You're as bad as Rebecca, both with your impenetrable silences.'

So I am on Rebecca's side now. Perhaps it's where I belong.

'I really am leaving.'

'For a while, perhaps,' he says with a sigh. Then he smiles. 'Just as well, really. Now that I'm writing the book, I have so little time for you. I know things have been difficult recently but once the book is finished, things will be different. I'll have all the time in the world for you, you'll see.'

'This time it's over, Ben. You must believe me.'

'The trouble is, sweetheart,' he says, leaning forward and capturing my hands, 'that I can't. I really can't.'

It is mid-afternoon when I reach Richard's office.

'Have you got an appointment this time?' asks the receptionist, staring belligerently through thick lenses.

'No, but he won't mind.'

'So you're clairvoyant too,' she grumbles, but picks up the phone.

When Richard comes downstairs we go outside, out of reach of her curious stare.

'You're looking very serious.'

'I feel very serious.'

'Good. Then let me ask you a serious question. Come and live with me.'

'There's my house, and what about Margaret?'

'We'll visit.'

'She needs looking after.'

'We'll visit every day.'

'She'd think we were prying.'

'Every other day, then.'

'Your flat's too small.'

'We'll live in yours.'

'Too many memories.'

'We'll buy somewhere else.'

It's impossible.

'It's not impossible.'

Richard always does that, answers my questions before they're spoken aloud.

'Be my love.'

'I am your love.'

'Then be with me.'

'You might not like it.' He might not like me.

'I will like you.'

'Will you stop doing that? Anyway, there's Sam to think of.'

'I never stop.'

I smile up at him. 'I know.'

His arms tighten round me. 'Why don't you come and stay with me, just for a day or two? Try it out. See if you like it.'

'There's something I have to do first.'

'Are you going to tell me what?'

'No.'

'Do you want me to come with you?'

Yes, oh yes.

'No.'

Richard takes a key from his pocket. It is just an ordinary key, tarnished with age, looped on a piece of string. He hands it to me. 'My spare key. May as well keep it.'

I put it in my pocket. May as well.

*

The Inspector looks exhausted. Does he never sleep?

'I wondered when you'd be back.'

I tell him what I have come to say.

As I turn to leave, I ask, 'Do you have a copy of the suicide note?'

'There's one on file.'

'Rebecca didn't write it. Ben did.'

'I see.'

'Do you? I wish I did.'

'The workings of the human heart, Miss Rose, are a thing of rare and curious interest.'

I always knew I liked that man.

It is past seven when I get to Richard's flat but the sun is still shining. I take the key from my pocket, stare at it. The light catches it, turning it gold.

I put it in the lock. It turns easily.

'Hello?' I call. 'Hello, I'm home.'

CONCERNING LILY

Sally Brampton

Three Friends, Three Relationships ... and one young woman without a conscience.

When Elisabeth Delaware, bored of her comfortable life, invites young, friendless Lily Clifton to meet her husband and friends, she cannot imagine the terrible consequences the invitation will have. For Lily is not just a stranger to London, she is a stranger to conscience.

Elisabeth does not see Lily for what she is, nor can she see that her marriage to solid, dependable Charles is slowly crumbling. Even Elisabeth's good friends, Bella and Daisy, both intent on salvaging the wreckage of their own relationships, are powerless to resist as Lily moves through all their lives, wreaking quiet but careless havoc.

'Completely absorbing and painfully accurate' *Fay Weldon*

LOVESICK

Sally Brampton

Harry and Martha had been together for seven years and met at the restaurant every Friday evening which, Martha had once calculated, amounted to three hundred and fifty Fridays. She had been thinking a lot about her life recently, which was unusual for her, but just lately the weeks had started to stretch into a grey sameness which made her feel as if she'd somehow got on to a motorway which had no exit lanes. That evening she calculated that, by her reckoning, she had sat for a whole year of her life and listened to Harry order prawns.

Bored of Harry's steadfast dependability, Martha leaves him in search of a more exciting life. But as her life and the lives of those around her begin to unravel the pitfalls of reckless passion become all to obvious.

A bitter-sweet, contemporary novel about friendship, love, the fun of a little danger and the danger of a little fun.

'*Lovesick* deals with the complexities of marriage, loyalty and friendship. A moving story that builds slowly to an explosive climax.' *Woman's Journal*

Also Available

☐ Lovesick	Sally Brampton	£5.99
☐ Concerning Lily	Sally Brampton	£5.99
☐ Tulip Fever	Deborah Moggach	£6.99
☐ Close Relations	Deborah Moggach	£6.99
☐ Moon Island	Rosie Thomas	£5.99
☐ Every Woman Knows a Secret	Rosie Thomas	£5.99

ALL ARROW BOOKS ARE AVAILABLE THROUGH MAIL ORDER OR FROM YOUR LOCAL BOOKSHOP.

PAYMENT MAY BE MADE USING ACCESS, VISA, MASTER-CARD, DINERS CLUB, SWITCH AND AMEX, OR CHEQUE, EUROCHEQUE AND POSTAL ORDER (STERLING ONLY).

☐☐☐☐☐☐☐☐☐☐☐☐☐☐☐☐

EXPIRY DATE .... SWITCH ISSUE NO. ☐☐

SIGNATURE ....

PLEASE ALLOW £2.50 FOR POST AND PACKING FOR THE FIRST BOOK AND £1.00 PER BOOK THEREAFTER.

ORDER TOTAL: £................................. (INCLUDING P&P)

ALL ORDERS TO:
ARROW BOOKS, BOOKS BY POST, TBS LIMITED, THE BOOK SERVICE, COLCHESTER ROAD, FRATING GREEN, COLCHESTER, ESSEX, CO7 7 DW, UK.

TELEPHONE: (01206) 256 000
FAX: (01206) 255 914

NAME ....

ADDRESS..

....

Please allow 28 days for delivery. Please tick box if you do not wish to receive any additional information. ☐
Prices and availability subject to change without notice.